P9-CSF-142

# Sweet Ruin

ALSO BY CATHI HANAUER

*The Bitch in the House* (editor)

*My Sister's Bones*

# Sweet Ruin

Cathi Hanauer

ATRIA BOOKS New York London Toronto Sydney

ATRIA BOOKS
1230 Avenue of the Americas
New York, NY 10020



Library of Congress Cataloging-in-Publication Data
Hanauer, Cathi.
Sweet ruin : a novel / Cathi Hanauer—1st Atria Books hardcover ed.
p. cm.
ISBN-13: 978-0-7432-7734-1
ISBN-10: 0-7432-7734-1
I. Title.

PS3558.A459S9 2006
813'.54—dc22 2005057123

First Atria Books hardcover edition June 2006

10 9 8 7 6 5 4 3



Manufactured in the United States of America

# PERMISSIONS

To Sweetbird and Moonbeam,

lights of my days,

and Daniel Jones,

love of my life.

And to Donna C,

with affection and gratitude.

*Hide me in your arms*

*just for this night,*

*while the rain breaks*

*against sea and earth*

*its innumerable mouth.*

—PABLO NERUDA

"Wind on the Island"

# Part One

# Chapter One

I suppose, for literary effect, I should start with how everything was dying that year—how the riverbed dried up into a brown Brillo pad, the wisteria shriveled on their vines. But the truth is, that brilliant April, after rain had soaked us all March, it felt to me as if the earth and the plants, the insects and trees just couldn't stay in their pants. Daffodils unfurled and grinned into bloom; tulips reached up their orange and crimson cupped hands. Across the street, the Japanese weeping cherry tree exploded into a firework of lilliputian pink clouds, while down the block Mrs. Zuppo's lily garden peeked out from its bed weeks early. All the world was a stage, and I walked around in a daze beholding the spectacle that was life. It seemed to me it had never been this way. But then, I was waking up again, after all that time.

During the more than two years since Oliver's death, my goal had been simply to get myself through the days. After dropping Hazel at preschool or kindergarten or first grade and dragging myself through the errands (grocery shopping, bill paying, dry cleaners for Paul . . . all those things that plague the work-at-home wife), I'd simply returned to my house and crawled back into bed, where, between the empty escape of deep naps, I did my editing work—its own kind of refuge—until it was time to pick up Hazel again. Then, with what felt like superhuman effort, I would act out the role of the cheerful, inspired mother I was not, somehow getting us through the hours until we were at last back in bed again—her bed, this time, where we'd both fall asleep, me half-waking only to switch to my own bed and continue my dreamless coma. I never felt Paul slip into bed hours later when he finally got home. Really, it was as if I were dead, except when taking care of Hazel or working, and then I operated on automatic pilot: numb, simply soldiering on.

But this year, with the first signs of spring in my New Jersey town—a slowly gentrifying commuter and college hub where octogenarian Dominicks and Guiseppes bordered thirtysomething Manhattan transplants like me, with handfuls of crunchy Gen X-ers tossed throughout—something had started to change. I felt my old self, the one I'd thought was gone forever, sending out tiny shoots from deep in my bones—stiff, strong, green tips to tell me the roots were still in there, *I* was still in there, somehow . . . and wanting, at last, out again. On the day this story begins, I had taken a morning walk, peeling my old Eileen Fisher cardigan from my arms to let the sun drench my pasty, winter-sapped skin. I'd headed to the fish market for two slabs of salmon, then to the bakery for a crusty ciabatta. Then a bottle of sauvignon blanc from the liquor store and a bar of fine dark chocolate for dessert. I suppose I was celebrating my rebirth. At any rate, when I got home I was ravenous, and by the time my piece of fish was done broiling I'd already sampled a few bites, standing at the oven forking the salty pink flesh into my greedy mouth, burning its tender skin. I didn't care. It was worth it to taste that delectable bliss, and to finally crave food again.

On the way to the table, I dragged my hunk of bread through the circle of salted olive oil I'd drizzled onto my plate, bit it hard, and swallowed it practically whole. Unlike Paul, who'd always been someone who eats to live, I had been—and now, it seemed, was on my way back to being—a happy fat person inside a genetically thin body: always anticipating my next meal, savoring it when it came. Today, I'd fixed Paul the other piece of salmon—lemon, olive oil, splash of tamari—and left it front and center in the fridge, just so he'd know, when he got home, having long ago eaten the dinner his law firm had called in from some trendy restaurant nearby in the financial district, that I had thought of him, that I loved him. *Elayna, the loving wife.* I'd also left him a salad and a couple of wedges of a perfect blood orange. Placing my dish on the table, I uncorked the wine, poured a glass, and sat down.

I ate in rapture, licking the plate at the end. Well, why not? I was alone, after all.

My work lay open next to me, a manuscript of the latest soon-to-be issue of *Popular Poetry* magazine. Each month, the journal reproduced classic and some contemporary poems in a palatable and accessible form for those who wanted to see what they'd missed in college or who wanted a tiny, digestible version of the contemporary poetry scene. My job, bestowed on me by an old English-major colleague at Barnard, was, frankly, a dream: I proofread and lightly edited the copy, not so much for mistakes or typos (thankfully, there was someone else for that) but for content and appeal. In essence, I was simply an early reader who each month sent back a detailed critique. I made minimal suggestions—"Flip-flop the two Hopkins poems," or "More of an intro on the Dickinson might be nice"—and sometimes I suggested stories. ("How about a feature on Edward Lear?") The pay was laughable, of course—the job amounted to half-time work for an hourly salary barely above minimum wage—but Paul's hefty lawyer paychecks made that okay, and since he worked heftily to *make* those paychecks, it had been more important, once we'd had Hazel, for me to do something close to home than to pull in a decent salary.

When Hazel was young, the job had provided me the perfect escape from the obsessive mothering and brutal self-examination full-time parenting can bring. Once Oliver died, the work kept me from descending into darkness when Hazel wasn't around. In fact, most of the time I'd looked forward to it—as much as I could look forward to anything then. But today, after my feast (for dessert, I melted squares of the chocolate bar in the microwave and poured them over a fat ball of coffee ice cream), I was distracted, unable to focus. I glanced out between the little white curtains in my kitchen and saw a smattering of dark clouds moving in. Trees blowing, swaying. Immediately, I grew anxious. Hazel was phobic about storms, and I couldn't bear to think of her panicked out there.

I glanced at the clock above the stove. Still almost two hours until I had to get her from Pansy's house, where she went on Wednesdays—half days at her school—from noon until three (more days in the summer or if I got busy). I got up, wandered into the living room, and glanced out the windows. This was the ugly side of our house, and the neighborhood canine Porta Potti—a small strip of dead grass between house and sidewalk, overly shaded by a big old hemlock tree. Anything that did manage to grow there the neighborhood dogs quickly dispensed with. I couldn't do much about their pissing, obviously, but the rest of what they did was illegal and infuriating when left there. Yesterday and today there had been fresh loads of poop to greet me, and looking out now, I spotted a third and felt the rage rise up through my blood, almost thrillingly. If I found out who was doing it, I'd tear the hair from his head.

I wandered to the back door and then outside, onto the deck, and I leaned over the edge of the rail, letting the balmy breeze breathe over me. It was unseasonably warm; the air felt pregnant with pollen and humidity. I closed my eyes and shook my hair down over my bare arms, then inhaled deeply, sucking in the splendor through every pore. The cicadas shrieked; the atmosphere seemed to vibrate. I could feel the charge seeping through my skin, making me tingle with life. *Life, at last.* I could have wept with joy.

Someone went by, walking a dog: I heard a collar jingle, loud panting, canine toenails on tar, and then I saw them, a silver Weimaraner with an orange sneaker in its mouth, leading a cute, crew-cut boy by the leash. *Guy,* not *boy,* I should say, though he was a boy compared to me. He was wearing jeans and no shirt, exposing his lightly freckled white chest. His arms were curved and ample for his otherwise lean frame. Maybe gay, I reasoned, but either way, a Gen X-er for sure, or was it Gen Y-er, these days? I watched boy and dog pass by, cross the street, and head into the driveway of the small apartment building Paul and I jokingly called the Tenement. With its Victorian charm and two sugar maples out front, it was as unlike the tenement where we'd lived in New York—broken buzzers, roaches, filthy stairwell—as our tree-lined enclave of a New Jersey town was unlike Manhattan. Anyway, they mounted the steps, boy and dog, and climbed to the top floor, the fourth, dog still carrying the sneaker. In they went.

I was surprised. I hadn't seen them before, and, ashamed as I am to admit it, I knew virtually everything about the area from my house to Hazel's school (and little, these days, about much of anything beyond)—and certainly who'd moved into and out of the Tenement. The place was filled with young people like him, not-quite-kids with tattoos and pierced noses, tongues, lips, ear cartilage, and (yes) chins, hair of blue and green and nickel gray and magenta that stuck up with faux messiness. They were soon-to-be graduate students at the nearby university, or philosophically inclined slackers, artists, aspiring "filmmakers," living off their parents till they figured out a bearable way to make a living or invented some iPod facsimile and set themselves up for life. I loved the Tenement; it reminded me that there were people in the world with obsessions other than their commute or what preschool was best. These were people waiting for their lives to begin, people who, for all their manifestations of depression and grunge and loneliness, were secretly full of optimism and promise and the blazing, glorious arrogance of youth. Their mistakes didn't count, because their Real Lives hadn't yet begun. Things could change for them in an instant.

I glanced up at the apartment boy and dog had gone into, but other than a couple of potted plants on the fire escape, there was no sign of life. Beyond the Tenement, houses speckled the hills; if you climbed a hill at night, you could see shimmering New York City, a million seductive points of light. I heard the commuter train wail, the cars, on the main drag a few blocks away, streaming toward somewhere—maybe only the new mega Home Depot near the highway. I went down into the yard, set up Hazel's T-ball apparatus, and whacked the crap out of a dozen balls, high and hard. I gathered the balls and did it again, and then again. Then I turned and stomped back inside, panting as hard as that Weimaraner.

I glanced impatiently around my kitchen, then took off my sandals and kicked them across the room. The floor—Italian tiles Paul had picked out on a business trip to Sicily—was cool and smooth on my feet. I peeled off my T-shirt and tossed that too, until I was down to the gray sports bra I'd chosen this morning, thinking maybe later I'd go for a run. My breasts were large and full and not too badly sagging yet, despite having nursed Hazel for a year. They were still my best feature, and I'd always made a point of standing straight, shoulders back, so I didn't turn into one of those slender, large-chested women being dragged floorward by her rack. The rest of my body was thinner than usual—no exercise and little appetite for two years will do that to a person—but starting, finally, to bloom back into its curvier shape, and I was glad.

In the living room, a Louis Armstrong CD was poised to play, but I wasn't in the mood. I tossed in Alanis Morissette's *Jagged Little Pill* and turned up the volume. Her twangy, pissed-off rock blared out. I listened a minute, feeling it loosen me and make me happy. And then I did something I hadn't done since before I'd had Oliver. I danced.

I danced, and—I kid you not—I sang too, because the words seemed to be speaking to me: words about being tired but happy, sick but pretty, messed up but moving on. I twirled around, letting this sweet young thing's tough voice and angry words take me back to thirty, twenty-eight, twenty-three. When the song ended, I played it again. I was hot. Melting, really. I peeled off my skirt and hurled it, leaving my gray cotton Calvin Klein briefs. Then I leaped and twirled in my underwear, a demented overgrown ballerina; if Hazel had been there, she would have rolled her eyes. Out the window, someone rode by on a bike. The song ended. I played it three more times, then flopped on the couch, spent.

By the time I thought to look at the clock, I had all of fifteen minutes until I had to pick up Hazel at Pansy's. I bolted upstairs to shower, then rushed down and grabbed my purse—big, leather, gift from Paul for my recent thirty-fifth birthday—and, digging for the car keys, started toward the door. But I happened to glance out before I opened it, and what I saw made me stop and stare. Gen XY Boy and his dog were back, and Dog—back arched into a sleek silver mountain, tail extended out behind him—was depositing a pile of fresh turds onto my Porta Potti strip. I watched until the canine had reclosed his butt hole and retained prepooping posture. Would his person rise to the challenge and scoop up the dung? XY Boy glanced at the turds, and then—as I'd somehow expected—turned and headed briskly back home.

I was out my front door in two seconds. "Excuse me!" I yelled, rushing down the steps.

XY Boy stopped and turned around; XY Dog turned too, wagging his tail. "Oh, hey," Boy called, stepping toward me again. Neither one of them had an iota of guilt on his (or her) beautiful face, which pissed me off even more—though my anger, I confess, was a bit subsumed by the excitement I felt at having come upon the criminal in action. "I was just—" Boy started, but I cut him off. "Can I tell you something?" I stalked toward him, hands on my hips. "I have a six-year-old daughter who plays on this lawn. If there's a pile of dog shit on it, she steps in it. Then she trails it through my entire house. Have you ever tried cleaning dog shit out of the rug in your bathroom?" I stared at him, furious.

He opened his mouth, presumably to answer, but I cut him off again. He was young, beautiful, irresponsible; he was my scapegoat for all the carefree people whose dogs had crapped on my lawn for the past five years. "Do I use *your* yard as *my* toilet?" I demanded.

He smiled a little, then shook his head. "No. Not that I know of, anyway."

I saw the gleam in his eye. "Oh, go to hell," I said, because I knew I was a pathetic cliché, the aging lawyer's wife getting angry at the cute-but-careless young renter who sullied her perfect property. I turned around and marched back up to my house, anxious to get inside now. But XY Boy called, "Wait!"

I stopped and turned again.

"I guess you'd never believe me if I said I always clean up after my dog."

I snorted. "Except this one particular time when I happened to see you? You're right. I don't think I would."

"Well," he said, "this one particular time just happens to be the time I gave away my plastic bag to someone just down the block"—he gestured with his head back in the direction from which he'd come—"because she happened to be in her own particular dog-do bind. I figured Sasha here would probably make it home without a problem, and if she didn't, I'd just go home and get another bag and come back and clean it up."

"And that's where you were going now?" I felt myself soften just a touch; at least he cared enough to try.

He shrugged. "But I guess I don't blame you for not believing that. It's like the kid caught leaving the candy store with a pocketful of baseball cards swearing he was on his way home to get his money."

I raised my eyebrows. Maybe he wasn't as dumb as he was beautiful.

"Forget it," he said, before I could respond. "Sorry about the mess. I'll be right back to clean it up."

I shrugged now myself, as if it were really no big deal and never had been. "Whatever," I said, stealing a phrase from Hazel's repertoire, which made me realize, with renewed panic, that I was already late to get her. I came back down the steps and started to walk quickly toward the garage, away from him. "By the way," he called, "I like Alanis Morissette too. I have a great bootleg concert CD, if you ever want to borrow it. I live right across the street. Fourth floor."

I was still walking, but slowly now, and for a step or two I actually wondered how he knew I liked Alanis Morissette. And then I stopped. I turned and stared at him, feeling heat creep into my face. Had he seen me dancing in my living room? Had he been just passing by, or actually stood there looking in my window? I thought about how I'd tossed off my shirt, peeled off my skirt, hurled my body around. *Oh my god.* I wanted to reach out and smack him.

He may have blushed then too, realizing what his offer had revealed, but I could be mistaken. At any rate, after a second, he jumped from a standstill to a trot, like a well-trained horse. "Be right back," he called, and off he went, his dog trotting after him.

*Son of a bitch,* I thought. I turned and hightailed it toward my car to get Hazel.

And that was the beginning.

# Chapter Two

Pansy Dougherty's in-home day care was held at her small clapboard cottage, which, painted conch shell pink with lemon trim, resembled nothing so much as a giant cupcake. This was the first lure for the hundreds of children she'd cared for over the years; the second was her two part-Persian cats, Pearly Dew Drops and Cuteface, which she'd rescued from the pound, and the third was the almost unfathomable stash of Barbies, Beanie Babies, Barney videotapes, Candy Lands (several versions), Thomas the Tank Engines, and red stuffed Cliffords she had inside, topped only by her own personal and proudly displayed collections of snow globes and British royal family paraphernalia. Stepping out of the car, I noticed two new pink pelicans added to the ceramic zoo on her lawn, which included a smiling frog in a top hat and a winking, cat-size bluebird. I passed the bird feeder, then the red-and-yellow windmill with the smiling face. These would remain, I knew, through the spring and summer, then be replaced by the scarecrow, the life-size plastic deer, and the many grinning jack-o'-lanterns that adorned Pansy's fall, to the delight of her tiny charges.

I climbed the steps, my muscles already aching from my dance marathon, and knocked on the door. After a few muffled measures of some preschool band shrieking a tinny, high-pitched version of "The Farmer in the Dell," the curtain behind the door was drawn aside and Pansy's face—wide-eyed but prim, framed by two silver blond braids—appeared and then vanished again. Several locks clicked, and the door opened a crack. "Come on, come on, before the bugs come in," Pansy scolded. She ushered me into her house, already cool with the air-conditioning she employed if the thermometer topped seventy. Inside, three well-shorn, saucer-eyed little boys sat at her feet, while one of the cats—huge, fat, apparently exempt from any rules—glared at me from on top of a toy piano. In the center of the room lurked an enormous toy fast-food counter, complete with cash register and napkin dispenser. Hazel and another older girl stood behind it, wearing brown-and-orange vests.

"Hi, puppet," I said, filled as usual with instant joy at the sight of her snobby, ravishing face. She ignored me, as she always did at Pansy's house; I was the enemy, come to take her away. "Today is food court day," Pansy announced as she relocked the bolts on her door. She dropped down next to the boys on the worn pink carpeting, crossing her legs Indian style. She wore loose jeans, a T-shirt with an appliquéd smiley face, and white Keds. "Okay, Hector, your turn," she said to one of the boys. "What are you having today—French fries, McFlurry, or Filet-O-Fish?"

Hector's lashy brown eyes darted around. "Um," he said. "Ummmmm—"

"Fish filet?" coached Pansy.

Hector nodded.

"One fish filet, *please,* counterperson," Pansy said. "Very good, Hector. You chose a healthy meal from the meat, fish, and poultry group."

Hector glanced at me, grinned, then ducked his beautiful black-haired head. I looked at him and felt a pinprick of sadness. I pushed it away, and instead thought, *How can his mother bear his cuteness?* I would have drowned him in kisses twenty times a day.

"How much does he owe?" Pansy asked, turning to Hazel.

Hazel consulted the register, as if it held the answer. "One dollar and ninety-five cents," she said—not unrealistically, I thought, swelling with pride.

Pansy nudged Hector. "Give her two of your dollars. Hazel, you'll need to give him five cents in change." She turned to me. "The two- and three-year-olds are focusing on sharing, as you can see. And their food groups. The older girls are doing their math. You can never start too young. Good, Hazel, give him his change. Hector turns four next week, so he graduates to using the register."

"Huh," I said, as if I hadn't heard this three hundred times before. Pansy had rigid rules for when each child could use each toy, sit in each chair, do each activity. She felt this kept the younger ones safe and imbued the older ones with a sense of pride and accomplishment. It all seemed a bit arbitrary to me—gel pens at age six, dot paint at four—but what did I know, as the mother of one? Anyway, with Pansy, you listened whether you wanted to or not. After thirty years of taking care of children, including three of her own, Pansy treated everyone like a child. And we acted accordingly.

I handed Pansy her money, then turned to Hazel. "Come, sweetheart, let's get your stuff."

Hazel ignored me.

"Hazel," Pansy instructed, "after you've given Hector his change and his ketchup, go get your things, please."

Hazel handed Hector a plastic coin and a small packet of real ketchup to go with his cardboard Filet-O-Fish box. She took off her vest and folded it neatly, then went into the kitchen to get her lunch box and sweater. I watched with my usual amazement. Pansy could get them to do absolutely anything, all without raising her voice or even repeating herself. And Hazel loved coming here, right down to the rules. She'd started when she was one and I'd gotten my job. I'd thought that once she reached kindergarten, Pansy's house would be a thing of the past, but when I told her this, both she and Pansy protested so vehemently that we'd compromised. Hazel would come on Wednesday afternoons, since she got out of school early that day, plus, at least theoretically, for the occasional sleepover when Paul and I had a late-night occasion together. Not that I could remember the last time we had.

"Now, I wanted to ask you," Pansy whispered to me loudly as Hazel and I headed out, "how's she doing in school? Because at this age, you know, they can pick up some questionable things there. I'll never forget the day Delilah came home from first grade and said"—she looked at me, cupped her hand to the side of her mouth, and mouthed "'fuck'—right at the dinner table. Her father hit the roof. And children are very vulnerable at this age, especially girls. You have to watch them for signs of trauma. I'm telling you, Elayna. I just came from a workshop about family catastrophes—very, very enlightening, I learned an incredible amount in one hour—and they told us that it's our responsibility, as a child's domestic educational facilitator, to alert the parents to—"

"Wait," I had to interrupt her. "As a *what*?"

"Domestic educational facilitator," she announced, straightening up and adjusting her jeans. "That's how we now refer to ourselves. And I can tell you, after thirty years of being called a babysitter, it's a welcome relief to have an appropriate title. All my friends who are DEFs agree. If I were just a babysitter, quote unquote, I could have been sitting on the couch all this time reading magazines or yakking on the phone while these kids watched TV. Now, I'll ask Hazel this for proof, because six-year-olds don't lie if you confront them point-blank. Do we ever, Hazel—*ever,* except for one half hour around nap time and during sleepovers—watch television in my house?" Hazel shook her head no soberly, and Pansy smiled. "That's right. Come here before you go, and give me a hug." Hazel rushed over, and the two of them embraced. "See you next Wednesday," Pansy said to her. "It'll be dress-up day and hair salon."

"Yay!" Hazel yelled, and then, before Pansy could finish telling what exactly it was she'd learned in her workshop that we were supposed to look out for, I ushered my daughter out of Pansy's cool pink house and into the heat and our car.

I started to search for my seat belt, but I stopped and turned around. Hazel was sitting on her booster seat, staring thoughtfully out the window. Her hair was a mop of orange tangles, curls and frizz, as it always was at the end of the day, and her lips were even redder than usual, as if she'd just eaten a cherry pop. "Buckle up, buzzworm," I said, tearing my eyes away. I listened for the click. "How was your day?"

"Fine," she said. "How was yours?"

"Very good," I said, thrilled she'd asked. "Thanks for asking, sweetheart."

"You're welcome. Mom, can you put on Broadway Kids?"

I paused. I was in no mood to hear a bunch of eleven-year-olds belting out tunes from *Cats.* Plus, I hadn't talked to Hazel all day, and sometimes the car was the best place. But I also didn't want to start with a fight. "In a minute," I said. "Tell me about school. What did you do?"

She shrugged. "Nothing."

"Not one thing? All day?" I laughed lightly. "Were all your friends there today?"

"Destiny wasn't," she said. "She has shingles. Dylan came back, though. He had lice. But it's all gone now."

"That's good," I managed. I turned the corner. "Did he—"

"Oh, Dunkin' Donuts!" Hazel yelled. "Can we stop, Mom? Pleeeze?"

"No," I said, automatically. "Let's go home and get a good snack."

"Dunkin' Donuts *are* good!" she said. "Clementine's mother gets her them, like, every single day. And Pansy got me them like three times already."

"She did?" This surprised me. Pansy was always advocating healthy snacks, reprimanding me for putting a cookie or a Hershey's Kiss in Hazel's lunch box.

"Yup," Hazel tattled. "Once in the summer, once in the fall . . ."

"Well, just 'cause Pansy does something doesn't mean I will. And Clementine's mother—" I stopped. I liked Adele. "Every mother has different rules," I concluded, unoriginally.

She was silent. I slowed with the traffic braking, no doubt to accommodate the cars streaming in and out of Home Depot a quarter mile away. "Clementine is going to a wedding," Hazel said. "She gets to be a flower girl."

"Really! Whose wedding?" I asked.

"Her uncle's. He found a wife. In another country. Her name is Nikita, or Brikita, or something. Anyway, Clementine gets to wear high heels. Mom?"

"Hm?"

"If I was in a wedding, would you let *me* wear high heels?"

"If you WERE in a wedding. Maybe," I said.

"If I was the flower girl?"

I resisted the impulse to correct her again. "Probably," I said.

She clicked the ashtray. "When WILL I get to be a flower girl?"

"Well, I don't know," I said. "I can't think of anyone we know who's the right age to get married anytime soon. Most of our friends are already married, on the road to divorce." I laughed again, then stopped suddenly, realizing this wasn't funny.

"Mom," she said, "do you like Pansy?"

"Sure," I said. "If I didn't, I wouldn't let you go to her house." I accelerated gently, then had to brake again as an SUV cut me off. "Pansy's patient, and careful, and energetic," I said. "She's sometimes a little eccentric for me, but—"

"Eccentric?"

"Unusual. But that's what gives her her charm." I assessed my answer and gave myself a silent nine out of ten.

"Pansy says the world has gone to heck in a handcart," Hazel said.

I glanced at her in the rearview mirror. "She does?"

"Yup. She says there's too much violence on TV, and it's making children grow up to be violent homick—homa—whatever, those people who shoot people when they grow up."

I sighed. "Well, I don't actually agree. I think some things have gotten more dangerous and others less. I think there are mean people and nice ones, and there always have been and always will be. If there's more violence now, it's only because there are more *people.* You know, in the quote-unquote good old days, things weren't so perf—"

"Destiny's hair is even curlier than mine," Hazel interrupted. "Don't you think?"

"Um . . ." I tried to switch mental gears. Her friend Destiny's hair was silky and straight, with a slight little wave at the ends; Hazel's was squash-colored fusilli, orange bursting pell-mell from her head. It went along with her freckles, which were equally gorgeously unruly, smattered over her face and body. "Not really," I admitted.

Silence, and then she yelled, "I HATE my hair!"

"Oh, Hazel," I said, and sadness drifted through me. "Love yourself, baby. If you don't, who will?" It was my own lecture, of course, the one I'd given myself for years, until it had finally sunk in. I wasn't perfect, but I could haul groceries home, move the occasional piece of furniture, carry my almost seven-year-old up to bed. And I could still dance. If you could call it that. I thought of Gen XY Boy looking in at me, and sweat broke out under my arms. What had he seen?

"Well, I like Britney Spears's hair," Hazel said flatly. "It's yellow and straight. That's the kind I want."

I turned onto our street. "How do you know about Britney Spears?"

"I saw her on TV at Pansy's house."

I shook my head, then slowed down to check out the houses of our neighbors as we passed by. Several were being worked on—new roofs, fresh coats of paint. Our house was stagnant. It needed a new screen door, a window repaired, probably a new roof.

"I wish I had a brother," Hazel said suddenly.

I winced.

"Everyone has a brother or sister except me," she said loudly, even though it was far from the truth and she knew it; half her classmates were only children.

I thought about how to answer. *Well, I wish you did too?* It had been almost three years since Oliver died. He'd had one day of life as a "normal" baby, and then he turned blue and began breathing as if he'd just run a marathon. That was our first sign.

I swerved a little to avoid an oncoming car, distracted now by the memory. He had been rushed into surgery—something called a Norwood operation—to try to fix his heart, the left side of which hadn't developed properly. The right side pumped blood to his lungs, but the left side couldn't distribute the oxygenated blood back to his little body.

*Eighty percent success rate,* we'd been told about the surgery. But Oliver was one of the other twenty. "I'm so sorry," my doctor had said, and she did look sorry, broken and teary eyed. But then her face shifted, that thing coming over it that gave her the resolve to be a doctor. "I know this isn't what you want to hear right now," she said, "but you're young and healthy and given that you already have one perfect daughter, chances are very, very good this won't happen again. So—mourn for a while, then make another baby. You could have him in your arms a year from now."

But we hadn't. Instead, Paul had escaped even further into his work, and I'd gone into hibernation. It was only around Hazel that I'd pulled myself out of my stupor. I was determined not to let her get mired in the sadness Paul and I felt. And though I thought I had mostly succeeded, at times like this I knew she still felt the loss, and that she probably never would completely forget it, even though she'd been only three. When Paul had told her her brother died in surgery—I couldn't bear to—she'd burst into tears and climbed into my hospital bed, refusing Paul's offer to go out and buy Jell-O, apple juice, toys. So he went out alone, and she fell asleep in my arms and I kept crying, dizzy with grief, my face pushed into her sweet little neck, my hands clamped around her arms, trying to gather strength from her presence.

Hazel had snapped back pretty quickly once I came home, though as with me, nothing ever really disappeared—only snaked deep into her mind, where it hibernated to resurface hours or years later in an explosion of anger or grief. I had tried to hide the change in myself from her—the expanding blackness and subsequent shriveling up I'd gone through inside—but clearly she sensed something, some loss of optimism or fun in our lives. Maybe it made her angry or depressed. Whatever she felt, it seemed to manifest now and then, usually as nastiness to me. People said this was because she was confident of my love—so sure of me that she could take out her darkest feelings safely in my presence—but that was a perky explanation, the sort I thought people gave mostly to make themselves feel better about a less-than-pleasant thing, though I tried to remind myself of it anyway when she lashed out. Meanwhile, I still thought about Oliver every day. He'd be almost three by now, jumping around, throwing balls, wearing little wide-wale corduroy pants.

"Aunt Cindi and Zach are coming over tonight," I said, not exactly changing the subject. The birth of my sister's boy not long after Oliver's death was another reason I'd been able to go on, to keep face for Hazel in between the long nights and long naps.

"They are? *Yay!*" Hazel yelled. "Can I take his picture with my new camera?"

"I suppose so," I said, but I half-hoped we didn't have any film. She had written to my father asking for a Barbie camera. In response, he'd sent her an expensive, complicated camera, completely inappropriate for a six-year-old. "If I can figure out how to work the thing."

"If you can't, Daddy will." She paused. "Will Daddy be there?"

"I don't know, puppet. He's working on a very important case. He probably won't make it home for dinner, but he'll give you twenty kisses when he comes in."

The ashtray clicked again. "He *never* comes home anymore."

What could I say? She had a point. "Well, maybe it'll be better next month." I pulled into the driveway, then into the garage. "Can you bring your lunch box inside for me?" I said as I turned off the car, but she was already running toward the house, leaving everything for me to carry in, naturally.

I struggled between calling her back (to teach her responsibility) and doing it myself (to let her be carefree while she still could, experience the pure joy of running to her swing), and opted, as usual, for carefree. I watched her race down the driveway and onto the front lawn. She jumped on the swing, a wood plank on long ropes that Paul had hung from a branch of our big oak tree, and I felt, at the sight, one of those brief flashes of happiness that always made me palpably aware of how crucial Hazel was to me, of how that black space inside me that never really went away would explode and devour me alive if anything ever happened to her. My beautiful house, my brilliant husband, all the things I tried never to take for granted . . . they would all be nothing without her. Or not enough to save me, anyway. That was what a child did to you, rendered everything else second fiddle, second string.

I gathered her lunch box, her backpack, her jacket, and the two stuffed animals she'd taken to Pansy's and carried it all, along with my own bag, around to the front door, just so I could watch her swing. Clomping up the steps, I dropped it all to dig for my keys. "Fifteen minutes till dinner," I said as I found them. I unlocked the door and half-carried, half-kicked everything in. "Don't step in poop. Someone's dog went here today, and I haven't cleaned it up yet."

She was swinging high now, ignoring me, her little stilt legs pumping back and forth. Inside, I hung up her jacket, took out the papers from her backpack and laid them on the kitchen table, then listened to the phone messages while I emptied her lunch box. The parent rep at the school, to tell me about a class meeting; Celeste, my best friend, saying to call her; the tailor to tell me Paul's pants were ready; and Paul himself. "Hi. Are you there?" Pause. "Oh, you're probably getting Hazel from Pansy's, it's Wednesday. Well, I'm heading into a long meeting, so no point calling back till after six, if you want to try me—oh, that's right, Cindi and Zach are coming over. Sorry. *Cynthia.*" He laughed, and I smiled. Paul remembered everything, right down to Cindi's recent whim to change her name. His mind was like a well-organized filing cabinet. "Well, don't call me back, then," he said. "I'm just calling to say I'll be late. Sorry. Can you tell Hazel I'll make it up to her this weekend? Thanks. Love you."

I hung up, looked at the phone, then went back to the lunch box, opening the untouched container of cantaloupe and popping two pieces in my mouth. I turned on NPR and put up water for more pasta. Wagon wheels, this time. And chicken nuggets, as usual. I took out the box, removed three for each of us, and stuck them on a plate to microwave.

I had already cooked and drained the wagon wheels, made a salad for myself and broccoli for her, and dumped plain tomato sauce—no spices, no chunks, no green specks of any kind—from a jar to a saucepan when the doorbell rang. By now, Hazel was inside watching *Mister Rogers' Neighborhood.* I waited a second to see if she'd run to the door—if so, I would give her some space, watching from down the hall until I was required—but she didn't go, so I headed down myself, wiping my wet hands on my jeans, squinting to see who it was, thinking that I had to get my eyes checked, that maybe it was time to get the glasses I'd avoided wearing for thirty-five years.

And then I saw him. Through the glass in the door, standing politely facing sideways, giving me a moment to take him in before he met my eyes. I almost stopped, but I caught myself and kept going, and when my hand reached up to undo my hair—I had shoved it into a messy knot—I caught myself again and managed to leave it alone and approach him, disheveled or not. I pulled open the door.

XY Boy raised his right hand, then dropped it again. He smiled. "Hey," he said.

Through the screen door, I glanced around behind him, as if someone else might be there too—the person who'd make me understand, instantly, the reason for his visit.

"How are you?" he said.

I raised my eyebrows. "Fine," I said. "And you?"

"Good, thanks." He smiled again, and I noted with relief his small ears, his vaguely protruding chin, his mildly hooked nose. He was not, thank God, a perfect specimen. Then I saw, with dismay that overwhelmed any relief, that in combination with the downturned mouth and shy-boy smile, the piercing green eyes, bony cheekbones, short light brown hair, and tiny silver ring in one ear, not to mention the dark T-shirt tucked into loose-fitting jeans . . . well, I saw that the overall effect was unspeakably dazzling. If he were an animal, he would have been a desert iguana, beaky, rough hewn, and stunning. "Um," I said, and then, because I felt too nervous to be straight, and because our earlier encounter seemed to call, now, for something less than straight anyway, "To what do I owe the pleasure?"

"Uh—forgive the cliché, but—I was wondering if I could borrow some sugar."

"I don't have any." I blinked in surprise as the lie spilled out. Perhaps my unconscious was simply protecting me.

He laughed. "You don't have any? Wow. I thought all mothers had sugar."

"How do you know I'm a mother?" Now I was absurd, a severely retarded version of my former self.

"You told me," he said. "Before, when you said your daughter steps in dog shit if I leave it on your lawn. By the way, I cleaned it up."

"You did?"

He nodded. "Anyway, I've also seen your daughter. I see her swinging, from my apartment. Right there." He turned around and pointed to the top floor of the Tenement. "That's a nice swing," he said, turning back to me.

"Thanks. Paul put it up. My husband." I shifted on my feet.

"Beautiful swing for a beautiful girl," he said thoughtfully.

I blushed. For whatever reason, it felt as if he were complimenting *me.*

Neither of us spoke for a moment. I still hadn't opened the screen door. "Anyway," he said, "I guess if you don't have any sugar . . ."

"Well—wait a minute. Maybe I do."

I went back to the kitchen, leaving him out there, rude or not. My hands were actually trembling. I took out the bag of sugar. What to put it in? If I used a Ziploc, he might think I wasn't environmentally conscious—and weren't Gen X-ers, and Y-ers, supposed to be so environmentally conscious? But if I used a plastic soup container, he might think I hoarded things (which I did, but he didn't need to know that). And if I used a nicer container—say, Tupperware—he might feel compelled to return it, which meant having to face him again. I shook my head, opting for the Ziploc. Maybe it was computers that Gen X-ers were into, not the environment.

I filled it with sugar. Then I straightened my hair and headed back to the door.

But I stopped halfway, hearing his voice—in the den, I realized, along with Hazel's. I felt something simultaneously thrilling and paranoid, protective, rise up inside me. That was twice in one day he'd come into my house uninvited, even if the first time he had been just looking through the window. I walked toward the den. He was standing at the edge of the couch watching TV, and Hazel was next to him, holding his hand. He turned to me as I approached. "Sorry," he said. "Hazel invited me in. She wanted to show me—"

"Hazel," I ordered, interrupting him, "go wash your hands for dinner."

"Now he's going to the land of make-believe," Hazel said to him, ignoring me. "Do you remember this part?"

He nodded. "The trolley, right? And that's Lady . . . what's her name?"

"Elaine!" Hazel said. "Lady Elaine Fairchild! Like my mom! Well—sort of. Hers is Elay*na*."

"Really? Cool." He looked at me, then at her. "Your name is cool too. Hazel. I like that."

"Well, *I* don't," she pouted. "I like my friend *Clementine's* name."

"Hazel, I *asked* you to go wash your hands, please," I said. I turned to him and held out the sugar. "Here. I did find some."

"You're getting sugar?" Hazel said to him. "For your oatmeal?"

He nodded. "Probably for that too. But actually, I was thinking of making some cookies." He took the bag from me. "Thanks."

"You were?" Hazel beamed up at him. "What kind?"

"Hazel, I'm not going to say it again," I said. "Say good-bye to—"

"Kevin," he supplied.

"Kevin," I said. "Say good-bye to Kevin, and go. *Now,* please."

Hazel glared at me, then ran off without saying anything.

Kevin looked at me and smiled. "Mister Rogers, god. That guy's gotta be, what, fifty now? Sixty? He even has the same sweater." He laughed. "He was on when I was a kid."

Like you're not now? I thought. "He was on when I was a kid too," I said.

I don't know what I expected him to say—No shit, THAT long ago?—but he just flipped the bag of sugar over itself, a little somersault. "I'll bring you a cookie," he said.

"Oh—that's okay."

He looked at me. "You don't want one?"

I shrugged. I did, actually.

"Can I bring one for your daughter, then?" he said, and then, "I won't if you don't want me to."

"No—that would be nice."

He made his way to the door, me following, and then out. Hazel ran up behind me. "Bye, Kevin!" she yelled through the screen.

He turned around and smiled at her. "See ya, Hazel."

I closed the door and came back in. "Wash your hands," I said to her.

"Mom! You said that, like, four times already!"

I stood there hopelessly.

"Mom?"

I nodded.

"Is that guy your friend?"

"He's our neighbor," I said quickly. I looked at her. "Why?"

"He's nice."

I sighed. "I guess. His dog pooped on our lawn today."

She giggled.

I smiled. "What did he do that was so nice, anyway?" I said, casually.

Hazel shrugged. "I don't know. He was funny. He knows how to play Chinese checkers, he said. He's gonna come back and play them with me." She ran into the den and leaped on the couch, jumping up and down as if it were a trampoline. I followed her. "Come on," I said vaguely. "It's dinnertime."

She continued to bounce.

"Hazel," I warned.

She rolled her eyes. *"Okay!"* She leaped off the couch, missing the coffee table by inches, then ran toward the kitchen.

I followed her in, where I rotely dumped the now tepid pasta onto our plates, adding broccoli to hers. I took out her milk from lunch and started to take out the seltzer for myself, then changed my mind and got out the wine instead. I poured myself half a glass and sat down with her, sipping.

"Can I have a napkin?" she said.

I reached and handed her one.

"Mom, can you cut my broccoli?"

I leaned over to oblige.

"Yum," she said, tasting the pasta, and then, "Mom, can I have chocolate milk? *Please?*"

I took a third sip of wine. I could eat cake with the best of 'em, but three sips of wine and I was corked. "Okay," I said, because if I was drinking wine, why shouldn't she drink chocolate milk? I got up and took out the Quik.

"Can I make it?"

I nodded, and she knelt up in her chair and scooped out a monstrous tablespoonful. I forced myself not to say anything. She glanced up at me through raised eyebrows, then quickly dumped the chocolate powder into her milk, spilling some onto the table. She licked the spoon, coating her lips with dusty brown, then leaned down and stuck her dark tongue on the table to suck up the rest. I watched in silence. She was so much like me it scared me. Even the behaviors I'd been careful never to show her seemed present from conception, ingrained in her brain from the earliest strands of DNA. "Mmm," she said, swallowing and closing her eyes, and then she looked at me. "How come you're being so nice tonight?" She forked up pasta, watching me as she chewed.

I laughed. "I don't know. I'm just in a good mood."

"Because Zach's coming over?"

I nodded. "That's one reason. Honey, don't talk with your mouth full."

She took another enormous bite. "I wish Daddy was home, though," she said, after swallowing this time. She finished her pasta and put down her fork. I still hadn't touched mine. "I'm still hungry," she said.

"Well, eat your broccoli, and your chicken—oh, shit. I mean shoot. I forgot to put in our chicken nuggets."

She smiled. "Moron."

I laughed, shocked she'd know that word, then made myself stop. It was one of my no-no mother things, laughing at her when I shouldn't. "That's not nice," I said, trying to sound firm. "It makes people feel bad when you call them a name like that."

"Sorry, Momma."

I nodded. "Where did you learn that word, anyway?" I smiled again; I couldn't help it.

"Clementine's dad yelled it out the window one time, in the car."

Adele and her husband were divorced. I'd never even met the father. And when had Hazel been in the car with him? I made a mental note to check him out, then got up to make the chicken.

"Be right back," Hazel said, running off. "I'm getting my gum, for after."

"Wait—Hazel!" I yelled after her. "You're not excused yet."

No response. I stuck the nuggets in the toaster oven to heat slowly, then sipped my wine. I wasn't hungry. I was—jittery. Jittery and a little buzzed. Happy, even.

My mind jumped to Kevin, and I couldn't help wondering whether, despite my age, he thought I was pretty. Immediately, I chastised myself for the thought. What was so great about being pretty, anyway? I'd spent years making myself look less pretty than I actually was, just to make a point. After junior high and high school—years of straightening my hair, coating my eyelashes with mascara, stuffing myself into too tight clothes—it was heaven to troll around Barnard in baggy jeans, big old sweaters belonging to whatever boy I was sleeping with at the time. Later, working at a trendy alternative teenage magazine, my sense of fashion—or lack thereof—fit right in. I worked all the time then, day and night. After work and sometimes a run in the park, I'd go home to my tiny apartment and read poetry, working my way once again through my old *Norton Anthology,* trying to memorize two or three poems a night, occasionally trying to write a few too. In the morning, I'd rise early, throw on all black—T-shirt, miniskirt, tights—and be at work by eight to get a jump on the rush. I was the copy chief at the magazine by then, leading a department of three women through irreverent little write-ups about skin cream, tampons, the latest hairstyle, cover lines like "50 Ways to Twirl Your Hair (Okay, Only Two)," or antimakeovers where they stripped off some girl's slutty makeup and tamed her Big Hair to give her a more "natural" look. It was still all about products, of course, but at least it had the *feel* of something a little less scary and annoying than the usual fashion magazine. There were pieces about incest and sexual abuse, divorce and dysfunction. Working there felt right. It was about the opposite of pretty, or so I told myself.

Later, after I met Paul, I had let myself be pretty again—or at least, I'd relaxed a little with the short tight dark clothes, bought a few flowy dresses, jackets that weren't black. My hard-assed look didn't cut it in the places Paul took me, nice restaurants and off-Broadway plays, the opera sometimes. Then I got pregnant, and we moved, and within a year I was a young suburban mother of the sort I never dreamed I would be, expensive shoes and clothes on my slightly puffy body, expensive haircut framing my romantically exhausted new-mother face. That was pretty too, I supposed, in its way, but after a while Paul wanted to go out and do things again, and I had to try a little harder to make myself look pretty the *other* way: put on a little makeup, do something to my hair. That's when it occurred to me that it was one thing to choose not to be as pretty as you might, and another altogether not to have the option of being pretty if you wanted to. Tiny forks were forming at the edges of my eyes, skin softening and melting high on my cheeks. Then I got pregnant again, and Oliver was born and died, and the mirror became a thing of the past. Paul was working a lot, and we weren't going out; there was no reason to dress up. I had entered my hibernation. And now—well, now I seemed to be coming out of it. But so far, when I looked in the mirror, I had no idea what I saw. Did I look sophisticated, or just old? Mature and knowing, or haggard and over the hill?

I took my last sip of wine and put down the glass. *No,* I decided. *It would not be a bad thing to be pretty now. Not at all.*

# Chapter Three

The chicken nuggets were done. I got up to take them out. "Hazel!" I called. The doorbell rang.

"Zachie!" Hazel shrieked from upstairs. She rushed down with a tremendous clatter, wearing my square-heeled leather boots and a billowing pink tulle and satin dress I'd found in a thrift shop. She reached the door just as Cindi opened it and Zach shot in.

"Hi, Zachie," I said, smiling at the sight of his perfect little form. I bent down for a hug, but he ran straight to Hazel.

"Want me to get you all dressed up too?" she asked him, after their passionate embrace. "I'll be Cinderella and you can be the wicked stepsister." She took his hand and dragged him up the stairs, joy spread like jam over both of their faces. Cindi and I watched them go. Then—reluctantly, I confess—I turned to her.

We hugged and kissed, she enveloping me in the cloud of her grape-scented hair gel, a smell I knew would linger on me until my next shower. "How are you?" I said.

Cindi stepped away from me and shrugged. "Okay, I guess, except swamped with work, as usual." She rolled her eyes dramatically. "And also, I just got my hair cut and it's horrific. I told him a trim, and I swear he cut, like, three full inches. I feel totally bald."

Cindi had been awarded Best Hair at our high school, back when she'd had natural mustard-colored locks that waved their way down to her waist. Since then, she'd shortened her Rapunzelesque do all of four or five inches, compensating for its eventual loss of color and luster with highlighting and the heavy use of sculpting products. To Cindi, there was no such thing as a good haircut. "I wouldn't worry," I said, after a bit of fake scrutiny. "It looks exactly the same as always."

"Really? You swear on your mother, I mean Mom?"

I laughed. You could take the girl out of Jersey, but clearly you couldn't take Jersey out of the girl—not that Cindi had ever left anyway. "If I must," I said.

"Thanks." She grinned. "Mm, it smells good. What are you making?"

"Kid food," I said. "Ragú, or whatever. Want some?"

"Maybe. Let me see it."

She followed me into the kitchen, where she peered at my still full plate. "That doesn't look bad," she said, bending to sniff it.

"Help yourself. I didn't touch it, and I'm not really hungry. Mike it if you want."

"No, that's okay. That's way too much for me." She got up and fixed herself a plate exactly like mine except with less on it. "Do you have parmesan?" she asked. I nodded toward the fridge, and she found it and pinched about three specks onto her food. Then she added salt, pepper, and about six different spices, heated it in the microwave, and sat down. She spread a napkin daintily on her lap and looked at her plate. I watched her, knowing she wouldn't eat more than two bites.

"So what's new?" she said, pushing the pasta around with her fork. "Anything?"

"Well, let's see. Paul's working late. Ha-ha." I sighed. "But how can I get mad, when he's working on a death-row case?"

"He is? That's so cool." She took a tiny bite, chewing at least fifty times before she swallowed. "I didn't realize his firm did cases like that," she said. "I thought it was a typical corporate law firm."

"It is. And they usually don't. They took this one on pro bono. Paul asked to be involved. It's an amazing case. Some guy in Arkansas accused of murder during an armed robbery and sentenced to death, all for a crime that took place when he was probably five states away, visiting his grandmother on her birthday."

"Get out. Really?"

I nodded. "The case was appealed, of course, in Arkansas, and they lost the appeal. So now Paul's firm is stepping in. And he and his friend Mark are the litigators. It's very exciting, but the work is endless."

She nodded and took another bite. "So I guess you haven't seen much of him lately."

I shook my head.

"And you're okay with that?"

I shrugged. "As I said, it's for a good reason. And anyway . . ." I glanced out the window. "I like being alone. And alone with Hazel too. It's good for us."

"But not all the time," Cindi prompted.

I sighed. Ever since she'd discovered therapy last year, Cindi was everyone's shrink. "No, of course not all the time." Then, before she could launch into some long soliloquy about denial, I said, "So let's see, what else is new— Oh! I met a new neighbor today."

"Really?" Her eyes darted around the kitchen, like, if I was going to bore her with new-neighbor stories, at least she might find something half decent to look at.

"Yeah," I said. "Cute. Young. His dog pooped on my lawn, and I told him off." I laughed. "He came back later to borrow sugar, though, so I guess he forgave me."

She looked at me again. "How young?"

"Fifteen." I laughed again. "No, maybe twenty-two, twenty-three? Just a kid. So no, alas, he's not the husband you've been searching for."

"I'm not *searching*, Elayna. I'm perfectly happy without some man in my life that I have to wait on hand and foot and then deal with his dick hanging in my face every time I walk in my bedroom, thank you." She put down her fork. "Really, though, that's *so* unfair. If *he* was thirty-nine and *I* was twenty-three, society would smile at me for dating him."

I tried not to smile at her myself. My role as her younger sister was and always had been to placate and soothe her, even when I thought her ridiculous. Which seemed to be more and more these days. "Well, yeah," I said. "Or, you know. Not."

"Why not?" she snapped. "I mean, look at Dad. He's, what, sixty now? And his new girlfriend is twenty-three? Or did he move on from her to one who hasn't hit puberty yet?" She sniffed. "My point is, no one thinks it's a problem, because he's the man. Plus, it's all part of his *art,* or whatever, for him to fuck the women he shoots. Ugh. Excuse me while I go regurgitate." She got up and went back to the counter. "What's this?" she said, opening a white bakery bag.

"Muffins," I said, glancing over. "Paul brought them last night."

She opened the bag and took out all three muffins, setting them side by side on the counter. Examining them from all angles, she plucked out the one in the middle. "Can I have this one? Is it oat bran? If I don't start my day with something fibrous, I don't poop all week, and this morning, I actually didn't get—"

"Have whatever you want, Cindi. Help yourself."

"It's *Cynthia,* Elayna, don't forget, okay? It would mean a lot to me if you'd at least attempt to embrace this change in my life. But listen, are you *sure* about the muffin? Because I don't want to take it if it's, like, the last one, or if Paul—"

"It's fine. They're just getting stale anyway."

"Thanks." She grinned, returning to the table. "So what were we talking about?" She snapped. "Oh yeah. Dad."

"Oh yeah," I said, unenthusiastically.

She looked at me. "How come you never want to talk about Dad?"

"How come you always do?" But I knew the answer even before she launched, with all the zeal of the converted, into the details about Judith, her shrink—some new age Freudian Buddhist a friend of hers had hooked her up with. "And frankly, it boggles my mind," she was saying, "how rampant the dysfunction was and basically still is in our family." She waited, and when I didn't respond, she continued. "Screwed up does not begin to describe, Elayna, I'm telling you. First of all, Dad was completely inappropriate. Especially with you, of course, since you were the quote-unquote pretty one, but really with all of us. And the way Mom was so utterly passive about it the whole time they were together? I mean, almost despondently so. Don't you think?" She broke the muffin in two. I watched her mentally compare the two halves, then reach into one and pluck out a fraction of a walnut. She popped it in her mouth. "Oh. These muffins are *fabulous.* Where did Paul get them?"

I shrugged. "New York, I'm sure. Want me to ask?"

"Oh, that's okay, don't bother, I'm sure they're absolutely loaded with fat."

"So?" I said. "You could use a little fat." Cindi weighed all of ninety pounds, a fact she accentuated by dressing in tight black clothes much of the time. She spent every waking hour she wasn't at work, on a date, or at home (ostensibly with Zach, though no doubt also sawing away at her StairMaster) at the gym, furiously working off any semblance of flesh that might have dared to stick to her skeleton.

"Elayna," she said, patiently, "I'm just trying to stay healthy." She looked at me. "You don't have to worry as much. You're not a single parent. Plus, you're tall." She plucked out another nut and ate it slowly. "Mm. Dee licious."

There was a crash from upstairs. I looked at Cindi, but she was absorbed in her muffin. I got up and went to the bottom of the stairs. "Hazel?" I called up.

She appeared at the top. "It's okay, Mom, that was just the dress-up basket falling over. With Zachie inside it. Ha!" She giggled, and then Zach appeared next to her, wearing only a diaper and a feather boa, the latter tied around his head Indian style. "Hi, Aunt Layna," he said, smiling, melting my heart.

"Hi, sweetheart. Are you okay?"

He nodded.

"Are you having fun up there?"

He nodded again. "Hazo dessing me up."

"That's good." I smiled. "Want me to come up and play with you guys?"

"No!" Hazel shrieked. "Mom, do *not* come up! It's supposed to be a *surprise*!"

"All right! But be careful, please." I went back to the kitchen. Cindi looked at me guiltily as I came in. "I took half of another muffin and put the first one back," she said. "It wasn't actually that good after all."

"What?" I looked at her.

"The muffin. I took—"

"Oh. Fine." I sat down. "Cin, did you talk to your new shrink yet about why you're like this about food?"

"Like what?" She stiffened. "Listen, if you were gonna get all pissy about the muffins, you should have just told me from the start. That's why I kept asking. God, Elayna! You're such a bitch."

"I'm *not* all pissy—" I stopped. What was the use? "Forget it," I said. I got up and turned on the kettle, just to do something.

"Just so you know," she said, "I *am* working on my food issues. And Judith says it's because I feel unworthy. Like I don't deserve to eat a whole muffin." As if to prove it, she pinched off a crumb and popped it into her mouth. "I have low self-esteem, in case you never noticed. Thanks to Dad." Another crumb. "Just be glad you don't. And why should you anyway, when you were always his favorite? But whatever, you have other problems." Another crumb. "For example, you're highly sexualized. I'm anhedonic."

I raised my eyebrows. "Twin sons of a different mother," I said, trying to lighten things up. "Or maybe I should say twin daughters of a different father."

Cindi stared at me, holding a crumb in midair. "No," she said finally. "*Not* twins. That's the whole point. And the *same* father." She gobbled the crumb. "Anyway, my point is, Dad was highly inappropriate with you—"

"You already said that. Maybe I should make an appointment with Judith too, and she can—"

"I'm serious, Elayna. The way he watched pornography in front of us? The way he talked about other women's bodies all the time?"

"He's a fashion photographer," I said. "Women's bodies are his job—"

"Oh, and so is watching pornography? In front of his children?"

I thought for a moment. "Well," I said, "I have to confess, I don't really remember him watching anything that was so incredibly—"

"Of course not," she said soothingly. "Because you're in denial, Elayna. Hello? *Denial?* You always have been. You've never been a good feminist, either, or any kind of feminist, really. Barnard or not. And that's okay, not everyone has to be political, but . . ." I started to protest, but she cut me off. "Listen, who's the first one who told me I was fat when I came home from college freshman year?"

I sighed. "Dad?"

"Exactly." She stared at me self-righteously.

"Well," I said, after a second, "you have to admit you had put on a few—"

"Of course I had. I was a goddamned tank, okay? I needed an entire new wardrobe, right down to the shoes, and frankly, if you'd stuck me with a pin I'd probably have popped. But did I need Dad to point that out? I mean, did he really think I didn't notice myself?" She shook her head. "If anything, he could have been a tiny bit supportive. But no. God forbid he should have been a grown-up for once in his life."

"Well, you lost all forty-five pounds, plus twenty more, so—I guess you win."

"That's right." She grinned. "He was such a dickhead. Still is."

"Is that what Judith says?"

"No. It's what *I* say. Judith just helps me find the clarity to recognize it. First she meditates me—"

"*Meditates* you?" I smiled.

She rolled her eyes. "Sorry, Elayna, but not everyone can be an English major like you. Anyway, that's half of the session, like twenty minutes, and then—"

"Is she in there while you do it?" I asked. "I thought meditation was solitary."

"Not necessarily. At Buddhist retreats, people meditate in groups. I may actually go to one, if I ever get a vacation again." Cindi was a higher-up on the sales and management chain of a Jersey-based cosmetics company, a job she considered on a par with being, say, surgeon general or a Nobel laureate. "Anyway, no, she's not in there while I meditate. She's out preparing for our energy work."

I started to ask, then thought better of it.

"After the energy work, I'm incredibly lucid," she continued. "It's like I can feel the blood flow into every part of my being. I can actually *feel* my brain cells revitalizing. Some of my biggest breakthroughs come then. You should try it, Elayna. You'd be astounded." She stood up, sat back down, recrossed her legs. "What about the photos?"

"What photos?"

"The ones of you in that red slip of Mom's. That Dad took."

I sighed once more. "Are we really back to Dad? I thought we'd finished with him."

"I'm telling you, Elayna, you should *want* to talk about this. This is for *you,* not me." The kettle whistled, and she jumped up and turned it off. " 'Right back, gotta pee."

I watched her leave the room. As with Pansy, her philosophizing, annoying or not, left a tiny thread of doubt inside me. Reluctantly, I thought—for the first time in years—about the photos she was talking about. My father had shot them when I was eight or nine, but I still remembered it well. I'd been wearing a nightie of my mother's I'd taken out of her closet—cherry red silk, low cut—and posing with my neck thrown back, then splayed in the splits, then bending down, leaning forward. My father was encouraging me, shooting away. I remembered the thrill I felt, doing what I'd seen the models do, and seeing his camera on me as if I were grown up. When the dress started to slip down my chest on one side, my flat round Band-Aid of a nipple peeking out, he didn't say anything, just kept clicking and shooting. Even later, when I saw the photos—black-and-white, sepia toned—the nipple seemed like less of a problem than an interesting phenomenon, something subtly there and vaguely thrilling, until Cindi yelled, "Oh my god, Mom, her boob is showing!" and my mother's face fell into an expression I couldn't read, and a moment later, she whisked the photos away. That night when I went to look at them again, the nipple shots were gone from the pile.

And so what? Maybe they were inappropriate, maybe not; I still wasn't sure. And maybe they contributed to my parents' divorce the following year, but did it really matter, in the long run? They'd have gotten divorced anyway eventually. You could turn everything into something dysfunctional if you tried. You could spend your days dwelling on all the ways we all screw up, or you could accept life's imperfections and move on to the good stuff. Couldn't you? I was ready. I was sick of depression and dysfunction. It had been with me for too long.

Cindi breezed back into the room, sporting a fresh coat of lipstick and dark brown lip liner—something I've always thought someone must have invented as a joke. "Ugh," she said, cheerfully. "I look like I've aged about a hundred years since last fall. Thank god it's getting warmer, so I can lay out on weekends—if I don't end up working every weekend from now until eternity. I'm so riddled with exhaustion these days, I don't know my ass from my elb—"

A door slammed upstairs, and Hazel came clomping down. "Mom!" she yelled.

"What?" I stood up as she skidded into the room, still in her pink dress, now with gold glitter smeared on her arms and face. "Hi, Aunt Cindi," she yelled.

"How are you, big girl?"

"Good. Did you bring me any perfume?"

"Hazel!" I reprimanded, but Cindi said, "I'm so tired right now, cupcake, I can't even move to get up and check. If you remind me in a few minutes, though, I'll see if I have some samples in my purse. Okay?"

Hazel clomped over to Cindi. "I love your hair," she swooned, running her palms over it. "Mom, don't you LOVE Aunt Cindi's hair? Can I brush it?" Before Cindi could answer, Hazel yelled, "Oh my god, your boots are *so* cool! Can I try them on? Pleeese?"

"If you lower your voice about ten thousand decibels *and* promise never to call me Cindi again when my name is *Cynthia,* then yes, I guess so." Cindi bent down and removed one boot. "But just for a minute, because if Zach sees you, he'll want to wear them too, and then—"

"Where *is* Zach?" I said.

"Upstairs," Hazel said, taking the boot from Cindi. "He's putting on makeup. I already put some on him, but he wanted more, so—"

"Oh shit, makeup?" Cindi looked at me. "Zachariah!" she screamed up, without so much as turning her face toward the stairs.

"Zach*ariah*?" I said.

"I changed his name too," Cindi said. "Names that end in *e* are derogatory. Besides, I always loved the name Zachariah. It was his father who insisted on Zachary, but now that that asswipe is out of the picture, excuse my French, I might as well—"

"You said a bad word!" Hazel yelled. "Asswipe! Mom, she said asswipe!"

Zach clacked loudly into the kitchen. "Look, Mom!" he shrieked.

"Look at me!" He was wearing Hazel's plastic high-heeled Barbie dress-up shoes, a glittery magenta sequined tank top, and his diaper. The boa was now twisted around his legs, and his hair was knotted into some sort of crippled dreadlock, cemented with gluey glitter gel. His cheeks were covered with what appeared to be pink lipstick. I stood up, laughing.

"He's my orphan stepbrother," Hazel explained. "And I'm Britney Spears."

Cindi jumped up. "Oh my god, Zach. What *is* that, all over your face?"

"Tiptick," he said.

To her credit, Cindi laughed. "It's *lip*stick, you goof." She sighed. "Oh, Zachie, I'll never get that off. Why did you have to—"

"It's okay, it's kids' makeup," I said. "It washes right—"

"The thing is, I'm supposed to meet someone in half an hour. I don't have time to hose him down."

"I'll do it. Come on, Zachie, want to take a bubble bath?"

"No, there's not time," Cindi said. "I'll have to take him with me like that."

"Well, where are you going?"

"Out to dinner, in Weehawken."

"*Weehawken?*" I smiled.

"Well, that's where the guy lives, okay?" She glared at me. "It's a blind date, actually. With a guy Judith knows."

Oh great, I thought. Another New Jersey Buddhist. "That's nice," I said. "What does he do?"

"He's a personal trainer. He's really nice on the phone." She smiled. Then her smile dissolved, and she sighed. "So, Zachie's coming with us. The sitter has the flu."

"Why don't you just leave him here?" I said. "I'll give him a bath and put him to bed. You can get him tomorrow morning."

Cindi looked at me. "*Really?* You'd *do* that?"

"Of course." I'd have kept Zachie every night if she'd let me.

"Oh my god, that would be *heaven,*" she said. "I could stay out, I could *relax—*"

"Yay!" Hazel yelled, leaping up and down. "Zachie, you're having a sleepover! You want to wear the Barbie pajamas or the pink and purples?"

"Baow-bees," Zach said.

"Okay. Come." She dragged him off again.

"Hazel," I called after them, "put all the dress-up clothes back in the bin, and I'll be up in a second to give you a bath." I stood up and started to put my dishes and Hazel's in the dishwasher, knowing better than to touch Cindi's.

"Thanks," Cindi said. "Really, Elayna. That's totally sweet of you."

"It's no problem. But I should go get them started. Want to come up?"

"Oh, that's okay, I'm gonna get going." She put her full plate in the sink.

"Okay," I said, a tiny bit glad. "I'll walk you out."

At the door, she yelled up, "Bye, Zachie! Kiss kiss! Be a good boy!"

No response. Cindi turned to me. "What time should I pick him up tomorrow?"

I thought a minute. "Why don't I drop him off. Around eleven? Because Hazel and I are meeting Dad for lunch, and I don't want to be late." It was out before I really knew what I'd said.

Cindi stared at me, aghast. "You're *what*?"

"Meeting Dad for lunch. In the city. Why?"

She continued to stare.

"What?" I said, finally. "He's our *father,* Cin. And Hazel's grandfather. And he asked to see her."

She shook her head, as if deeply disappointed in me. "I don't know, Elayna. Do your really want to expose Hazel to that?"

"To what?" I would not be brought down by her hysteria. I simply would not. "It's fine," I said. "Really, Cindi. What's he gonna do?"

She bit her lip dramatically, then shrugged and turned away. "Listen, it's your life. It's your daughter." She sighed. "I just wish you'd go see Judith sometime. I'm telling you, Elayna, she could help you so much."

"Well, I don't actually need help right now," I said, slightly annoyed. "I actually feel pretty good at the moment, for a change. But thanks," I added, halfheartedly.

"I'm just saying, she might help you see some things that you can't right now, or maybe never could. That's all."

*And she might help me see things that were never there at all,* I thought.

She was struggling to pull on her enormous coat now, apparently unaware that it was practically summer outside. "Funny how he never asks Zachariah and *me* to come in for lunch," she said, giving the coat a final yank.

*Aha!* I thought. *So that's what this is.* "Maybe that's because he knows you'll say no," I said. "You haven't agreed to see him in years. And Zachie's too young anyway. It's not like he asked us when Hazel was two—"

"Listen, he wouldn't be asking us if Zach was six either. Now, if Zach was a *girl . . .*"

She paused. "But it's fine," she said, her voice suddenly lighter. "I have no desire to see the guy anyway." She leaned out to air-kiss me, and now, amazingly, it was as if she'd dismissed the whole thing. Not like her. For a second, I couldn't help thinking that maybe Judith was doing her some good after all. "You do what you need to do, sis," she said breezily. "I'm just saying, I hope you'll be careful. I don't trust him."

*Well, you never have,* I thought, but I said, trying to keep things light too, "Thank you, oh Mean One." It was a longtime shtick we had going, that she was the "mean" sister and I was the "nice" one. But really, I thought, it was more that she was the angry sister, and I was the—what? Depressed one? Not anymore. Happy one? Well, I did feel happy, at that moment, but I wasn't sure I'd go quite that far. Highly sexualized one? I thought about that one for a second. "*Mom!*" Hazel called down.

I glanced upstairs. "Coming!" I called.

Cindi grinned at me. "Have fun," she said breezily, and out she went.

# *Chapter Four*

Later, after I'd bathed the kids, read them a book and four poems, given them milk and brushed their teeth and located Clod, the stuffed donkey Hazel had seized on years ago and Paul had named on a whim, played them "Bye Bye Miss American Pie" (small effort to combat Britney Spears) and kissed them each dozens of times until they finally fell asleep, curled together like hamsters in Hazel's bed, Zachie practically swallowing his thumb, Hazel's nose pressed into Clod's dilapidated fur, and I'd wondered ever so briefly if I should put Zach on the floor, where he couldn't fall out, then decided to leave him with her—they were too perfect, huddled together this way—after all that, I went downstairs and stood there a moment, trying to decompress. *Tick tick tick.*

But my mind was still whirling. I couldn't calm down. I pulled off my shoes and padded around barefoot, looking at things: the small pewter horse, a wedding gift from Paul's famous doctor aunt; the pile of magazines on the coffee table—*Harper's, The New Yorker,* the *New York Law Journal*—all of which I liked to think I'd flip through but, let's face it, would not. I went back to the sculpture, its front legs and hooves reaching as if it were galloping hard toward something, and I imagined myself on its back, flying through the night. Outside, I could hear the trees blowing. I was jumping out of my skin. I went to the base of the stairs and listened. Silence. I turned and walked out the front door.

I confess, I looked first at the Tenement. The top floor was dark. Kevin must be out, probably with some punky chick with green hair. I glanced around to make sure no one was looking, then walked out to Hazel's swing, the grass cool on my feet, and sat down. I leaned back, letting my head drop. Oh, it was heaven! The full moon—alternately veiled behind the fast-moving clouds and then sliding into view, exposed once again—was a dazzling jewel, a ripe orb. And the wind, oddly thrilling (dare I admit?) in its blood-warm, greenhouse-effect mutancy, was coming from somewhere, bringing something. Hazel would've cowered under its ominous hand, and right then, I was glad; better that she be cautious. But me? I was ready to have it, whatever it was bringing, to have at it all. I opened my arms and swooned as it lifted my shirt away from my body, coaxed my hair off my neck and whipped it around, teasing and tickling.

Was Cindi right, then? Maybe I was "highly sexualized." But she was describing my past. It had been years, really, since I'd thought of myself as a sexual creature. And whose fault was that? Hazel's? Paul's? Little Oliver's, poor baby boy? But it had happened before him; before Hazel, even. I squinted up, catching glimpses of stars flashing, hiding, flashing again. Certainly, in my premarital days, I'd had lots of sex. Men had liked my body—the big boobs, no doubt—which was fine with me, since I liked their bodies too. And I'd liked the seduction, the chase . . . *so long ago now*! I swung the swing so high I was almost horizontal, my hair sweeping the ground when I descended again. In my midtwenties, one man—a middle-aged hippie who played saxophone and smelled of brass and valve oil and tasted deliciously of cigarettes—had told me I "exuded sexuality." My relationships back then were heated, passionate. After the seduction, the high lasted weeks, occasionally months, and then it fell away, and perhaps because I picked men I knew from the start I wouldn't love, I simply moved on to whoever was next. I had no interest in love then, and I told people that. When the sax man made noises, albeit sheepishly, about a real relationship, I was disappointed with him, as I knew he was with himself; we parted shortly afterward but got together once a year for a drink in some murky bar, just to remind each other the spark was still there, that we could always dip in again. But it wouldn't have been the same, and we knew it.

With Paul, though. With Paul, it had always been different—perhaps, if I want to give myself credit, because I knew a good thing when I saw one, though it could also be the timing was right to let someone like him into my life. I was twenty-seven, as autonomous and self-sacrificing as I'd ever been. I wasn't even sleeping with anyone. I worked all the time, even weekends; at night, I ran miles through Central Park. My life felt simple and pure, admirable, I thought, in a librarian sort of way. I liked my solitude—though I admit that occasionally I felt a twinge of panic. If I died, if one day I didn't wake up, who would even notice I wasn't around, let alone care? I had Celeste, of course, but we didn't talk every day, and I had my work colleagues, but none of them were good friends or people I saw outside the office. Sometimes, usually in the middle of the night, I had visions of growing old alone in that little apartment, slowly going out of my mind—coming downstairs and outside once a day in the filthy minidress I'd worn for the past twenty years, staggering to the local deli to get my tuna sandwich. What was to stop me, except for my job? And magazine copy-chief jobs were precarious. There was always someone else coming up the pike, some eager new smarty wielding her pen. My mother was married to Walter by then, still in Jersey, and the two of them did their own thing, oddly removed from me. My father was on the Upper East Side, living in the expensive condo he'd bought after the divorce, shooting supermodels for *Sports Illustrated* and *Elle.* He stayed out of my way and I stayed out of his, moving through my days focused on my job and my body in that way a single working person with few obligations can be.

That was when I'd met Paul. His firm was in midtown then, near my office, and one day we were both in the same mega sushi/pasta/salad/burger/Korean market/deli place buying lunch, weaving through a million darkly dressed New Yorkers filling their plastic containers. Paul was in front of me, moving down the assembly line toward the register, where a Korean cashier rang up orders in a fraction of a second and her cohort bagged them equally fast. I noticed Paul's tray before I did him, filled as it was with tortellini and artichokes and black olives, a fresh peach, some expensive sparkling drink. Next to his container were two dark chocolate bars from the gourmet section in back, a section I frequented myself for those very bars, though I'd been trying to cut back lately, an effort to even more fully librarianize myself. But I'd never done well with deprivation, so of course I noticed his chocolate right away, and then I noticed his hands: medium large, nicely groomed. No ring—not, I told myself, that I particularly checked. His tie, dangling just over his tray, was silk, royal blue. An electrifying feeling went through me.

He turned and smiled, probably noticing me drooling over his tray, and his smile—pretty and genuine—had an instant calming effect on me. "Those are awesome," I said, indicating the bars with my chin, and immediately I was horrified I'd used that word, smacking as it did of bong-smoking geek or horribly misplaced early nineties valley girl. He took the bars off his tray and placed them on mine, next to my salad, my little crate of tekkamaki, my package of sesame-seed bread sticks. "Good," he said, meeting my eyes with his lovely brown long-lashed own. "I was hoping to give them away so I wouldn't have to eat them myself." By the time I could protest, he was handing the cashier a twenty and telling her to charge both lunches to him, keep the change, and then he received his bag and smiled at me and moved out of the store with the crowd, expensive suit creasing in all the right places.

I took the candy back to my office, oddly thrilled. The next day I went back to the deli, where, naturally, he wasn't. I went every day for a week before I saw him again, and then there he was: cranberry tie, this time, but same brown curls and brown eyes, tallish, solidly built, a look of half pleasure, half stress on his face, as if only what was in his head kept him from being a purely cheerful, happy guy. Anyway. My heart stopped.

I made myself go up and say hi. "Thanks for the chocolate," I said, and was suddenly overcome by a horrible feeling that he wouldn't know who I was.

But he looked at me and smiled. "You're welcome. I actually know you, I think. Didn't you go to Columbia?"

I blinked, then nodded. "Barnard."

"I knew it." His smile grew wider, and I saw that it created a striking dimple under his left eye. "I went to Columbia Law School," he said. "I used to see you around now and then, you and another woman, dark, sort of Cleopatra hair . . ."

"Celeste," I said. "My best friend. Roommate, back then."

"Huh. So she still lives here too?"

"Where else?"

He nodded. "We actually took a class together, you and I. A poetry seminar, on Blake. With that nutty, brilliant guy with the beard, what was his name?"

"Bob Glavin. You're kidding. You were in that?"

He nodded. "I audited the class. I love Blake."

"You *do*?"

"Es-kuze me, you can plees talk somewhere else?" It was the cashier. We were blocking the flow.

"Want to sit a minute?" he asked. "My name is Paul, by the way. Paul Slade."

"Elayna. Leopold. Nice to meet you." We shook, then sat down. We talked for an hour before we went back to work.

I sat up on Hazel's swing now, remembering, slowing my pumping a little to let the crazy breeze toss me around. How long since I'd thought about all this? Years. And I loved thinking about the beginning; it could always give me a rush. We didn't sleep together for a long time—at least compared to all the other guys. We didn't even kiss. We'd have dinner and he'd walk or cab me back to my apartment, where I'd invite him up and he'd say no, he had to go, had to get up for work tomorrow, had to, I don't know, go water his plants. He'd kiss me on the cheek, wait until I was inside, and then he'd be jogging down the street, hailing a cab. At first I was charmed, and then miffed (Was he gay? No. No way.), and then slightly insulted. What was the problem? But he always called the next day, by midmorning, to say he'd had a great time and when could we do it again, how about early next week?

I'd liked him more and more. He was my intellectual soul mate, my sharer in sensibility. His eyes were rich, dark, vaguely troubled in all the right ways, yet never without a gleam that made me imagine the kid he'd once been. When I told him about the boy in the sailor suit I'd seen peering intently at a window display of stuffed birds and a nest with a perfect little blue egg in it, and how the boy's mother, dressed in a suit and heels and talking on her cell phone, dragged him away without noticing, he understood why this made me want to cry. I told him about Cindi, about my father, my mother. He listened and nodded, reserving judgment, perhaps until he could meet them himself. He was a lawyer, after all. He bought me a dozen bright green carnations from Gristedes when I told him he had tacky taste (which he didn't), just to prove me right. We fought about books and movies all the way up Broadway, through the Seventies, the Eighties, over to Eighty-ninth and Columbus, to the door of my dilapidated brownstone.

So one night, I didn't invite him up. It was a warm, humid night, and I was full of food and wine, giddy from our walk, a little sweaty (I was wearing the jacket I'd worn to work, too lazy to take it off and carry it), buzzed and high from his presence. I wanted—I wanted more of him. I wanted the whole thing. I wanted to know what was going on in that part of his brain that wasn't so decent, so perfectly polite. But I wasn't about to be rejected again. As we approached my building, I felt myself getting pissed off at the very thought. "Well—bye," I said, before he could peck my cheek as usual, and I turned and started to go in.

He reached for my arm, tugged at a strand of my hair, and that tug woke my entire body. "You're not inviting me up?" he said.

"No." I raised my eyebrows and shot him as snotty a look as I could muster.

He grinned—some combination, I thought, of amusement, regret, confidence, and something else, maybe (I hoped) lust. Then he put his hand inside my jacket, the bastard, and rested it, palm open, lightly on my waist. "Please?" he said.

"It's hot up there," I managed.

He laughed. "Oh. Forget it then."

So he came up. He came up the stairs behind me, hand still on my waist, burning through whichever one of my T-shirts, black or white, I was wearing that day, no doubt with some little black skirt. At the first landing, he turned me around and kissed me once, lightly, on the mouth. *Okay,* I thought, and I stood there, trying not to respond but feeling that kiss work its way through me. We continued up, three flights, four, five, until I was fumbling with my keys, trying to get us inside. Maybe this was where he'd tear off my clothes and ravish me. But he wandered in respectfully, looked around, took off his jacket and put down his briefcase and loosened his tie. I could smell him in that room, his expensive leather belt, the starch on his shirt, the mildly minty lotion he used after he shaved.

I got out some cheap red wine I had stashed somewhere for just this sort of thing, and he took the bottle from me and opened it and poured us each a glass, handing me mine. As he drank he walked around, looking at framed photos, asking me things. Was this my father? Me as a kid? Yes, I said, yes yes yes. I clutched my hair up off my neck in back and fanned myself, blowing air down my T-shirt. "Sorry I don't have air-conditioning," I said. "I'm sort of environmentally opposed, but it's not like I wouldn't blast one right now if I had it."

He laughed. "It's nice like this." He was looking at a volume from the collection of Shakespeare my mother's father left me, flipping through it. He put it back and looked at me, hard.

"What?" I said finally, blushing a little. I wasn't a blusher, but you have to understand the atmosphere.

He came over to me, closer than he'd ever been. I could smell the wine in his mouth. He raised his hand, as if to touch my hair again, then let it drop. He shook his head. "What am I gonna do with you?" he said softly, almost as if he were asking himself.

My stomach unzipped; my whole body did, really.

"I've wanted to come up here every time you asked," he said. "But—I don't trust myself with you. I don't want to rush, but I'm not sure I can stop once I start."

My body was one big, fat, pounding heart. "Don't worry," I said, and I laughed nervously. He should only know.

"Give me this." He took my wineglass and turned to put it down somewhere, and I saw his back through his shirt, his shoulder muscle through his expensive white shirt, and then his cool, wine-tinged mouth was on mine, and I could finally kiss him back, channel all those weeks of waiting, of wondering, the heat of my body and that stuffy little room, all of it, all of it, into this man I liked so much who was standing there waiting for me.

Well, you know how it is at the beginning. I won't go on and on, but can I just say this? He was like a wall I butted up against, protective and unyielding at once, something that both held me firm and held me back. Isn't that what love is, the real, long-term kind? But I was ready for a wall, defensive, flaky wisp that I was. I had been like a kite, flying high in the wind, picking up things—men—and dropping them the second they couldn't hang on, not wanting to be weighed down or steered anywhere.

Not wanting to go anyplace but where I wanted in that obstinate, twenty-seven-year-old way. But for all my autonomy, I was random, I could have disappeared or hit a tree and gotten tangled or floated too high and lost myself in the clouds, and he was the boy who took my string and held on and flew me—anchored me, yes, but also gave me direction and substance and heft. What's a kite without a kid? A brilliant glimpse, a striking eclipse, and then gone.

For a while, the sex was as good as it gets. There was the rush, the chemical high, the soapy showers together and obligatory takeout in bed and wearing of his clothes to my job so I could smell him all day. And then one day—a year, maybe fifteen months later—I realized something had changed. *I* had changed. Perhaps I had only just come down to earth, but I didn't want to jump his bones anymore. I was shyer in bed—more submissive, less adventurous. Was it because I no longer needed to conquer him, because I had him now, all of him, and he had me? There was no awkwardness to our relationship that sex needed to smooth out. It was already smooth. I respected and loved him. I felt *loving* toward him. But I craved his presence, not his body, and when I had his body, I approached it physically, not passionately. I had to close my eyes and fantasize about someone else when we had sex, because if I saw *him,* I felt loving and affectionate, not charged and horny.

For me, you see, love and sex had always been two different things, opposite and often contradictory. With the other men—none of whom I'd been in love with—I'd been free to be slutty, dirty, to debauch myself, but that was the opposite of being *loving,* and now, in the face of the real thing, I couldn't connect the two. It embarrassed me to try. I felt overly self-conscious, self-aware, when I started to lose myself in passion, and so I pulled back, slowly becoming a boring, passive, prudish *wife,* in my mind and in the bedroom. I wanted the lights out during sex. I wanted to do it quickly, not luxuriate. Don't get me wrong, we were still having sex, still getting off. The physical part was okay. But we had it down to a science, and a science is what it became: two substances in a beaker, shake until they explode and then move on to whatever, the laundry.

Paul didn't protest, though I can't imagine he didn't notice the change. And in all fairness to myself, maybe some of it came from him too. He was tired, he was working hard—trying to make partner at the firm—and also, his passion had always been for the intellectual, the cerebral; for fighting what was wrong in the world at large. Which is not to say he wasn't present or loving with me, when we both were around. He liked sex just fine and he always gave as much as I wanted, but when I stopped wanting—when I checked out mentally—he didn't really seem to mind. And I was glad for that, because, perhaps arguably, I don't think his demanding more of me would have helped. How can someone tell you what to feel? And it might have made things worse.

But I wondered: Did this always happen to wives (I considered myself his wife already, as our marriage was imminent), or was it just me? I spent the obligatory few sessions at an overpriced shrink trying to figure out the answer to that, though mostly wondering if she knew it and wouldn't tell me so I'd keep coming back, or if she was as clueless as I (in which case, why go?). Eventually I realized that, regardless, my contemplating ad nauseum the reasons I didn't long to have passionate sex with my longtime love—cute as he was, much as I loved him—was a rather solipsistic and indulgent pastime. Which might have been okay if it was making me change somehow, but it wasn't; it was only making me dwell on it all, and soon I grew impatient with the whole therapy thing. We were both working ten-, twelve-hour days—at least that much, in Paul's case—him supposedly saving the world while also saving for our Life Together, me supposedly saving the world's teens. And then we were married, and quickly I was pregnant, and then we were here, thirty-five minutes outside the city in this New Jersey suburb where Paul could commute in and out easily, not have to leave too early or get home too late, and I could raise my babies.

Or baby, as it turned out, who had grown into a girl as Paul, now a partner, left-earlier-stayed-later anyway, and our sex life further dwindled, in that way that was maybe a Problem or maybe just what married sex lives do, in the suburbs, with jobs and children and houses. Or anywhere, with anything, for that matter? Yes, we were busy, yes, we were exhausted in that new-parent way, but most of all, we were spouses now, our love was the *married* kind—years beyond that passionate, chemical-bath thing at the beginning when the sight of his suit or the sound of him taking a shower could make me go instantly weak. We were partners now, good partners, sharing a bed, a bathroom, a bank account. I loved Paul, as I love Paul now.

But we were down to having sex four times a month, then three, sometimes two. Was this okay? I didn't really know. But I didn't particularly miss it, and if Paul did, I didn't know it. He didn't have time to miss it. And I found my passion in Hazel: in the soles of her buttery feet and the tiny folds of her ears; in the sweet French-toast smell she emanated and her snotty, entitled little grin. And then her voice, and the way she laughed, and even the way she cried—that shrieky sandpaper roller coaster wail so wrenching and lovely I cried myself sometimes at its sound—and her fat little sausage-link arms and baby-ham thighs, propelling her around the house like an earthy slug, then a crippled turtle, a pregnant ladybug, a guinea pig, a gerbil, a mouse, and finally, standing, toddling, a chimpanzee, then a sprite leprechaun as she grew tall and thinned out, got surer and more deft on her feet. I was enraptured. And then I was pregnant with Oliver, first sick as a dog and then large and luxurious and excited, and then he was born, and then he died. And I plummeted. How could I bear this? *How?* I reminded myself that mothers had been bearing this for all time, sometimes four, five, six times in a row. It helped not at all. All my passion, all my everything—except for what little I was able to reserve for Hazel—all else became sadness. Passion was a thing of the past.

But now, now, oh, *now,* in the heat of the night, perfume from my lilac bushes wafting over me . . . something was brewing. I felt it from my scalp to the tips of my toes, on my skin and in the meat of my bones. I saw it in the moon and I smelled it in the air, I could hear it on the wind and in the impending rain.

A car was coming. I blinked into the headlights as it moved slowly toward me, until I was sure it was Paul's Saab, till I heard his music, opera music, pounding away inside it, the way he always blasted it when alone in the car. I felt a moment of joy as the car turned into our driveway and cruised past me, just as I felt the first drops, wet and wonderful, splash onto my bare arms, my bare feet. I pumped harder as Paul pulled into the garage, and then I heard the car door slam, and then the garage door come down, and then his shoes on the pavement as he headed toward the back door. "Paul!" I yelled. Cool rain pelted me.

He came around front, carrying his jacket in one hand, his briefcase in the other. "Elayna? What are you doing out here?"

"Swinging in the rain," I said, and laughed at my pun.

He smiled too, lifting his briefcase up over his head. "Where's Hazel?"

"Inside. Sleeping. Zach is too." I slowed down a little. "I thought you'd be later, actually."

"I bagged it once I realized I'd never finish tonight." He sighed. "I have to go back tomorrow."

"I figured."

"I know. I'm really sorry."

"It's not me, it's Hazel. But we have plans for tomorrow anyway—plus, she's so happy Zachie's here, she probably won't even notice."

"Thanks."

"Oh—I didn't mean it like that." I slowed to a stop. "Also, the house could use some work. It's sort of crumbling around us—"

"I know. I know. Sunday I'll do everything, I promise."

"What, call all the men? They're closed on Sunday."

He laughed. When we'd first moved here he'd tried to do all the house projects himself—usually for about five minutes per project, until he realized he simply didn't have time. Then he'd give up and call someone in. Or rather, I'd call someone in. After a while, he skipped even the trying; he'd just tell me who to call and why—the roofer, the electrician, the stonemason—and I'd set it up and let the guy in and let him back out when he was done, and Paul would come home later and admire it and, at bill-paying time, write the check. But lately we hadn't done anything. We had barely looked at the house. The paint was peeling, one front step was cracked, the screen door was sliced through with a tear. The garage window was still broken where I'd whacked a Wiffle ball through it last summer. And so on.

"I'm going in," Paul said. "Come on, you're getting soaked. How long have you been sitting out here?"

"It just started raining," I said, in lieu of answering his actual question, because I didn't know that answer, I realized. Had I been out here ten minutes? A half hour? I jumped off the swing and followed Paul up the front steps. But as soon as he opened the door, I froze. A low, moaning cry was coming from upstairs. "What's that?" I said.

Paul looked at me. Then he dropped his briefcase and jacket and took the stairs two at a time. I ran up behind him.

It was Zach. He had fallen out of bed and was lying on the wood floor, crying softly but not fully awake. "Oh, Zachie," I said, and I pushed past Paul to pick him up. "Oh, little sweet boy. You fell out of bed! Are you okay?"

"Bring him here," Paul said, motioning me into the hall. "Is anything bleeding?"

I carried him out. He'd stopped crying and was now asleep on my shoulder, his breaths steady and even—as opposed to mine, shallow and panicked.

"Is he okay?" I said, as Paul examined him. "Do you see anything? Oh my god, Paul, what if he has a concussion?"

Paul was carefully moving Zach's limbs, extending each arm, gently bending his wrists. He felt all over Zach's head, then neck, then shoulders. Zach continued to sleep.

"Should we wake him?" I said. "Aren't you supposed to, if they could have a concussion?"

Paul considered, looking at Zach. "I don't think so," he said, finally. "He seems fine. Let's just put him back to bed."

"Are you *sure*?"

"No, but I'm pretty sure. No part of him seems injured, and he didn't fall very far." He sighed. "You could call the doctor, but he's gonna say to take him to the emergency room." He looked at me, like, *Do you really want to go that route right now?*

"No," I said. "I think he's okay, if you do." I trusted him, though I don't know why; he was a lawyer, not a doctor. But he had good judgment. Better than mine. "I'll make him a bed on the floor," I said. "That's what I should've done to begin with, but—"

He was still looking at me, waiting, and I thought it was an odd look, perplexed. "How long were you outside?" he asked again.

I felt my defenses rise in spite of myself. "Not long. I checked them both before I went, and they were fine." It was half true. I had listened up the steps. Hadn't I?

He nodded. Then he reached up and squeezed the bridge of his nose, closing his eyes. He got migraines sometimes, and I wondered if this was one of those times.

Zach was breathing his hot little breaths on my neck. "Paul?" I said, suddenly.

"Hm?" He opened his eyes, still pinching his nose.

"Sometimes I can't bear it that Oliver died." Tears sprang to my eyes. Embarrassed, I tried to sniff them away.

But Paul nodded, as if he knew what I meant. He reached out a hand and rubbed my shoulder, the one Zach wasn't on.

"Should we try to have another?" I said, and it was only then that I realized how desperately I wanted another child, another boy. It was like a splinter, a piercing pain that had been there all along, but I'd only just noticed it.

Paul stood perfectly still, but he wouldn't look at me—that was the giveaway—and forgive the cliché, but my heart sank. "It's okay." I said, trying to spare him having to articulate an answer that I didn't want to hear anyway.

"No, it's just—I'm not sure I could go through that again. Not that we *would,*" he added quickly.

"We wouldn't. It would be fine this time. The doctor said the odds of this happening again are—"

"I know. I know." He looked straight at me now. "I'm just not ready, I guess."

"Well, it's not like I'm getting any younger," I said, my voice rising a little.

"I know," he said again. "But it's not like you've brought this up before, either—"

"I've thought about it, though," I said, even if that wasn't completely true. I hadn't been able to, really. "Haven't you?" I asked. "Really, how could you not?"

"Of course I have." He put his hand up, as if to caution me to calm down, and even though I knew he was right—I would surely wake Zach if I didn't shut up—the gesture annoyed me.

"Listen," Paul said, "do you want me to put him down? You must be tired."

"No. I can do it."

He watched me for a second more. "Okay. I'm gonna get something to eat, then." He went in and bent down to kiss Hazel, then proceeded back past me and on downstairs.

I went into the room and laid Zach in the middle of the bed, close to Hazel. Then I got two spare blankets from the closet and folded each one over once, then again, setting them on the floor next to the bed but not so close that she'd step on him if she got out. I transferred Zach down to them, covered him up. I didn't want to be angry at Paul. He didn't deserve it. I looked at Zach and tried to change my mind-set, to focus instead on how grateful I was that he hadn't been hurt, and after a minute, it worked. Who was it who'd once told me that raising safe, healthy children is 25 percent conscientiousness and 75 percent luck? I had failed the conscientiousness part, but luck had stepped in to save me. What did I have to complain about? Nothing. At least not this time.

I went downstairs to Paul. He was sitting at the kitchen table, eating Honey Nut Cheerios from my faded yellow mixing bowl. "Do you want a real dinner?" I asked. "I made salmon today. There's a plate for you in the fridge I could heat up."

He smiled tiredly. "Thanks. I'll have it tomorrow."

"You mean Sunday. You'll be working tomorrow."

"I know, but—I won't have time Sunday. I'll be too busy calling all the men to fix the house."

It was his way of saying he both apologized and forgave me. Paul and I rarely fought. We were friends. He was my best friend. And what was friendship, if not love? I sat down across from him and moved my bare feet over and onto his lap: an affectionate gesture, not a sexual one. He put his spoon down and obediently began to rub my feet—he knew I loved a good foot massage—then looked down and stopped abruptly. "Your feet are filthy!" he said, half amused, half grossed out.

He was right, I saw. "Sorry," I said, halfheartedly. "I've been barefoot all day. It's so warm."

He got up and washed his hands. I guess I didn't blame him—he was eating, after all—but still, I felt rebuffed. "Sorry," I said again.

He sat back down, picked up his spoon, and took a bite, chewing thoughtfully. He was staring at me without really seeing, lost in thought, his spoon in midair. Work, probably. I watched him, almost curiously. His hairline was receding a little in front, but not much for someone pushing forty-one. He still had most of his thick hair. But his usually rosy-tan skin was sallow, the color of someone who spent much too much time indoors. "Did you get out at all today?" I asked.

He snapped out of his daze. "What? Oh—yeah, Mark and I took a walk at lunchtime. The air's so thick, though. Brutal. You almost feel healthier staying in."

I nodded, though I didn't like the idea of him being up in that building for sixteen or seventeen hours at a stretch. Plus, going out with Mark—his colitigator on the death-row case—wasn't exactly taking a break. "How's the case going?" I asked.

He smiled a little, shaking his head. "It's as depressing as it is fascinating. The lawyer for this guy last time was unfathomable. Do you know that he actually said, at the trial, 'I'm not sure I can honestly say that Leroy Clark deserves not to die'? His own client!" He put down his spoon. "This is Arkansas's idea of a defense attorney for a man on trial for murder. A man who's the father of three little kids, with only one prior conviction—for a convenience-store robbery."

"Wait—I thought you said he had something like five prior convictions."

"That's how they presented it. Turns out it was all the same crime. They charged him for five offenses based on that crime, and then the prosecutors in the murder case kept referring to his 'five prior convictions,' misleading the naturally all-white jury to believe that this guy is a career criminal who's been convicted of violent felonies on five occasions." He gave a quick, bitter, silent laugh. "His own lawyer didn't bother to dispel that misimpression. Wouldn't want to waste breath."

"Wow," I said. I was starting to get a sense of what he was dealing with.

"I know. It's unconscionable." He was getting worked up, as he always did when discussing this case. "And there are all these relatives and friends who have the most amazing things to say about this guy," he said. "He mowed his sister's lawn, he brought his sick aunt groceries . . . even his ex-wife talks about how he sent her money for their daughter whenever he could. His lawyer didn't bring one of them to the stand."

I clucked my tongue.

"Well, we'll get them all up there at the hearing," he said. "Lots of people to prep, though. I'll be spending a fair amount of time in Arkansas over the next few months." He blinked, as if just remembering I'd be part of that. "Unfortunately," he added, for my sake.

I shrugged, gave him a small smile.

He took a deep breath. "Anyway," he said, picking up his spoon again, and I knew he was trying to come back to earth, to his Other life. "So what's up with you? How's Cindi?" He took another bite of cereal.

I sighed. "Cindi's Cindi. Hyper and furious." I picked up a pencil and doodled on the table. "She was going on a date."

"Ooh." He grimaced, then swallowed. "Hope the dude drank his coffee."

"Doubtful. He's a personal trainer. And a Buddhist, I think. He probably drank his valerian tea."

Paul laughed.

"I know. Her shrink fixed her up."

"You're kidding."

I shook my head. He was finishing his Cheerios now, neatly spooning milk into his mouth. I'd have picked it up and drunk it from the bowl, slurping as I went. I licked my finger, rubbed at the pencil marks I'd made on the table. "I met a new neighbor today," I said, and something inside me tightened, as if I'd just committed some faux pas. *Ridiculous,* I told myself, and I booted the thought.

He got up and put his bowl in the dishwasher, not really listening anyway. "Should I run this?" he asked.

"Is it full?"

"Yeah."

"Then . . . yeah." I resisted adding, *unless you'd like breakfast in a dirty bowl.*

He poured in the soap and turned the thing on. "I'm going up," he said.

"I've gotta get back fairly early tomorrow. Mark's coming too. We'll probably be there through dinnertime." He looked at me guiltily.

I sighed. "Don't worry," I said, after a moment. "We're having lunch with my father in the city, and then he's taking Hazel for a little while so I can see Celeste. Oh—that reminds me, I need to call her back." I stood and reached for the phone.

Paul nodded. He gave me a quick kiss, then left the room.

*He was nice, the neighbor,* I added silently, to his disappearing back.

I called Celeste and my father, leaving them both messages asking where we should meet; then I wiped down the table, tossed the sponge in the now running dishwasher, and picked up Hazel's shoes, coloring book, doll's tights, and Tweety Bird Pez dispenser from under the table and carried them all upstairs. Paul was snoring lightly, his stuffed-up springtime snore. He'd left my bedside light on for me. I went in and brushed my teeth, splashed my face. I thought about washing my feet, but decided against it. To hell with that.

Back in our room, I climbed into bed and pushed rudely up against Paul's big warm body. Without missing a beat in his snore, he moved to accommodate me. The last thing I felt before I drifted off was his big, clean, well-groomed foot wrapping itself around my grubby one, holding on to me.

I woke to the feeling of someone breathing directly into my face. I opened my eyes. Zach and Hazel stood, bride and groom style, about an inch from the bed, both wearing sunglasses. I closed my eyes again. "What time is it?" I mumbled.

"Um—big hand on the four, little hand on the six. No, the seven. No—well, sort of a little closer to the six," she said. "No, wait, it's—"

"It's practically the middle of the night," I said. "Go back to sleep."

"We can't!" Hazel said. "It's light out, and anyway, Zachie's pull-up leaked, it went all over the blankets on the floor. Mom, how come you took him out of my bed? We wanted to sleep *together.* We were playing *married* people."

"He fell out of your bed," I mumbled, and then I forced my eyes open.

"Zach, let me see you. Are you okay?" He stood there while I blearily looked him over. "Thank god," I said, falling back to my pillow.

"Mom, can we come in with you?" Without waiting for an answer, they both climbed roughly onto the bed and then in, Hazel between Paul and me, Zach on my other side. Paul groaned now, slapping his hand over his head. But I didn't think he minded. He'd gotten seven good hours. And he'd barely seen Hazel all week.

We lay there like that for a while, four warm bodies in a bed, heaven on earth. And then I thought of Oliver, and suddenly I didn't want to be there anymore. I struggled out of the bed and went downstairs. I opened the front door and blinked into the sunshine, already warm. Another scorcher on the way. "Mornin'!" someone called, and I squinted out to see Mrs. Zuppo, my neighbor, waving from the sidewalk in front of my house.

I waved back. "Out early today?"

She nodded. "Well, the doctor says if I don't walk, I'm gonna have a heart attack and die. So, what are you gonna do? Walk, I guess." She laughed, huffing and puffing.

"Well, good for y—" Something silver caught my eye, protruding from the mailbox. "—you," I finished, snatching the foil-covered package. Lumpy, the size of a small loaf of bread. There was a note sticking out of the foil, folded white paper ripped from a spiral pad. I pulled it out and read it: "*Hazel—Here are some cookies. Hope you like them. Love, Kevin.*"

I dropped the note, picked it up, dropped it again.

"Anything good?" Mrs. Zuppo asked.

My heart, that traitor, beat its little wings. "Cookies," I said. "Want one?"

"Oh no, I couldn't." She waved a fat hand. "Give 'em to the baby." Mrs. Zuppo's five children were all grown up. To her, I imagined, Hazel would be a baby at eighty-five.

"Please," I said. "There are plenty here for the baby, not to mention the rest of the neighborhood." I glanced into the packet. "They're enormous too."

"Well . . ." She took a small step up my walk. "Okay, if you're sure. But just one." She lumbered up the walkway, sweat glistening on her forehead. I felt a pang of guilt at stunting her weight-loss efforts so directly. But really, what was I supposed to do? Sweet Mrs. Zuppo, with her lovely gardens, her old metal swing set that she'd never removed so that her grandchildren and my daughter could use it anytime.

I peeled back the foil and held out the packet, and she took one, as did I. We smiled at each other as we chewed. "Oh my," she said. "I'll have to get her recipe."

"I'll ask her." I bent to pick up the paper, so she couldn't see my face. "Well, have a nice walk," I said, straightening up, and I slipped the note back in the foil, sealed up the packet, and went inside.

They were all downstairs now, Paul giving the kids horsey rides around the living room, Hazel and Zach screaming with joy. I stuck the packet in a kitchen cabinet, then proceeded to make whole wheat pancakes while Paul dressed the kids. Then I took a long, hot shower, leaving him in charge. When I got out, there were messages on the voice mail—Celeste saying she was free all day until six, and did I want to go shoe shopping? And my father saying we should meet him for lunch at a place called the Parlor, on West Fiftieth Street. "Have Hazel wear something appropriate, of course," he instructed. "And bring her camera, I'll show her how to work it." I sighed as I erased the message, wondering why he couldn't take her to Serendipity or some other normal spot for a six-year-old. But she'd probably love this. I had, at her age, when he'd wined and dined me. And then he'd take her off and entertain her, and I could go see Celeste. Win-win. How could I refuse?

My mind shifted gears. I hadn't given Hazel the cookies yet, and I knew it was because I didn't want to do it in front of Paul. *And why not?* I asked myself, and, as if to prove I had nothing to hide, I opened the cabinet and took out the foil packet and placed it on the counter this time, albeit toward the back, and knowing Paul probably wouldn't be in the kitchen again before he left. *There,* I consoled myself anyway, and I pushed any further thoughts of anything illicit right out of my mind.

# Chapter Five

My father, Devon Richard Leopold, was as prompt as he was immaculate. So when Hazel and I arrived at the Parlor at 1:03—she in her ankle-length plum chiffon gown, I in brown cropped slacks and a white linen blouse—he was already seated at a choice table in what struck me as a vaguely brothel-like room (think low light, red velvet curtains, drippy chandeliers), sipping his trademark double Stoli with lime and thoughtfully observing a table of ferociously chic women to his left. He stood when he saw us, and with his subtly perfect tan, slimly toned body, close-cropped silver hair, and black linen suit with expensive T-shirt underneath, he was the picture of the thriving middle-aged New York Man in the Arts, be he architect, editor, fashion photographer, or ad writer. "Hello, my darling," he said, bending to kiss Hazel Euro style, on both cheeks. He did the same to me, but afterward I reached out and hugged him anyway—something that must always have caught him a little off guard. My family were kissers, not huggers; I had learned hugging from Paul and his mother, before she died.

It had been a while since I'd seen my father, and the last few times other people, including one or another of his girlfriends, had been around, flanking him, distancing me. "You're looking well," he said, when we'd finally settled in, ordered drinks, and dispensed with the tactfully hovering host. "Not as thin as you have been, but on you that's a good thing. Your face was gaunt last time I saw you."

"Thanks," I said quickly. "You look healthy too."

He smiled. "I just got back from a week of shooting in Monaco. It's tough not to return from Monaco looking better than when you left, working or not."

"What's Monaco?" Hazel said. She picked up the pepper shaker and shook pepper onto the table.

My father reached out and took the shaker from her. "Monaco," he said, sweeping the spilled pepper into his palm and discreetly discarding it under the table, "is an exotic and beautiful place on the French Riviera that's full of exotic and beautiful people—particularly women. Someday, if you'd like, I'll take you there."

"Cool!" she said. "Like, this summer?"

He glanced at me, amused. "A few years would be preferable," he said. "Then I could take you into the casinos with me."

"Try a decade for that," I said. "At the very least."

"A decade, then." He shrugged at Hazel.

"What's a decade?" she asked.

"Ten years."

"I'll be . . ." She began to count on her fingers. "Fifteen—no! Sixteen!" she yelled.

"Shh! But very good!" I said, impressed as always with whatever prowess, intellectual or otherwise, she cared to display.

My father took a sip of his drink. "She's as brilliant as she is ravishing."

"Thank you," I said, accepting the compliment for myself—after all, I had created her—and pleased with it against my will. I could do without the commentary about my weight, especially in front of Hazel, but I relished it when he was impressed by her.

"Not unlike her mother at that age," my father added.

"I wasn't close to her on either count," I couldn't resist mumbling.

"I beg to differ," my father countered.

Again, I felt a flash of the ambivalence I always felt around him: the thrill of being attended to and adored combined with the discomfort of such close scrutiny. His clear gaze at me, so blunt and intimate—and so coveted when I was a kid and he wasn't around much—now, as lately, felt a little too close. It was what had made me separate from him in my twenties, when I needed space to screw up with no one watching. When I married Paul, the distance with my father stayed. Paul liked him well enough, but he didn't entirely trust him; and my father was enmeshed then in a social world—models, agents, fashion editors half his age—that I had no desire to enter or even see.

But when Hazel was born, I'd inched closer to him again. I wanted her to know her grandfather, and him to know her. It had been slow at first; he didn't know what to do with a baby except photograph her. And after Oliver died, I couldn't face him any more than I could face anyone, so I'd taken a hiatus from the more frequent contact. Only recently had my father and Hazel started to get to know each other in any real way. And—just as I had, as a child—Hazel adored him and the sophisticated attention he focused on her. "So what else is new?" I said, trying to steer the subject away from either Hazel's or my appearance. "How's—I'm sorry, I forgot your girlfriend's name."

"Sandra? She's fine, I think, although I've been feeling a little, I don't know." He took another sip of his drink. "Restless, I suppose."

"Really," I said, not making it a question, because frankly, I didn't want to know.

"Mm." He looked up contemplatively. "I went out last night with an older woman. Lavinia. To the opera, and then out to eat." Another sip. "Well, old compared to the others, I mean. Your age, probably. Midthirties. A photographer, actually."

"Huh. Was it fun?" Again, I didn't need the details but didn't want to be rude.

He frowned a little. "Fun? No, I wouldn't say that. It was more amusing than fun. She was beautiful, of course, but completely distracted. An intriguing topic would be introduced, and before you could sink your teeth into it, she'd leap up to go to the restroom or make a phone call. Things kept stopping and starting, rather than building. So the whole meal had the feeling of, say, premature ejaculation rather than foreplay."

"What's foreplay?" Hazel said.

I turned to her, actually surprised by her presence; she'd been sitting there quietly listening. "Nothing you need to know," I said, and I looked at my father. "Could you edit your conversation? She's six, don't forget." *And I'm your daughter,* I almost added.

"Forgive me," he said, and, as always, I did. I don't know why. Perhaps because he forgave me everything, all the time, and one good turn deserved another. Or perhaps it was because, his offenses and inappropriateness notwithstanding, I didn't think he really meant to harm anyone. Even when he'd philandered, even when he'd left us, he'd still loved my mother. You could see it in his eyes when he'd come to pick us up—the way he glanced around us in the doorway to see if she was there, the way he waved to her when he drove us away in the car. I think he'd have stayed if he could have without hurting her, but his job, his needs, his very presence in our house were sucking the life out of her. He'd had to betray either her or himself, so he'd chosen her, but the way I saw it, it wasn't so much a choice as his sad destiny.

My father picked up his glass and finished his drink. "Anyway, enough about me, how are *you*? Still feeling run-down? Did you see that doctor I told you about?"

I shook my head. "But only because I'm so much better lately."

"Good! You did those things I said with your diet, then? Cut out the chocolate, added the pomegranate juice?"

"Not really," I confessed.

He smiled. "Well, I'm hardly one to criticize. I have my own vices, as we know."

"What's a vice?" Hazel said, and again, I found myself turning to her in surprise. No doubt she'd realized that if she remained unobtrusive while scanning the conversation carefully, she'd hear all sorts of juicy tidbits.

"A vice," my father answered, "is something depraved. Something bad. Though bad is all a matter of degree, of course. It really depends on whom you ask. Where one person might think a vice is, say, littering or smoking a cigar, another might think it's, you know, bopping someone over the head with their shoe." She giggled, and he grinned at her. "And how are *you*, my dear? Are you in love?"

"Eww!" she shrieked. We both shushed her immediately. "I do have a boyfriend, though," she said, in a slightly lower voice. "Roger Simprey. But I kind of hate him. Clementine hates hers too. Hers is Ethan Wilson."

"Ah," said my father. "Unfortunate, if they're your boyfriends."

"I know. But I like him *sometimes*. Just not every day."

"I know what you mean." He nodded sympathetically. "And your girlfriends? Who are they, besides Clementine?"

"Destiny, Sage, Jenny, Willow, and Cray."

"*Cray?*" he said.

She nodded. "Cray Emerald Jones. But she's not my best friend. Clementine is. I love her. She's going to a wedding. And she taught me Jacob's ladder. Want to see it?"

"Of course," he said.

"But you have to have a rope, I mean a string, I mean yarn. Yarn."

"Naturally," he said. "We'll buy some."

She grinned.

"And how's your father?" he asked. "Well, I hope?"

She nodded. "But he works twenty-four seven."

I laughed. Surely she'd heard me say that (in one of my dorkier moments), but still, even the *way* she said it, her expression, her intonation . . . just like mine.

"He could've joined us," my father said to me. "He knows that, of course."

"Thanks." I smiled politely. "He had to work today, actually. He's working on a death-row case that's got him consumed. But he likes it, I think."

"Well, of course. What's not to like about hard work, if it's good work. It's buoying. Ego affirming."

"Yes," I agreed.

A woman walked by the table—tall, striking, tight black floor-length skirt and neat little braids held back with what appeared to be a glittery silver sock—and my father watched her until she'd disappeared into the restroom. *No doubt imagining how he'd photograph her,* I thought, giving him the benefit of the doubt, but I felt myself shift in my seat. Had he gotten worse—his appetites, his lack of shame about them—or had I gotten more conservative? Or simply more aware?

A waiter arrived with my wine, and I accepted it with relief. He placed a tall Shirley Temple in front of Hazel, ordered by my father. "Whoa!" she yelled. She started to reach in for the cherry, then looked at me. "Can I?"

"Of course you *may,*" my father answered for me. "Just don't drip cherry juice on that stunning dress, please. Here, I'll help you." He slid her cocktail napkin from under her glass and held it below her chin as she popped the cherry into her mouth. "Delectable, no?" my father said as she chewed.

Hazel nodded. But then her face changed, and she turned to me in a panic. I grabbed my napkin and held it under her mouth, and she spit the chewed-up red bits into it. "Sip your water," I said, and she did that too. She put her glass back and frowned. "That was *disgusting.* It tasted like *cough* medicine."

"And that's probably more or less what it is, minus the medicine," my father said. "Red dye and a few choice chemicals." He looked at me. "Nicely handled."

I raised my eyebrows. "How would you have handled it differently?"

"Good question. I probably wouldn't have handled it, actually. Your mother generally took care of that sort of thing."

"You didn't like messes," I offered.

"Well, no. I didn't. I credit my father for that, actually." He picked a piece of invisible lint off his jacket and flicked it away. "Apparently, when I was two, I would make myself vomit when I was angry. One day, in his care, I vomited all over the place. He picked me up by a clean part of my vest, removed all my other clothes, and spanked me. According to him, I never vomited again. And I don't believe I did." He took a sip of the fresh drink that had somehow appeared in his hand.

Hazel and I both stared at him. "He *hit* you?" Hazel said, echoing my thoughts. "For *throwing up*? When you were *two*?"

"That he did." He looked almost pleased about it.

I felt a wave of sadness for him, his poor little-boy self. "Things were different then," I said to Hazel. "Lots of people spanked their kids." I thought about Zach—his pointy little shoulder blades, his paper-thin baby skin—and I had to blink several times. I thought about Oliver. I gulped at my wine, and then at my water.

Immediately, a waiter appeared and topped off my glass. "Would you like to hear the specials?" he asked.

"Absolutely," said my father. He tipped his head back and closed his eyes lightly.

The waiter began: braised this and flame-grilled that, scallops and sea bass and some caviar thing. Fennel and rosemary. I didn't listen carefully to any of it. I felt vaguely unsettled.

The waiter finished, and my father opened his eyes. "We'll start with the two special appetizers," he said. "The feta and spinach, light on the cheese, and—"

"Do you have any French fries?" Hazel interrupted.

"Don't interrupt, baby," I said.

"I'm sure I could drum some up," the waiter said, without smiling.

My father nodded. "We'll take the shrimp too, please. We'll need another minute for the rest." The waiter departed. My father looked at me. "You'll stay for lunch, then?"

I shook my head. "I was thinking I'd finish my drink and then go see Celeste, if you were serious about that offer."

"Absolutely," he said. "Hazel and I have plenty to do together."

"Can we take pictures?" Hazel asked.

"Of course. We can do whatever you want. I was thinking we could maybe go over to the Met and pick out our favorite impressionist paintings, and then we could go to the park and shoot some photos of ducks or maybe interesting people, if we see any, and then we could go have a Coke. Your mother can meet us back at my apartment whenever she wants. Sound okay?"

Hazel motioned me closer. "He said he'll get me a Coke!" she whispered loudly.

I shrugged. "When you're with Grandpa, he makes the rules."

Her eyes widened with joy. My father stirred his drink, eyes fixed on her. "So then," he said. "Let the wild rumpus start."

"*The Wild Things!*" she yelled.

"Exactly."

Hazel beamed. Then her expression shifted, and her eyes slid over to me. "Mom, you can go."

I hesitated, as I always did before leaving her, anywhere. Then I stood up. "I'll be back at—let's see. Five?"

My father nodded, and I reached into my bag. "Take my cell number," I said, scribbling it twice—once for him, once for her. I leaned down to kiss her. "Call if you miss me. And listen to your grandpa." I started to amend it, just as a joke—*unless he tells you something absurd*—then thought better of it, I don't know why. Instead, I kissed my father—only one cheek this time, no big hugs—and made my exit just as the waiter headed back to the table with two artful appetizers and a heaping plate of French fries.

# Chapter Six

I took the number two subway downtown, refusing to let further thoughts of my father interfere with the bliss of my ride. I had never minded the subway, but now that it wasn't a regular thing in my life, I had come to relish it: the decadent blast of cold air upon entering the train, the motley clusters of people huddled together, standing, slouching, tired or angry, frowning or anxious or bland. It cheered me no end, all these different faces and bodies, all the thoughts and lives. I spotted a seat and lurched over, squishing between a plump woman in a red sari and a skinny old—man? woman?—holding bags of leafy vegetables. The train screeched forward, and I smelled bodies, sweat and perfume and hot dogs, saw ads for milk and vodka, a plea not to give to panhandlers, a number to call if you've been sexually abused. In front of me, a large guy with a shaved head clung to a pole, tattoos covering both of his arms, and I stared at them for a while, imagining the pleasure/pain of having them put on, especially inside the elbows and just under the armpits. Below him, a baby stared up from its stroller, cartoon-round white eyes in a creamy round face, and I caught his attention and made faces at him until he smiled at me, and then his mother did too. After a while, I leaned back and closed my eyes. The subway, with its blunt, no-bullshit beauty and ugliness. There was nothing like it in the suburbs. Absolutely nothing.

I got off at Fourteenth Street and Seventh Avenue and headed toward Sixth Avenue and Eighth, continuing to soak in the buzz around me. Like the poet mouse Frederick in Hazel's book, I would store it away to take out on a tedious day when I was stuck at home doing laundry, paying bills, dusting the TV. At B. Dalton, Celeste's and my regular meeting place before I'd had Oliver—it was now Barnes & Noble, of course, but we still called it Dalton's in amused protest of enormous chains taking over slightly less enormous ones—I went in and spotted her in the new fiction section devouring some book, her coolly chopped straight black hair falling into her face, which was heart shaped and very white with full berry-colored lips and extremely dark, long-lashed eyes. I headed over happily, waving when she saw me.

She hugged me, the corner of her book pressing pleasantly between my shoulder blades as her arm came around me. "Anything good?" I said, jumping right in.

"No—bad, actually," she said. "This new novel by Curt Blonfield, have you heard about it? It's the story of a sexually harassed woman who ultimately falls in love with her harasser. Written from the woman's point of view by the ever sensitive, empathetic, and versatile Blonfield."

I laughed.

"It takes place half on a plane to India and half *in* India," she continued, "so there can be the requisite India scenes from Blonfield's year in India that his parents funded between funding his college education and funding his MFA. Oh, and there's a sixty thousand first printing, in case you needed to ask."

"I didn't."

She nodded matter-of-factly, then closed the book and hid it behind several other books on the shelf.

"But you don't hold a grudge, or anything," I said.

She looked at me for a moment, then suddenly smiled. "And how are *you*? You look great. So much better than last time."

"You think?"

She nodded, still assessing. "It suits you, that moneyed, casual-chic look of a rich bitch in the burbs."

"And you yourself are looking very Williamsburg," I returned. "Love the new glasses. Very nouveau nerd."

"Oy. I've gotta get out of that town, now that all the fashionably clad twenty-two-year-old video artist-slash-trust funders have taken it over, pushing out all the exceedingly more noble thirty-five-year-old novelist-slash-temps such as myself. I swear, you can't even smoke on the sidewalks anymore. Everyone's all about, like, yoga and chai."

"Shame."

She smiled. Then she reached over and hugged me sideways. "I'm so glad you came in. I was starting to think you'd found a new best friend. I was envisioning someone with pastel jogging suits, frosted hair, a book group that reads all the Oprah selections, and a very perky dog, or something. To match her upbeat personality."

"Never," I said.

"Well, thank god for that." She glanced around briefly. "Do we want to go to this Starbucks, the one down the block, or the one across the street? Or walk a block and pick from the ones over there, so I can have a cigarette on the way back?"

"Cigarette, if you want."

We crossed the street with a small army of people, went in, and got in line, listening to the clatter and whir of the coffee machines. Celeste ordered a double espresso, I a hot chocolate. I paid for both drinks over her protests, crushing a dollar into the tips cup for the corporate counter slaves. We made our way down the assembly line to retrieve our drinks.

"Well," I said, as we settled at a table, "should we get the small talk over with?"

She nodded, sipping her drink. "I'll go first. Paul?"

"Eight," I said, as in eight out of ten, and then, "well, actually, more like six. He's working too much—but . . ." I shrugged. "Could be worse, I guess."

She made an invisible check mark in the air. "Work?"

"It's okay. I still like doing the work, though I never talk to my boss anymore. I hand in my edits and never hear back. I hope that doesn't mean they're about to ax me."

"The opposite. It means you're so good they don't have to micromanage you."

"Well, thanks, but . . . I actually used to sort of *like* talking to her. It was nice to hear that I'd done decent work." I sighed. "I feel like a Stepford editor now."

She clucked in sympathy. "And Hazel, that raucous little beast?"

"Ten, of course. Except when she's being a two. She actually said to me the other night, 'Mom, I love you as much as a snow cone. And *so* much more than Jack Pim."

"Who's Jack Pim?"

"A kid in her class who she hates."

We both laughed loudly. "So how about you?" I said, sipping my drink. "How's your apartment, your mother . . ."

"Apartment, fine. Mother?" She made a face. "I'd rather be kind."

Celeste had grown up in a small town in Minnesota, in a house with six kids who had three different fathers, one of whom stuck around to beat up her mother every few days. She was the only one of her siblings who'd gone to school consistently; at age fourteen she'd landed a scholarship to Andover, raised money for plane fare by babysitting, then left Minnesota and never looked back. At Barnard, where we'd met, she'd taken out massive loans and worked as a cocktail waitress to put herself through. While we were there, her mother married and divorced again. Celeste had skipped the wedding. "Okay, then," I said, happy to change the subject. "Work?"

"You mean the day job? Two. Barely bearable, hate every minute—but can't quit, need the money . . . the usual."

I gave her a sympathetic look, but she shrugged cheerfully. "I know, you can hear the little violins, right? Don't worry, I don't mind. It keeps me tough." Three days a week, Celeste worked twelve-hour shifts as a highly paid temp for Palm Wireless International; one day a week, she volunteered for several hours at a shelter for battered women. She wrote her novels at night and on weekends, churning out about one a year, and between those and the temp job, paid her bills and student loans with some left over to feed her expensive-clothing habit, take occasional exotic vacations, and still stash some away. She designed her own schedule at the temp job, partly because she typed about ninety-five words a minute and partly because her boss, an aging alcoholic executive, had lusted after her from the second she appeared in his office five years ago, fresh from the temp agency. "Boss still a lech?" I asked.

She nodded. "Still dropping paper clips so he can bend down and look at my crotch, then go whack off in the bathroom. Though it's getting harder for him to get up once he's down. The other day I practically had to go over and help him— Oh! I almost forgot! They hired a new temp, a *boy*! Absolute eye candy. He's a um—*poet,* of course." She smiled. "He's the type who tells people he grew up in Harlem when he was born in a luxury high-rise in Morningside Heights and then moved to Westchester at age three. You know? The type whose book jacket will say he hails from Washington, D.C., when in fact he lives in suburban Maryland?" She sighed. "But I forgive it all, because he's so luscious and I'm so damn shallow."

"You are."

Looking pleased, she sipped from her minimug, pinkie high in the air.

"Speaking of which," I said, "are you still seeing the editor? Stephen. Right?"

She nodded, smiling.

"So when do I get to meet him? It's been what, like, four months? Unheard of!"

She shrugged pleasantly and took another sip of coffee.

"Well, what's he like?" I pushed. "Are you in love?"

"I am, actually. I like him. It's very fun, and very liberating. It's—intense."

I felt a wave of envy. "Why liberating?" I said. "Do you mean compared to the others?" Celeste's answering machine was always full of male voices offering to fix her broken air conditioner, take her out for dinner, lend her this or that. "When do I get to meet him?" I said again.

She shrugged once more. "I don't actually see that much of him."

I narrowed my eyes. "Celeste, tell me the truth. Did you meet him online in a chat room, or some horrible thing?"

She laughed. "No! I told you, he works with Susanna." Susanna was her editor, at Viking.

"So then why don't you see him more?"

She played with one of her many silver bracelets. "He's busy, I'm busy, we respect each other's space . . . you know. Like that."

I decided to let it go and come back to it later, maybe after I'd revealed something juicy and she owed me one. I sat back. "Well," I said happily, "I have a mystery man in my life too. Except he's not a mystery, really.

He's actually just the opposite. Ringing my doorbell, bringing me cookies, and—"

"Wait—*what?*" she said.

I debated, but only for a second. And then, in a rush of nervous excitement, I told her about XY Boy's dog pooping on my lawn, me rushing out to scold him, his comment about Alanis Morissette, which made me realize that he'd seen me dancing in my underwear, that he'd actually watched me.

"Wow." Celeste laughed, her black eyes alight. "Were you furious? Or—"

I shook my head. "The thing is, I *wasn't.* I was mortified, of course, but . . ." I sighed. "I feel like a jerk even saying it. Like I'm betray—"

"You liked it." She grinned. "You got off on him having watched you."

"Well—it didn't bother me. Or if it did, I got over it pretty fast. I mean, he's this gorgeous young thing. Why would he waste his—"

"Because you're the gorgeous older woman! The kid has a Mrs. Robinson fantasy."

I laughed. "God, we actually probably *are* around that old now, aren't we."

"Sadly, yes," she said flatly. "Anne Bancroft was thirty-five when she played Mrs. Robinson."

"Are you serious?"

She shrugged. "As serious as the internet, anyway. There's no such thing as real fact anymore."

I told her the rest of the story—how he'd come back later to borrow the sugar, how he and Hazel had made friends. She listened, rapt. "Wait," she said at one point, and she reached down and opened her purse, took out a cigarette, and placed it between her lips, then said, "Okay, go on." I told her about the cookies, his note. She removed the unlit cigarette from her mouth and sat up straight. "Wow. He's hot for you, Elayna."

Her words filled me with panic and joy. "He is not."

She put the cigarette back in her mouth, took a dry drag, then held it between her first two fingers, blowing out nothing. "Does he know you're married?"

"Of course. He lives across the street."

She shook her head, smiling. "So what are you gonna do?"

"What do you mean?"

She looked at me. Neither of us moved. "What!" I said, finally. "Are you asking if I'll have an affair with this guy?"

She held my gaze a second longer. Then she reached down and took out a silver cigarette lighter. "Of course not," she said, closing the purse, and I felt as if she'd closed a door then too, one I wasn't sure I wanted closed yet.

"Why?" I said. "Would *you*?"

To my amazement, she lit the cigarette. She took a long drag, then held it under the table. I glanced around. Luckily, nobody seemed to notice. "First of all," she said, exhaling real smoke now, "I'd never be in the situation, since I'm not getting married."

"Never say never."

She gave me a look. "You know I don't believe in marriage, Elayna."

She had, it was true, always said this; in fact, it was one of the things we'd bonded over at Barnard. But I'd always figured she'd come around—as I had, as most women do.

She took another drag of her American Spirit, looking thoughtful. "Second of all—"

"Excuse me," called a frizzy-haired woman from a nearby table. "There's no smoking in here."

"Oops—sorry," Celeste lied. "I'll put it out." She extinguished the cigarette into her saucer, then turned back to me. "Want to go?"

We headed out, blinking into the sun. "Why are you so antimarriage?" I asked, more curiously than defensively.

She looked at me. "You mean, besides the really obvious reasons? Besides the whole, 'If two people love each other and want to be together, why can't they just *be* together, rather than making such a big 'until death do us part' deal about it, with aunts and uncles and second cousins, not to mention the toaster ovens and tablecloths and Calvin Klein sheets, while the rest of us—"

"Humans are fallible," I cut in. "And just maybe that commitment helps us to not fail. You sign up for a semester of school, and you have grades to keep you from bailing midsemester when you're tired and burned out. Right? Or you join a church or temple, where the members nag you to pay your dues, go to potlucks, complete your little rituals and ceremonies . . . all so you don't just go there three times, get bored, and call it quits. And in the end, it pays off."

"Or not." She shrugged. "Let's face it, Elayna, of the half of married couples who don't divorce, how many do you think stay faithful *and* actually care about each other, as opposed to simply staying together because they're too lazy or humiliated or afraid or financially strapped to go out and get a divorce?"

I thought a second. "I could name a few. My mother and Walter—"

"Two long, bitter, heartbreaking divorces, one happy marriage."

"How do you know Walter's was heartbreaking?"

She gave me a look, like, *How many aren't?*

"Okay," I said. "Me and Paul." I wondered why I hadn't said us first.

She nodded, looking down again. Was she failing to meet my eyes, or was I imagining it? "You and Paul," she granted.

"Pansy and her hus—"

"Pansy?" She laughed. "Who the hell is that?"

"Hazel's babysitter."

"Oh. Okay. Pansy." She smiled. "Do you know," she said, "that forty percent of men and thirty percent of women in this country acknowledge having had at least one extramarital affair? And those are just the ones who *admit* it!"

I looked at her skeptically. "Is that true?"

She nodded. "Eighty percent of human societies throughout the world practice some form of polygamy. Ooh! Let's go in!" She pointed to a store called Shoe Explosion.

The place was absolute chaos. Shoes lined every wall, littered floors, protruded from the hands of frantic customers awaiting help. Large red signs in front of racks touted MASSIVE SALE! and WE'LL BEAT ANY COMPETITOR'S PRICE!! A sweaty salesman swooped down on Celeste and me. "You want those?" he yelled at Celeste, in some thick Middle Eastern accent. "What size?"

"Eight," she said. "And those too, please." She pointed to a pair on a chair.

"You got it, doll. Hey, José!" he yelled into his headset, "get me 06817, 14935, and 02134, in an eight." He winked at me, then went over to a cluster of similar-looking men hovering in a corner, where shoes emerged steadily from a hole in the floor.

I glanced at Celeste to see what she made of all this—because it seemed to me that the city had turned into even more of a circus since I'd left—but she seemed unfazed. Our man reappeared with a stack of boxes, dropping them to the floor. Celeste took off her shoes and stuck a foot toward him. "Those are fabulous on you," he said, the second he'd fastened them. "I were you, I'd take two, three pairs of that shoe. It's buy two, get a third half price."

Celeste frowned. "I don't like them. Let's see the next ones."

Obediently, he removed them and placed the next pair on her feet—dark brown platform sandals, clunky as bricks. Celeste stood. "Better," she told him. "Definitely possible, though I'd prefer them in black—"

"Gone!" he yelled. "Sold out the second they arrived. Take the brown while they last."

Celeste gave him a look. "Lemme see the next pair."

It was like a game, New York. Everyone played his role, with pride if not glee. Once more, the salesman bent to oblige, and once more Celeste stuck out her foot and then turned to me. "It's only very recently in our history that people got the idea that marriage should be monogamous," she said to me, as if there'd been no break in our conversation from before. She switched feet for the salesman. "And, like I said, most of us fail at monogamy. Look at your father. My father. My mother. Look at—"

"Meg Ryan," said the salesman. "Liz Taylor. Kate Hepburn. Nicole Kidman, for Christ's sake. There, walk in those."

Celeste clomped around. "That was never proved, was it? That Kidman cheated?"

"Proved?" He clucked. "It was obvious."

"Well, Tom left because he was gay." Celeste sat back down. "And weird. These are good. I'll take these."

"How many pairs you want? Two, or three? It's buy two, get the—"

"I'll take six." Celeste laughed. "Just kidding. One, please."

Outside, we headed east on bustling Eighth Street, which felt virtually dead compared to inside the store. Celeste looked at me. "Do you need shoes? Or do you want to go sit in the park?"

"Park."

We continued east, then turned right onto Fifth, heading toward the arch, then into the park, then over to a cement wall near the amphitheater, which was filled with punks and grungers, someone riding a unicycle, someone juggling three bowling pins. We sat down. A man walked by carrying his cat against his chest in a black trash bag to its neck, its triangle head peering out, marble eyed. Celeste laughed. "Sick place, New York. Don't you miss it?"

"Yeah," I said, though it wasn't that simple. I had loved living here, but I'd been ready to leave when we did; now, I loved it perhaps even more, but with the nostalgia of being on the outside looking back in.

"That's kind of what Stephen looks like," Celeste said, pointing to a stocky man walking by with a red-blond goatee. "Except older and thinner and more—editorish."

I nodded. "Why won't you tell me more about him?"

She gave me an odd look. "Well, for one . . ."

"What?"

She sighed. "He's married. There, I said it."

"He *is*?" It all made sense now: why I couldn't meet him, why she didn't see him much, why she was suddenly so revved up about polygamy.

"Technically, yes," she answered. "Although he thinks his wife is probably cheating too. But that's beside the point, as far as I'm concerned." She looked at me. "Just for the record, it's not like I pulled him into this unwillingly. He pursued *me*."

The juggler, pins now at rest on the ground, was coming around collecting money in a sneaker. Celeste dropped in a dollar. He looked briefly at me, then moved on. "Does he have kids?" I asked.

"Boy and girl. Ten and eight, I think."

"Ugh." The word slipped out of my mouth. "Sorry," I said immediately. "I didn't mean it like that. I just—I was one of those kids, you know. And my mother was the wife. And I have to tell you, it was pretty crappy for her. And for us too. We all knew. My father was—it was so obvious."

Celeste cocked her head, looking genuinely sad. "Oh, honey. I know, it was heartbreaking." She paused. "But Stephen is not your father. Not by a long shot. It's *not* obvious, in his case. He would never let it be. I see him three, maybe four times a month max. And we're very, very careful. We meet in very private places. My apartment, usually, or little restaurants in Brooklyn. I would never call him or blow his cover. I'm not needy like that, and he knows it. So, I'm basically just a few extra hours he's at work, that's all. And when he goes home, he's a happier guy. And I'm happy too."

My eyes wandered to a young couple on a bench nearby, making out. His one hand was in back of her head, twisted in the hair that fell down her back; his other hand caressed her side through a thin white tank top, an inch or two under the bra she wasn't wearing. "That's all you see him?" I said. "Three or four times a month?"

"Usually, yeah."

"And it's been going on for, what, three months?"

"Almost four." She took a deep breath. "It's the best sex I've ever had, Elayna. This guy is so hungry for me, he's so amazingly horny. And so grateful afterward. Do you know, he told me he and his wife haven't had sex for four years? He doesn't dislike her, mind you. They're very amicable. They just don't want to fuck each other. And he still wants to fuck." She shook her head, smiling a little. "Four years of celibacy for a guy not even middle-aged. Only marriage or, like, leprosy can inflict that on somebody."

The couple got up and moved on, his arm around her waist. "That's such a sad view of marriage," I said.

"I know. And I'm sorry, because I know they're not all like that."

But I thought again of my father, breezing into our house after spending the day shooting beautiful women, slinky dresses with nothing on underneath, and suggesting to my mother in his calm, even way that she could stand to lose a little weight, that maybe she should henna her hair. The phone would ring, and the person would hang up when my mother answered. Or my father would answer and go into the other room to talk.

But I hadn't hated him. How could I, when he adored me so much? I think I even convinced myself that if he was treating her this way, she must have deserved it. After all, he took me to fashion shows, to the Plaza for tea, to photo shoots where real makeup artists put makeup on me and I got to pose under the lights. He bought me flouncy dresses, shiny shoes, a wide-rimmed pink Easter hat. I twirled around at Saks, modeling the new clothes while he watched me, eyes alight, hand clasped to his chin. Later, after the divorce, he'd show up when he knew my mother was at work, with bouquets of parrot tulips for us. Cindi would glare at him and go close herself in her room, but I'd take them, knowing they were for me anyway, and stuff them into a big glass vase and bury my face in them, drowning my thoughts in their colors, their peppery smell. He brought me a diary, pretty hair clips and bracelets. Once, he brought me a dictionary, and I remember him carefully printing my name on the inside cover. I still had that dictionary.

How could I hate him?

But I hated him now, thinking about what he'd done to my mother.

I stood up suddenly. "I should call Hazel," I said to Celeste. She was leaning back, eyes closed. Fantasizing about her adulterer, no doubt.

I took out my cell phone and dialed, first his apartment, then his cell, both times getting his voice mail. *They must be in the subway,* I told myself, but I thought that was odd, as my father generally took only hired cars or cabs. I left a quick message—*Hi, Elayna calling to check in, call me back if you get this*—then hung up. Celeste opened her eyes and looked at me. "What's wrong?" she said.

I shook my head. "Nothing. I just suddenly got nervous about having left Hazel with my father for all this time."

She looked at me curiously. "Why? What are you nervous about?"

"Oh—nothing. I'm just being neurotic." It seemed easier than trying to explain something I wasn't even sure of myself. I forced a laugh. "Ridiculous, right?"

She shook her head. "Not if you feel that way. What, you think she might wear him out?"

"Well, yeah, that too. But I also think he might—that he might not be totally appropriate around her. You know?" I thought for a moment. "At lunch today, for example—in front of Hazel—he described the quality of the conversation during one of his recent dates as being like 'premature ejaculation.' "

She laughed, which relieved me, but then shook her head. "What did Hazel say?"

"It went over her head, thank god. But—it's that sort of thing." I thought briefly of telling her about the photos Cindi had reminded me of, but decided against it. For one, the whole thing sort of embarrassed me now, and, as before with Cindi, I just didn't want to think about it. But also, after all, Celeste's father had knocked her mother senseless, then walked out for good. Mine had taken a few artsy photos of me in a slip. BDN, as Hazel would say. Big Deal—NOT.

Celeste stood up. "Come on," she said. "If you're nervous, you should go. I'll walk you to the subway."

We headed toward Astor Place. "How *is* your father?" she asked. "I can't believe I haven't asked until now."

"Very friendly, actually." I shrugged. "Anxious to have a relationship with Hazel."

She looked at me to try to gauge how I felt about this, so she could figure out how to react. "Well, that's good," she said, after a second. "Right?"

"I think so. I mean, I'm happy about it, I think." I took a deep breath. "We'll see how today goes."

She nodded, and we finished the walk to the subway in silence. "Elayna," she said, when we arrived, "I hope you don't hate me for what I told you about Stephen. I hope you haven't lost all respect for me. Not that, you know, you had much to start."

I laughed. "I could never hate you," I said, after a second. "I love you too much."

She smiled, then grew serious. "But you hate what I'm doing, right?" She shook her head quickly. "Don't answer that, I don't want to know." She sighed. "You know, I almost didn't tell you, even though I was dying to. I've kept it from you all this time because I had a feeling you'd disapprove. But then today, when you mentioned . . ." She stopped. "I don't know, the timing just seemed right. But the fact that you can't relate—well, that's a credit to your marriage. And to Paul. You're lucky, you really are."

For some reason, tears came to my eyes. I reached out to hug her. "Thank you."

"For what?" she said, after a second.

"For coming out to see me after Oliver died. And for putting up with me these past few years. I know I haven't exactly been a barrel of laughs."

"How could you be?" She looked at me thoughtfully. "But I knew you'd come back to yourself eventually," she said. "Some version of yourself, anyway."

I looked at her. "So—have I, then? Because I—I'm—I can't really—"

"You're getting there."

I let out my breath. "Well, that's good, I guess."

"It's great. And you know what? Thank you too. For not forgetting me in all this."

"Oh, please. As if I ever could."

We both laughed, suddenly embarrassed. "Now go," she said. "Go to your baby."

I nodded, then turned on my heel and took off. "I'll call you later," I shouted as I raced down the subway steps.

"Yes," she called. "I want the update on Cookie Boy."

For a second, I froze. I'd forgotten I'd told her about him, and now, after all we'd just talked about, part of me wished I hadn't. And yet, at the sound of those words in her mouth, something electrical ran through me, a tingle deep in my flesh—something completely separate from what I felt about Hazel, Celeste, my father . . . anyone.

The train was coming. I ran the rest of the way down the long, dirty steps, into the steamy underground of the subway. I fumbled for my Metrocard, pushed through the turnstile, and jumped on the train. The doors slammed behind me.

# Chapter Seven

Even as I told myself I was being histrionic, I ran crosstown from the subway stop all the way to my father's building, a modern high-rise that cut like a gleaming sword into the sky of far East Eighty-sixth Street. I halted before the uniformed doorman, panting. "Hello, Elayna," he said, as if I were nothing more than the usual sweating harridan landing breathless at his post. "Nice to see you. Everything okay?"

I tried to smile. "Fine, thanks. Good to see you too. Luis, did you notice my father and daughter go up recently?"

He thought a moment. "About two hours ago, I think." He grinned. "Beautiful girl. She likes those cherries, huh. My daughter used to love those too."

I thought of Hazel spitting the chewed-up maraschino into my napkin at the restaurant, and I almost asked him to explain. But I nodded and slipped past him. "I'll phone up to let him know you've arrived," he called after me.

In the elevator, I smoothed my hair and tried to calm down. The doors opened, and I proceeded to my father's apartment—unlocked, I found. Slipping quietly inside, I beheld—what? Hazel watching the end credits of the Frances McDormand version of *Madeline.* She didn't notice me come in, nor did my father. He was arranging his magazines into a tidy tabletop pile, erasing the only two traces of anything resembling disorder in the otherwise immaculate apartment, which was bachelor sparse and sleek-modern, with white walls, pale gray trim, furniture made of metal and glass, and, among other expensively framed modern art, a medium-size original Mapplethorpe that he'd acquired years ago—a striking photo of the back of a naked man sitting but leaning forward, legs spread apart. Even the photo contributed to the place being all of a piece, with maleness and order its two main ingredients. My father worked hard to keep disorder from entering his life, though he was aided by his prim housecleaner, Bev, who also shopped, took messages, picked up tonic and limes and dry cleaning and even cooked dinner on the rare nights my father didn't go out or entertain a woman at home. A wife without the hassle, I sometimes thought about Bev, leaving my father free to proceed with his days unrestricted by the boundaries of either family life or housework.

I observed silently for a few more seconds. He had changed from his black Levi's into looser, faded (but still ironed and perfectly creased) blue ones and a plain black T-shirt, garb that both displayed the fruits of his daily gym time and brought out his sexy-aging-man traits: the tanned, slightly weathered skin, the teeth as straight and white—and eyes the same icy blue—as they'd been when he was twenty, but in a face that registered both the experience and the amusement of a life of thought, pleasure, creative work. It was easy to see how he scored the women he did. "Hello?" I said, over the TV. Hazel turned and saw me. "Momma!" she screamed.

She rushed over and embraced me, and I bent to hug her. My father ceased his organizing for a moment. "You're back early," he said. "We didn't even get to play Barbies yet. That was next on the agenda."

"Mom!" Hazel yelled, "Grandpa got me Wedding Barbie! Can you *believe* it? And he let me watch *Madeline,* and we went to F.A.O. Schwarz, it's the most giant toy store! You should see Wedding Barbie, she's *so* attractive." (*Attractive?* I thought.) "And I got to take pictures in Central Park, we took them of, like, *everyone,* plus all the little duckies, they were *so* cutie cutie—" Here her voice rose an octave, taking on the squeaky squeal she reserved for talking about small furry creatures. "—plus I got to feed them crackers Grandpa bought—oh yeah, and I like those red cherries now! I saw them in a store and I wanted to try them again, so Grandpa bought me a jar and I *liked* them! He took pictures of me eating them, just to prove it to you. But they're not developed yet, right, Gramp?" She turned and looked at my father.

"Correct," he said.

"Well, that all sounds fantastic," I said, relieved. "I'm glad you had a good time." I felt a wave of sheepishness at my worry and urgency, followed by shame, followed by annoyance at myself, followed by annoyance at Cindi, who I felt had made me overly cautious about my father for no reason but her own neurotic tendencies. I don't know what I'd expected to find, but whatever it was, it was miles from the truth. Both of them were glowing.

"And Grandpa only said one swear," Hazel said. "When I spilled my orange juice, he said the S one. But I told him he shouldn't get mad if it's an accident. Right, Mom? Because no one is perfect?"

"Right." I nodded, glancing at my father. He allowed a small smile.

I excused myself and headed down the hall. Inside the spotless white bathroom, I looked at the magazine rack. It was divided in half, with one part containing a coffee table book of Diane Arbus photos and the other recent issues of *Playboy.* I pulled one out and opened it to the centerfold. The woman—yellow blond with an equally yellow, perfectly triangular patch of snatch hair and enormous yet pert breasts with pink aureolas the size of poker chips—reminded me of a lollypop. Or an Easter egg, maybe, with all her pastelly colors. I pictured a miniature version of her sitting on a doily at a table place setting. And yet, despite this image and my firmly hetero ways, I felt a wave of sexual desire pass through me. I shut the magazine, stuffed it in the rack, and went back out.

He had set out a pewter square of dark chocolate balls on the coffee table, and he and Hazel were playing Barbies—her Barbie, naturally, the bride, while his was the groom, and mine, she told me, the "best maid." As we played, I couldn't help noticing that my father was animated and involved in a way he'd never been with me as a child. Back then, he'd pulled me up into his world rather than coming down to mine. But with Hazel, he knew how to play. I couldn't quite believe it, and my pleasure must have been obvious.

Hazel struggled a little with her Barbie, attempting to adjust the miniature wedding dress. "Those are Belgian truffles, by the way," my father said to me, gesturing toward the chocolate. "The model Tatiana brought them back for me. Please, have one."

"Oh—no thanks," I said, and then, looking at them, "well, maybe just one." I popped the biggest one into my mouth. "Oh my god," I said, chewing.

He smiled, then took one himself. He closed his eyes as he rolled it around in his mouth. In spite of myself, a twinge of annoyance and then repulsion echoed through me.

Hazel was watching him. "Can I have one?" she said.

My father looked at her. "TGFTC."

"What does that mean?" She frowned.

"Too good for the children," he said. "However, I never much liked that expression. If we so-called adults can have them, why shouldn't you? Help yourself, my little bride."

Hazel grinned and reached out a fist.

"You may have *one,*" I said, and then instantly regretted it, as it meant I couldn't help myself to six or seven more.

The phone rang. My father ignored it, and his answering machine clicked on. We made out his short message—it was loud enough to hear his voice, but not what he was saying—and then it beeped, and a woman's voice came on. She yakked for a while, and it clicked off again. "So," he said, casually, "have you heard from your mother?"

I shook my head. "Haven't called her in ages."

"And she hasn't called you?"

"She almost never calls me."

"Really," he said, with interest. "Why, do you think?"

I sighed. "Well, she's got her job, and they're pretty involved with Walter's kids now . . ." I stopped. I'd gotten used to the situation and let it go—mostly, I thought, by refusing to dwell on it. Plus, even after all these years—even with my father having been the one who cheated, the one who left, the one who had some ridiculous model on his answering machine right now—even with all that, I still felt guilty talking about Walter in front of him. The fact was, my father still loved my mother. And for all his girlfriends and big jobs and fancy garaged car, I sometimes got the feeling he was really just a lonely old soul longing for connection. Sometimes, when I looked at his bold blue eyes—still striking, yes, but soon, he must realize, to grow pinker, softer, *old*—I got the feeling that behind them, thinly veiled by his surface perfection, lurked a sadness that would make the two and a half years I'd just gone through seem like mere hours in a day.

"*Mo-om*," Hazel was saying, "stop distracting Grandpa! He's supposed to kiss the bride now."

My father raised his eyebrows, then stood up. "Well!" he said, and he smiled at me. "That chocolate made me thirsty. What can I get us. Perrier? Wine? Mango nectar?"

"That one!" Hazel said. "The nectar! What's mango?"

"Quiet," I said to her, and, to him, "Water is fine, for both of us. But don't get up, Daddy, I can get it. And then we need to go." I turned to Hazel. "Run and use the bathroom before we leave."

It wasn't until she'd already closed the door that I remembered the *Playboy*s. I debated a second, then decided to leave it alone. Chances were she wouldn't try to get the magazines out of the rack, not knowing what they contained. Besides, who was to say she hadn't seen them earlier anyway? Quickly, I gathered her stuff and stuck it into my bag. "So when can I see her again?" my father asked. "I want to help her develop the film." He watched me. "I hope we can do this more now that she's older. She's a great kid."

Once again, my thoughts shifted to a better place. "Well, not next weekend, because Paul's hardly been home. But maybe the one after that?"

"Perfect. I'll take her to the Met, since we never made it today. She'd love Monet and Degas at this age."

I liked the idea of Hazel at the museum. "Let me ask Paul," I said. "Just to make sure he doesn't have anything planned." I had made my way to the door. Hazel was back. I kissed my father on the cheek. "Thanks for everything."

He stepped back, looking surprised. "You're overheated, Elayna! You should've told me. I'd have turned up the air."

"Oh—that's okay. I'm always hot these days." I shrugged, then glanced at Hazel.

"Have you tried Maca?" he said. "It's herbal, for hot flashes. You just have to make sure you get good stuff, because it can be contaminated. I can get you some, if—"

"Dad, they're not *hot flashes*!" I laughed. "How old do you think I am, fifty?"

He smiled. "Of course not. You're not a day over twenty-five to me." He turned to Hazel. "How 'bout a hug for Grampa?"

She leaped into his arms and squeezed his neck hard.

"Christ!" he croaked. "I said a hug, not a strangling."

She giggled, and he kissed her hard on her cheek.

I let them finish. And then I took her hand, and we made our way out.

# Chapter Eight

It was weeks later when I ran into Kevin again. The flowers had changed: The daffodils and tulips were now naked stalks, while the poppies reigned, peach and red, their tissuey petals as flowy as a schoolgirl's prom dress. And deepest blue irises, and handfuls of pansies, and red-orange columbine, dainty as tiny giraffes. Anyway. It was night. Paul had turned in. He was crashing earlier and earlier, then getting up and taking off in the morning sometimes before Hazel and I even awoke. In contrast, I had miles to go before I would sleep, so I went out to walk off some of them.

I went to the university, then down to the pond, where, through the quiet night air, I made out the regal black water, white geese sailing by. I perched briefly on a bench to watch them. Seconds later, a yellow tennis ball flew past, and then a silvery canine blur chasing it. The dog whizzed to about fifty feet ahead of me, then stopped, chomped the ball, and carried it back to the fast-approaching person who'd thrown it. Kevin, of course.

I couldn't quite believe it. I turned toward him, waiting for him to notice me, and promptly he did.

"Hey!" he said. "It's you! What are you doing here?"

I smiled; couldn't help it. "Just—getting some air. Hey, thanks for those cookies. I was hard-pressed to share them even with Hazel."

"Glad you liked them. It's my mom's recipe." He sounded about sixteen. "Mind if I sit?" he asked, approaching my bench.

Flustered, I moved even farther to the end I was already near. He sat down in the middle. Sasha nudged his knee with the ball, and he took it and hurled it far into the pond. She thrashed in after it, scattering ducks.

Kevin sat back to watch her, and I watched too, squinting to make her out as she retrieved the ball and turned back, her pointy face poking out of the water. "Don't you worry about doing that at night?" I asked, then wished I hadn't. If he was sixteen, I was sixty.

He shrugged. "Night, day—it's all the same to a dog. This is amateur stuff for her. Right, Sash?"

The dog, who'd just reappeared before us—dripping wet, ball in jaw—gave her half hot-dog tail a wag. "Can I throw it?" I asked.

Kevin extricated the ball, wiped it off on his jeans, and handed it to me. I stood up and whipped it as far as I could. *Ow,* I thought, as pain shot through my arm, but it was worth it. "Whoa," Kevin said, on cue. "Where'd you learn to throw like that?"

"High school. I played shortstop."

"Yeah?" He looked at me, impressed.

Sasha was back. Kevin offered me the ball, but I knew enough to decline this time. He whipped it himself, then turned back to me. "Where did you grow up?"

"Here," I said. "New Jersey. Bergen County, though. You?"

"Oh—everywhere. Pittsburgh, Vermont, upstate New York . . . I was an army brat. At least until my parents divorced. Then I was the son of an aging hippie."

"Your mother?"

He nodded.

"My parents divorced too," I said.

"Yeah? How old were you?"

"Nine," I said. "How old were you?"

"Thirteen."

"Wow. That was hard."

He shrugged. "Not as hard as when they were together."

I looked at him. "I know what you mean. My mother could stop trying to please him once he was gone. We could all relax."

"Yup." He laughed quietly, bitterly. "My father was a jerk too," he said, as if I'd said that about mine.

"Mine was—mine's . . ." My voice faded as I tried to think of how to explain something I wasn't even sure I knew myself.

"Luckily, my mom's the greatest," he said. "And I got to stay with her. My father took my brother."

"They split you up?"

"We split ourselves. We each picked the parent we wanted. And vice versa."

I thought about that for a while. Cindi and I had never been particularly close, but still, I wouldn't have liked being separated from her.

"So where is she now?" I asked. "Your mother."

"Atlanta. She's a shrink."

Sasha appeared, dropped the ball, then flopped down in front of the bench and set her head on her paws. Kevin sat up straighter and reached into the pocket of his jeans. He came out with a neat little joint and a matchbook with two matches in it. He cupped the joint and lit it.

I watched him in hungry disbelief as the nutty smell wafted over. Getting high was one of those things that simply didn't exist in my world anymore. He took a drag, then held it out to me. I hesitated very briefly, then took it and inhaled.

"Do you get high a lot?" I asked, handing it back.

He shrugged. "Depends what you consider a lot."

"Like, every day?"

"Definitely not."

"Once a week?"

"At least."

I laughed, letting my head loll back a little. Stars stars stars, twinkling like sparkling salt. Above him, a sliver moon hung askew in the sky, a smirking grin. I felt wonderful, floaty and surreal, sitting with this beautiful boy and this beautiful dog on this insanely gorgeous night. "What's your mom like?" I said, using his term. Everyone I knew had always said "mother," not "mom."

He shrugged. "Really smart. Really pretty. Not afraid of anything." He smiled a little. "She saved my life."

I wanted to ask how, but suddenly I felt overcome with longing for a son who would someday say that about me. I stood up. "Shoot. I've gotta go home. What time is it?" I began to walk, fast.

Kevin jumped up and caught up to me, Sasha pulling to a trot behind us. "Do you do this a lot?" he asked as we walked.

"What?" I turned to him.

"Walk at night."

"Oh. Well, lately I have all this—energy. Which is good, actually, since there was a long time when I didn't."

We turned onto our block, passing one of the splendid Betty magnolia trees that somehow hadn't yet shed its enormous rich, purple blooms. There were streetlights on our block, and this plus the looseness of pot on the brain allowed me to study him more bluntly than I should have: his sparkly green eyes, his cheekbones pushing against his lovely pink cheeks. He took the tennis ball from Sasha and threw it far down the block, which put him enough ahead of me for my eyes to make their bold way down his back, and then, less obtrusively as he faded back into step beside me, his profile. He was shorter than Paul, and thinner. Not so much taller than me. He wore a T-shirt, old jeans, black high-top sneakers. I looked—I couldn't help it—at his arms, or the one closest to me, particularly at his bicep, round and strong, rolling under his freckled white skin. I had always loved a man with nice arms. When I was young, in my town in New Jersey, a man's status was almost entirely determined by the number of pounds he could curl and bench-press. You wanted a guy with arms so massive they split the seams of his shirt. Later, thankfully, my taste got more subtle: smaller arms, but still nicely formed, sleek and curved, biceps round as a fist.

And still later, of course, it wasn't about arms at all. That's when you knew you were a grown-up, maybe. But this arm on this guy next to me on the street . . . it was like something from my youth. Something that, like that joint, had no place this close to me now. And yet, here it all was, near enough to reach out and run my palms over.

"So where was your energy for a while?" he said.

"Sorry?"

"You said before that you didn't have energy for a long time."

I felt my heart speed up. "I was sad," I said, after a moment. "For a long time. But I think I'm coming out of it now."

"Why were you sad?" He was blunt, blunt, the unwavering son of a shrink. His green eyes stared at me, naked and unnerving.

"I was sad because my baby died." My throat closed, as it did every time I said those words. But it opened again. "My son," I said. "Oliver."

His eyebrows shot up, his mouth shut. "Oh, man," he said. "That's so terrible. How old was he?"

"Four days."

"Four *days*?" He shook his head. We walked a few steps, not talking. "What did he die of?" he said, and then, "Don't tell me if you don't want to."

"No. I do want to." I loved him for asking, for offering his small, neat, silver-ringed ear and inviting me to let it all out. And I did. I told him everything. About Oliver, and his life, and his death, and my retreat into sadness. About how you think losing a baby so young wouldn't be that big a deal, but it tears you apart. The words spilled out, pent-up words that had been inside for so long, words Paul and I couldn't say to each other because my pain plus his pain, together, were too much to bear. We were almost at my house. "I'm sorry," I said suddenly. "I didn't mean to burden you with all that."

"You didn't burden me. I asked. It's nice to know something about you, finally. I'm just sorry it has to be a sad thing."

*Finally.* I tried to push the word out of my mind, but it stuck there, loaded and thrilling. There was an awkward second, and then, almost reluctantly, I took a step toward my house. "Well—bye," I said. "Thanks for the—you know." I couldn't say pot. It was too ridiculous, and also, what if by some weird chance Paul was up and listening?

"You're welcome. Anytime." He smiled, and I swear, his eyes bored into mine.

I went inside, locking the door behind me. I was high as a kite. I had that fluttery, empty feeling in my limbs, that jittery rush in my brain. My wrists tingled, my eyes focused and refocused. My heart danced.

But my mind was racing too. And the answering machine was blinking. There were dishes in the sink. The trash was at the top of the can. I felt a tiny pinprick in my bubble of giddy glee. Paul hadn't dealt with any of it.

*Well, why should he?* I asked myself. *He supports us. He has a job, out in the world. He's trying to save a man from being put to death.*

And me? I was out smoking pot with the neighbor boy. What did I know from the world? My world was myself and my daughter, my needs and hers.

I took out a glass, filled it with water, chugged it, filled it again. I took out the mint chocolate chip ice cream and a spoon and stood at the counter mining for chips. When I was done, I tossed the spoon in the pile in the sink, shoved the carton in the freezer, and headed upstairs.

I went to Hazel's room first. She was asleep, of course, her snooty nose aimed up at the ceiling, her lips open like the seductive little nymph that she was. "Mama's home," I whispered hotly into her ear, and I kissed her luscious cheeks until she shoved me away. I pulled her quilt up over her; she kicked it off with her skinny white legs. Then she opened her eyes wide and bolted upright. She grabbed my neck, kissed me hard, clenched me into a hug, then let go and fell back down, instantly out again.

In my room, Paul was asleep in his boxers on top of the sheet, a file folder and some newspaper clippings scattered around him. Glasses nearby on the bed, face pressed into a pillow in the front and on most of one side. From the back, his dark hair curled around his neck, longer than he usually let it get. It was hair you wanted to touch, like a spaniel puppy's. I reached out, straightened a curl with two fingers, let go, and watched it curl again. His back was big, soft, olive, neither flabby nor too thin; he was well built, but more flesh than muscle at this point. He had good bones, and he still looked handsome and sharp in a suit, but he didn't get to exercise much these days, and he was no sapling anymore.

I leaned down and sniffed him. He smelled clean and familiar: hints of mint shaving cream, rich white paper and ink, the silk of his tie, his car's leather seats. My eyes suddenly stung. Why hadn't he covered himself? His back looked sad and vulnerable, naked on top of the covers like that. With a rush, I forgave him for everything. I picked up his glasses, folded them carefully, placed them on his bedside table. I gathered all his papers, put them back in the folder, and tossed it gently to the floor. I stripped to my underwear, climbed in next to him and pulled the quilt over both of us—

climbed in without washing my face, brushing my teeth, even taking a pee. *There.* My mouth tasted delicious, all frosty, chocolatey mint, and I was still slightly buzzed from the pot. I pushed up against Paul's back and threw my leg over him, shivering rapturously from the combination of his hot body against me and the cold ice cream inside. I wrapped around him like a catfish against a warm rock, a child with its favorite stuffed thing. *There. Now he'll be all right.*

And then I let my mind go, away from my house, to the outside world I'd discovered tonight. It was delectable. I was in heaven. Here, in my conjugal bed, my body had Paul—my love, my husband—and my mind was full of Kevin, beautiful young boy-man across the street.

I drifted off into a half sleep of fantasy I couldn't stop and didn't want to. Kevin standing face to my face, wearing his jeans but without the T-shirt, rim of white boxers just visible over the waistband. I sank down before him, brushing my thumbs lightly over his chest as I knelt, and then moved my mouth to his right flank, just a couple or three inches—just enough to taste him and make him respond. I ran my mouth over and over him, sampling and sucking his skin, which was white and soft, sublimely delicious, salty and fragrant and sleek. Up and down, up and down, just that one small space; I could have spent an hour on just those few inches of him. Was it wrong—is it wrong now, given everything that's happened—to say it was maybe not unlike the way a mother might devour her baby boy? Had his mother ever done this to him? Teased him to hear his beautiful gurgley laugh, felt him fold in on himself with glee?

In this bliss—Paul on my body, Kevin on my mind—I drifted to sleep.

# Chapter Nine

I awoke around five in the morning, in the midst of a nightmare I'd had before, though I could never remember the details—only Oliver, falling off of something (a cliff? changing table?), and I reach out to catch him, and he slips through my hands.

I took a deep breath, then got up.

I needed a shower—or, better yet, a hot bath. I tiptoed into the bathroom and grabbed my towel and some of Hazel's bubble bath, then slinked up to the third-floor bathroom—the guest bathroom, not that we ever had guests—and turned on the water softly, dimming the lights to a mustardy glow. I cocked my ear and waited. No sound from below. I dumped in some bubble bath, a lively blue goo that smelled like cherry gumdrops, then peeled off my clothes and stood naked, shivering, until the tub was half full of steaming-hot water. Then I stepped in and, wincing, lowered myself until I was submerged, shuddering with the ecstasy of the heat.

I lay back and closed my eyes. In the magazine this month, they'd invited readers to submit their favorite poems, so I'd gotten to reread Langston Hughes, Dorothy Parker, Sharon Olds, Tony Hoagland, Ha Jin. I thought about my own favorites, the lines my young heart had filed for safekeeping in my head. The Romanian poet Nina Cassian: *I am greedy. Puritans scold me for running breathlessly over life's table of contents and for wishing and longing for everything.* And, later in the poem: *Well, that's my way! I'm hungry, I'm thirsty. I rush through the world like a living sound. I refuse to walk slowly, to crawl, or to remain indebted for a kiss.*

I moved the washcloth down my body, rubbing the stinky-sweet bubbles under my floating breasts, over my rounded belly. I imagined Kevin sitting on the edge of the tub watching me, and a warm spark shot through my body, beginning and ending between my legs. I was dizzy, sweating, in and out of the sparkly blue haze of bubbles, cool and then warm again.

I fell asleep. I don't remember the falling, only the waking up—to the voice of Hazel, calling me. "Mom? Mom? Mom-*AH*! Where *are* you!"

I sat up. "Hazel?" I called back. She must have gone to my bed, as she usually did in the morning for our last hour or so of sleep, and climbed in and found me not there. "Up here!" I yelled. The water was freezing. I turned on the hot and put my feet under it. Her footsteps raced upstairs.

She burst in. "*Mo-om!* I didn't know where you *were*!" She glared at me. "Why are you up here, anyway?"

"I took a bath here so I wouldn't wake you and Daddy. And then I fell asleep—"

"You fell *asleep*? In the *bath*? Mom, that is *totally dangerous*!"

Was she six, or fifteen? "You're right," I said, and then, lying, "But I wasn't completely asleep. Just resting."

She continued to glare at me, until she spotted her bubble bath on the floor. "*Mom!* And who said you could use my Clifford bubble bath!"

I laughed. "Oh, come on, Haze. It's first thing in the morning, and you're already this mean to me?"

She considered this a moment—*Did feelings truly exist outside of her own?*—then suddenly smiled. "Well, can I at least come in with you, then?"

"Sure—what time is it?"

"I don't know."

"Well, look at a clock."

"I can't tell time yet!"

"Oh!" I laughed. "Right. Um . . . bring me the little clock from the guest room."

She did. It was 6:35. "Daddy's gone already?" I asked, and only then recalled his coming up about a half hour ago, our brief mumbled exchange—*Why are you up here? Didn't want to wake you. Call you later—* then a quick kiss and him rushing off.

She nodded. "He's not in the bed."

I sighed. "Well, okay. We have some time. Come on in."

She threw off her clothes and plunked her bony butt smack down onto my stomach, then began flailing all over the place, a feisty little fish tearing up my quiet pond. But I didn't mind. In another year or two, she wouldn't fit in the tub with me—or want to. She stared at my boobs for a while, then poked one nipple. "Hazel! Stop it!" I said, but I laughed. I couldn't help it. She had such nerve. "You know you don't touch other people's private parts," I said, trying to sound firm now.

"I have private parts too. See?" She spread her legs and stuck her finger on her vagina.

"That's lovely. You can close your legs now."

She giggled, snapped her legs shut, turned over, and swam all over me, paddling on both sides with her hands. She was a physical, sexual little creature; that's all there was to it. I grabbed the washcloth and began scrubbing her back. "Ow!" she yelled. "You have scratchy cactus legs!"

"Sorry. I haven't shaved them in a while."

"Why not?"

"Because, um—'cause it's a pain." *And no one feels them anyway.*

"Can I shave them?" she asked.

I looked at her. "Of course not!"

The water had warmed up again; it was almost to the top of the tub. I turned it off with my foot. "Hey, let's do *The Jumblies,*" I said.

" 'They went to sea in a Sieve, they did,' " she recited, obediently. " 'In a Sieve they went to sea: / In spite of all their friends could say, / On a winter's morn, on a stormy day, / In a Sieve they went to sea!' "

She shot me a beatific smile, which I returned. " 'O Timballo! How happy we are,' " I said, " 'When we live in a Sieve and a crockery-jar, / And all night long in the moonlight pale, / We sail away with a pea-green sail . . . ' "

"What's a crockery jar?" she asked.

"Um—like earthenware."

"What's earthenware?"

"Um—it's like ceramic."

"What's ceramic?"

"Hazel!"

"What? Momma, I don't know what it is!"

I sighed. She was right, of course. So many things for a person to learn.

I squeezed past her and got up and out of the tub, my fingers shriveled into raisins. She tumbled out and downstairs after me.

I told her to get dressed, and then went in and dressed quickly myself. Down in the kitchen, I put on water for oatmeal, poured orange juice, got out her vitamins. "Haze, come on down!" I yelled as I found her lunch box, put on more water for pasta. I got out her thermos. "Hazel!" I yelled up again.

The phone rang. "I'll get it!" Hazel yelled, rushing into the kitchen wearing only pink polar bear underpants.

"Hazel!" I wailed. "Why aren't you dressed?"

She grabbed the phone, ignoring me. "Hello? Hi, Grampa! No. Yes. No. What?"

This was new, his calling to talk to her at length; it had started after our last New York visit. But it wasn't usually in the morning. I listened while I dumped pasta in the water, stirred the oatmeal, sliced cantaloupe. "Yes!" Hazel yelled. "I *totally* want to. Oh, okay. Just a minute." She thrust the phone at me. "He wants to talk to you. Mom, can I be in a fashion show? Pleeeeze?"

I took the phone. "Go upstairs and get dressed *this second.* I want to see you down here in exactly two minutes, or—"

"Or what?" She put her hands on her hips.

"Take your hands off your hips. I'm not sure what yet," I said. "But it will be very terrible, I promise you."

She rolled her eyes, then pranced out of the room.

My father wanted to know if Hazel could be in a children's fashion show he was shooting, sponsored by *The New York Times.* Mostly professional models, but a few pretty children of VIPs whose eager parents had wormed their way in. My father had shown Hazel's photo to the director, and she too had been invited to participate.

The pasta was boiling. The oatmeal was about to bubble over. I reached quickly to turn it off. "I don't know, Dad," I said, but I was leaning toward no. "When is it?"

Hazel rushed in, dressed in tight flare floods, an aqua shirt, platform sneakers, and sparkly magenta socks flashing just below each pant leg. She looked like she'd actually just walked *out* of *The New York Times Magazine*—those ads with kids dressed like minihipster adults, complete with sultry little pouts. And yet, I felt a burst of pride.

"Please, Mom?" Hazel yelled.

"Shh!" I said. "I can't hear Grandpa!"

"It's next Wednesday," he was saying. "It starts at two o'clock."

Hazel dragged a chair to the stove to peek into the pots. "Yum, pasta," she said out loud to herself. "I *like* bow ties, though they're not, like, my best pasta in the whole—"

"Quiet!" I yelled to her. And, to my father, "Well, she is off from school on Wednesday afternoons . . ." I moved to the fridge to search for the butter. "But I'd have to cancel her sitter."

"Pansy?"

I paused. "How did you know that?" The fridge door closed to tap at my back.

"Hazel told me. The woman sounds vaguely neurotic, Elayna. Does she really need to go there anymore?"

"She *likes* to go." I found the butter and closed the fridge door. "What do you mean neurotic? What did she say?"

"Well, the way she has all the kids doing all the same—"

I suddenly glimpsed the scene at the stove. Hazel was dishing out oatmeal into a bowl, using a tablespoon. With each scoop, the pot slid closer to the edge of the burner, and now it teetered precariously on the absolute edge. "Hazel!" I yelled, rushing over, and I caught the pot, dropping the phone, just as it started to fall. Hot oatmeal splattered onto my jeans. "Ow! Shit!" I yelled. I dropped the pot on the counter, grabbed a dish towel, and began to wipe the oatmeal off my thighs.

"Sorry, Mom!" Hazel yelled. "I didn't mean to!" She burst into tears.

I took a deep breath. My thighs were hot and damp through the pants, but not burned. I was fine. I went over to Hazel. "It's okay," I said, hugging her. "I'm okay. Just—next time, let me dish it out, okay?"

She nodded tearfully, then sat down at her place, for once not talking back.

I returned the pot to the stove and picked up the phone. "Dad?"

"What happened? Jesus."

"Nothing. Hazel almost spilled the oatmeal, but I caught it. Listen, can I call you back? I should ask Paul about the fashion show anyway."

"The thing is, I need an answer pretty fast. They want a head count by noon."

"Today?" I looked at the ceiling.

"Sorry. I found out late last night that she'd been invited, and I didn't want to—"

"Well, I'm volunteering in Hazel's school this morning, and I'm not sure what Paul's morning is like. He may not be available until I get back."

He paused, and I could almost feel him thinking, *Why does she need to ask Paul?* He had never made a decision like this about us as kids. He hadn't even known what we were doing 99 percent of the time.

But now, with Hazel, it was as if he wanted to make up for all that. It pleased me, the interest he was showing in her. And she loved it. She loved him.

"It would be fun for her, Elayna," he pushed. "Interesting if nothing else. She'll get exposure, and—"

"Exposure to *what*?"

"Oh, I don't know. To the world beyond the suburbs."

I didn't answer. I felt vaguely insulted, but I also saw his point.

"And you wouldn't have to stay. You could, I don't know, go shopping, or—"

"Who would help Hazel, though? Who would get her dressed, and—"

"Oh, there'll be plenty of people for that. They probably won't even let the parents backstage, to tell you the truth."

I felt myself tempted. I could use some clothes. New underwear and bras, for one thing; now that I'd bought a couple of sets a few weeks ago, I felt like replacing the whole tired drawer. And I could grab a drink with Celeste, and then, after the show, Hazel and I could meet Paul for dinner. We could take her somewhere special, Little Italy, Chinatown. I glanced at Hazel. She stared back, round eyes pleading.

The pasta was boiling. "Okay," I said suddenly. "It's fine. But I have to go, Dad."

"Excellent. I'll call you with details over the weekend."

We hung up.

Quickly, I handed Hazel her oatmeal and the tub of brown sugar. While she dumped about fifteen spoonfuls into her cereal, I dialed Paul's office.

The line was answered on the second ring. "Paul Slade's office." It was his new secretary, Marisol, a young woman who, from what Paul had told me, was so smart, hardworking, and interested in his work, she might as well have been his partner. I hadn't met her yet, but she had a nice phone style, friendly but professional, taking her cue from me about how chatty to be with each call.

"He has you in before eight in the morning?" I said to her, after identifying myself. "I'll have a word with him about that. Just because he's a workaholic doesn't mean everyone has to be."

She laughed. "Oh, I don't mind. As long as he brings me a cup of coffee when I get here."

I raised my eyebrows. When was the last time he'd brought *me* a cup of coffee? "Well, he *should,*" I managed. "Is he there?"

"He is, but I'm not sure where he is at the moment. He ran out a minute ago—"

"Maybe to get your coffee," I couldn't help saying.

If she caught anything, she covered it beautifully. "No—we're way past that hour already. I think he's in a meeting with Mark. They're working so hard on this case," she said. "It's very exciting. I feel lucky to have been hired just as this is all happening."

"Yes," I said. "I can imagine."

"Anyway—can I have him call you as soon as he's back?"

"Actually, I'm about to take Hazel to school. Can you ask him to try me later this morning?"

"Sure."

We hung up. I stood for a second, my hand on the phone. "What's wrong, Mama?" Hazel said, through a mouthful of oatmeal.

"Oh. Nothing." I glanced at the clock. "Oh shit—shoot, I mean—it's late. Finish up, we have to get going."

"Mom!"

"What, baby?"

"You forgot to eat breakfast!"

"I did? Oh—I guess I did. Don't worry about me, I'll grab something later."

She rushed over, reached her arms around my middle, and stuck her head into my diaphragm. "I love you I love you I love you," she said.

I gazed at the top of her orange-and-white scalp. From this angle, you could see her messy part, as crooked as the line a drunk walks. "I love you too," I said, hugging her.

"I love you more."

I laughed. "Okay, puppet. At this point, I'll take all the love I can get."

# Chapter Ten

I was back home from her school by eleven thirty, where the first thing I did—the first thing I always did, after a morning in Hazel's classroom, a buzzing, thriving, captivating, and utterly draining place—was reward myself with several squares of very dark chocolate. Afterward, I played the messages on the machine. Deborah—my editor—for a change, inquiring about one of my edit marks she couldn't read and didn't see why I'd made, and Paul, brief, tense, returning my call from this morning. I called Deb first and left an explanation on her voice mail. Then I called Paul, and got Marisol once more.

"Oh shoot, you missed him again," she said cheerfully. "He just jumped into a meeting. Want me to see if I can get him out?"

I hesitated. What did I really have to tell him that couldn't wait? That was more important than maybe saving someone's life? "No," I said. "Can I grab his voice mail? Actually—never mind. I'll just try back."

"He may be a while. Should I tell him you called?"

I hated this, the secretary, the phone tag. Why didn't Paul just let his voice mail pick up his calls? Then I could say whatever I wanted, or hang up and call back until I reached him in person. "No," I said. "Thanks. I'll catch him later."

We hung up. I thought for a second, then picked up the phone and dialed Pansy.

Her machine answered. I waited through the high-pitched rendition of "Singin' in the Rain"—an activity, I couldn't help thinking, that Pansy would never do—then left a quick message saying Hazel wouldn't be there this Wednesday, as she was meeting my father in the city.

I hung up and counted. Forty-four seconds later, the phone rang.

"It was bathroom time," Pansy said. "All three of them had to poop. So now she's not coming Wednesday?"

"Right. She's going to New York to see my father. He's anxious to spend time with her these days. And she loves it, so . . ."

"Uh-huh," she said. "Well, we're anxious to see her here too. This is a family too, you know. Once a week isn't very much time to see her—wait, hold on. Hector, it's Josh's turn! You just had your turn. I'm on the phone, boys, as you can see."

"Listen, I'll let you go," I said. "I just wanted to tell you in advance."

"Well, I appreciate that," she said. "Because I do plan very carefully, you know, depending on how many I have here. If there's three, we can walk to the Target and buy treats—and school supplies. If there's four, forget about it."

"Uh-huh." I reached for the sponge and began to wipe the table.

"Anyway. So tell her I said to have fun with your father, though I hope this won't become a regular thing."

She paused, as if for reassurance it wouldn't, but I was in no mood.

"What are they doing in New York?" she demanded.

I thought about lying. "He's taking her to a fashion show," I confessed.

Silence on her end, except for kid sounds in the background.

"Actually, she's *in* the show," I said, coming completely clean now. "My father's photographing it. For work."

More silence, and then, "I'm gonna have to go in a minute. I'm very busy with all three boys."

"Okay," I said. "I just wanted to let you kn—"

"What kind of fashion show?"

"Children's clothes, I guess. It's sponsored by *The New York Times.*" I sighed. "Listen. She's dying to do this, and so is he. I think they'll have a great time."

She cleared her throat. "I'm all for a great time, Elayna, you know that better than anyone. Just not at the expense of routine. Children crave routine. They need it. We all do, actually, but if we want to mess up our *own* lives, that's our per-og-a-tive. But we don't have a right to play around with the lives of innocent—"

"I know," I interrupted, "but—"

"So, that's all I'm saying. I hope she has a great time with her grandfather, and let's just not let this become a habit."

"No," I said. "Of course not. Well, bye—"

"What will she be wearing?"

"Sorry?"

"Wearing. In the show."

"Oh. I don't know! Whatever they put on her, I guess. Pansy, this isn't some sleazy operation. It's *The New York Times*! These are top child models, and she's been invited to join them." *My god!* I thought. *Listen to yourself, defending child modeling!*

"I understand all that," she said. "I just want to make sure they're not planning to put her in those ridiculous shoes the kids all wear these days. Platforms, and high heels . . . It's irresponsible. Did I ever tell you about the time—"

"I know. The girl was wearing high-heeled shoes, and she fell on your—"

"Front steps. Practically broke her nose."

"I know. You've told—"

"Well, I'm not in the habit of repeating myself. And I don't want Hazel's head swelling up, either. She'll come in next week all about New York this and high-fashion that, and pretty soon I'll have six girls here all wanting to be in a fashion show. I need that like I need a hole in the head." She sniffed. "She's young, you know, Elayna. You don't want her to grow up too fast. Believe me. I've raised—"

"I know," I said. "More than a hundred and seventy-five chil—"

"More like a hundred and eighty-five, at this point in time. Not to mention three of my own. And I've seen what happens when a child is exposed to things before it's ready. Let me tell you, it is not something you want to have happen with your own daughter. Especially Hazel. She's a very aware child, very sophisticated and smart, yet extremely sensitive too. That's a potentially dangerous combination, and you have to be careful. She already knows much more than she needs to, for her age."

I thought, *Resist the bait.* "Like what?" I asked anyway.

"Oh, don't worry about that now. We'll talk about it some other time, when I don't have three active boys here." She took a deep breath. "Anyway, let's just say children talk. They notice everything, and they don't hesitate to say it, here in family day care. You wouldn't believe some of the stuff I've heard. Parents would be horrified. They'd—"

"What did Hazel say?" I cut in—a tiny bit horrified myself, I confess.

"I'm not saying Hazel per se," she said. "I'm saying, all of them. Every single one, at some point or another, will open up to me, because that's the kind of atmosphere we have here, and that's the way the children view me, as a confidante, of sorts. And Hazel is no exception. That's all I'm saying."

"Right." My eyes glazed over again. "Listen, I should get to work—"

"You and me both." She laughed suddenly. "What about a makeup? Since she won't be coming Wednesday."

I thought a minute. "I'm happy to pay you anyway."

"Oh, forget that, I could care less about the money. But I don't want Hazel to go two weeks without being here. She'll lose track of the routine, and the other kids will—"

"The thing is, she gets home from school so late the other four days, and I like to see her after—"

"How about an evening? Hector and Josh stay till eight anyway most nights. She could come for dinner. I could take them all out for pizza for a special treat."

I shook my head, smiling, in spite of myself, at her persistence. "Okay! Fine. I'll go see a movie, or something."

"How about next Thursday? That way, it's only one day past her routine."

I hesitated. If Paul by some chance made it home for dinner that night, he'd be upset not to see Hazel. But really, he hadn't made it home to have dinner with her in ages. Why should next week be different? And on the rare chance it was, we could always go out, he and I, for a real, grown-up dinner. It had been weeks. Months.

"Next Thursday," I said. "Great." I hung up, exhausted by the call.

I wanted to talk to Paul. I wanted to ask him what he thought about Pansy. Did he think she was pushing too hard? Was it time to stop with her, as my father had suggested? I wanted to hear his voice, for a change, to feel like he cared or even thought about my life, and Hazel's. But really, what *was* my life, at the moment? I couldn't compete with his death-row case, his brilliant secretary, exciting colleagues, best-of-everything take-out menus.

I thought of Kevin. Quickly, I went over and turned on NPR to get my mind off him. While I listened, I cleaned up the kitchen, put away dishes, scrubbed the pots. Heading upstairs, I looked out the window. Sunshine, red maples, glorious new grass. *To hell with work*, I thought, and I went to my room and dressed in running clothes, then went out for a long, fragrant run. When I came back, I slipped off my sweaty stuff and jumped into the shower. Remembering Hazel's comment about my prickly legs, I shaved them closely, then shaved my armpits and bikini line. I toweled off quickly, feeling smooth and free of all extraneous nubs, then smeared cucumber body lotion liberally all over myself. By the end, I smelled downright edible.

Back downstairs, I worked for a couple of hours, then drove to the school, Juice Newton music pounding through my car as I sang along. When Hazel saw me, she flung herself into my arms. "Bye!" she said, waving to Willow and Sage and Destiny, girls of the trees and the earth and of fate, and they all turned to wave happily back. We sang some more on the way home, Hazel's festive little warbler's voice joining in. Thirty minutes, arrival to departure, and I was home with my girl, safe and sound.

I made popcorn and washed strawberries, then watched her eat her pretty red and yellow snack, smacking away. " 'There were suitors at my door,' " she sang, " 'Oh lay oh lakia. Six or eight or maybe more.' " It was a song I hadn't heard before; she must have learned it in school that day. " 'And my father wants me wed, oh lay oh lakia. Or at least that's what he said. Oh lay oh lakia'—Mom, can I watch TV?" She turned to me.

"Absolutely not. It's beautiful out." I grabbed a strawberry and devoured it.

"Can I go to hamsters-dot-com, then?"

"No—let's do something fun together, something that doesn't involve a screen. Maybe outside. Just you and me."

She glanced out the window, then at me. "Do you think a storm is coming?"

I shook my head. "Absolutely not. It's as still as, I don't know. A blanket."

She laughed. "I know! Let's make a baking-soda volcano!"

I pictured the supplies, the hassle, the mess. The bright sun outside. "Let's save that for when Daddy's around," I said. "Want to ride bikes?" She shook her head no. "Or paint? We could take the watercolors outside and paint still lifes."

"Yeah! Or no, wait. Let's do Play-Doh! All different colors!"

"Okay," I agreed.

We had a recipe, a variation on the flour-water-salt mixture I'd made as a kid. Flour-water-salt still, but now you added oil and cream of tartar too, fancy-fancy, and you heated it up in a saucepan. It came out smooth and easy to shape, the color blending in fast and evenly, the dough supple and warm in your hands.

We made four different colors, the primaries and chartreuse, and took them outside with a blanket, cutting board, rolling pin, and our snack. We spread the blanket on the front lawn. Two weeks ago, it had been too cold and wet to do this; in another few weeks, the mosquitoes would be out. This was it, the year in its prime, days of utter perfection; the zenith before the descent.

" 'So I told him that I will,' " Hazel sang, continuing her song from before, " 'when the rivers run uphill, oh lay oh lakia, and the fish begin to fly, oh lay oh lakia, and the day before I—' Yuck!" she yelled, looking at her project. "This is coming out *disgusting*! I was *trying* to make a hamster, but it's so *stupid.*"

Her tone was an arrow, aimed at the balloon of my high. "Maybe it's just not done yet," I tried. "You have to keep working at it, Haze. Here, let me try to—"

"No!"

I raised my palms. "Sor-REE!"

She laughed, at least. "I'm wrecking this one anyway," she said. "I want to start over." She smashed the Play-Doh, put it down, took up a blob of chartreuse.

I watched her for a while: her orange-lashed eyes focused intently, her freckles, her beautiful hands. She was sticking with it this time, molding and sculpting, concentrating. I lay back, kicked off my shoes. The warm sun, the thin breeze, the honey-liquor smell of hyacinths, my little girl next to me. The sky was so blue it was like a parody of itself. I closed my eyes, imagined drifting down a stream in a boat, then taking off my clothes and diving in, pushing my body through water, a current, diaphanous plants. " 'And the rivers ran uphill,' " Hazel sang, " 'oh lay oh lakia. And the fish began to fly. And the day before I died, oh lay oh lakia, I became a blushing bri—' *Mom!*" she yelled suddenly. "Stop *sleeping*! You're supposed to *make* something with me!"

"I know," I mumbled. "I was just listening to you sing."

"Momma!" She stuck a blob of Play-Doh on my closed eye.

I pulled it off and, opening one eye, stuck it on her arm. She laughed and stuck it back on me. I grabbed her arm and mashed it into her skin. She shrieked with laughter.

"That looks fun," a male voice called.

I froze.

"Hi, Kevin!" Hazel yelled. "Hi! Oh, look at your cute doggie!"

I unfroze and sat up quickly, squinting at him under the visor of my hand.

"This is Sasha," he called. "Want to meet her?"

"Yeah!" Hazel said. "We're doing Play-Doh. Want to do some?"

"Sure. If it's okay with your mom."

They headed over, Sasha tugging at her leash. She licked Hazel's face, and Hazel screamed happily. Kevin turned to me. "Hi, Elayna."

I raised my hand and smiled in spite of myself, and he smiled back. He sat down next to Hazel; the dog slumped down next to him. "What are you making?" he asked her.

"Well, I *was* making a hamster," she said, "but it came out really stupid, so I smushed it."

"Oh." He watched her for a minute. "So what are you making now?"

"I don't know. Maybe a dinosaur, or *maybe* Hermione Granger . . ."

"Who?"

She stared at him in disbelief.

"From Harry Potter," I supplied.

"Oh." He nodded.

"Well, I might not make her," Hazel said. "I'm still deciding."

"Can I make something?" he asked.

"Yes! What color do you want?"

"Um . . . You decide for me."

"How about red?" She handed him the red blob.

"Thanks," he said. "I'll save a little bit out, in case your mom needs some." He looked at me and smiled, and I felt myself blush, ridiculously.

He turned to his Play-Doh, pretending not to notice, if he did. He divided the dough into two pieces and began to mold the larger, his hands fast and intent.

Hazel and I watched. It was turning into something, his creation; something with contours, shadows, depth. "What are you making?" Hazel asked, for me.

"You'll see." He kept sculpting. When the first piece had obviously become something—it wasn't yet clear what—he took up the second piece, lengthened and flattened the middle, made a ball-like shape on each end. It looked like a barbell, then I wasn't sure what.

"It's a phone!" Hazel said delightedly. "Momma, he made a phone!"

He raised his eyebrows. "Very perceptive. Can I use some blue, please?"

She handed it over, and he broke some off and shaped it into a small, thick pancake. Using his pinkie, he made holes around the rim. Then he stuck it on the larger red piece, and I saw it at once: the dial of an old-fashioned phone. The smaller piece was the earpiece. He placed it on the base, as if hanging it up. It was adorable and brilliant.

"There," he said. "All we need is some twisty phone cord, but we may have to use the real stuff. I don't think I can reproduce that."

Hazel's mouth had fallen open; I was trying hard to keep my own closed. "Oh my god, that is *so* cool!" she yelled. "Can I have it?"

"Sure," Kevin said. "I made it for you. I already have a phone."

Hazel clapped her hands delightedly. Then she jumped up, climbed onto his lap, and threw her arms around his neck. "I love it!"

He laughed, putting one hand on the small of her back. "I'm glad."

She backed her face away from his, but held on to his neck. "But I have to let it dry first, right?"

He nodded. "If you want it to last."

She let go of him, finally, and I let out my breath, realizing only then that I'd been holding it. And then the three of us sat looking at the phone, though in my peripheral vision I was looking at him: his ears, the meat of his neck. He reached out and adjusted the receiver a little. Then he looked at Hazel. "Now should we work on your hamster?"

She shook her head. "I don't want to make a hamster anymore."

"Oh." He shrugged. "Okay."

A robin descended nearby, did its hoppy little dance to make the worms come up for a drink, thinking it was rain; when one did, he yanked it hard from the ground and flew off with it. "You're an even better artist than my *mom,*" Hazel said.

I laughed. "And that's saying a lot, let me tell you."

"Well," Kevin said, looking at Hazel, "your mom probably doesn't practice as much as I do."

"You practice a lot?" Hazel asked. "With Play-Doh?"

"More with clay, actually." He looked at her. "Did you ever try a potter's wheel?"

"A what?"

"A potter's wheel. It's like a thick plate, sort of, that spins, and you put a ball of clay on it and shape it into something— bowls and mugs and things."

She shook her head. "I've never even *seen* one."

"Do you want to?" he asked.

"Yeah!" she said. "Mom, can I?"

I blinked. "You have one?"

"Yup. Right in my living room." He looked at me now, finally. "Come on. I'll show you."

I hesitated for all of two seconds. Then I got up and slipped back into my shoes.

We left everything and followed him, Hazel taking my hand to cross the street, Kevin holding Sasha, who tried to bolt for a squirrel. At the Tenement, we climbed the three flights of steps. It felt odd to be up there after all those years of looking at it from across the street, like entering a movie set or the stage of a play. His landing was rustic white wood: old straw doormat, small, paint-spackled wood bench on which sat several plants in glazed ceramic pots of varying sizes and shades of blue. His door was unlocked. "Sorry about the mess," he said, entering. He released the dog from her leash.

Hazel stepped in, pulling me behind her. He had flipped on the light, but my eyes hadn't yet adjusted, and it felt dark, cool, slightly earthy in there, a smell I'd later learn came from the clay. We were in a main room, like a living room—wood floors, futon couch on a frame—but there was an old picnic table against the wall with drying clay objects spread out all over it. To the right was a small kitchen, where Sasha drank sloppily from a bowl and then flopped on the linoleum floor. Kevin had hastily gathered some clothes from the furniture and disappeared, no doubt to toss them somewhere else. I glanced through one of the two large windows and was surprised to see our house just right there, looking coiffed, trimmed, more modern and finished from this angle than I'd ever envisioned it before. *A grown-up house,* I thought, with a sudden tug inside: I didn't feel old enough to have a house that nice. Our bushes looked pretty, the rhododendrons in cottony fuchsia bloom, the bleeding hearts bleeding away. I saw our blanket and all our stuff abandoned on the lawn, and that felt more like me somehow—not quite responsible, not all *there.* I looked up. A few rain clouds had appeared from out of nowhere, and the sky had grayed suddenly.

I turned back into Kevin's dark house. As my eyes adjusted, I saw, smack center, the promised potter's wheel. Smaller and lower than I'd imagined, the wheel itself was like a silver turntable atop a fiberglass base. It was covered—the wheel—in powdery pale gray residue, and around it was a splash basin, behind which sat a small bucket of what looked like muddy water. A cord extended from somewhere and plugged into the wall. Underneath it all, a large piece of plastic protected the floor.

"Whoa!" Hazel marveled as she walked around it; she was pulling my hand, holding tight, so I had to walk around too. I maneuvered her over to the picnic table, which, I saw now, was covered with unglazed mugs, bowls, and pitchers on one side, big plastic bags of clay on the other. On the floor to the left of the table was a small wooden set of shelves that held more mugs and bowls, but this batch was glazed—reds, turquoise, some silvery black. Carefully, I picked up one of the smaller ones and examined it. It was rustic but delicate, its handle slender and smooth. I put it back and picked up a bigger mug. A small round insignia was scrawled into the bottom, the initials KC inside a circle that extended from the C. *Cannon? Connelly? Callahan?*

"Let *me* see!" Hazel said, stretching for the mug, but I lifted it out of her reach.

"I'll show you," I said. "But you can't touch. It's fragile."

"*You're* touching."

"When you're my age, you can touch too."

"Thirty-five?"

"Shh! Yes. Don't yell." I showed her the mug, then carefully put it back. Kevin came out, holding a small wooden stool, which he placed in front of the wheel.

"Did you make all this stuff?" Hazel asked him.

"I sure did." He moved to the picnic table, took the rubber band off a big bag of clay, and rolled back the opening so that the gray block emerged.

"It's very good," Hazel said, in her "Aren't-I-Mature" voice.

"It's beautiful," I echoed, wishing she hadn't beaten me to the punch.

"Thanks." He removed a chunk of clay from the brick, using a tool that looked like a spatula without the handle, and transferred it back and forth between his hands, making it rounder. It was the size of my fist, more or less. "Here, Hazel, you want to feel it?" he asked. Uncharacteristically, she shook her head no and hid behind me.

He shrugged. "Okay, then. I guess your mom gets to have all the fun." He held it out to me, and I closed my thumb and fingers around the clay, molding it with my hand, switching hands, back and forth, feeling my arm muscles work. Kevin was watching me. "It feels nice, doesn't it?" he said. "I remember the first time I ever got my hands on some clay—I was around Hazel's age—and I didn't want to let go. It was at my mom's friend's studio. I took it home and hid it in my lap during dinner. My mom had to pry it out of my hands when I went to bed. I loved how it felt, I loved the idea of this solid thing you could shape and reshape . . ." He laughed. "Freaky kid, right?" He reached out for my clay, and I handed it back to him.

In two seconds, he had it smooth and round. He sat down on his stool, legs spread apart, and slapped it on the wheel, where it sat waiting to become whatever he decided to make it. I thought of what some famous sculptor, Michelangelo, Rodin, had said about his work: that to him, a block of marble appeared not as a block, but as a sculpture surrounded by excess that had to be chipped away to get it to its natural state.

"What are those?" Hazel said, peeking out from behind me. She pointed under the table, and I saw several large buckets that held shapes and shards of dried clay—broken fragments of pieces already made.

Kevin glanced over. "Those are things I made that I didn't want to keep. When I add water, they'll turn back into clay. Then I can start all over again. It's called slaking."

A frown came to her face. "That's sad."

He looked at her. "What is?"

"That you throw it away if you don't like it."

He considered a moment. "I guess I never thought about it that way. I was always just thinking about what I'd make next." He looked at the clay on the wheel. "Want me to show you how to throw?"

We both nodded.

I heard a click and a gentle whirring sound, and the wheel began to spin. Kevin reached into the muddy bucket and wet his hands; then he put one hand on each side of the ball and bore down gently on the clay, and the whirring got louder. "First I center it," he said. He leaned down over the wheel, elbows braced on his thighs, arms still, fingers tight against each other. He was using the fingers of one hand and the side of the other, forcing the clay down from the top, in from the sides. Every few seconds he reached up to scrape his hands on the bucket edge, sometimes pushing water onto the piece. Or he held a scrap of sponge to the wheel and the clay was sucked up, exposing silver again.

"Normally this is a pretty messy thing," he explained. "But I've learned how to do it neatly, so it doesn't get all over the floor and my clothes. There, it's centered. That's the hardest part sometimes."

"Do you do this professionally?" I asked.

"I have a few people who order things, but . . . it's basically for fun, at this point. Otherwise, I'd need a studio." He pushed his thumbs into the center of the piece now, which made the sides rise up into his hands, the middle open up. "I have a place I can fire stuff, at least. They let me use the kiln because I work there sometimes. Teach a few classes, help clean up the place."

"This *feels* like a studio," I said, and then, "I guess you don't have a roommate."

I was kidding, but he answered seriously. "Not at the moment. Now, see how the sides are coming up? This is called pulling." He had one hand inside the pot, the other outside, guiding it up evenly. He dipped the little sponge into the water, touched it to the side of the clay. "Why are you doing that?" Hazel asked, watching intently.

"I'm using the sponge to keep the clay wet. If it gets too dry, it sticks to my hand. And if it gets too wet, it could collapse. You want to make it slip between your fingers, but not make it soft." He looked at her. "Here. Want to try?"

She smiled but shook her head no.

"Are you sure?" He cocked his head at her. "It's pretty fun."

She thought a minute, then let go of me and stepped toward the wheel.

"Thattagirl." He scraped his hands off on the bucket edge once more and got up. "Sit here," he said, motioning toward the stool. He looked at me. "Is it okay if her clothes get a little splattered? It should wash off."

"Oh—that's fine." It was the first time I'd felt I had any power in this scene, and I admit it gave me a tiny jolt, a faint but nonetheless thrilling buzz. Kevin was helping Hazel onto the stool. "Hold on, I'm gonna make you a little closer," he told her, and he picked up the stool, with her on it, scooted her right up to the wheel, and turned it on. "Good. Now I'll help you make something." He had stayed right behind her when he put down the stool, and now he put his arms around her and leaned over, his chest to her back, arms engulfing hers, hands outlining her hands. Face right next to hers. "We'll do it together," he said. "First, you want to wet your hands in the bucket, just a little bit. Good, that's good. Now we touch the clay while it turns. Don't worry, it feels nice and smooth. See?" She had put her fingers gingerly on the sides of the clay, and he placed his over hers to steady them, his thumbs inside the piece, guiding it. "Good," he said. "You're doing great. The clay feels a little cold, right? Because it's losing water. That's why we have to keep adding more. What do you want to make?"

Her face was a mask of concentration.

"Want to make a mug?" he prompted. "Or a bowl?"

She shook her head.

"How about . . . a pencil holder?"

She nodded, not taking her eyes off the piece.

"Pencil cup it is. Let's see, we need to make the bottom of it, then, and bring the sides a little higher. You don't want the top to flare out, and you don't want to make it too thin either."

He continued to talk, perhaps to make Hazel relax, or perhaps for my benefit. Their piece was morphing, getting taller and then flatter again. I watched it, trancelike, feeling my body relax into the motion of his hands, of the clay ebbing and evolving on the wheel. "Okay," he said finally, and as the wheel slowed I saw the neat little object they'd made, a minivase with smooth little ridges, sitting there.

Hazel smiled.

"Do you like it?" He looked down at her.

"Yes," she said.

"Now, don't touch it, okay? I'll get it off the wheel. After it dries, I'll take it and fire it for you. You can come back in a couple of days and glaze it."

It was my turn to take her over, but I had to force myself to snap back into mother mode. "Come on, Haze," I said. "Let's go wash your hands." I moved behind her and picked her up, carried her into the kitchen, her soiled hands extended before her. Sasha watched us from the floor, her stumpy tail wagging as we passed. In the kitchen, I held Hazel up to the deep, old white sink, washed her hands around a dirty pan and a couple of bowls. I dried her hands on my shirt bottom—no sign of a towel—and we came back out. Kevin had removed her piece and was back at the wheel, a new ball of clay before him.

He looked at me. "Your turn."

"Oh—no. That's okay." I was trying to think of a reason. "We should get home."

"You don't want to?"

*Want*, I thought, *is not the word.*

He looked like a hopeful little boy. I wanted to cup his face in my hands and tell him it would all be okay. "Can I take a rain check?" I managed. We did need to get home, actually; get Hazel fed and to bed. Maybe I'd cook tonight. Maybe I'd wait up for Paul and we'd eat together, open some wine. Even if it was eleven o'clock. Even if he was tired. I'd stay up. And I'd make him stay up too.

Kevin nodded, but he looked disappointed. "Don't get up, your hands are dirty," I said quickly. "We can let ourselves out."

He hesitated, then shrugged. "Okay. I'll get that pencil holder fired, though, so she can glaze it."

"Thank you," I said. "And thanks for showing us all that. I can see how you'd want to do it all the time."

He smiled a little.

"Hazel," I said, "What do you say to Kevin?"

"Thank you," Hazel recited.

He grinned at her. "My pleasure. Come back and do it again, okay?"

"Can we, Mom?" Hazel looked at me.

"Of course we can," I lied.

# Chapter Eleven

Outside, it had begun to rain. "Run!" Hazel yelled, and we ran, climbed our steps, burst through the door. "Daddy!" she screamed.

Paul came toward us, smiling, and Hazel leaped into his arms. "Hi, kitten," he said, kissing her hair. "Long time no see." He stretched around her to kiss me.

"Wow," I said. "Home by six o'clock? To what do we owe this luxury?"

"Exhaustion. I couldn't take it anymore." Paul looked at me. "Where were you, in the rain? You left some stuff on the lawn. I brought it in, but not before it got wet—"

"Daddy!" Hazel burst out. "I made something on the pottery wheel! At Kevin's!"

"Wow," said Paul. "That sounds fun." He put her down gently. "Who's Kevin?"

"He's our neighbor," Hazel said. "He's really nice."

"He lives in the Tenement," I said.

"Mom, can Daddy give me my bath?"

"Sure." I looked at Paul. "Okay? Then I'll start dinner."

"What are we having?" Hazel asked.

"Um—" I tried to think of what I could dredge up. "Spaghetti and meat sauce," I said, hoping I had meat in the freezer. "And bread, and—let's see. Red wine."

"That sounds perfect," Paul said. He looked tired but happy.

Hazel tugged at his hand. "Come *on*, Daddy!"

"Easy, sweetheart," he said. "Daddy's old." But he let her drag him up the stairs.

In the kitchen, I found a package of hamburger in the freezer and—consciously not looking at the date—stuck it in the microwave. I set some oil in a pan to heat, took out an onion and began to chop it. Tears filled my eyes.

I could hear them upstairs, laughing, the bathwater running, Hazel prancing around. "Hey!" Paul yelled, teasing. "Who said you could wear my tie, thief? Give me that!" She shrieked with laughter. I thought about Kevin's hands on Hazel's hands, his bare arms next to hers. And then I imagined myself in her place, feeling his hands on mine, his breath on my neck. I took out another onion and chopped it. The tears ran down my face.

I took out the meat, broke it into cold chunks, and threw it in the pan with the onions. I added a can of crushed tomatoes, oregano, salt and pepper. While it simmered, I made the pasta, tossed a salad, heated a frozen loaf of bread. I wiped sweat from my upper lip, wiped my eyes with the dish towel.

Paul and Hazel were in the living room now; he was reading her *Yertle the Turtle*. Hazel was freshly scrubbed, skinny as a twig in tight black pajamas, hair a tangly bird's nest. Paul could bathe her, but he couldn't begin to deal with her hair. I watched them a moment. "Dinner's ready," I said.

"Finally! I'm starving," Hazel said. She jumped off his lap and ran into the kitchen.

But she didn't like the sauce—too spicy, too many lumps—and after about twenty minutes, she climbed onto Paul and dozed off. He carried her upstairs as I sat sipping wine, but in the end she yelled for me anyway, and up I went for the ritual of bringing her drink of water, ten kisses exactly on each cheek. She still wanted me most, and I reveled in that, though tonight it also made me sad for Paul; with three, someone was always left out. In the hall at last, I took a deep breath. I'd been up for close to eighteen hours, give or take the few minutes I'd dozed in the bathtub. And the wine wasn't helping. But really, how often did I get to have dinner with Paul? Besides, there were things we needed to discuss. I went back downstairs.

Paul was soaking up pasta sauce with his bread, leaning slightly over his plate. I watched the top of his dark curly head, his throat as he swallowed. "That was great," he said, sitting back. "Best meal I've had in a month."

"Better than El Rosario takeout?"

"Kicks its ass."

"Well, come home more often and you'll get more of them."

"I wish I could." He had changed to a T-shirt and taken off his shoes, though he still wore his suit trousers. He pushed his chair slightly back from the table and leaned back, looking at me. He had new glasses, wireless rectangles that exaggerated both his eyes and the lines around them, but I liked them, I decided. He looked better than he had lately. Not quite as frantic. Calm, even. "So what's up?" he said. "Sorry I never called you back this afternoon. I'll save the litany of excuses, but believe me, I wanted to."

I shrugged. "It's okay. I'm used to it."

He winced. "Ow."

"Sorry. I didn't mean it like that." I picked up my fork. "I just meant, you know, that I *am* used to it. I mean, I know it's not your fault. And it *is* okay. More or less."

"Well, it's not, I know that, but unfortunately there's not a whole lot I can do about it right now." He looked at me. "I just wish you could take my place for a day, so you'd see how it is. There's never enough time. There's always more you can be doing, more you *should* be doing. And I don't mean in order to do a great job; I mean, just to do it decently. Just to give this guy a shot."

I resisted reminding him that he'd worked this hard before the death-row case.

"Oh, whatever," he said, perhaps catching something in my eyes. "I don't need to bore you with more details."

"You're not," I said. "I like to hear about it."

He sat still a second, looking at the table. "I know it's been hellish for you—"

"But it hasn't," I said. "Really. Hazel and I do just fine. I mean, we miss you, but—don't add guilt to your roster."

"Okay," he said. "I won't, then." He reached for his wineglass, twirled the stem lightly between his thumb and forefinger. "Anyway, if it's not too late to ask, what were you calling about? Marisol said you sounded like you had a question, not like you just wanted to say hi."

I resisted asking how Marisol knew any fucking thing about me. "I did, actually," I said. "I wanted your opinion on something, but—I ran out of time, so I made the decision."

He waited for me to continue.

"My father got Hazel into a kids' fashion show he's photographing in the city next week. For *The New York Times.* He was asking if she could do it, and he needed an answer by noon, of course. So—" I reached for my wine. "I said yes."

"What day next week?" Paul said.

"Wednesday. Afternoon. After school. I'll drive her in, or we'll take the bus."

Paul nodded. "That sounds great. She'll probably love being in a fashion show."

"Oh, there's no question she'll love it. The question is, should we *let* her."

Paul shrugged. "I don't see why not."

I felt—unfairly, I know—simultaneously annoyed at and relieved by his casual attitude. If he'd objected, I might have been angry he'd questioned me, but I also thought he might be a little more concerned about Hazel so clearly entering my father's world; that he might show a little more concern for her welfare.

"Well, Pansy wasn't too pleased about it," I said.

"You asked Pansy?" He laughed.

"I thought you like Pansy," I said, annoyed again.

"I do like Pansy, but—Pansy wouldn't be pleased about a hot fudge sundae. Pansy sees the local swimming pool as nothing but a breeding ground for warts. Pansy—"

"She's concerned for our child," I said. "She cares, at least."

He blinked, surprised. "Let me rephrase. I think Pansy's great. She's perfect for Hazel. I'm just not sure I want our lives to be guided by a world view based on paranoia."

I didn't answer.

"You do agree she's paranoid," he said, "do you not? I mean, I'm getting most of my information about her from you." He looked at me. "Is something wrong? You seem suddenly pissed off at me."

I took a deep breath. "I'm sorry. I'm just tired. I had a nightmare last night, and I couldn't sleep after that."

"Is that why you took a bath so early this morning?"

I nodded. At least he'd noticed that.

"Come here," he said gently, and he motioned me over.

I got up and went around the table to his side. He opened his arms and I sat down on his lap. He reached up to massage my shoulders, and we sat like that for a little while. "What did you dream?" he asked.

"About Oliver. Same as always. He's falling off of something—I'm not sure what—and I can't save him." I shrugged. "Pretty transparent, right?" But the tears from before suddenly pricked again at my eyes.

I felt Paul stiffen. Just the mention of Oliver. After a little bit he relaxed, but not as he'd been before. "What makes you dream it?" he asked. "I mean—now?"

He was trying, anyway. "I don't know," I said. "I took a late walk last night. Maybe that got me revved up."

"Maybe." He paused. "How late?"

I shrugged. "Ten, ten thirty."

"Where'd you go?"

"To the pond."

"The pond?" He turned me slightly toward him. "Did you have your cell phone?"

"Of course not."

"Why not?"

"I don't know!" I looked at him. "Who would I call? You were already asleep."

"Well, what if I woke up and didn't know where you were? Or what if you got in trouble?"

I thought, *Like what? Someone tries to jump me, and I'm like, Hang on a second, I need to make a quick call?* I laughed. And he was calling Pansy paranoid? But a part of me was flattered too. Again, at least he cared enough to have a fight.

He frowned. "What's the point of having the phone if you don't take it at a time like that?"

I sighed. "Then let's get rid of it. I'm sick of cell phones anyway. They make people twice as annoying as they already are."

He laughed in spite of himself. He lifted his glasses, rubbed his eyes, let the glasses drop to his nose again. He shifted me a little on his thighs. "How's your job?" he said. "You don't talk about it much these days."

I shrugged. "It's okay. I still like the work. It's just that I never talk to Deborah anymore. They cut back staff, and she's overworked. . . . So I hand something in and never hear from her, unless she has a question. If I call, I get her voice mail." I reached for his wine, having polished off mine. "I guess that's good, right?"

He nodded. "As long as they're not complaining."

"Although, it is nice to get credit when you do something."

"True."

"That was one of the best things about working in an office." I twirled a piece of hair around my finger, remembering. "People were always giving you credit, even if it was for ridiculous things. They were like, 'I love your pages, I love your haircut, cute dress.' " He laughed, and I smiled. "You felt human, at least. Female, even."

"Well, I can do that for you," he said. "I like your outfit. Your hair looks cute."

"Gee, thanks. I feel so much better."

He laughed. I finished his wine, and we sat another minute. Then he shifted and started to stand, pushing me up gently. "Sorry," he said. "My legs are falling asleep."

"Oh." I rose quickly and began to clear the table.

"I didn't mean you had to clean up," he said. "Stay. Here, I'll bring over a chair."

I shook my head. "That's okay. I should get this stuff put away."

"Well then, I'll help you, at least."

We cleared off quickly together. "I'll do the dishes," he said, but I said, "No, you should relax." I was being a martyr, I knew. Maybe I just wanted to feel angry at him. Maybe I was trying to pick a fight.

"Are you sure?" He was looking at me.

"Yes," I said, more gently. "It's fine. I don't mind. I'll leave you the pans."

He shrugged. "Okay. Whatever you want."

He left the room, and I heard the TV go on, his shoes plunk to the floor.

I cleaned up quickly, leaving the pasta pot and the saucepan to soak. I wiped down the counters, hung up the dish towel, looked around. I felt like calling Celeste. But I preferred to talk to her when Paul wasn't home—not that he was listening, but still. What I'd have said to her would have sounded silly, even to me, just knowing he was in the house.

I turned off the kitchen light and went down the hall. Paul was sitting on the couch facing the TV, but he had a document in his hand, his briefcase open before him.

"I think I'll go up and read," I said.

" 'Women Who Read Too Much,' " he said, quoting a button I owned.

"And proud of it," I said. "At least I read interesting stuff."

He looked at me, surprised. "This isn't interesting? Saving an innocent man sentenced to death?"

He had a point, of course; I turned away, feeling ignorant and narcissistic. But I thought of something, and suddenly it seemed so perfect I couldn't believe I hadn't thought of it earlier: that the vengeance with which he was fighting this case—indeed, with which he'd taken it on in the first place—might have something to do with losing Oliver. That his way of coping was to throw himself into his work, just as mine had been to tune out, to sleep and sleep. But—somehow—it had never occurred to me that, having seen a life lost, he now wanted to save one. It was perfect, really, given our natures. I wanted to start a new life, he wanted to save one already out there.

"I didn't mean it like that," I said, and I went over and kissed him gently on the lips. "Good night," I said. "In case I fall asleep before you come up."

"Good night," he said. "No nightmares tonight, okay?"

Something deep inside me stirred, a little firefly of light, of love for him. I kissed him once more. "No," I said. "No nightmares."

# Part Two

# Chapter Twelve

Another week or two, and it was lupine, lupine . . . oh, the lupine were everywhere! And the peonies, those stuffed little balls of pink fluff, bursting out of their tight green jackets then puffing up like fat Easter chicks, seducing young and old alike—I among the many. I was outside, resting on my front steps, a slave to the glorious day. It was warm, not too damp, I was showered and slathered in my cucumber scent. I wore a red tank-top sweater, dark brown capris, pretty sandals, vibrant blue feather earrings on little gold hooks that I'd dug up from college days. I felt the accomplishment of a morning of work and the anticipation of picking up Hazel and taking us to New York, of seeing Celeste and of wandering the streets alone, losing myself in the city.

A milkweed puff blew by. I reached out and caught it, made the same wish I always did—for Hazel, Paul, me to be happy, healthy, and together, adding then the rest of my family, Cindi and Zach and my parents, Paul's parents, everyone else, everyone's pets—then sent it on its way. A luscious breeze kicked up from out of nowhere, stirring the heat. And then a car pulled up to the corner, an old, loud, retro-chic silver Saab, and Kevin stepped out of the passenger side.

As he came around to the driver's side, I stood up to sneak into my house before he could see me, but not before I saw the person at the wheel—a girl, long dark hair, sunglasses perched on her pretty head—lean out her open window to Kevin, who had now arrived there. "Bye," she said, and he bent down and smooched her briefly on the lips. "I'll call you," he told her.

By the time the car pulled away, I was in the house. I closed the screen door gently, then moved away so he wouldn't see me.

I went into the kitchen. I filled a glass with iced tea, drank it, poured another, drank that too, breathing hard afterward. Then—when I was sure he'd be gone—I walked back to the hallway and sat on the bottom step of the stairs, where I could catch the air from outside without going out myself, and where the cool wood floor would help the iced tea cool me.

But footsteps were coming up my front walk. Before I could disappear again, there was a knock on the screen. "Elayna?" Kevin peered in at me.

"Oh!" I stood halfway, trying to act surprised—not that I wasn't.

"Hi!" he said happily, and then, "That's okay, you don't have to get up."

I sat down again, helplessly. I took a tiny sip of tea, then held the glass in his direction. "Want some iced tea?"

"Sure. Thanks." He opened the screen door and stepped in, and I saw now that he too was hot, his face flushed and slightly sweaty, making his eyes look even greener than usual, almost demonic, and gluing portions of his short hair in tiny boyish points to his forehead. I handed him my glass, and he took it and drank, Adam's apple sliding up and down. He jiggled the ice at the end. "Oops—sorry. I didn't leave you much."

"Try, you didn't leave me any."

He laughed. "Sorry."

"That's okay." I smiled, finally. At least I'd cracked a joke. "Do you want more?"

He shrugged. "Sure. If you have it."

I got up, went to the kitchen, refilled the glass for him and poured another for myself. I delivered his and sat down again on the bottom step with mine. He sat down near me, not too close, but close. Close enough that I had to turn my head to see him, close enough that I was glad I'd just shaved my legs. He was wearing jeans, despite the heat, and sneakers, and the usual T-shirt. "I have Hazel's pencil holder," he said. "It's fired. Now she just needs to glaze it. So anytime you want, bring her over."

"Thanks. I will."

He took another long drink of tea then put the glass on the floor near his feet. Neither of us talked. His sideburns were damp, and I noticed a drop of sweat coming down from the one facing me. "Where were you coming from?" I asked, and then wished I could take it back. I didn't want him to know I'd seen him get out of the car.

"The studio," he answered. "It's downtown, sort of near the library. Behind it."

I nodded. "Did you get a lot done?"

He smiled. "Depends what you consider a lot, I guess. I was mostly just messing around." He looked at me. "How 'bout you? What are you up to today?"

"Well, I worked this morning. I help edit a poetry magazine."

He made a face like he was impressed. "So who's your favorite poet?"

I thought desperately. "That's a horrible question," I said, after a second.

He laughed. "Well, who do you *like*, then? Is that better?"

"Well, I like Blake, to start with the past. Deborah Garrison, Sharon Olds, Edna St. Vincent Millay . . ."

"What's something she wrote?"

"Edna St. Vincent Millay?" I thought for a second. "'Safe above the solid rock the ugly houses stand: / Come and see my shining palace built upon the sand!'"

"That's nice," he said, after a moment.

"Yeah."

"How 'bout Deborah—"

"Garrison? 'God forgive me— / It's the firemen, / leaning in the firehouse garage / with their sleeves rolled up / on the hottest day of the year.'"

He was watching me, smiling. "That's a chick poem."

I laughed. "Well—yeah. I guess it is."

"What about the other one you mentioned?" he said. "Susan, or—"

"Sharon. Olds." I paused, debating whether to go on. "She has this one poem, about her daughter and son," I said. "It's called 'The Couple.' The sister's older, bigger . . . healthier. It's a beautiful poem. Kind of breaks my heart, though." I stopped suddenly.

"Tell me some of it," he said softly.

I took a breath. "'Like a small royal bride and groom,' she describes them. Her 'big hard head' and his 'narrow oval skull, until they are crown to crown, brown hair mingling like . . . ' " I stopped again. I thought, *Would Oliver have grown up to be more delicate than Hazel? If he'd grown up?*

"What?" he said. He was looking at me, looking, looking.

I shook my head. "Nothing."

"I love that you know all that by heart," he said, after a second.

I swallowed. "I wish I could write them, though. I never was any good at that."

He was still looking. "Well, never too late, right?" he said, slowly. "Carpe diem, or whatever. If not now, when?"

I didn't answer. After a second, he put his hands behind him and leaned back on his palms. From outside, a hint of a breeze stirred the air, and I caught a faint smell of sweat and of something astringent, alcohol or maybe lemon. The drop of sweat was still there. He turned to me. "Elayna?"

Some sort of wall came down inside me, a trapped door opening up; my sad thoughts, my name on his lips, his body this close to mine. And I couldn't take it, suddenly. My senses were loaded and overflowing. I felt as if I were on the edge of a diving board, leaning into the air but not allowed to fall in.

"What?" I managed.

"That girl who dropped me off? She's just a friend."

I laughed. I didn't know what else to do.

"I just wanted you to know that," he said.

"Okay," I said.

We sat in silence then, the inside heat around us. On the other side of the door was the brightness of day, but in here it was cooler, darker, still as glass, except for my heart, which was banging, thrashing, misbehaving. I reached for the tea, just for something to do, took a sip, and put it back near his feet. And again, that droplet of sweat on his temple. I reached up and wiped it off with my first two fingers, as if I were smoothing ice cream off Zachary's chin.

He turned toward me.

"Oh! Sorry!" I said, recoiling.

He raised his eyebrows. "What for?"

I shook my head.

"Sorry for what?" he said again, but I knew that he knew; something palpable had passed between us.

"It's okay," he said, after a second.

I looked down, took a deep breath, then jumped up. "I have to go get Hazel. We're going to New York, to see my father."

"Oh." He got up too and took a step back, but I could tell he was still looking at me. He picked up the glass, as if to carry it into the kitchen, like the good boy he was.

"That's okay," I said, taking it from him. I met his eye for the briefest second, then looked away.

Kevin wiped his palms on the butt of his jeans. "Thanks for the tea." He took a step toward the door. "Have fun."

"Thanks. You too."

I grimaced at my line. How much did he realize? How much was I showing? Was my face purple, transparent, my heart reaching its pulsing arms through my chest toward him? "Well—bye," he said, and he passed through the door and out into the sunlight again.

# Chapter Thirteen

My father had told us to meet him at one thirty at the back entrance to a club called Gigi's on West Forty-fifth Street, where the fashion show would be held. We arrived with time to spare, and as we stood waiting, I looked Hazel over one last time. Last night, I'd washed and detangled her hair; today, in the schoolyard before we drove to the bus stop, I'd combed her curls neatly back off her face, capturing them with a tight barrette. Then I'd fought her into a pretty, white Laura Ashley dress, clean white sneakers, and a white cotton cardigan and scrubbed her face with the damp washcloth I'd brought along. I wasn't sure quite what had come over me—normally, I let her wear whatever she wanted—but I was determined that she arrive looking clean, the perfect pure, naive suburban girl.

My father arrived promptly, of course. Hazel rushed at him, and he allowed her to cling briefly to his neck before peeling her off and plunking her down for appraisal. "Angelic," he said. "Pure as new-fallen snow. Now, are you ready to be a fashion star?"

"Yes!" she screamed.

"Good." He looked up at me then, and we kissed briefly on each cheek. "Hello, Elayna," he said. "You're looking well. Exceptionally well, actually."

I smiled. "Thanks. So are you." He was pumped up: cheeks flushed, hair freshly cut and standing like a putting green, so thick I wondered if he'd been dipping into the Rogaine along with his daily pomegranate juice. He wore his trademark black jeans and black T-shirt, expensive soft leather shoes, a Nikon and a Polaroid around his neck. If it weren't for his silver hair, which only added to the effect, he could've passed for forty, not to mention gay. "So what's new?" I said.

He looked off into the distance. "I was at the Frick yesterday, with a friend. I'd forgotten how exquisite the Vermeers are, especially. Mm." He shook his head, lost in whatever brand of rapture he experienced, and once again I marveled at his need to be constantly titillated, constantly devouring the world.

"Are you going, Mom?" Hazel asked impatiently, for she too needed to be continually entertained, intrigued, fed. As did I.

"She wants me all to herself," my father said, matter-of-factly.

I rolled my eyes. But I was pleased he was fostering this.

"Go, Elayna," he said. "Enjoy your day. Do some shopping, or go see a movie. Or get a massage. I know someone fabulous, if you're interested."

I pictured some hot young thing, barely clad, massaging his supine body. "No—thanks," I said. "I have things to do."

Hazel was holding his hand now. "Well, good," he said. "The show doesn't start until five thirty anyway, and you'll be bored out of your mind if you stay here."

"But who will watch her in there?" I said. "Won't you be working?" I was questioning, not insisting. I wanted to leave; I was ready to be gone; I was just covering my bases, doing the mother thing.

He picked up one of the cameras, pointed at me, and shot—something he hadn't done in years—and I took a step back, caught off guard. "I won't let her out of my sight," he said. "And she'll have the time of her life. There are a bunch of girls I know in there dying to meet her, friends of mine. Believe me, she'll be well taken care of. Now go. Have a good time. Come back at five thirty, if you want to see the show. Otherwise, let's see . . . Call my cell later and we'll figure it out."

"Bye, Mama!" Hazel said, and now that it was clear I would in fact be departing, she reached up to throw her clean little hands around *my* neck. "I love you!"

I heard my father's camera click twice.

"I love *you,*" I returned.

She removed herself from me and took his hand again as his camera dropped back to his chest. I waved to their backs until the door closed behind them.

And there I was: alone, free, in New York. I felt my body fill up with it, as if I were being slowly inflated; at the end, I was floating on air. Where should I go? I had four luxurious hours. Celeste had said to call her at work, that she might be able to meet around three forty-five for a quick walk or drink. I took a few deep breaths, relishing the gray, the smog, the Con Ed workers blasting propane torches from their hole below the sidewalk, the faint smell of brick and pavement, of endless people and newspapers and pizza baking and cookies cooling and even of oozing, steaming trash. Bodies streamed by, cell phones attached to their heads like some required new form of ear. I watched it all with the rapture of being able to view and participate without anyone engaging me, needing me, noticing. Then I opened my own cell phone and called Celeste, joining the fray.

"Hey," she answered. "Where are you?"

"West Forty-fifth. I just dropped Hazel off with my father."

"Excellent. How is that ravishing little diva?"

I smiled. "Snotty as ever. Listen, want to meet?"

"Yeah. Three o'clock?"

"Really? Can you leave?"

"No, but who cares? I'll tell him I have an appointment. Where were you going from here?"

"I don't know. I was thinking of going underwear shopping."

"Grown-ups call it lingerie, Elayna. Bloomingdale's, then. I'll meet you in the café on the seventh floor at three. You can show me all your gorgeous new edible undies." She laughed. "See you soon." The phone clicked.

It had been years—okay, months, whatever—since I'd bought myself a piece of clothing. Arriving at Bloomingdale's after a brisk walk across town, I cruised past one makeup counter after another, refusing all offers to be spritzed with perfume. But as I passed the last assaulter, I stopped suddenly and walked back to the closest makeup display. "Can I help you?" said an exotic Hawaiian-looking supermodel posing as a lowly Bloomingdale's salesperson.

"No, thanks." I waited for her to disappear, or at least pretend to, before I approached the massive lipstick drawer and pulled it open: endless samples of peaches, pinks, browns, like soldiers heading off to kill or be killed. I honed in on reddish browns and tried four, smoothing them onto my hand. I chose one, wiped off the no doubt billions of germs on its surface, painted it on my lips and peered in the mirror. Whoa. It really *had* been years since I'd worn lipstick. I had never cared much for makeup, always thought it screamed out, *I'm trying! Really! Don't I look good today?* But now . . . well, now it was time for something different. I glanced at the clerk, who instantly glided over. "I'll take this one," I said.

"Would you care for some eyeshadow, mascara, or skin toner with that?" she asked, in a heavy accent.

"Nope. Thanks. This should do the trick."

She nodded and clipped her long red nails onto my credit card.

After that, I proceeded to the shoe department, where I promptly bought two pairs of black sandals: one platformy chic, the other more practical but not completely old fart. I didn't even look at the prices until the cashier, a razor-cheeked brown-skinned man in an exquisite suit whose name tag said JAN, announced, "That's three hundred and sixty-five, with the tax."

"It is?" I blinked. "How much is the tax?"

He gave me a look, then frowned down at his tie, smoothed it, and glanced back at me. "The one pair is Prada. Still want 'em?"

"Yes," I said, after the teensiest pause.

He rang it up and handed me the shopping bag, then went back to guard what I now knew was the All Too Special Prada display, of which I now, like every other half-rich New York woman, was a victim. I checked my watch. I still had thirty-five minutes.

I went to designer sportswear—or whatever you call it—where, in the Calvin Klein section, I found a few summer sweaters and a breezy little blouse on a sale rack. I proceeded to the jeans, where I took variations of my size—thin end, big-butt end, the short end, the long end. Outside the fitting room, two middle-aged black attendants—one of them drop-dead gorgeous, the other attractive in a toothy, big-featured way—were talking and laughing, so loudly I smiled watching them.

"How many items?" the gorgeous one finally asked me, wiping away her tears.

"Um—" I tried to count my items, dropping a couple on the floor, stooping to pick them up, dropping another in the process. They both watched me, amused, not deigning to help, but not unfriendly, either. "Ten?" I said. "Thirty-five? I don't know."

They both cackled. "Sorry, you can only have six," Gorgeous said. She handed me a big plastic number 6. "But go ahead, take them all."

The first six pairs made me look either fat or flat butted. The seventh was perfect. I checked myself out at least twelve times from every angle—sixteen or twenty from the more flattering ones—then took them off and tossed them on the floor to start a yes pile. My god, how long since I'd been alone with time in a dressing room? I tried the sweaters next. All great—or at least they would be, once I got some new bras. I narrowed it down to two, a teal and a deep cranberry, then glanced at my watch. Fifteen minutes to go.

Now the blouse. I eyed it skeptically. Handkerchief thin, sleeveless, with tiny blue flowers, a tie at the midriff . . . something that could have migrated here from the juniors department, except for the price. I shook my head. Only Calvin Klein could get away with charging $110 for about 10 cents' worth of cotton—not that all the other designers didn't do it too. I maneuvered my arms into it. They popped out of the sleeve holes, looking not as bad as they might, and I imagined Calvin watching me, grinning, saying, *It's not what you have, hon, it's what you do with it.* And then Calvin was Kevin, and the grin was a gaze, intense and longing. As I buttoned the blouse, I imagined him unbuttoning, his thumbs and fingers maneuvering my hands and the buttons the way they'd maneuvered the Play-Doh, the clay, Hazel's fingers a few days ago. I moved closer to the mirror, my face almost touching the glass, and looked at myself as if I were him watching me; I raised my chin and parted my lips and thought of his hands on my neck, his thumbs passing over my breasts through the soft, thin cotton, until, to my own amusement and embarrassment, I visibly flushed, my chest as pink as rare meat.

Oh, the power of the mind! But it was time to go. I took my purchases to the register, signed the slip without looking at the amount, and got up to the café by 3:35. No Celeste. I bought an iced decaf and a slice of chocolate cake—I hadn't been hungry since Kevin left, and if anything would tempt me, it was this—then sat down to wait. Instantly, I thought of this morning, of him sitting next to me in my house, saying my name.

Celeste showed up promptly at 3:42. We dispensed with the pleasantries, and, after I forced down a few bites of cake, proceeded straight up to lingerie. She was visibly pleased that I was showing signs of joining the rest of the female race in caring about shopping, at least for a day. Plus, she needed stuff too—or so she said—and so, when we reached the department, off we both went (me to the C cups, she to A), convening shortly to assess each other's stash and snag side-by-side dressing rooms.

I had picked out some standard, everyday bras, and then, on impulse, grabbed a few extravagant pieces off a rack: black lace bra/thong sets, lacy (okay, slutty) slips and bustiers. After choosing two white bras, I moved on to the good stuff. First, a blood-colored silk camisole, dark tan lace on the cleavage. It looked hot. *I* looked hot. I *was* hot. In fact, I was sweating. Who the hell was I buying this stuff for? Paul would laugh. I had never worn this sort of thing in my life. Then again, I'd never been thirty-five. *It's now or never,* I thought, fingering it. In a few years, it would be too late.

I peeked out around my curtain—no one in the hall—then sneaked into Celeste's room. She was standing before the mirror in a dark crimson lace bra—or rather, a fraction of a demibra, which, in her case, was about a millimeter of material, like a ribbon of lace, under each silver-dollar breast. Above them, her dark nipples were two intense bull's-eyes, daring anyone to resist. Her underpants matched, ribbons of red lace barely covering her perfectly trimmed black pubic patch.

"That stuff was conceived exactly for you," I said. "No wonder he cheats on his wife."

As soon as I said it, I wasn't sure I should have. But Celeste laughed.

"And that's exactly what it's designed for. Mistresses such as myself. Can you imagine a married woman wasting her time with this nonsense?"

"Of course. Lots of them do."

"Point taken," she said. "Otherwise the stores wouldn't be so loaded with it." She smiled. "So, like, this is what you guys wear most of the time?"

"Yup. I parade around in it every evening and morning. And then we fornicate on the kitchen table while Hazel is brushing her teeth for school."

We both laughed.

"But I'm not your typical lingerie customer anyway," I said, suddenly defensive. "I never buy this stuff. I'm just saying, lots of women do."

"And you will too, now. Right?" I didn't answer, and she said, "You can't possibly not buy that, Elayna. He'll come just looking at you."

I thought of Kevin, and I swallowed. "Well. I came in for white cotton bras."

Celeste rolled her eyes, justifiably, and I stole another peak at the mirror.

"Oh, go ahead," she said. "Buy it. Live a little, Elayna. And then go home and put it on for Paul tonight. Maybe something good will happen."

"Maybe I will," I said, wondering if he'd even be home. "Anyway . . ." I started to pick up something, a bra or whatever, then dropped it again.

Celeste was watching me. She sat down on the bench in her underwear, or lack thereof, and looked at me. "Do you want to talk about it?"

"About what?" But I slid down and sat on the floor, scratchy carpet rough on my bare thighs.

Celeste watched me for a long moment. "Did you sleep with him?" she said.

My heart stopped. "Sleep with who?"

"Cookie Boy."

I barked a laugh. "God, Celeste! Of course not."

She actually looked relieved. "Then, okay. You have nothing to worry about."

"I'm *not* worried."

She smiled. "I know. I was just making sure."

I picked up a piece of underwear, fondled it. "So it's that simple, then? If I didn't sleep with him, I haven't done anything wrong?"

"I guess it depends on what you consider wrong. I mean, I know women who think anything shy of penetration isn't even worth going to confession for. And others who say if you so much as fantasize about someone else, you might as well—"

"That's ridiculous. Even Dr. Ruth says you can fantasize."

"Listen, you don't have to convince me. I mean, who *wouldn't* fantasize? To be married to the same person for months or years or decades and not even *think* about anyone else? Now, *that's* dysfunctional. *That's* something to worry about."

I didn't answer, and after a second she turned away. "Well, maybe that's just me. I was born the wrong sex in the wrong country. I should've been an Italian man."

I smiled. "Well, I'm glad you're not."

"Me too, actually." She looked at me, then sighed. "I have to go back to work. And you probably need to go back to Hazel too, right?"

I nodded. But I didn't want to go. I wanted her to ask me more about Cookie Boy.

"Listen," she said, reading my thoughts, "whatever you're doing, I'm sure it's not nearly as bad as you think. You always were the most absurdly moral person I knew."

"I'm not *doing* anything!" But I was glad she'd said that.

She shrugged, then stood, and I stood too, went back to my own dressing room and plucked out a few of the sexy items I'd picked and added them to the yes pile without trying them on. I got dressed and took it all out and bought up the lot of it.

Celeste had gone off to the bathroom, and I proceeded there now, hauling my bags. In a stall a few away from Celeste's feet, I dug in my bags for the black lace bra and underwear, put it on quickly, and dressed again.

Celeste smiled as I emerged, I'm sure knowing what I'd done. We washed our hands and headed out. "I wonder when they'll start offering Botox shots at the cosmetic counter," she said as we dodged the perfume brigade. "Not soon enough, if you ask me."

"Oh, Celeste. You wouldn't." I looked at her. "Would you?"

"What, do something fast, easy, and relatively painless that would make me look instantly ten years younger? Oh no. Why even ask?"

We exited on Third and Fifty-ninth. She put up her hand, and immediately two cabs screeched to a halt. She chose one, then leaned over to give me a hug. "Call me," she said, getting in. "And don't worry. As long as he doesn't penetrate, you're golden."

I laughed in spite of myself, which pleased her. She slammed the door and kissed the window from the inside, and the yellow cab whooshed her away.

# *Chapter Fourteen*

And then it was 5:05, rush hour, and I was halfway across town from Gigi's. Once more, I ran, Bloomingdale's bag handles digging red lines in my hand as I dodged briefcases, purses, newsstands, overflowing trash cans, high-heeled miniskirted secretaries smoking in clusters outside tall silver buildings, beefy men in tank tops yelling more nothing into cell phones, baby strollers pushed by young Hispanic mothers or black Caribbean nannies or rich Waspy Upper East Side rail-thin aging Barbie clones. By the time I arrived at the club, the line outside the entrance extended around the block. I rushed to the front. "Excuse me," I said to the bouncer, an ape of a man with a beeper on his belt and, for some reason, a chopstick stuck behind one ear. "I need to get in. My father's the photographer."

He assessed me, pausing at my boobs, and I wished briefly that I had on Celeste's favorite T-shirt from college, a skintight, hanky-thin white thing that said, in bold letters printed across the chest, LOOK UP. "Sorry," he said, his eyes finally deigning to meet mine. "You'll have to wait. Doors don't open until five twenty-five."

I felt a tiny surge of panic. "But my daughter's in the show. My father told me I'd be able to get in anytime." Was this true? Now that I thought about it, we hadn't even discussed this.

The bouncer regarded me, chewing his gum. "Got a ticket?"

I shook my head.

He sighed. "Name?"

"Elayna. Leopold. My father's Devon Leopold."

"Wait a minute." He hauled his muscles up and slipped inside, the door closing behind him. I stood still, my bags dangling, trying to ignore the resentful stares of the people around me. After ten decades or so, he returned. "Okay," he said blandly. "Go in."

The club was bigger, darker, more upscale than I'd expected—I don't know why, this being *The New York Times,* this being My Father. There was a stage with a large runway protruding from it, rows of mostly empty chairs, enormous speakers onstage. No sign of Hazel or Devon.

A teenage girl appeared briefly on stage, outfitted in some yellow feather number with a headdress. Then a woman came out: small, thin, short black skirt, black shirt unbuttoned to below the breast line, revealing much of the black bra painted onto her chest. She scurried to the end of the runway and looked around, black spectacles atop her head, before rushing backstage again. Lights were being tested, and the runway kept changing color: lime green, purple, bright white. Anticipation crackled the air.

I wove through the chairs toward the stage. Hazel had to be back there somewhere, didn't she? But I stopped at the edge; it was too high for me to get onto without hoisting myself up with my hands, something I wasn't sure I could accomplish even if doing so *wouldn't* have gotten me hauled out of there.

"Can I help you?" A man—white blond, black clad, faggy—was tapping my arm. He had a pile of what appeared to be programs in his hand.

"I'm trying to find my daughter," I said. "She's in the show."

He pointed to the side of the stage. "Try that door."

I went to it and knocked. No answer. I tried the knob, but it was locked. I knocked again, much harder. There was a loud clatter behind me, and I turned to see people from outside streaming into the club. Just then someone answered the door, a tall, skinny hipster—female, it seemed—with dreadlocks and a nose ring. "Um—yeah?" she said.

Once more, I explained that I was looking for my daughter, blah blah.

The person waited, expressionless.

"I'm her mother!" I said.

Suddenly she could barely restrain her VIP annoyance. "It's a really bad time," she said, letting the dreads fall tediously in front of her face. "The kids are getting their makeup done. The show's about to start—" She glanced back behind her. "In fact, it is starting. It's starting." She closed the door in my face.

I stood for a second, stunned, then raised my hand to knock again. But the seats were filling up. I glanced around, slightly panicked, for my father. And there he was, standing on the other side of the room with his cameras, talking to someone. I rushed toward him, grabbing a seat in the process. "Dad!" I yelled.

The room was full and abuzz now, lights flickering. People in seats were flagging down friends, screaming into cell phones, flipping through their programs. "Dad!" I yelled again.

He turned and saw me.

"How is she?" I yelled.

He raised his thumb. "Perfect. They love her."

The lights dropped, too dramatically; for a second, the whole room was black. Dawdlers and latecomers scurried blindly to find seats as the lights returned, much more dimly, for all of ten seconds; then they disappeared for good, music booming through the speakers, white light shooting onto the stage.

"Welcome," hummed a smooth, loud, slightly nasal male voice, "to a preview of the fall line of children's and junior wear for Jenni Kline, Donna Zoler, Michael Michielli, Austin Jones, and Stephen Mirauder."

Immediately, two teenage girls who could only have been identical twins sashayed onto the stage from opposite sides, met perfectly in stage center, and began down the catwalk together, like yin and yang: both leggy, rail thin, flanks as long and flat as ironing boards, topped off by just-budding breasts, perfectly evident through their tight, transparent clothes. One was dressed in white from head to toe—boots, leggings, short skirt, spandex top with sequins in a band across the waist, feather hat—the other in black. They both wore bright red lipstick. I have to say, the effect was spectacular. At the end of the runway, they turned perfectly and reversed direction, sauntering back like a pair of lynx. I felt a pang of dread. There was no way Hazel could do this. What had my father been thinking? What had *I*?

But the next models were coming, and then more after that, mostly girls but some boys too, teenagers and preteens and just a few younger ones, none who looked as young as Hazel; she would be the baby of the show. I crossed my fingers and told the powers that be that I'd behave for the rest of my life if they'd just let her do okay this one time, if they'd just . . . but by then I was mesmerized again, riveted to the stage. As far as I could tell, the job of the girls, besides to show off the clothes, was to elicit awe and envy among the women and perhaps the gay men in the crowd, and lust among the rare heterosexual male. The boys—the gorgeous, shaggy-long-haired teenage boys—were to put the fire in the women's and queer men's loins. One in particular, a raven-haired, lionesque stud quite possibly part feline, sent a ripple through the crowd when he appeared, in tight white jodhpurs with no sign of an undergarment and a white waist-length jacket, also worn against his velvety brown chest.

Did he look right at me? Of course not, any more than he looked right at any other woman there—he wore the bored, jaded look of a wealthy budding snob who, at seventeen, already has the world wrapped around his finger and is just killing time till he can be off to Rome or Bhutan or somewhere that, god willing, will thrill him—but reality wasn't the point here. It was fantasy, pure and sweet, and I was happy to submit. Skin was rampant: exposed legs, backs, midriffs, with the covered body parts cellophaned with stretchy-thin wraps of aqua, magenta, lemon peel. Lighting, makeup, accessories—feathers, fur, sequins, glass beads—in the same wild colors. For the second time that day, I felt my general disdain for all things fashion related pushed to the back of my brain, replaced by that ever more mundane thrill caused by Things That Look Good. Tacky or not—and I suspected it was not, though of course, the now diminished but never quite vanished voice of reason and intellect in my brain wanted to believe it was—the show was unquestionably thrilling and beautiful; the human animal at its most seductive and attractive, perfect flesh and bone structure, eyes, skin, teeth, nostrils, decorated and displayed.

And then there came my Hazel, my own baby human, the flesh and blood of my own, sauntering onto the stage in a long white tube skirt and a short, tight, hot pink midriff tube top, her belly button peeking out like a wink from the thin belt of white skin between. Her hair was arranged in two braids, Pippi style, antler style, sticking (drumsticks? hangers?) straight up and out. Her freckles were an exotic, bold wash, her lips a dark fuchsia, her eyes magnified and pulled practically out of her face with mascara, bold shadow, black lines. Was I imagining it, or did a murmur rise when she came out? At any rate, she was miraculous; all the shyness she'd ever had seemed utterly vanished as she stalked to the edge of the runway, slit her eyes and glared out at the audience, put a hand on her hip and did her side-to-side swirl, Pippi with an ax to grind. My mouth was open. How the hell did she know how to do this?

I felt an odd thing in the pit of my stomach, extreme pride mixed with a sort of dread. It was a little like being hit by lightning, I imagined—that simultaneous feeling of astonishment, horror, naiveté, and an absolute zeal for life. I stood up. "Hazel!" I yelled, and I saw her eyes shift in my direction, her lips tremor with some hint of satisfaction, and one part of me, at least, relaxed—the part that had been disconnected while I was away from her and until she knew I was back again, and I knew she was okay.

She came out three more times, each in an equally thrilling outfit. It was an odd fashion show, or at least it seemed that way to me, not that I'd seen many. At the end, they played music from *West Side Story,* and a teenage boy and girl did a seductive little number in which they chased each other around (but mostly he chased her) and then she succumbed and they embraced and danced together, ending with a kiss that was just awkward enough to communicate that scintillating, terrifying thrill of first love. So what if he was already a troubled homosexual and she anorexic? I was as riveted as every other sucker in the place.

When it was over, we all clambered backstage into a mass of bodies and clothes and makeup, of champagne and lavender punch and tables full of sushi and crudités and little pizzas, Cokes and Cokes with rum and perhaps the other coke, too, being snorted just out of view. Kids were disrobing, changing back into T-shirts and shorts, unraveling their hairdos and having their makeup removed by mothers or nannies or friends. And there was Hazel, rushing up in a crowd with another little girl, a striking white blond with, I swear, emerald eyes, and two teenagers—one of them clearly the blond's sister—herding them like shepherds. "Is that your mom?" one of them said to Hazel, pointing at me.

Hazel ran over, but stopped short of her usual embrace, aware of her urbane company. "Mom," she said, coolly. "Did you see me?"

"You were amazing! I was blown away, Hazel. How did you know what to do?"

She couldn't conceal her pride, but she kept her poise. "It was easy. Maude taught me the walk, and once I got it down, it was no big thing."

"Maude?"

"Her." She pointed to White Blondie the teen.

"Don't point, Haze," I said, smiling. "It's not polite."

"Oh please," Maude said, flipping her hair dramatically. "My sister's exactly her age. Anyway, she was a breeze to teach. She picked it up in, like, five seconds. You should be in another show, Hazel. You're an absolute natural."

Again, pride permeated Hazel's face, but she said, as if she were the perfect twelve-year-old, "I don't know, it's, like, up to my mom. And it depends on our schedule, and stuff." But she looked at me pleadingly. "Can I?"

I shifted. I didn't want to be the dork mom any more than she wanted to be the dork kid. "We'll have to see," I said.

"There's another one in, like, two weeks," Maude said. "Same time, I think. I'm not sure where, but you could call our booking agent, Esther. Here, I have her direct dial on my cell." She reached into her purse and pulled out a pink phone. "She could rep Hazel too, if you want. I'm sure she'd *love* you, Hazel, with that fabulous hair." She smiled, a striking, radiant train of endless teeth, and ran her hands through Hazel's curls, now loose and wild, released from their daggerlike braids. "I would *kill* for that hair."

"Well, I hate it," Hazel said, unable to hide her pleasure. "I'd kill for *your* hair. And Chloe's." She glanced at the little sister, then back at Maude.

I was starting to find this all a bit much. "You know," I said to Maude, who was now holding the tiny cell phone to her ear, "maybe I'll just take your agent's number and call her at a better time."

"What? Oh. Whatever." She pressed a button and snapped the phone shut, dropped it back into her purse. "Anyone want a Pellegrino? I'm getting one."

"I'll take one," Hazel said, as if she had any idea what one was.

I cleared my throat and reached for her hand. "You know what, Haze?

We need to find Grandpa and say bye, because we need to go down and get Daddy."

"But I don't want to!" Hazel pulled her hand away from mine. "I want to stay! There's a party! Why do we have to go?"

I felt a pang. Empty-nest syndrome, phase one. "Because we're supposed to surprise Daddy and take him out to dinner," I said. "Remember?"

She sighed, and I could tell she was mildly torn, emphasis on mildly, for about three seconds. "Can't you and Daddy go just this once without me?" she said. "Pleeeze, Mom? You could pick me up right after. Or no, wait—I could sleep at Grandpa's! And he could drive me to school tomorrow."

I laughed. "Have you told your grandfather that plan yet?"

"What plan?" my father said, gliding up. He was aglow with excitement. "Does this plan involve me, by any chance?"

"Yes!" Hazel yelled. "You would drive me to school in the morning if I sleep at your house—so I can go to the fashion-show party."

"Ah," he said to me. "So I see you've met my two favorite girls—after Hazel, of course. Their mother is Kay van Morgan. Old friend of mine. Harvard girl, like her husband, Dick. Excellent family. Enormous philanthropists. They're responsible for the Van Morgan library on East Ninety-eighth Street. Have you been there yet, Elayna? You must go."

Maude smiled at him, then tossed her creamy head. "Hazel could stay at our house if you don't have room, Mr. Leopold. The guest room is always made up. Our driver picks us up for school at, like, seven fifteen, but Hazel could stay till whenever, our nanny could watch her."

My father seemed amused. "Is that right?"

"Absolutely. My mom, like, *loves* visitors. Well, not all visitors, obviously, but I know for sure she would love Hazel. Wouldn't she, Chlo?"

Chloe nodded dutifully. "Antoinette could make her a protein milk shake." She looked at Hazel. "They sound gross, but they're totally yum."

"Unfortunately," I cut in, a little nervously now, because this thing seemed to be taking on a life of its own, "Hazel can't stay. Her father likes to see her, and she's tired—"

"I am not!" Hazel yelled, reverting briefly to her old self.

"Please don't yell, Hazel," I said. "You can't sleep in the city tonight."

"Okay!" she yelled. "Then can I at least stay for the party?"

"Oh, let her stay," my father mumbled to me. "You can go out with Paul and have a nice dinner. I'll watch her. I'll be photographing the kids anyway—"

"You don't have to *watch* me," said Hazel. "God!"

"Hazel," I warned.

"Okay! Sorry!" She sighed. "But can I stay, Mom? Please?"

I sighed too, considering. On the one hand, I knew I probably shouldn't give in, since I'd already sort of said no and Hazel's snottiness would make my giving in that much more pathetic. On the other hand, why *should* I drag her kicking and screaming to some dinner with Paul where she'd hate all the food, be bored after five minutes, and keep the whole thing from even mildly resembling romantic or relaxing? Plus—well, it was nice she'd made some new friends. Friends from a wealthy Harvard philanthropist New York family. I tried but failed to be above being impressed. My father's Ivy League snobbery was something I'd always hated, which I knew meant it was only a matter of time before I acquired an even worse case of it.

"Okay," I said, giving in. "You can stay. But I'm coming back around nine, and you'd better hop on that bus home and go *instantly* to sleep. Understand?"

"Yes!" She leaped up and hugged me, then let go and grabbed Maude's hand.

"Okay with you too, Dad?"

"Of course," he said.

"And you'll absolutely watch her?"

He smiled, patronizing me. "My eyes won't leave her immaculate face, except to take the occasional shot of another stunning child." He motioned toward the door. "Have a nice dinner, and we'll see you at ten. Good-bye."

"Wait!" Hazel yelled. "I have to tell her something first!" She rushed over to me and pulled me down. "Momma," she whispered in my ear, "did you see what they did to my hair? Wasn't that sooo cool?" She pulled away to look at me for an answer. "Yes," I whispered back, and for a second my love for her almost brought me to tears. She nodded, then pulled my ear back. "And you know what else? They put *mascara* on me! *Blue* mascara! I didn't even know they *invented* that yet!"

Again, she withdrew to gauge my response. "Very cool," I whispered. "I couldn't believe it when I saw you. You looked at *least* seven, maybe even eight or nine."

She beamed, giddy with joy. She was in heaven that night. And who was I to rain on her parade? I know what Pansy would say to that question, but even now, I don't think I would have dragged her out of there.

Hazel planted a kiss on my cheek. "Tell Daddy I love him, and I'm sorry I couldn't come to dinner," she said, all sophistication now.

"I will. I'm sure he'll forgive you, just this once."

She considered a moment, then nodded. "Okay, well. Bye."

"Bye, baby." I turned to my father. "Take care of her."

"Naturally," he said.

# Chapter Fifteen

Christensen, Schulman, Berzoff, Myers & Schappell was located on the thirty-second, thirty-third, and thirty-fourth floors of a forty-four-story tower on lower Broadway. I swung through the heavy glass doors and entered the lobby—high ceilinged, palm treed, befountained, marble up the butt—walking against traffic as dark-suited men and the occasional skirted woman clacked out past me. I gave a wave to the door-man, got my pass, and headed for the elevator. As I rose in the sleek silver box, I took out my new lipstick and applied it to my mouth, then poked a tiny dot on the top of each cheekbone and rubbed. It looked good, I thought, peering into the elevator doors; dramatic, sultry. I flipped my head and fluffed my hair, adjusted my blouse, aware of my new lingerie underneath. By the time the elevator opened and I stepped out into Paul's office, I was ready to be the New Me.

I sniffed the sanitized air (plush carpeting, Xerox machines, a trace of perfume) and looked around. The main receptionist was gone, as were, I assumed, most of the secretaries, but lights were on all over and I could see the occasional person coming briefly into view as he or she passed through the hallway leading in. I had planned to pick up the phone and dial Paul's extension—that was the best I could do for a surprise, I supposed—but then I noticed someone coming down the hall to go out, and I moved closer to the glass door. He opened it, assessing me. "Aren't you Paul Slade's wife?"

I nodded, surprised. "Yes. I'm sorry, you're—"

"Graham Jackson. We met last year at the Christmas party."

He was tall and lanky, with disheveled long hair—unusual at a law firm like this, I thought. His pale blue shirt matched oval-shaped eyes set so close together they almost touched his nose, one eye—interestingly—slightly higher than the other. "Oh—right," I said, trying unsuccessfully to remember meeting him.

"You edit a poetry magazine."

I raised my eyebrows. "You have a good memory."

"For certain things." He smiled, then said, "But yes, in general too, unfortunately. Otherwise, I wouldn't be at this place."

"Oh come now," I bantered. "It can't be *that* bad."

"No, of course not," he countered. "I mean, I could be home dining with my wife then retiring to my room to, I don't know, read a novel." He made a face of exaggerated disgust.

"Provided your wife made a healthy six figures."

"Provided I had a wife. She left me long ago, alas."

"Oops." I smiled. "Sorry."

"Please. It's hardly your fault."

"Well—thanks for letting me in."

"Anytime, doll."

I moved past him through the doorway, wondering if I'd get to flirt like that every day if I worked at an office like this. The magazine office had been almost all women, and the few men were dramatically nerdy, fun but not sexy. But here? I maneuvered my way through the brightly lit hallways. The offices seemed to contain hardworking men and a few women—lawyers, not secretaries, I figured from their clothing, demeanors, and stress-lined faces. They were, I decided, either too young, too unattached, or too conflicted to have children yet . . . or else they were those rare women who can relegate the complete care, feeding, and even bedtime rituals of their offspring to a husband or an au pair. The dark office was the exception at 7 PM. I rounded a corner, passed a skirted woman at a copy machine—one foot held slightly aloft its expensive beige pump—and headed for Paul's office. I stopped just outside his door, savoring the suspense of surprising him at work, lipsticked and lingeried. Then I stepped into his doorway and, after a second, walked in.

He was sitting at his desk, looking down at some papers, and Marisol was standing next to and close behind him, looking over his shoulder at them too. It could only have been Marisol: skirt not so professional that it didn't reveal her youthful thin legs, hair in a ponytail not quite so hard core as to avoid suggesting it could be yanked out with one good, hard tug to descend into a sultry black mess. He hadn't bothered to tell me she was a knockout too, but I saw now that this was the case. Paul looked up and spotted me, and some combination of interest, surprise, and what seemed like genuine gladness crossed his face. I saw, I confess, no sign of guilt or deception. But still, why was his secretary still here when all the others had gone?

"Hey!" he said, smiling, pushing his chair back and standing. "What are you doing here?"

His own hair, I noticed, was in need of a cut. His tie was loosened, and, I saw now, his trousers were big in the waist. When had he gotten so thin?

Marisol blinked, smiled, walked toward me, hand extended. "You must be Mrs. Slade."

I made a cringing motion. "Elayna! Please."

"Elayna, then. It's so good to meet you."

It was the "so" that elevated it from a small-talk cliché to what seemed like a genuine expression of her pleasure that I was here. *She's no dummy,* I thought, and I smiled and took the hand, mumbling, I'm sure, some similar pleasantry. Then she vanished discreetly. "Hi," Paul said again, and we kissed, because the atmosphere seemed to call for it. "Nice to see you here. It's been, what, six years since you've been up?"

I laughed. "It has not."

He smiled, always pleased when I laughed at his jokes. "Sit," he said, gesturing to one of the two seats on the other side of his desk, the side for everyone but him and Marisol. I sat. He sat down in the second chair and moved it a few inches closer to mine, so our knees almost touched. I smiled. "Hey," I said, "remember when we were dating and we had to go to that company dance, and you sprained your ankle, and—"

"Wait," he said. "*I* sprained my ankle?"

"Right after we first met. Remember? And your company had that dance, and first you forced yourself to dance with me even though you could only stand on one foot, and then we finally sat in folding chairs somewhere and you leaned over and picked mine up, with me in it, and put it back down right in front of you, so you could reach me?"

He looked pleased. "I did that?"

"I can't believe you don't remember! It was a pivotal moment for me!"

"Why, because I was such a macho stud?"

"Exactly. Of course, I had to act like I barely noticed, like I was way above being impressed by something as clichéd as, you know, male strength. But secretly . . ."

He laughed, then sighed, looking wistful. "Those were the days. Six days a week at the gym or on my bike. I *was* a stud, wasn't I."

"Well, don't take all the credit yourself, for your big, manly arms," I said. "I was a stud too. Not an ounce of fat on me. That's probably why you could lift me."

He laughed. "Well, I'll take you now any day."

I frowned. "Do I detect an insult buried in that compliment?"

"Absolutely not. You look perfect just like this."

I wondered if he meant that or if it was just rote praise of the husband variety. Still, it was nice. "In other words, you won't trade me in for a younger, sexier model with, like, perkier boobs?" I said, fishing.

He looked thoughtful. "Maybe next year or the year after, but not yet. You still have a good year or two before I put you out to pasture."

I laughed. It was nice to see him up here, in context, all dressed up, neither rushing to get off to work nor having just come home from it, exhausted. I reached for one of the photos on his desk that faced the other way—not our wedding photo in the tiny silver Tiffany's frame, but the one of Paul in a hospital gown holding Hazel hours after her birth. She was looking at the camera with that same "don't mess with me" sneer she still has. And he was gazing at her with a look at once thrilled, relieved, and vaguely terrified. Looking at that photo always made me smile. I put it back and reached for a third, dark green frame, one I didn't remember seeing before: Hazel and me—she was two or so—wearing matching denim overalls. I was holding her close to my face, and she was hugging my head, and we were both wide eyed and smiling, staring at the camera. "Oh!" I said, laughing. "Where'd you find this?"

"I don't know. In a drawer, I think."

I shook my head. "She's incredible. Isn't she?"

"Which she?" He smiled.

I smiled back. "To what do I owe all these compliments?"

"I don't know. I'm glad you came up, I guess."

"Well, good! Maybe I'll come up more often." He nodded, but didn't say anything. "How are you, anyway?" I said. "What's the status?"

He sighed. "It's gonna be another late one."

"Can you take a break for dinner?"

He shook his head. "Shit, I wish I'd known you were coming. Mark and I already ordered in food. We're supposed to meet in the conference room in"—he glanced at his watch—"well, *now*, actually. We're working on who we want to call for witnesses, who will interview who when we go down." He looked at me. He must have seen something there, because his expression changed, suddenly. "Listen," he said, "if it's really important, I can tell Mark to start without me—"

"Oh—no. That's ridiculous." I don't know why I should've been surprised he couldn't go. In fact, I don't know why I'd thought in the first place that I could yank him out of his office with no notice. And I certainly wasn't about to beg him to come. Still—and despite it all—I almost couldn't believe he wasn't.

I stood up. "Well, I should let you get back to work then, I guess."

"Wait," he said. "Stay another minute."

I sat back down.

He sighed again. "Come on, Elayna. Don't hate me. The hearing will be over soon, and then things will lighten up, at least for a while."

I nodded blandly.

He was quiet for a minute, perhaps contrite. Then he said, "That's not the only reason you came into the city, is it? Just to—"

"Of course not. I came in to take Hazel to the fashion show."

He slapped his thigh gently. "Right. The fashion show." He frowned, annoyed with himself for forgetting. "How was it?"

I felt my guard melt a little. "Incredible, frankly. She was—" I searched for a way to describe it. "All her spiciness and flare and arrogance . . . it's the perfect medium for her to use all that. And she does it! She's not shy. I've never seen her have such poise and confidence. But it's more than that. She's got the right *attitude*, or something." I sighed. "I'm not sure whether to be happy about that or terrified, but—you should've seen her."

"I wish I could have."

I knew he meant it. My guard slipped a little more. "You will!" I said. "There will be more of these shows, and—"

"You think so?" He looked at me. "I sort of thought this was a one-time deal."

"Apparently they have these things fairly often. And she was begging to do another. And if they're on Wednesdays, and my father's into taking her . . ." I trailed off. "She's made some new friends already," I said. "Cute kids, from some philanthropic Upper East Side family. They offered to have her over tonight."

"You said no, I hope."

I looked at him. "No, Paul, I said yes. I told them to keep her for a month."

He blew out a breath. "Sorry." He reached over and gave my arm a squeeze.

"It's okay," I said, finally. He looked sad and helpless. Or did he? I thought of Marisol, leaning over his shoulder, her smooth, perfumed neck millimeters from his rough one. When was the last time he and I had been that close, except when one or both of us was sleeping? When had we last danced, taken a walk, done anything fun together?

*And when did you become a cliché of a wife, nothing better to do than nag your husband to come home earlier?*

I stood up just as someone knocked on his door frame—the door proper was still open—and there stood Marisol, in the flesh. "Excuse me," she said. "Your dinner's here, Paul. Mrs. Slade—Elayna—can I call you in something? They're very fast."

"No. Thanks. I was just leaving."

Paul stood up too. "Are you sure?" he said. "You could sit in on the meeting. Or just hang out in my office. I have my Blake in the drawer."

I gave him a look. "Thanks, but I'll go." I held the look a second; I couldn't help it. "So what time *will* you be done?"

"You know—I won't be, is what it comes down to. But I have to leave sometime. The meeting should be over by nine or nine thirty. What time are you and Hazel going home?"

"I was picking her up around nine." I said. "I guess we'll catch the nine thirty bus."

"You took the *bus* in?" He looked surprised. "I don't want you guys going back on the bus at that hour—"

"Why not? My car's parked at the bus stop."

"Forget it." He looked at his watch. "Give me an hour and a half. No—give me two. I'll pick you and Hazel up wherever she is at nine fifteen. Write the address down." He handed me a pad and a silver pen. "I'll call you when I'm on the way up, so you can be waiting and I won't have to park. Oh, but—should I come in and say hi to your father?"

"That's okay," I said. "He'll understand."

He nodded. "And then I'll finish the other stuff when I get home."

"Okay," I said. "That would be great. Hazel would love it if you picked us up." I knew I should go. But I added, "She wanted to come with me down here, to surprise you, but she was having so much fun there. But she was really torn."

He smiled, no doubt grateful I'd thrown him a bone. "Well—I'd better get over to the meeting, then, so I can get back out of it." He was about to turn away, but instead he stopped and looked at me once more. "You look different. Did you cut your hair?"

"I'm wearing lipstick," I confessed.

"Lipstick?" He looked baffled. "You don't need lipstick," he said, after a minute. "You don't need any makeup."

I blinked. "Well, maybe I *want* it. Maybe I like looking, I don't know, *different,* once in a while. Maybe I'm sick of my old self."

Perhaps I imagined it, but I could have sworn his eyes welled up. "I don't want you to look different," he said. "I like you the way you are."

"Well, this *is* the way I am, today," I said, and *I* felt like crying now.

He caught the tone. "Sorry. Sorry." He looked sheepish. "You do look really good, though," he added.

"Nice try, Paul." I laughed, and after a second, he did too.

We kissed good-bye then, to prove to ourselves or to Marisol that we still loved each other. And then he went back to his meeting, and I to the street once again.

# Chapter Sixteen

I walked until I found a cute Vietnamese place a few blocks away, where I ordered lemongrass chicken and a glass of white wine. I took out my book and cracked it open, looking around. Deep red carpets, drippy gold chandeliers. It was nice, now that I was here. I'd never minded eating alone, especially with a good book by my plate. What I minded was never being able to choose. I took a sip of my wine, remembering a quote I'd once heard: "*Solitude is vastly preferable when it's voluntary.*"

The food arrived, fragrant and steaming, and I picked up my chopsticks and carved a cave in my sticky rice. While I chewed, I thought of Hazel in the show. How had she ended up with that hair, those freckles, those eyes? And if we had another child, what would it be like? Oliver hadn't really had a chance to show himself before he died; his eyes were the blue-brown haze of a newborn, his hair almost black, but I knew that that hair would have fallen out and different hair eventually grown in. Would he have had flaming orange hair too? I thought of his little body, rigid and blue, and my blood grew thick and dull, my brain heavy, as it always did when I thought of him. But I shook my head this time, trying to push the thoughts away. So much time I'd spent heartbroken, mourning my boy, and he'd deserved every minute. But now it was time to come back to my life, to put him into a room I could visit—and would—but that I no longer lived in.

I bit into a piece of the meat, tender and juicy, and thought instead about my father—how, when I was Hazel's age, he'd introduced me to impressionism, cubism, baroque, Van Gogh's sunflowers, Picasso's blue period. My mother was our bread and butter, always there, in charge of our care and daily upkeep, but my father was the spice, the glittering colored jimmies, the one who took us out of our daily lives and showed us the rest of the world. When it came time for college, he helped me make a list of where to apply and drove me up to see them, though of course it was Columbia, his own alma mater, where he hoped I would go. He got me the interview, and if there were strings to pull, he quietly and cleanly pulled them.

But there was more than that, really. He wanted me to live, to love, to share his passion; he wanted me to see and experience New York and beyond. He saw life as a giant 3-D photograph, a multisensory exhibit, and himself as the man with the camera, seeing it, touching it, taking it in. And when I was young, he had tried to show me this world, to show me life in this way, and I'd seen a glimmer of it and had reveled in it as he did. And now—now, he wanted to do that for Hazel. So why shouldn't he?

I finished my meal and opened my book. I read for a good half hour before the waiter appeared with a check and more tea. I paid and left, made it back to the fashion-show party by eight forty-five.

The place was emptier than I'd thought; Hazel's friends had gone home, as had most of the kids, and though Hazel—dressed back in her white dress, I was happy to see—showed no signs of waning, my father seemed tired and ready to hand her back. I retrieved my Bloomies bag from the coat check, where I'd stored it before I'd left, then gathered Hazel's things and Hazel herself, assuring my father we'd be fine here until Paul arrived. Then we walked him out to a cab and all kissed good-bye on both cheeks. "Thank you," I said, meaning it. "She had a great time."

"Thank *you*," he said. "I enjoyed it immensely." His cab drove off, and Hazel and I stood under the awning to wait for Paul.

The air was cool now; I caught a whiff of what smelled like sweet sliced lemons in the breeze. Hazel was holding my hand. "And I had these little rainbow cakes," she jabbered, "they had three different colors of cake in one. But I didn't like the green cake. Only the pink and the white—oh! Mom, didn't you love Maude's hair?"

"Um—yeah," I lied, not really remembering it.

"Me too! When I get, like, your age, I'm gonna dye my hair exactly like—oh! There's Daddy's car! *Daddy!*" She ran to the curb, hopped up and down while he pulled up and opened the back door from the inside for her.

He turned around to hug her while I got in the front, my bags at my feet. He glanced at me, then at her again. "How did it go?" he asked.

"It was *so* cool!" she yelled, bouncing on the seat. "I got to wear these excellent clothes, and real makeup, not just stupid pretend baby stuff, like at home. And all these lights were shining in my eyes, and I had to walk really slowly and do a spin like a real, live model, on a stage—"

"Mom told me. That's awesome. Haze, can you climb onto your booster and buckle up now, so we can go?"

She hopped onto the seat Paul kept in his car for her and snapped on her seat belt. "I was, like, *famous,*" she said.

Paul laughed. "I bet you were. I bet you were the star." He moved into the line for the Lincoln Tunnel, benevolently let one car into his lane but held firm after that.

"No," Hazel said. "Actually, Maude was the star. She's my new friend. She's a *teenager.* She says I can sleep over their house anytime I want."

Paul glanced at me. "Sleep over? Then when would I get to see you?"

"Daddy! Like only the next *morning*!" But she seemed pleased he'd said that.

We rode in silence for a few minutes, till we came out of the tunnel and wound around to the Jersey side. And now it was New York, not New Jersey, across the river, sparkling like a silvery lit-up toy city. "Dad?" Hazel said, surprising me; I'd thought she'd fallen asleep.

"Yes?"

"Which would you rather do—burn to death, or freeze to death?"

"I don't know," he said. "That's not really a question I can answer now."

"Why not?"

He pushed his glasses up and rubbed his right eye, as I'd noticed him do earlier, and I wondered if he was getting conjunctivitis; he'd gotten it once from Hazel, and had ended up with a horrible case. "It's too hypothetical," he answered her.

"What's hypothetical?"

"Um—like fake," he said, wearily.

I waited for him to elaborate. "It's more like a created situation," I said, when he didn't. "You make up something as an example of what might be, to make a point. Like, '*What if* . . . the world were flat, or aliens came to earth.' Or something."

"Oh," she said. Silence, and then, "Mom, what about you?"

"What, puppet."

"Which would you rather do? Burn or freeze?"

"Um—probably burn," I said.

"Eew! You would?"

"Well—no. Freeze, I guess. But I hate being cold! At least burning is fast."

"Yeah, but your skin would all, like, melt off, and you'd be—"

"Haze," Paul said. "Do we have to talk about this?"

"Which would you rather do," Hazel said, ignoring him, "have to pee really bad, or poop really bad?"

"*Really* bad?" I said.

She nodded.

"Pee, I think." I giggled.

She giggled back. "Me too!" She sighed with contentment. Then she began to sing " 'You're a grand old flag.' " She sang the entire song, loud and clear.

"Wow," I said. "I didn't think they taught that in schools anymore."

"They don't," Hazel said. "I learned it at Pansy's."

"Oh. Of course."

She was quiet for a minute. Then, in the same tune, she began to experiment. "You're a grand old fag, you're a high-flying hag. And forever in snot may you gag."

"Hazel," Paul said, in a warning voice.

I glanced at him. "Fag isn't a nice word, Hazel," I allowed.

"Why not?" she said.

"Um—it's a mean thing to call two men who love each other. It's much nicer to call them gay, or—"

"You're the emblem of," she sang, interrupting, "the dork I love. The home of the fools and the nags."

I laughed. She was so damn creative.

"Hazel!" Paul said, raising his voice. "That's enough."

I looked at him.

"Why?" she said. "What did I do? Momma, what did I—"

"I don't like that kind of talk," he said.

"Why *not*?"

"Because I said so."

It was the wimpiest parent answer, one I hated. I felt myself taking her side.

"What*ever,*" she said, with a big, snotty sigh.

"And don't take that tone with me," Paul yelled. "Do you understand?"

I looked at him. "Paul," I said quietly, "she's tired. Give her a break."

"Give *me* a break," he muttered back. He turned on the radio—NPR, some blues singer—and I sat stewing while annoyingly mellow blues notes filled the car. Paul was stewing too. Unfairly, I thought. We passed some tidal flats, and then a string of dilapidated, long-abandoned apartment buildings near or in East Orange, their windows broken, open, cavernous black holes. I turned to look at Hazel. She was sound asleep, head tilted to one side, mouth open. *Poor baby,* I thought, though she was neither of the two. I turned back to the front seat.

"Can I turn the radio off?" I said, not exactly pleasantly. "It's giving me a headache."

He shrugged the shoulder closest to me. "If you want."

I snapped it off. We rode in silence for a while, and I wondered if he was letting it go, the whole conversation from before. But then he said, softly but not kindly, "Whatever happened to parental solidarity?"

"That only works if we agree," I said. "I'm sorry, but I don't think she did anything wrong."

"She was being inappropriate."

"She was being *funny.* That's how kids are funny at that age."

"By talking about pee and poop?" he said. "And fags? And snot?"

"Yes! Well, not fags, but I don't think she knew what she was saying. But pee and poop? And snot? Absolutely."

He glanced over at me, then back to the road. "And how is she supposed to learn she can't just say that stuff if we don't reprimand her? If we encourage her by laughing?"

He had a point, I supposed, but I didn't feel like conceding it. "Oh, Paul, lighten up," I said. "Not everyone's on death row, you know."

He didn't answer, but I saw his jaw tighten.

"Sorry," I said, after a second. But I wasn't that sorry. I was angry. I was thinking, *How dare he?* "It's just that you're so hard on her," I said, trying to rein myself in. "You don't see her all week, and the one time you do—"

"It's not like I have a choice!" he exploded. "I'm not exactly electing to work this hard. I'm not exactly relishing it."

"No?" It was a low blow, I knew, but I was in a low-blow kind of mood, by then. And I could've gone lower. *Well, it sure beats sitting home thinking about your dead baby,* I could've said, because that's what I was thinking.

He stared at me for a good several seconds before returning to the road. "No, I'm not," he said. "Believe it or not."

I took a deep breath, trying to calm myself, but I only got more fired up. "I'm just saying," I said, "sometimes you have to come down to her level, instead of expecting her to rise to yours. Or at least you have to meet her halfway. She's a kid!"

His hands were gripping the wheel, knuckles white. "And you're the mother of the year, right?"

"Fuck you," I said. It was the first of two times in my life I'd ever said that to him.

We were home. He pulled into the driveway, too fast, and then into the garage. I got out of the car, grabbing my bag and my purse on the way, and slammed the door. It occurred to me then that we'd forgotten to go to the bus stop and pick up the other car, but by this time I didn't care; I'd deal with that in the morning. I started to storm inside, then remembered Hazel, asleep in her seat. I pivoted and turned back. Paul was leaning into the car, already removing her seat belt and preparing to carry her in.

"Do you want me to take your briefcase?" I managed.

"No. I'll come back for it."

He kicked the car door closed, hard, but he was careful on the steps as he carried her into the house. I rushed ahead of him, unlocking the door and flipping on lights. In her room, I turned on her lamp and folded down her covers so he'd be able to slip her right in. Then I stormed out. I couldn't remember the last time I'd been that mad. Certainly not at Paul. It felt good, in a way. "Is she asleep?" I said, passing him in the hall. I was red faced, I knew, and steaming.

"Yes," he said. He looked at me, then away.

"Good," I said. "I'm going for a walk." I stalked downstairs, grabbed a few dollars from the drawer where I stashed loose change, and slammed out the door.

# Chapter Seventeen

The air was sweet, balmy, heavy with mist; pollen-filled flowers craned and leaned and virtually burst forward, engorged with bloom. I smelled lilies, more like sex than sex itself, and roses, which evoked red velvet sofas, lavishly wallpapered bathrooms. It had finally cooled off a little, and the scratchy chirp of crickets made the night air vibrate. I turned right at the corner and headed downtown.

Paul and I fought like that about twice a year, which I considered—and I think he did too—not bad at all for a Happily Married Couple. I didn't mind the fighting so much—it was an adrenaline rush, if nothing else—but usually I hated the aftermath, his disappointment and anger making me feel sad and guilty, as if I were some raging, irrational shrew. (In the end, I always felt it was my fault, even if it wasn't.) Most of all, I hated his absence during those postfight times; the feeling that we weren't a team, that I couldn't just call him up and tell him some stupid thing about Hazel, or our house, or just me. For all his unavailability and Big Lawyer schedule, he had always dropped anything for me when I needed him to—not that I asked very often (which, of course, was part of the deal), but the few times I had, most of them right after Oliver, he'd been instantly there. And so when we did fight, we both tried to make up as soon as we could, which made us both feel a rush of love and a huge sense of relief.

But this time was different. This time I wasn't anxious to make up. He had started the fight—of that I was sure—and he was clearly the unreasonable one. So I got not only the moral upper hand, but the go-ahead to act irrationally, without guilt. Or at least that's how I saw it then.

I was almost downtown. Suddenly I changed my mind and began

walking back in the other direction. I don't know why. I'd have to go back past my block and then at least twice as far in that direction to get to anything except streets and houses, and even then, there wasn't much to get to: a little strip mall, an all-night 7-Eleven. Still, I walked, hard and fast, anger pushing one foot in front of the other. After a half hour or so, I got to the 7-Eleven and went in.

Behind the counter, an older man—bulbous nose, greasy slate-colored hair—was reading the paper. He glanced at me wearily as the bell on the door tingled, then back down at his paper, neither of us feeling obliged to say the perfunctory hi. I picked up a magazine, flipped through it, put it back. I moved to a food rack, where I examined a package of Hostess Suzy Q's before returning that too. I glanced around until my eyes fell on the shelves of cigarettes. "A pack of Marlboros, please," I said to the man. He tossed the box on the counter, and I paid him and left.

Outside again, sharing the fluorescent lights with moths, big and small, silver, white, green, I slapped the pack against my palm a few times, then peeled it open and shook out a cigarette. I ran two fingers over its stem. Then I lit it and took a long drag. My throat clenched but I didn't cough, and then I relaxed into it.

It had been years—fifteen, sixteen, maybe more—since I'd so much as held a cigarette. In college, I'd smoked socially now and then, but I'd always thought the risk of it outweighed whatever else it provided, and though I never was an antismoking freak—how could I be, living with Celeste?—I had at times found it vaguely repulsive. So why, now, was I relishing it? I took another drag, felt the harsh air fill my lungs, blew it out and sucked more in.

I'd smoked three cigarettes by the time I turned onto my block, and I suddenly panicked for a second. What if Paul was still up and smelled the tobacco on me? I took a deep, long breath and then another, hoping the night air would cleanse the smell from my clothes, my hair, my body. I jumped a little, trying to air out; I bent over and shook out my hair. There was my house, my home, same as always. I extracted the pack of cigarettes from my back pocket and looked at it. There was no way I could take it in. I glanced around, and then up at Kevin's apartment. It was dark. Maybe he was asleep. Doubtful, though. Probably he was out with his girlfriend, if he had one. Or maybe with the babe from the Saab. I walked quickly up to the side of his building and placed the cigarettes under a bush. Then I strolled calmly up my own front walk and into my house.

"Elayna?" Paul called, from upstairs.

My stomach lurched. "Yeah?"

"Where the hell did you go?" He sounded furious.

"For a walk," I said, trying to sound casual.

He appeared at the top of the stairs, topless in dark blue boxer shorts I'd bought him. "To where? Fucking Mars?"

So now he was using the F word too? "No," I said. "To the 7-Eleven."

"You *walked* to the 7-Eleven? At this hour? Are you *crazy*?"

"Not last time I checked." I sounded like a sullen teenager, and I didn't care.

He stared down at me, shaking his head. "Five more minutes and I'd have called the police." He stormed away. I heard our bedroom door slam.

I raced upstairs and burst into the room. He was in bed, lights out.

"Why?" I demanded, hands on my hips. "Why shouldn't I go for a walk?"

"Oh, you should," he said, his voice sharp with rage. "You should do whatever you want, Elayna, not that you seem to need me to tell you that. And don't worry about letting anyone know. Don't ever think anyone might be *worried* about you, or anything."

"Oh, Paul," I said, a little more mildly. "Come on. I go out for walks at night all the time."

"Right," he said. "Sure. And I bet you always lock the door too, just like you did tonight. Right? And take your key? And your cell phone?" He gave a loud sigh. "Now, if you don't mind, I'm going to sleep. I have to get up tomorrow."

"Oh, like I don't?"

He didn't answer. I waited, staring through the half dark at our bed, at his clothes on the floor, papers and his laptop scattered on top of them. I waited. But he didn't answer. "Fuck you," I said. That was the second time. I backed out, slamming the door behind me.

I went out to the front porch. I thought of retrieving the cigarettes and lighting up again, but it was too risky down here, and anyway, I was too angry to smoke; my hands were trembling with fury, if not also nicotine. My eyes caught something shiny—a rock with some mica, whatever—and I picked it up and whipped it into the street. I found another and whipped that one too. Insects buzzed under the porch light, gnats forming a fluttery cloud. I looked for a third stone to throw, but couldn't find anything.

So I sat. I sat fuming for a moment, and then another, and eventually my anger began to evolve into a more rational form of self-questioning. And I thought, *How is it that marriage comes to this?* I loved Paul. I did at the beginning, I did six hours ago, and as far as I could fathom, I always would. And yet, at that moment, my marriage to him felt ugly and claustrophobic, a cage with windows that let me see out to what I wanted and needed but kept me from getting to it. I wanted—forgive me—to be transported, up and out of my pain and beyond. I wanted to live again. Was that such a bad thing?

I looked up. Kevin's light had gone on.

*Okay,* I thought. *Okay.* I got up, crossed the street, and climbed his rickety wooden staircase.

I hesitated then, at least. I'll give myself that. It was late, for one thing, though probably not for him. But I glanced at my house. Dark and quiet, sleek and well kept, pretty garden, pretty swing Paul built. Something trembled inside me. *Poor house.* But my eyes switched back to Kevin's door, and I knocked three times, fast.

Only in the ten or twelve seconds it took him to answer did it occur to me that he might have someone up here, and I almost fled. But then there he was—no nubile doll in his arms, just Sasha, lying on the rug, and him, bright eyed, wide awake. "Hey!" he said, smile spreading as he registered me. "Elayna! Hey."

He was wearing jeans, as usual, and a button-down short-sleeved shirt, untucked. His feet were bare, one of them streaked with grayish-white clay. "Oh," I said quickly. "You're working—"

"No—I'm not. I'm just fooling around. Here, want to come in?"

He opened the door, but I shook my head. "That's okay. I saw your light on, but—I don't want to bother you."

"You're not," he said. "You wouldn't be. I like company."

I didn't answer.

"I promise," he said. He opened the door farther. "Come on. Come in."

So I walked in and stood there. *What are you doing?* I asked myself silently.

"Sit," Kevin said. "Do you want—um." He laughed. "Ketchup. I do have ketchup, I think." Another laugh. "Oh, or a beer, of course. Want a beer?"

I hesitated for only the briefest second. "Yes," I said. I sat down on one end of the couch, at the edge. "That sounds great."

He went to the fridge, took out two beers, and tossed the twist-off caps in the sink. He handed me mine and sat down a few feet from me.

His place smelled musty: the earth, his sweat, something smoked at some time. I noticed faint music, low and male, deep and raspy—Tom Waits, maybe Johnny Cash, aging men with voices like the last embers of a fire. I sipped my beer. Sasha looked at me without moving, big gray eyes that seemed to know everything.

"So, what's up?" Kevin said.

I laughed suddenly. The absurdity of this.

"What's so funny?" Kevin smiled, turning his body sideways, so he could look directly at me.

I shook my head. "Nothing. Listen, I should probably go—"

He looked at me curiously. "Why? You just got here— Oh. Wait." He jumped up. "I have something for you." He went over to his table of pieces and returned with a little white ceramic cup. "Hazel's pencil holder," he said.

I took it from him, and as I examined it, I felt some combination of love and sadness fill me up, the way it did when I looked at anything Hazel had made. I don't know why the sadness. Maybe because it was so exquisite in its childlike imperfection, or because I knew the years were passing in which she'd make things like this. Pretty soon, they'd all be made; her quota would be filled, and she'd be on to whatever, dating and bad music. It was temporary, this crooked, lovely, child's art.

"She needs to glaze it," Kevin said, sitting again. "Remember? You should bring her over."

I nodded. "Right. Yes. I will."

He looked at me, then around the room, then back. He smiled a little, took another sip of beer.

"So what *were* you making?" I said. "Before I—"

"Oh. I was just trying to figure out some new stuff that's not really working yet."

"Like what?"

He took a breath. "I have a woman who wants some very delicate teacups. Too delicate, I think. The ones she likes wouldn't last a week. But when I make them stronger, she says they're too clunky, too thick." He shrugged. "Well. I have to find that fine line, I guess. So that's what I've been doing. Playing around with different designs."

I nodded. "Can I see?"

"Nothing to see, at this point. I tossed 'em all back in the slop bucket."

"All of them?" I asked, surprised.

He shrugged. "They were ugly. They sucked, basically."

"Well, maybe she'd have liked them," I reasoned.

"All the more reason not to show her." He laughed.

I got up and went over to the bin of clay and picked out a small, thin mug with a handle. "Is this one of them?"

"Actually, that's the evolution of one." He took a sip of beer. "It started out completely different. Wider, thinner walls. Too precarious. So I made it taller and narrower, a little thicker. That looked better, but—it still pretty much stunk." He shrugged and smiled. "So I said fuck it and made a big fat pasta bowl, which is what I felt like doing in the first place." He pointed to it, drying on the table. "And then I started to make a nice little bowl to go with it. For salad, or something. Clementines."

"Is that what that is?" I pointed to the wheel, where sat a wet mound of clay, raw but slightly molded.

He nodded. "I guess I didn't get very far."

"Will you finish it?"

He shrugged. "Probably. Eventually."

"Why not now?"

He looked at me, cocking his head. "Because you're here." He smiled. "I'm taking a break," he added, more for my sake than his.

I took in his face, the pink of his beautiful skin, two star-shaped flushes under his eyes. I noted his small, folded ears, the almost girlish lack of hair on his cheeks and chin. I wanted to touch him so much it was painful. I forced my eyes off his face, looked at the gray clay pushed under his short nails, hands atop his thighs. Was he on fire, like I was—or just being friendly? Trying to tell me something, or just enjoying the night? Suddenly I couldn't bear this not knowing, not being able to move to the next stage, whatever that might have been. I needed to touch him, to kiss him. We needed to kiss. And we couldn't, and it was torture—not just not doing it, but not knowing if he wanted to. But it was exquisite torture, raw, sweet, thick passion, loading the air.

I cleared my throat. "Would you finish it? I could watch. I'd love to."

He took a last sip of beer, then got up obediently. "Okay."

He moved past me and sat down at the wheel. I took a quiet, deep breath, then perched on the arm of the couch as he started the machine. He wet his hands in the pail, studied the clay for a second, then went to work. I watched the ball go from an unformed blob into a curved, perfectly rounded shape. It changed and changed, getting shorter, taller, wider and flatter again. His hands stayed steady, though his arm muscles rolled in and out, moving under his skin. His eyes focused, eyebrows lifting and lowering as he worked, until he seemed to forget I was there. The music ended, and then the room was quiet, just the hum of the turning potter's wheel. I could hear myself breathe, and then I lost track of time. Minutes went by. Maybe half an hour.

He stopped when there was a bowl—a half soccer ball, give or take, but a little more curved, more interesting. He turned off the wheel and assessed it. Then he used a piece of wire to take it off.

I swallowed. "That's amazing."

He laughed. "It's pretty basic, actually. Maybe I'll do something more to it someday. I don't know." He looked at me suddenly. "Your turn."

I opened my mouth to protest.

"It doesn't bite, you know." He smiled. "Come on. I'll help you."

So I got up and went over to him.

He took out some new clay and made it into a ball, slapped it down on the wheel with a smack. "I'll center it for you," he said, and I stood back and watched him bear down with concentration. Finally, he stopped the wheel and stood up. We switched places, me moving to his still warm stool.

"Wet your hands first," he instructed. I stuck my hands in the bucket, and despite the heat of the room, a shiver went through me.

"Now turn on the wheel. That lever, right there."

The ball began to spin.

"Go ahead," he said. "Whenever you're ready."

I started to reach out, then pulled my hands back.

He laughed.

"Shut up!" I said, laughing too.

He was standing to the side of me. I reached out again and touched the clay with one finger. Immediately, a little ridge appeared in the blob. "Oh no," I said, yanking my hand back. "I messed it up already."

He laughed again, softly this time. "There's nothing to mess up. It just evolves. It changes. You can do whatever you want. That's the beauty of it. And then you can undo it, or change it again."

I nodded, though I wasn't sure about that.

"Go ahead, get your hands in there," he coached. "Be firm. Like this." He held his hands up stiffly in the air, palm facing palm, then bent them into two curved lines, as if surrounding a bowl.

I did as he said. Immediately, the clay shot up in my hands.

"Good," he said. "Now you can work it back down. Bring your palms up on the sides, and bear down on it a little from the top."

"Whoa," I said softly, as the clay flattened again. The initial wetness and coolness had disappeared; it felt natural on my hands now, as if I were touching a part of myself.

He stood back, nodding. "Good. Excellent."

I flipped my head, trying to shake my hair back, away from the clay. "Maybe I missed my calling," I managed. "What am I doing messing around with editing poetry?"

"Good point. Way too snooty. Come in a little with your right hand."

I pushed at the clay, felt it give in my palms. "Not if you know where to look," I said. "There's plenty of accessible poetry."

"Yeah?" he said, softly. "You'll have to turn me on to it."

*Turn me on to it?* My heart fluttered. "What should I make?" I said, not looking at him.

"What do you want to make?"

"Something easy." I laughed nervously. "How about a mug? An easy one."

"Wait a minute, though. Let me do something first." He went to the sink and washed and dried his hands. I watched him walk back toward me and then behind me, but close. I swallowed. My fingers were buried in clay. What was he doing? I felt his hands come around my neck, toward my face, from behind. I held my breath. And then I felt him touch my hair and pull it gently back on both sides, and my eyes closed as I let out my breath. "Once," he said, as he began to form my hair into a loose braid against my neck, then my shoulders, "I saw someone's hair get wrapped around the wheel. Not something you want to see twice." His fingertips brushed my neck.

I made a sound.

"There," he said softly. "That should hold awhile. How's your mug?"

I waited desperately to be able to talk. "Good," I finally croaked. "It's— it looks more like a bowl. A really ugly one. Like for dog food, or someth— oops. Sorry, Sasha."

She raised her head at the sound of her name, then lowered it again.

"That's okay, she forgives you," Kevin said. He was still behind me. "Work the sides up. Apply pressure with the base of your palms. Here." He leaned down, and I felt his chest over my shoulders, not touching, but there. He put his hands outside of mine, again not touching. "Like this," he said, and his hands came onto mine, and he began to work on the clay through my hands.

Thank god it was dark; thank god I couldn't see him; thank god there was something we had to do, to attempt to concentrate on, besides him. I smelled the beer on his breath, felt his breath on my neck, his hands on my hands, pushing mine in. He was young, a boy, but his hands were so confident. Words jumped into my mind then, words from a Tony Hoagland poem that I loved:

*I think there must be something wrong*
*with me, or wrong with strength, that I would*
*break my happiness apart*
*simply for the pleasure of the sound.*

"Stop," I said suddenly.

"What?" His hands came off mine, and mine off the clay, which kept spinning. "What's the matter?"

"Nothing. I just—"

He reached over and flipped off the wheel. I felt his body back away from mine—and again, that feeling of being on a diving board, leaning over but not allowed to fall in. I wanted his touch back; I couldn't bear it moving away.

But I had to stop this.

I rose, my hands wet with clay. "I'm sorry," I stuttered. "But I just realized—it's so late. It's the middle of the night. I have to go home." I stepped away from the wheel.

He raised his eyebrows, then shrugged. "Okay."

I took a step toward him, then back again. Sasha looked up. "Sorry," I said.

He was watching me, a confused little boy again. I pulled my eyes off his and stumbled toward the door.

"Don't you want to wash your hands first?" he asked.

I shook my head quickly. "I'll just do it at home."

He smiled a little. "I'd better get the door for you, then." He opened the door, and I pushed myself through. "Bye," he said, as I staggered down the steps.

I moved into the street, fresh sweat slick on my neck despite the cool air. I stood still for a moment, taking deep breaths. Then I hurried across the street and up my own steps and into my house, getting clay all over the front door.

I think I expected all the lights to be on and Paul to be sitting there, arms crossed, saying, *Where the fuck have you been?* Instead, all was dark and quiet. I could smell the clay on my hands, smell his house in my house, even smell the beer—or was I imagining that? No matter. I had brought him in here with me.

I went into the kitchen and, without turning on lights, washed off my hands. I dried them on the dish towel, then went back to the front door with the towel and wiped off all the clay I could find in the half dark.

Back in the kitchen, I threw the towel in the trash, then reached in and buried it.

My hands were shaking. I sat down at the kitchen table, still in the dark. It was eleven forty-five. It felt like three in the morning. I picked up the phone and called Celeste.

*This is me,* her voice mail said. *You know what to do.*

"Celeste." I swallowed. "I'm going down a road," I said softly. "A hill, actually. With—with Cookie Boy. And I need to know how to turn myself around." I hung up.

My answer would come the next day, via email. *How far down that hill have you gone? And do you really want to come back up? If you do, I will try to help you. But, and don't kill the bearer, I will probably fail. You know I love Paul, right? So I can say this. True love notwithstanding, you're only human in needing a little mystery now and then.*

*Call me on my cell. I promise to pick up. xxx Celeste*

In fact, she would call *me*—in the morning, after she'd sent the email—and I would screen the call. She'd call again in the afternoon, and again that evening. And I wouldn't answer any of them.

By then, of course, I would regret having left that message.

For one thing, it felt like a betrayal of Paul—amazingly, a more concrete betrayal than anything else I had done.

But for another, as smart as she was about people, Celeste couldn't fully understand this. Her arguments were theoretical, because she hadn't lived inside marriage. And so her permission, if that's what she was giving me—and certainly, it seemed to be what I was seeking—was meaningless.

If I was going to turn around, I had to do it on my own. That's what it came down to. I had to find a way to keep myself from flying headlong down that hill—flying like some runaway trolley, gravity at its back, sweet cool wind rushing to meet it.

# Chapter Eighteen

For the rest of the week, my interaction with Paul was rare, surface, and brief. He worked late, I went to sleep early, and in between, we said what we needed to say. As for Kevin, I went out of my way to avoid any possibility of an encounter. Thursday morning, I took my laptop downtown and worked hidden in the back of a coffee shop, picking at a chocolate chip muffin and drinking cup after cup of black tea. Then, when it was almost time to get Hazel—at noon, one, or two now that it was summer, depending on my workload each day—I ran home, propelled by sugar and caffeine, and jumped in the car for Pansy's. Thursday afternoon I took Hazel to the playground, out for ice cream . . . anywhere but home. Friday afternoon we went to see the latest Disney film, which delighted her as much as it annoyed me (the enormous blue eyes, the one-dimensional villains, the moralistic ending). When we got home from the movies, Paul was there, with a steak marinating, a salad made, and something that wasn't quite a scowl on his face. It was a nice surprise, and a welcome relief; I'd made it through the week, each day finding it that much easier to convince myself anew that nothing out of the ordinary had happened with Kevin Wednesday night. And now, it seemed, my husband might even love me again.

Which is not, alas, to say I didn't think about Kevin constantly. I walked around in a state of nonstop arousal, thinking of his beautiful arms, of the way he'd smiled when I'd come through his doorway that night, of his hands coming around to cover mine over the clay . . . and I literally broke out in a sweat. I imagined kissing him, imagined the taste of his tongue, the feel of his sleek, bony back; I pictured the slight outward curve at the tail of his spine, his muscles tensing as he fucked me. I imagined what he'd feel like, and what I'd feel like, and I swooned in my kitchen, my bathroom, my bed. It was impossible not to think about him, and thinking about him made me instantly drunk with that pure, sweet, poisonous juice that flows through your blood and swirls around your brain, leaving all reason and intellect crushed in its path. And then I'd reprimand myself, as guilty as I was fired up. Here was Paul, my loving, good husband, who provided for me and loved me, who told jokes that made me laugh, who threw his warm arm around me at night and loved my baby girl as much as I did. Why wasn't this enough?

It all made me want to call Celeste—who I knew would reassure me that I was not a horrible person—but I refrained. If I talked about my feelings, they became that much more real—and besides, she would push me for details about That Night, about my phone call to her, and I would have to break down and confess. (*Confess what?* I instantly asked myself. *That he'd shown me how to use his potter's wheel? Big deal.*) So instead, I ignored her calls and emails—I was never home to answer them anymore anyway—and I sat down and ate Paul's nice steak, and asked about his work, and watched him laugh with his daughter. And together we began the process of letting the fight dissipate, like cigar smoke or thick perfume that finally creeps out under doors, past cracks in windows, through vents, and out to the world and its vast, endless air.

Which is not to say I thought this was the greatest approach, even then. The truth is, we needed to finish the fight we'd started. After all, it had begun as a rational disagreement over our daughter and how to handle her. But neither of us wanted to risk going back to the ugly place that fight had found us in that day. So we skirted it, and then there we were, in that position that, for better and worse, marriage forces you into sometimes: co-owners of a life (house, kid, take-out menus) making your way through a less than ideal period, pretending everything's fine.

We ate our dinner Friday night, inching toward the weekend. Cindi had called earlier in the week to ask if we'd take Zach on Saturday and overnight into Sunday—she and Joey, the Buddhist personal trainer Shrink Judy had fixed her up with, were going to the shore for a "romantic getaway"—and I'd of course said yes, always happy to see Zachie's sweet face and have someone for Hazel to dress up, manhandle, and otherwise occupy herself with. And so, early Saturday—Paul, uncharacteristically, still asleep, Hazel up for hours already, waiting—the doorbell rang, and Cindi and Joey clomped in, Zach in green sandals and tiny plaid shorts; Cindi in an enormous lime green straw beach hat, tight white shirt, white capris, and spiky white mules; and Joey, a buffed-out lug of a guy in some sort of polyester one-piece body-gripping nut-hugging workout garment that put me in mind of the high school wrestling team, along with, to remind us of his Zen side, a pair of Birkenstocks. He had several rainbow-colored woven-thread friendship necklaces around his meaty neck, along with one, I was amused to see, around his ankle. He was hauling Cindi's enormous pink beach bag.

I invited them to stay for coffee, which Cindi declined and Joey accepted but edited to herbal tea. Then we all proceeded to the front stoop—I wielding two tea mugs, the children racing for the swing—for the obligatory six minutes together before Cindi and Joey could depart, leaving me with my babies.

"Anyway," Cindi said to me, after we'd finished discussing the weather and the best kind of sunscreen, "he hasn't taken a poop yet today"—I assumed she meant Zach, not Joey—"which means he'll probably need to take one the second you get in the car to go anywhere. Yesterday, I swear, we had to stop for him to take a dump in every single skeevy toilet I passed." She made a face. "Well—at least he's not constipated anymore, thank God. Last week he couldn't go at all, this week he can't stop." The subject of Zach's excretions had always obsessed her, probably because she herself was stuck in the anal stage. "Anyway," she was saying, "make sure you ask a lot if he needs to go. Ask him—let's see." She glanced at her watch. "Once in about a half hour, and then at least once an hour after that. Okay?"

"Okay," I said, suppressing a yawn. I glanced toward Kevin's apartment, pictured him shirtless, working at the wheel.

Cindi pulled a compact out of her makeup bag, opened it, sucked in her cheeks like a fish, and applied blush to each cheek with the flat little brush. She examined her face from both sides, then closed the compact and dropped it back in the bag. Then she stood up, teetering on her heels. "Well—we should go, so we don't miss any sun. I'm so sick of being white as a ghost. I'm, like, still using foundation every day! On July first! It's *horrible*!" She looked at Joey. "Ready, hon?"

"Whenever you are, hon." Joey stood and picked up Cindi's bag. "Are revoir, kids," he yelled toward the swing.

"Bye, Zachariah," Cindi echoed. "Be a good bunny." She turned to me. "You have my cell number, right? I'll call you on our way back tomorrow."

"Sounds good," I said.

"Thank you again for doing this, Elayna. I owe you one." She smiled, genuinely. "Tell Paul sorry I missed him. We'll catch him mañana."

I endured a Coppertone-scented kiss from her, and then they were off, pulling down the street in Joey's car, his bumper reminding the world to "Follow your bliss" and that "The best things in life aren't things" and that "Life isn't about finding yourself, it's about *creating* yourself." Maybe for his birthday, just for fun, I'd get him the one that says, "Save a tree. Wipe your ass with an owl." The car turned out of sight. I went over to the swing, sat down on the grass, and closed my eyes.

"Momma!" Hazel yelled instantly. "Momma, *watch*!" I cracked my eyes open a hair. She was twisting Zach around and around, then letting him go so he unspun quickly. He was laughing uproariously. His laughter was contagious, putting me in an instant good mood. The front door opened and Paul came out, wearing a red-plaid robe I'd once bought him. "Are they gone yet?" he mumbled, heading over, rubbing his eyes.

I laughed. "Stop it! That's Zachie's mama you're making fun of."

"Sorry." He grinned sheepishly, then yawned. It was good. We were friends again, more or less. All was well, or at least back to the status quo. After a while, I went inside and left Paul out to watch the kids while I packed bathing suits, towels, goldfish crackers and drinks, sunscreen, hats, flip-flops, a sippy cup and diaper stuff for Zach, plastic buckets for the pool, plastic toys and crayons and books for the car. Then I came back out and Paul went in to dress, and then we herded everyone into the Subaru and drove to the swim club.

And there it was, suburbia at its best and its worst. The big, blue, chlorinated pool, only a few half-dead bees, bloody Band-Aids, and foil gum wrappers floating on its surface; the zinc-nosed, overtanned lifeguards in tinted imitation Guess shades soaking up the hot noonday sun; the smell of the snack bar, with its pancake-thin burgers and greasy French fries, mixed with the smells of hot tar, hot cement, suntan lotion, bubble gum, mown grass, clean towels, plastic lawn chairs. Van Morrison's "Brown-Eyed Girl" buzzed nasally from the speakers, which were placed strategically in the corners of the pool, so you couldn't escape their racket. And the people! The same people, again and again: Pansy and her husband, Ed, who emerged on weekends to lumber along behind Pansy until he could park on a chair and fall asleep; Adele, Clementine's mother, with another mother I recognized from the school; Mrs. Zuppo, a presence in a purple bathing suit in the lap lane, swimming long, slow laps, I was pleased to see. Paul and I scoped out two of the more hidden chairs in the back; he, like I, preferred to avoid the scene, though he generally ignored it while I observed. "Come on!" Hazel yelled, and she and Zach took off for the kiddie pool. "Hazel!" I yelled. "Wait!" She kept running. "Shoot," I said to Paul. "I could kill her when she does that."

Paul dropped his bag. "I'll go. Just give me the sunscreen."

I fished for it. "Thank you! Here, take their buckets too." I tossed it all, and he caught it and jogged off after them.

I moved my chair even farther back, then sat down and took off my shirt as the music switched from Shania Twain's "You're Still the One" to Tina Turner's "What's Love Got to Do with It," barely a pause in between. Two very tan women with dark ponytails and full makeup walked by in bright white tennis skirts, and I caught a snippet of their conversation, in full Jersey accent: "I says to him, I says, 'Dawnie,' I says, 'if you think I'm gonna put up with this BS anymore, you got another think comin' . . . ' " I took out my book, but didn't open it yet. A teenage boy, perfect body, face riddled with acne, ascended the diving-board steps and dove in.

Pansy, wearing a dark one-piece bathing suit and a blue visor over her hair, was getting in the water now, going slowly down the ladder holding on to the railings while one of her younger charges (so much for it being the weekend) waited patiently at the edge. She reached up and he climbed into her arms; she held him firmly, straight-faced herself, while he laughed and splashed and gently kicked. I thought about when I'd done that for Hazel: She'd complain I wasn't holding her right, she'd want to get in and out of the water ten times, but when I said we should stop, she'd protest and demand that I do it again, which drove me nuts. Pansy, in contrast, looked completely comfortable in the water—which is not to say she looked thrilled to be there. "Not too much splashing," I heard her tell the boy. "Don't disturb the other swimmers."

Mrs. Zuppo hauled her bulk up the pool ladder and collapsed onto a chair not far from mine, flipping her tiny white towel onto her enormous shoulders. She was still oddly beautiful, with her wide face and round, dreamy eyes, her downturned mouth and small upturned nose, but she'd been a *real* babe once, I knew; I'd seen her wedding picture, a mischievous bride beaming at the camera sensuously, ready to have a great time with her cute new husband, half her size.

I caught sight of a blond woman I'd seen before, around my age, sitting at the side of the pool in an aqua one-piece suit cut low in the breasts and high on her hips. She was flirting with a dark-haired man in the water, laughing loudly at whatever he was saying; he, in turn, was keeping the jokes coming, a grin glued on his face. I thought of the woman's daughter, a chubby first grader with a long blond ponytail, and then I saw the girl, splashing around in a blow-up vest in the shallow end, not far from her mother's painted toenails. "Mommy, watch!" she called out, and the mother turned and obediently watched her kid splash for a minute or two. "Good, honey," she managed, before her attention returned to the man. He said something else, and she laughed loudly. "Oh my god!" she said, wiping her eyes.

I got up and took off my shorts, wrapped a towel around my waist to cover my butt, then went over to the pool, where I dropped my towel and dove in quickly, letting the cool water steal my breath.

I swam for a solid half hour, till my muscles screamed for relief, till, after forcing myself to sprint the last half lap underwater, I shot to the surface and clung to the side of the pool desperately sucking in breaths. Pansy was back, this time sitting on the edge of the pool, the little boy sitting next to her. "Not yet," she was saying, patiently but firmly. "You have to wait a half hour after you eat. You have ten more minutes. See that clock over there?"

After a minute, I released the wall and breaststroked down toward her, waving as I approached.

"Oh, hello, Elayna," Pansy said, without smiling. "How are you?"

"Not bad, thanks. And you?"

"Fine thank you. Elayna, this is Joshua Evan Jacobs. His mom had to work this morning, so I'm watching him until she gets here. Josh, say hello to Elayna. She's Hazel's mom."

"Hi, Elayna," Joshua said shyly.

"Hi, Josh." I smiled. "Are you going swimming?"

He nodded. "In ten minutes. After I digest my lunch."

"Di*gest* your lunch," Pansy corrected. "And it's down to nine minutes, now. You're being very patient today. Thank you for that." Pansy looked at me. "Hazel is doing well too, this summer," she said, firmly. "She talks about her grandfather quite a bit." She paused, as if actually considering whether or not, or maybe just how, to say the next thing. "She mentioned some, uh, M-A-G-A-Z-E-N-S he has in his house. Elayna, I'm not sure if you know about them, but—"

"Oh—those." So Hazel had seen them after all. "Yeah, I do," I said, stalling for time. "They're not my favorite either, but—" I shrugged, making lighter of it than I felt.

She looked at me for a long moment. "Those magazines aren't appropriate for her to see at this age, Elayna," she said, finally.

I sighed. "I know, but—"

She waited.

"I don't know. I mean, do you really think they'll do any major damage? I remember when I saw my first *Playboy,* and I never—"

"Shhh!" she shushed, and she gestured toward Joshua. "S-P-E-L-L it."

"Sorry. Anyway, I don't remember being majorly damaged by it. Just—curious."

Josh was sitting patiently, moving his feet in two circles in the water. "Listen," Pansy said, finally. "I'm glad for Hazel that she's reconnected with her grandpa. I just don't advise you to let her spend too much time at his house."

I felt a red flag go up. Instantly, it was knocked down by a feeling of defensiveness. "Why not?" I said. "He's her grandfather. And my father."

"Of course he is. I'm just saying, I think he might not have a sense of—" She looked at Josh, then back at me. "I just think you'd better keep your eyes open."

"Thanks," I said, feeling not at all grateful. "I'll keep that in mind."

I heard a peal of laughter, and I glanced across the pool to see the woman in the aqua suit still sitting there. The dark-haired man was now sitting next to her. Her daughter was climbing in and out of the water, up the slide and back down, the adults talking, not watching her. Pansy frowned. "I don't like those floatie vests," she said. "They give a false sense of security. If you're gonna let a child who can't swim get in the water, you need to be in there holding them."

"Well, she seems to be doing okay," I couldn't help saying. "And the mother's right th—"

Pansy looked at me. "What if that child falls off those steps? That's concrete down there. Who's gonna catch her?"

"But she probably *won't* fall," I said, wondering why I was suddenly so worked up. "I mean, she's already done it twenty times, and she hasn't fallen yet. It just doesn't seem that risky to me."

"Joshua, four more minutes," she said to the boy and, to me, "You want to take a risk with your own life, go ahead, but you don't have the right to do that with a child. Children need to be protected by the adults around them." She was glorious, glorious in her self-righteousness. And why not? Every minute of her life was devoted to living out this ideal. I wondered if she'd ever had any passion for anything else besides raising children, or, for that matter, if she even had passion for *this*—or if it was more like a set of rules she needed and followed, and passion didn't even figure in.

I stood up. "Right. Well—see you later," I said to Pansy, and I waved to Joshua.

"Bye," he said, glancing up at me.

I made my way down to the kiddie pool, a vast, shallow, cement-bottomed puddle of toddlers, babies, sweaty, tired parents, and grandparents, firmly divided, it seemed, into camps of Absolutely Firm and Completely Permissive. Paul was there with the kids, sitting in the water cringing while Hazel and Zach poured, directly over his head, buckets of the half-piss half-chlorine solution I'd always imagined the water to be. I laughed at the sight. "Hey," I said to him, and I sat down on the side of the pool near him, letting my feet drop into the water.

"Momma!" Hazel yelled. "We're playing barbershop! I gave Zachie a goatee! Do you like it? Zachie, show her!"

Zachie closed his mouth, raised his chin, and posed for me. "Breathtaking," I said. "Did he give you a good tip?"

"Fifty percent," Hazel announced.

I laughed. "Well, that is good. You must have done a great job."

"I did. And now I'm doing Daddy's, and Zachie's my assistant." She scooped up a bucket of water and dumped it on Paul's head. "Ahh!" he yelled, wincing. I laughed. He glared at me, water dripping from his face. I laughed again, and he laughed now too, in spite of himself, perhaps sharing my thought about what idiots contemporary parenting made of us.

"Zachie's favorite planet is Uranus," Hazel said. She looked at me. "*Your* anus," she said, pointing to my crotch. She giggled.

"Actually, I think it's pronounced Urine-us," Paul said—graciously, I thought.

"Eew! Urine!" Hazel yelled. "Zachie, give me that bucket. I need that."

He shook his head no. "*I* need dat," he said.

"Zachie!" Hazel yelled. "*Give* me it! You're supposed to be my *assistant*!" She tried to grab the bucket from his hand. He clung on. It was the first time I'd ever seen him stand up to her, and I cheered him on silently.

"*Zachie! Give* it!" With a final pull, she yanked the bucket from him. He fell back, plunked into the pool, and began to cry, though he wasn't at all hurt.

"Hazel!" I said, and then, to Zach, "Oh, sweetheart." I reached out to him. "Come here. Come to Aunt Layna." I picked him up and stuck him in my lap, wrapped my arms around him. "Come here. How's your goatee, little man? Huh?"

He turned his face away from mine, trying to be stubborn, but his body defied him as he relaxed into my arms, stopped crying, stuck his thumb in his mouth, and let his head fall against my breast. "My sweet corn cake," I murmured to him. "My tiny tree lemur." I kissed his forehead. He was so simple. All you had to do was feed him, cuddle him, love him. His needs were predictable and easy to meet; he was a baby man already, just waiting to unfurl. Hazel had always been infinitely more complicated. You never knew if meeting her needs would please or infuriate her. And her needs seemed to change constantly.

Zachie was falling asleep on me now. "Mom, can I get a frozen Milky Way?" Hazel said.

"Um—okay," I said, too lazy to protest.

Hazel looked at me, joyously surprised, as did Paul. "Yay!" she yelled. "Zachie, want a frozen Milky Way?"

His eyes popped open. "Yeth," he said, through his thumb.

"They didn't have their lunch yet," Paul said to me.

I shrugged. "Whatever. They'll have it later."

Paul frowned. Zachie had already climbed out of my arms and taken Hazel's outstretched hand. They ran toward the snack shack. "I can take them, if you want to go swim," I said to Paul as I got up, but he shook his head no and got up too. "Why didn't you make them have lunch first?" he said.

"I don't know," I admitted. "But it's not a big deal. They'll have lunch later." I looked at him. "They'll remember this," I said, trying to justify my "decision." "They'll remember the day I let them have candy for lunch. And then later, they'll have lunch for dessert, and it'll all even out, except this way they have the memory."

He shook his head, but he let me win this time. Like I said, the smoke was supposed to be dissipating. In the shack, I found Zach at a table playing with a sticky ketchup dispenser, Hazel at the ordering counter being handed three large candy bars by the teenage clerk. She picked them up and shuffled back toward our table, dropping one, awkwardly picking it back up. I didn't help her, knowing she wouldn't want that, and after a minute of struggle she reached us and dropped them, victorious. "I got you and Daddy a frozen Snickers," she said. "I got me and Zachie our own frozen Milky Ways. You have to go pay seven dollars and some cents. Okay?"

"Perfect," I said, not glancing at Paul. I went over and paid, then got a plastic knife. Back at the table, I attempted to saw the Snickers bar in half, first without removing the wrapper, then after taking it off. The knife jerked, bent, then snapped, the top half of it flying across the room.

"Oops," I said, smiling.

Hazel cackled, which made Zach crack up too.

"That's okay," Paul said, obviously not sharing our delirium at my mishap. "You can have it. I'm gonna go get a sandwich, or something. Anyone else want one?"

The kids stared at him with their large oval eyes, faces already covered in chocolate. Zachie was holding his candy bar in his fist. I had a sudden vision of Cindi seeing this, and I almost cringed.

"Don't all yell at once," Paul said, walking away.

Hazel looked at me. "Is Daddy mad?"

I shook my head. "He's just nervous. He has to go away this week."

I glanced out the screened window of the shack. The sun was high in the sky now; it was the height of the day, a cloudless day, the sun beating down. Overhead, a plane flew by, very high, a tiny silver cross, a splinter in the sky. I watched it until it disappeared. I thought—God, forgive me—of Kevin, of his hands over mine on that wheel. Sweat beaded on my upper lip.

But Pansy and Ed were coming now, his black bathing suit too high on his tall waist, no little boy between them this time. As they approached the snack bar, I saw with surprise that they were holding hands. They came in and went to the counter, where Pansy ordered, presumably for both of them, then began to talk animatedly to him. And then Paul was back, with a burger, a salad, a strawberry milk shake. He sat down and began to dress the burger, carefully placing onion, lettuce, tomato slice, then squeezing ketchup on the whole thing. "Yum," I said, looking at it.

He nodded and took a big bite. Juice dripped down his chin. He reached for a napkin and wiped it away.

"I can't have a bite, right?" I said, and I thought that if I were Paul right then, I'd have smacked me.

But I wasn't him. *He* was him, and he'd never not shared with me. He pushed the plate my way, and I took a big bite. Hazel and Zach were starting to slow down on the chocolate; they both had that glazed, sugar-dazed look in their eyes. I swallowed, took another large bite, and handed the plate back to Paul. "Thank you," I said, my mouth full of meat. "I'll save you half my frozen Snickers."

He looked at me without smiling. "Damn straight you will."

# Chapter Nineteen

And then it was Thursday, and Paul was kissing Hazel good-bye as his black town car waited, idling, to whisk him to the airport, where a plane would take him to Arkansas. "Good-bye, babe," he said to Hazel. "Be a good girl and listen to your mother." He leaned to kiss me too. "I'll call you," he said.

The car pulled away, leaving Hazel and me, blinking into the already steamy day. Another week had gone by, and I hadn't seen Kevin. Relief and also dismay, this time. He probably thought I was ludicrous, a desperate housewife on the prowl. How could I seriously have gone up to his place that night? I shook my head in self-disgust before rushing Hazel inside to get her ready to go to Pansy's.

That day and the next, I finished up the "Favorite Poetry" issue in the mornings and drove Hazel to the pool in the afternoons, the second time taking Clementine with us. Friday night, over dinner, I reminded Hazel that Celeste was coming tomorrow—Saturday—to visit. Hazel seemed pleased. She was happy these days, long summer days of just enough time with Pansy, plenty of time with me, no school, little stress. We had rented *Little Shop of Horrors* and were watching it together while eating our hamburgers and peas and milk shakes. It was campy and cozy, a perfect summer mother-daughter night—and yet, I was impatient, antsy; I kept glancing out the window. *It's too nice outside to be in,* I told myself, for lack of a better explanation, though I knew we'd already had enough sun today; too much, probably, for Hazel's light skin.

"Yay!" she announced, when I mentioned Celeste. "What do you think she'll bring me?"

"Wrong question, petunia. You should be happy to see her for *her.*"

"I *am* happy," she said, patiently. "I'm just wondering if, like, you think she'll, like, *bring* me anything."

I shrugged. "We'll have to see. But don't ask, and if she doesn't, do *not* say, 'Celeste, where is my present?' "

"*Duh,* Mom," she said.

Celeste came in the late afternoon on Saturday, a hazy, hot day that was well over ninety, air thick and steamy. Hazel and I had spent the morning food shopping in the cool of ShopRite, then cleaning up the house in the cool of central air-conditioning, which she'd convinced me to turn on. At four thirty or so, when the sun was a little less brutal, we'd squeezed into our swimsuits—mine with cut-offs thrown on top—and ventured out into the yard, where we now sat in her round plastic pool, me on a child-size chair I'd plunked into the water, Hazel in the water itself, holding the hose and running the fresh, cold stream over my feet. She'd shed her suit already, as usual, and now, buck naked, was singing a song from her school that I loved, about a man who gets up in the middle of the night and sneaks out to dance with bears. At the chorus, I joined in, and we sang at the top of our lungs:

*He goes wa wa wa waltzing, waltzing with bears*
*Raggy bears, shaggy bears, baggy bears too*
*There's nothing on earth Uncle Walter won't do*
*So he can go waltzing, wa wa wa waltzing*
*So he can go waltzing, waltzing with—*

Hazel stopped suddenly. "She's here!" she yelled.

Celeste walked into the yard, a hip princess from some faraway land. "Hi, dolls," she said, unslinging the black sack from her shoulders. "Is this the party house?"

"Yes!" Hazel screamed.

"Hey!" I said. "You were supposed to call from the bus stop!" I got up to hug her, and she leaned over the pool to reach me. She was wearing a short black cotton dress and black flip-flops, hair piled on top of her head, pieces cascading down.

"No need," she said. "I met an old friend on the bus, believe it or not, and he drove me. I can't believe I remembered how to get here."

"I know. It's been—well, years, really." I remembered that the last time she'd come was right after Oliver died. It had been hellish for her, I'm sure, but she'd stayed for a couple of days anyway, reading Hazel stories, watching me cry, shopping for groceries for us.

"Maybe," she said, shrugging, probably remembering too.

"Go grab her that red chair, puppet," I said to Hazel. "And then bring me your bathing suit and let me stick you back in it, so Celeste can see how gorgeous it is."

Hazel ran and got her suit, which she'd thrown on the ground, and I helped her put it back on. Then she retrieved the chair for Celeste and placed it in the pool next to mine.

"Why thank you, ma'am," Celeste said, smiling down at her. "With service like that from friends in gorgeous bathing suits, who needs servants? All the more reason to splurge on gifts." She reached into her bag and made a show of rooting around, then handed Hazel a small white paper sack. She pulled out another bag, larger and flatter, and handed it to me.

I looked at her, surprised. "What's this for?"

It was a pair of beautiful, sexy white pajamas, a lacy cotton tank top and capris. "Celeste, these are gorgeous!" I shook my head. "How dare you spend this kind of money on me!"

"It's nothing, they were on sale," she said, pleased. "You like them? They'll be incredible on you. Plus, white is the new black, and all that."

"Thank you!" Hazel was screaming. She had unveiled her own gift, a clear plastic bucket containing a dozen tiny bottles of nail polish, in colors from yellow to gray. She climbed out of the pool, sat down on the grass, and, after making Celeste open several of the bottles, began to apply a different color to each toenail.

Celeste had dropped her bag, kicked off her flip-flops, stepped into the pool, and sat down on the chair. "Aaah," she said, dunking her feet. "Suburban heaven. All I need now is a whiskey sour and some peanuts, and I'm good for at least a month."

"Funny you should say that," I said. "I was just about to make some cocktails. I'm not sure I have whiskey-sour mix, though. Would a margarita suffice?"

"Perfectly," she said. "Can I help?"

"Of course not."

She leaned back and closed her eyes. "I should do this more often. I already feel that tense, scowling, bitchy city thing disappearing." She opened her eyes and looked at Hazel, and then me. "Can I smoke?" she whispered to me, behind her hand.

I nodded. "Just make sure to tell her it causes cancer, and cancer makes you throw up," I mumbled. "As long as throwing up is involved, she'll stay away."

I went in and made frozen margaritas in the supersonic blender Paul had bought, going heavy on both liquor and ice. I filled three tall glasses—one with orange juice for Hazel, the others with the perfect cold green slush—and put them on a tray. In the living room, I turned on Lucinda Williams and cranked the stereo so we'd hear it outside. Grabbing a bag of blue corn chips and the tray of drinks, I made my way back out.

Hazel was kneeling at Celeste's feet, one hand spread on Celeste's smooth, tan thigh as Celeste polished Hazel's nails dark purple. "I wish I had your hair," Hazel was saying. I put the tray down and handed out the drinks.

"If you did," Celeste said, taking her drink, "you'd wish you had *your* hair."

"Would not."

"Would so." Celeste took a big sip of margarita.

Her nails finished, Hazel jumped up and ran out to the lawn. She did a cartwheel, and then another. "Don't smear your nails," Celeste called.

Hazel bent down, picked a white fluffy dandelion, and blew seed puffs all over.

"Don't, Haze," I said. "It makes more dandelions grow."

"But they're pretty!" She picked up another one and blew it.

"They're weeds," I said.

"But *why* are they weeds?" she demanded. "Why aren't they just flowers?"

"Well, they are flowers," I said, thinking. "I mean, they *have* flowers. But they're considered weeds because they grow where they're not wanted. People want pure lawns."

She paused, considering this. "So, if you *planted* them—like say in your *garden*—they'd be flowers, but because they plant their own selves, they're weeds?"

"Well—sort of."

"Well, then, I'm *planting* these now. So they're not weeds."

"Oh my god," Celeste groaned. "I could never be a mother."

We drank for an hour, till the sun was a pink egg yolk low in the sky, and then a sinking fiery red ball. The mosquitoes came out, so Celeste and I switched to adult-size chairs outside of the pool, lit some citronella buckets, doused ourselves with Off and refreshed our drinks. Hazel was sitting between us in a big chair now too, wrapped in a towel and listening as we talked about college, my father, Celeste's unfathomable childhood. (A version heavily edited due to Hazel's presence. She had once told me her mother's last husband would make her take out her dentures to give him a blow job, a fact that Celeste's mother shamelessly told her.) Her little sister was now living in L.A., she said, and Celeste was worried about her. She was sending her money, but—she wasn't sure how her sister was spending it.

I wanted to ask more, but it would have to wait. Instead, Hazel told Celeste about the fashion show. There was another one soon, she said, and she was wearing a flowered miniskirt for one outfit. Afterward, my father was taking her to see *Hansel and Gretel.*

I sipped my drink. Neither Hazel nor my father had actually asked me if this was okay, and because they hadn't presented it as a question, but as a given, I hadn't really thought to protest. I wasn't looking forward to mentioning it to either Paul or Pansy. But when I thought about that, it annoyed me. I was her mother, after all. I was the one who was with her 90 percent of the time. Who the hell were either one of them to decide?

I focused back on the present. "More drinks, girls?"

"I shouldn't," Celeste said flatly.

"Aw, come on," I responded, deadpan.

"Well, if you insist."

She laughed, and I laughed, letting my head fall forward weakly, half drunk. This was so much fun. I would be hungover in the morning, but who cared? Paul was gone. It would be Sunday. Hazel and I could watch movies all day long, *Curly Top, Bye Bye Birdie.* "I'll go make another pitcher," I said.

"Knock yourself out," said Celeste.

I looked at Hazel. "Babysit her while I'm gone, will you, Haze?"

"Yup," Hazel said. "What if she tries to smoke, though?"

"Tell her we love her too much to let her die of cancer. Make her stop."

She nodded importantly.

I went inside, to the bathroom. Washing my hands, I saw that I had gotten some sun. *Crap.* My aging process hardly needed extra help . . . but it did make for pretty pink streaks under each cheek. I splashed cool water on my face and patted it dry, shook out my hair. In the kitchen, I made another batch of drinks, then found the bag of cherries I'd bought yesterday, which I washed, dumped in a bowl, and carried out, along with the newly filled pitcher.

It wasn't until the door slammed behind me that I noticed Kevin, standing talking to Celeste and Hazel. Sasha stood beside him, wagging her tail.

"Look who's here, Mom!" Hazel screamed, as if I were blind as a bat.

"I see, Haze. Hi," I said, feeling a blush creep onto my face.

"Hey," he said, smiling, and his smile lit me up, a ray of sun at the end of a storm.

"I see you've met Celeste," I managed.

He nodded. "Hazel introduced us."

"She did?" I blinked.

"Yup," said Celeste. "She said, 'That's my mom's drunk best friend.' " She laughed.

"I didn't say that!" Hazel said, and then, "*Is* she, Momma? Drunk?"

"Of course not," I said. "Hey, anyone want a drink?"

Kevin laughed. "Sure."

"You need a chair too," Celeste said.

"I'll get it!" Hazel yelled.

Kevin glanced at me. "I'll help her." He attached Sasha's leash to the railing, then went into the house with Hazel. I fell into the chair, tense and fluttery.

"Oh my god," Celeste whispered. "That's *him*! He's absolutely mouth-watering. How old is he? Twelve?"

"Shut up!" I hissed. The door opened and they came out, chatting, Kevin holding a kitchen chair in one hand, Hazel holding his glass. He put down the chair across from mine and Celeste's, poured himself a drink from the blender, sat on the edge of his seat, took a gulp, and looked at me. "I haven't seen you for a while."

I blushed and looked down, not daring to glance at Celeste.

He snapped his fingers and turned to Hazel. "I have your pencil cup. You need to come glaze it."

"Yay!" She looked at me. "When can I?"

"Whenever you want, I guess."

"How about now?"

"No, Haze," I said. "We're talking now. Kevin's talking."

"I can take her now," Kevin said. "It'll only take a few minutes."

Hazel looked at me. "Can I, Mom? Pleeeze?"

I tried to think straight. "Do you want me to come?" I asked Kevin.

"No need to. Hazel and I can handle it. Right?" He looked at her.

She nodded and reached for his hand.

"Well, get your flip-flops, at least," I mumbled in Hazel's direction.

She ran inside while Kevin finished his drink and freed Sasha's leash; five seconds later, she returned wearing my black platform flip-flops. "I couldn't find mine," she said. "I'll be very careful." She took Kevin's hand again.

"Bye," he said, looking at me. "We'll be back in a little bit." Out they went.

I let out my breath. Celeste was looking at me, a small smile on her face. "He's in love with you," she said.

You know those fireworks, the white ones with a million waterfalls of cascading sparks? "He is not!" I blurted out. "Shut up!" I didn't know whether to laugh or to cry.

She shrugged, took a sip of her drink. "Okay."

So we sat there. It was almost dark out now; the sun was a tiny purple slit, sinking fast. Celeste lit a cigarette and smoked it slowly. "Why did you say that?" I couldn't resist asking.

"I can tell," she countered—instantly, as if she'd been waiting for me to break. "His eyes, and his hands. The way he looks at you, and the way he doesn't know what to do with his paws when he's around you. He's smooth, but not that smooth. Too young to be."

I held my breath, praying for her to go on.

"You're not in love with him, though," she said, as if hearing my thoughts. "You're in love with how he sees you, but not with him personally. I mean, beyond the physical. Physically, what's not to love? He's like a fucking cupcake." She set her drink on the ground. "So—what are you gonna do?"

I looked at her. "What do you mean?"

She kept looking at me.

"Nothing!" I said, finally. "What *would* I do?"

She shrugged. "Nothing, of course." She took a drag of her cigarette, then a sip of her drink. I sipped mine too. And then we were silent, in our alcohol haze, under the coming night. Neither of us had mentioned the phone call yet, and I wanted it to stay that way. But I couldn't get her words out of my mind. *He's in love with you.*

"How's your book going?" I asked her, pointedly. "When's it coming out?"

She was looking at me again. "Elayna," she said quickly, "I just have to say this. It'll sound like the most hypocritical thing in the world coming from me, but I have to say it, as your friend. Be careful. Because rule number one about affairs—and obviously it can be broken if you're very, very careful, as I am, but—rule number one about affairs is, never have one with someone in a different situation than yours. If you're married, make sure he's married too. If you both have kids, all the better. This guy's young, and he's single, and he's carefree as hell. You're the one with something to lose. Everything to lose."

"Celeste!" My heart was pounding, pounding away. "I am *not* having an affair with him!"

"Shh! I know!" She waved her hand quickly in the air. "Forget it. I was just projecting. I know you wouldn't. Of course I know that."

"We're friends, if anything!" I insisted. "Not even friends, really. We're—" I stood up. A wave of dizziness washed over me, and I reached for the chair back to steady myself. I was drunk as a skunk. "I should go see what Hazel's doing," I slurred.

Celeste held up her hand. "Wait—is that them?"

It was indeed Hazel's voice, a ways off but coming closer. Soon enough, the gate opened and in they came. "Hi, Mom!" she said. "I glazed my pencil holder! It's gonna be blue—well, it doesn't look blue now, but after it goes in the kiln. Right, Kevin? Blue like the sky. No, like the ocean. Well—like both, kind of. You like blue, Mom, right?"

"I do," I said, trying to focus.

"Is it your favorite color, though? I thought it was black!"

"Oh yeah. Well, it was, but—it changed recently."

"Oh. Good. Because—oh, never mind. Wait—Kevin, come here!"

Kevin bent down, and she reached up and put her hands around his neck and whispered something in his ear. She was still in her bathing suit, I realized. The right side of the bottom pushed between the cheeks of her butt, exposing a round half-moon of perfect white flesh. I thought of Paul, for some reason. Kevin nodded, then whispered something back in her ear. She giggled and nodded.

"Haze, it's time to go in," I said. "Time for your bath."

"What about the fireworks?!" she yelled. "*Mom!* It's Fourth of *July*!"

"Oh shi—shoot," I said. "I forgot all about them."

Kevin looked from Celeste to me. "Are you going?" he asked. "I'm heading over there later, to meet some friends."

"*Can* we, Mom?"

"Um—wait. Just—let me think, for a minute."

Celeste looked at me. She stood up. "Come on, Hazel," she said, picking up her drink. "Let's go in and shower while your mom decides. You can try on my new shoes." The two of them exited stage left, Hazel neglecting to thank Kevin or say good-bye.

So—he stood there, hands in his pocket, a sweet, happy, slightly searching look on his beautiful face.

I pushed my hair out of my eyes. "Thank you for helping her glaze her thing," I said. "Cup. Or—pencil holder, I mean. Sorry. I'm just—actually a little drunk." I laughed.

He smiled. "Yeah, that margarita wasn't exactly a virgin. Did you make those?" I saw the flash in his eyes. He was flirting now. Torturing me.

"Listen," I said, trying to think. "Let me go in and get dressed, make dinner, and see what Celeste wants to do. If we're still up for it after that, we'll head over with you."

"Great." He bounced on the balls of his feet. "I'll swing by in an hour and a half?"

"Okay."

"Don't forget a blanket."

I nodded, wasted, trying not to blush. "See you later," I said.

# Chapter Twenty

We went, of course. The fireworks were held at the college every year, and on the walk over—showered, fed, dressed, and amply revived, though still slightly drunk—I made a point of sticking tightly to Hazel, telling her jokes, stories from my childhood . . . anything to keep her by my side. That left Kevin and Celeste to pair up, which they did, lagging behind so Celeste could smoke a cigarette and Kevin a joint without Hazel noticing. By nine o'clock, the four of us had arrived on campus and teamed up again. As we entered the sea of bodies—walking, sitting, lying on blankets—and searched for a place to spread our own, Kevin spotted his friends. I saw him say something to Celeste, and then he made his way over to two guys and a girl, all of whom looked about twenty-two. Did his eyes linger on me just before he left? "Where's Orion's belt?" Hazel said, as she flopped down on her back. I lay down next to her and looked up. " 'Star light, star bright, first star I see tonight,' " she recited, and then, "I wish my daddy was here."

I felt a pang of sadness. "He'll be back soon," I said. "A couple more days."

"Will I see him that day?"

"I don't know, baby. Depends on what time he gets home."

A firework went up, a silent missile shooting high in the sky, then exploding in blue and pink streaks. "Ooooh!" Hazel yelled, with the rest of the crowd. Another one went off, this time loudly. Hazel winced. "Mom," she said. "I have to go to the bathroom."

I looked at her. "You're kidding me, right?"

She shook her head.

"Oh, Haze! You really, really can't hold it?"

"No! I have to go bad!"

I sighed. "Okay, come on. Celeste, we'll be right back."

Celeste lay on her back looking up at the sky. "Okay," she said. Another loud firework went off, and Hazel squeezed my hand.

There were probably Porta Potties but I couldn't find any, so I took us to one of the campus buildings. We were sweating by the time we got there. In the bathroom, Hazel picked a stall and opened the door. "Ew," she said, backing out. She moved to another, went in, and came back out. "Mom!" she moaned. "It's automatic flush! I *hate* automatic flush!"

I sighed. "Just go, please."

"No. I don't have to go anymore."

I slit my eyes at her. "I did *not* walk all the way here for nothing, Hazel."

"Only if you come in with me."

I refrained from shaking her. "Okay! I'm in. Now go."

"You have to cover up the flusher so it doesn't flush. Promise?"

"Yes! I promise! Please go, already. I don't want to miss the whole show." I moved to the back of the toilet, holding my breath, and covered the sensor with my palm.

Gingerly, Hazel pushed down her pants and sat on the edge of the seat. "Hurry up," I said, stretching to keep the thing covered.

"O*kay*! God!" Silence for a moment. "Don't look at my butt!" she yelled, as if she didn't parade the damn thing half the rest of the time.

I had to laugh. She was impossible. I was craning to cover the sensor on the back of the wall, and now I had to turn my head away too? "Hurry, Haze," I pleaded. "I can't hold this position much longer."

"Okay. I think I'm done— No! Wait! I have more!"

I looked up at the ceiling and counted silently to thirty, holding my breath.

She hopped off the toilet. I must have moved my hand slightly, because it flushed loudly as she did.

"Mom!" Hazel wailed. "I didn't even wipe yet!"

I couldn't help smiling. "Sorry, I didn't mean to let go. Go ahead, just wipe."

The toilet went off three more times while she did. Then, after she'd thrown in her last enormous, crumpled wad of toilet paper, it refused to flush at all. "That was efficient," I said, kicking the bowl. "Twenty gallons of water and a mess in the bowl at the end. Another one for the list of most retarded human inventions of all time."

Hazel laughed, and then I did too.

We made our way back. The fireworks were coming more steadily now—it was almost time for the warm-up to end and the actual show to begin—and I noticed that each time one went off, Hazel stopped walking for a second and tightly squeezed my hand. Finally, we reached our blanket and Celeste. "Oops," she said, stabbing out her cigarette when she saw us. But Hazel hadn't noticed. She was looking up worriedly. I glanced around. Kevin was a few blankets away, with his friends, but I saw him look over. Our eyes locked, and we both looked away, my pulse jumping out of my skin.

I sat down next to Celeste. Hazel lay down next to me. There was a loud *boom,* and then another. Hazel sat up, hands on her ears.

I looked at her. "Pretty, right?" I said.

She shook her head no.

"No?" I asked, surprised.

She shook her head again, her face tight with anxiety.

Another pop, followed by an "Ooh!" from the crowd.

"It's too loud!" Hazel yelled. "I want to go home!"

I stared at her in absolute disbelief. "We just got here!" I said. "You'll get used to it. Give it a minute."

Another loud bang, and then another. "I don't like it!" she yelled, panic in her voice. "I want to go home!" She stood up. "Come *on,*" she said, pulling at me.

For the past two years, I remembered then, we'd skipped the fireworks; the year before that, she had sat on Paul's lap and he'd held his hands firmly over her ears the whole time. Still, I hadn't expected this. "Hazel," I said, trying to stay calm, "get a grip, okay? It's not dangerous. It's loud, but it's totally safe. You can try covering your e—"

Another loud bang, *bam bam bam.* "Mom!" she shrieked. People were starting to look at us. One woman whispered to her friend, and they both turned our way.

"Hazel, *stop it*!" I hissed. Like in the bathroom, I knew I should be more sympathetic, but by then I just wanted to scream. Kevin's friend was smoking a joint now; I saw the friend hand it to Kevin, and him take a drag. "Mom!" Hazel yelled. "I *hate* it here! I want to *go.* Can we please go home?" Her eyes filled with tears.

Somewhere deep down I felt a hint of compassion, but not enough to ease my anger. I looked at her and shook my head. She was such a head case. Maybe I should call Pansy and ask what she thought . . . but Pansy would just blame me for not exerting more authority. I could almost hear her voice. *You have to hold firm, Elayna. You have to let her see that you're in charge. And you have to give her boundaries. All children want boundaries. It's when they don't have them that they get scared, because then they feel they have to be in charge of themselves, and they don't know what to fear, so they fear everything.* "Hazel," I said, more firmly than I felt. "We're staying here for ten minutes. If you're still upset then, I'll take you home. But we just got here, and I think you should give it a chance. I'll hold you on my lap and cover your ears, if you want."

She began to cry. Tears ran down her face. Immediately, I wished I hadn't said that. Now I'd have to stick to it. A loud boom sounded, and she literally jumped. And then, before I could react, she took off through the crowd.

"Hazel!" I yelled, standing up. "Hazel! Get back here!"

"Oh my god," Celeste said, sitting up. "She's actually going."

I watched her for another few seconds. Then I stood up and took off after her.

It was quite dark by then, with blankets and people everywhere, fireworks exploding away. I had to keep an eye on Hazel and also watch where I ran, trying not to trip or step on people's hands. I was apologizing to everyone, squinting to see where she went, while she, being smaller and less self-conscious about invading anyone, wove through the crowd easily. After a minute, she had gained on me considerably. I was panting, enraged, but also panicked. *What if I lost her here? What if she just disappeared?*

But she didn't, of course. Near the end of the crowd, she slowed down, and then, lucky me, she turned in my direction. I took three steps and grabbed her arm, hard. "Don't you ever, ever, *ever* run away from me like that again!" I yelled, in her face. "Don't you *ever*! I don't care *how* scared you are. I don't care *what* your problem is! You *never* run away from me in a crowd! Do you understand?"

She was bawling loudly. "Sorry!" she said, hugging my thighs. "Sorry, Momma!"

I was shaking. People were looking. I bent down and hugged her, tears coming to my eyes now too. "It's okay," I said. "It's okay. But, Haze—do you understand me? You can't do that anymore. It's *so* dangerous! You don't know where you're going, and someone could—I don't know, you could get lost, or someone could snatch you." Paul hated when I told her stuff like that: histrionic things that eventually would make her realize I was full of it. Well, Paul could come deal with this, then.

She didn't answer, anyway. She probably wasn't even listening. Her face was buried in my legs. "Can we please go home now?" she begged.

"Yes. Yes. I just—I have to go get Celeste. I left her there."

"I don't want to go back!"

"I know. Um—let me think." I thought for several seconds, getting nowhere. "Maybe we should just wait," I said, finally. "Maybe she'll come."

So we did. We sat and waited, and I held her with my hands over her ears, and it seemed to work, perhaps because we were a little farther from the noise, perhaps because she knew, now, that we were in the countdown to leaving. After a while I spotted Celeste coming through the crowd, dragging the blanket, the thermos, the bag of cherries I'd brought. I waved to her, and then somehow we all made it home, me apologizing profusely to her.

I apologized once more after I'd put my crazy daughter to bed. We were sitting at the table, drinking tea with the Tylenol we'd taken to ward off our hangovers. "I'm so sorry that turned into that," I said.

She wagged her hand. "Please. It's not like it was your fault. I saw what happened. I just felt sorry for her."

I shook my head. "I never can tell if she's a spoiled brat, or a true head case."

"Probably a little of each. Like all of us."

I sighed, exhausted. "I guess."

"Anyway, I didn't care if we stayed. I just wanted to get a taste of it."

"What'd you think?" I said, after a minute.

"What'd I think? It was sweet. I loved it. All those families." She smiled—wistfully, I thought. "The road not taken, for me. Always good to see what you missed."

"Well, you could still take it," I said. "You could still get married. Have kids."

She shook her head. "No thanks. I have no regrets."

"You don't?" I looked at her.

"Definitely not. In fact, the more time I spend around kids, the more I'm sure it's just not for me." She looked at me thoughtfully. "What you did tonight? I am so not cut out for that. I just could not handle it."

"You could if you had to. That's what I would have said before I had them too." Had *her,* I should've said, but I left it alone. I took a sip of my tea and felt it fall, warm, all the way down inside me. "How's your boyfriend?" I asked, after a moment.

"Stephen? He's fine." She smiled.

"Do you love him?" My words were so sudden I was appalled at myself.

Celeste reached for the pack of cigarettes on the table, shook one out, and lit it. "I love being with him," she said. "I love fucking him. I love sitting across the table from him in some restaurant and knowing he has a hard-on because of me. I love when he comes over in the middle of the night and tells me he couldn't get through the night without, you know. Fill in the blank." She took a drag, blew it out. "So—what is love? Is it being able to take a shit in front of someone? Because no, I don't have that with him, and frankly, I hope I never do. I could do that in front of my cat, if I had one, which I never would, because I hate cats."

We sat for several moments. It was cool, quiet, pleasant. I sat back and looked at her. We had always been utterly honest with each other, and I felt it was my role as her best friend—one of her only friends, I knew—to tell her my worries about this highly unorthodox life she seemed to be choosing. But the thought of that exhausted me. "Celeste," I said. "I think I have to go to bed."

She nodded. "You go, honey. You've had a long day."

"So have you."

"Not as long as you. I slept in this morning." She stood up. "I'm gonna watch TV for a while. I'll put myself to bed when I get tired."

"Are you sure?" I stood up too.

She reached out and gave me a kiss on the cheek. "Good night."

I hugged her. "Thanks for keeping me going. I mean it."

"It's mutual," she said. "I live vicariously through you. I love being here. And I'll love going home again, to my smoky cave in Brooklyn where I can write my fucked-up books and have my fucked-up love affair and be content only now and then."

"Well, that's all that I'm content too," I said, wanting to be generous.

She let go of me and smiled. "Exactly."

# Chapter Twenty-One

The next day, Hazel and I walked Celeste to the bus, then went grocery shopping. Afterward, I plugged her into a movie so I could clean up the house, and another one so I could get some work done. Paul was due back late that night—he'd left a message that they'd finished sooner than expected and moved up their flight from the next day—though he wouldn't get in until close to midnight. "Daddy's coming home tonight," I said to Hazel, as I tucked her into bed.

She was half asleep already, but her eyes popped open. "He is? Can I stay up to see him?"

"No, sweet. He'll be very late. But he'll give you thousands of kisses."

She smiled and closed her eyes.

I gathered her dirty clothes and put them in the hamper, took a bath, started to put on an old T-shirt of Paul's then remembered the white pajamas from Celeste and put them on instead. They were gorgeous, a soft, white cotton spaghetti-strap tank top with cotton lace at the cleavage-exposing chest, and loose white capri pants; it all fit just right, and the top looked perfect against my dark hair. I ogled myself in the mirror for a while, holding my hair up in different styles and pretending to be a Victoria's Secret model, as if. Then I went downstairs with my book, where I made a mug of peppermint tea and helped myself to two dark chocolate truffles from my stash. I sat down happily at the kitchen table to read. I was looking forward to sitting there like that for an hour or two and then going to bed, probably long before Paul arrived. Not that I wasn't also looking forward to seeing him, to telling him about Celeste's visit and about what had happened last night with Hazel and everything else . . .

but better to do all that tomorrow, when I wasn't hungover and he wasn't exhausted, as he surely would be tonight.

But fifteen minutes later, there was a knock at the front door. I got up to answer it, wondering why he didn't use his key (too much luggage, maybe, or he didn't want to scare me) and why he was so early (probably caught an earlier flight) and why he wasn't coming in the back way—but of course, the car service would have dropped him in front. I made my way to the door, looking up, as I opened it and peered through the screen, for Paul's weary face. There stood Kevin.

I sucked in my breath, clasped my hands to my chest.

Kevin's smile melted. "Oh—shit. Did I scare you?"

I shook my head no, because of course, it wasn't so much that he'd scared me as simply that he was here. "It's okay," I lied, as my heart tried to leap from my chest and throw itself onto him.

"I'm sorry," he said.

"No—it's fine." I forced my hands down. "Really."

He looked at me, and I saw his eyes quickly notice my chest in the thin white cotton. "Anyway," he said, "I just came to give this to Hazel. I promised her I'd bring it as soon as it was fired, and I just got back from my studio, so . . ." He held out her pencil cup, blue as advertised.

I took a deep breath. "Hang on a sec." I went upstairs and got a white Oxford shirt out of Paul's closet, slipped my arms into it. Another deep breath. *Okay.* Back downstairs, I opened the screen and took Hazel's cup. "Too bad you can't give it to her yourself," I said. "She'd love that."

"Oh. I can." He glanced beyond me, then back to my eyes. "Is she here?"

I laughed. "She's asleep! It's almost ten o'clock."

He smiled. "Oops."

I looked at the beautiful little cup, and then at him—looked with something like rapture, I admit. He was lovely, clean and sloppy, all cheekbones, sweat, and sinew, standing there like a goof, smiling at me.

"Well," he said, "I guess I should let you get back to . . . whatever you're doing."

"Reading." I cocked my head at him. "And drinking peppermint tea."

His eyes stayed on mine; his little silver earring glinted in the scant moonlight. "Did Celeste leave?" he asked.

I nodded. "She had to go to work tomorrow."

"She's nice," he said, after a second.

"Thanks. I mean, not thanks, but—you know." I laughed.

"Have you been friends for long?"

"Since we were roommates at Barnard."

"You went to Barnard? Wow." He looked dreamy. "I wish I'd gone there."

I started to ask him where he had gone, but it seemed like a ridiculous question to ask through a screen. "Listen," I said instead, "do you want to come in for a minute? I could make you some tea."

"Sure." He smiled. "Thanks."

I pulled Paul's shirt a little closer over my chest (immediately, of course, it fell right back open), then pushed the screen door toward him. In he came. I headed back toward the kitchen, aware of him behind me. "So how's she doing?" he said.

I turned around, still walking. "Who?"

"Hazel. Didn't she have some sort of crisis last night?"

"Last—oh, you mean when she took off at the fireworks? You saw that?"

We'd reached the kitchen. I put Hazel's pencil cup on the counter and turned on the kettle as he maneuvered around, looking at things here and there: a small framed watercolor of a black couple dancing that I'd once bought on the street in New York; my grocery list (juice boxes, chocolate, Annie's macaroni and cheese); a picture Hazel had drawn of a mermaid neighborhood, featuring baby mermaids trailing mothers, a queen mermaid on a throne, and a mermaid UPS driver. In this room, he seemed bigger than usual, thrumming with nerves and energy. "Too bright," I said, giving the dimmer a whirl, and I leaned back against the stove in the relative dark as my eyes adjusted, as the water began to simmer. "Hazel's fine," I said, remembering his question. "Actually, that sort of behavior is nothing new for her. She's always been a little, um—"

"Phobic?" He paused at the counter, picked up Hazel's pink pencil with the cat-shaped eraser, two glittery eyes, and smiled at it.

"Well—yes, actually," I said.

"My mother's a shrink," he reminded me. He put the pencil back down, picked up a light-up yo-yo and shot it down its string and back up again.

"Oh. Right," I said.

"Plus, I had tons of phobias myself as a kid."

"You did?" I looked at him. "Like what?"

He put down the yo-yo and picked up Hazel's paper fortune-teller. "Cars, for one," he said, slipping the four sections onto his fingers, moving them in and out. "For, like, a year, I wouldn't get into a car. I was scared to death of it. I'd get panicked if I had to, and then dizzy. I'd feel like I was suffocating." He smiled. "Drove my mom nuts."

"I can imagine."

"Yeah. I think that's partly why she became a shrink. Man, I remember these things." He lifted a flap, read his fate out loud—" 'You will fall in the toilet'—ha!"—then replaced the fortune-teller on the counter. "She started her degree when I was in grade school," he continued, moving to the table. "After she divorced my dad."

"Huh. So—did that help?"

"Definitely. I was much more relaxed when he wasn't around."

I laughed. "I meant your mom becoming a shrink. Did that help with your—problems."

"Oh." He shrugged. "Probably. I mean, at least she knew the terms for what I had, even if she couldn't cure me. I was a human guinea pig right in her own house." He picked up the salt and pepper shakers—red ceramic roosters we'd gotten as a wedding gift from Paul's aunt—and examined them.

"Oh, come on," I said, giving him a look. "You couldn't have been that bad."

He looked at me, shrugged, and smiled adorably.

I thought, *Be still, my heart.* "What else were you afraid of?" I managed.

"Dogs," he said, putting back the rooster shakers. "All animals, really, except, like, fish."

"Get out!"

He laughed. "I was."

"So you had a fish tank, then?"

"Nope. I had *a* fish. Two goldfish, actually, but then one of them died.

One was always dying. I wanted to have two, so they'd have company, but every time I'd get a new one, one of them would die. Finally someone told me you can't have two at once, unless it's a huge tank where you pump air in. In a regular fishbowl, the bigger one will always die, because it doesn't get enough air."

"Really? I had two fish in a bowl growing up." I thought a minute. "Though, now that you mention it, one of them always *did* die."

He laughed. The kettle whistled. I took out two mugs and two fresh tea bags, poured the water, and handed him one. "Sit," I said.

He sat down obediently, last seat at one side of the table, and plunked down his tea. After debating a second, I sat at the head of the table, next to him but with the corner between us, so our mugs were side by side but our bodies weren't, quite. "So—in the end, you just had one fish?" I picked up my mug, blew at the tea, replaced it. My hand shook ever so slightly.

"No," he said. "In the end, I had none. I filled the water too high one day, and he jumped out and died on the rug."

I laughed, then covered my mouth with my hand. "Sorry."

"It's okay. It was thirteen years ago. I'm almost over it."

He worked on the tea for a while. With each minute he didn't get up and go, I was a little more confident, or at least a little less nervous. I was aware of my body, full in the pretty pajamas; my mouth felt fresh with mint. I sipped my tea, flipped back my hair. I felt pretty, flirty, light as a kite, and it was rapturous, that feeling, after all these years.

Kevin fidgeted with a spoon, with the handle of his mug, with a Juicy Fruit wrapper from somewhere, and I thought, *Ten thousand dollars for your thoughts?* because I figured they were probably about me. But I wanted to know: Did he think I was sexy? What was this really about? He looked at me. "Do you ever wish you were a guy?" he said.

I blinked. "What?"

"Sorry. That's probably a dumb question. I was just—I was thinking about when I came to the door, and how—"

"No," I interrupted, because I wanted to answer the question. "It's okay. I don't, though. Wish I were a guy. Though sometimes I think I was meant to be."

His green eyes looked into mine. "In what way?"

Behind him, the wall clock ticked quietly. "In the way my mind works, I guess," I said. "Or used to, anyway."

"How?"

I laughed a little at his bluntness. "I didn't like waking up with anyone," I said, plunging in. "When I was younger, I mean. In my twenties." I sat back, thought a second. "I wrote some poetry back then, stop laughing—"

He laughed. "I'm not laughing."

"—and in the morning, if I wasn't rushing off to work, I just wanted to write. Or go for a run, or see three or four movies in a row, or just lie there and *think.* You know? It's not that I had such profound thoughts. But I needed to have them, and I needed to be alone to do it." I smiled a little. "You know all those magazines about holding on to a man? My thing was always, how do I let go of one. I mean, without being a jerk. Because I wasn't a jerk, I don't think. And I liked men, I liked going out. I just didn't—I didn't want . . ." I sighed. "Well. Your mom would probably say I didn't love myself so I couldn't let anyone else love me—that whole thing. But I don't know if it's that complicated. I think I just wanted to be free while I could." I took a sip of tea.

He was nodding, looking at me, apparently finding nothing inappropriate about our conversation. "That's the opposite of me," he said. "Not that I mind solitude, but—I love waking up with someone."

Something inside me unraveled. I imagined—how could I not?—waking up with him some morning, sunlight streaming through the curtains of wherever, his rosy, optimistic face right there staring into mine. "Sorry," I said, after a second. "I didn't mean to go off."

"Are you kidding? Not at all." He sat for a moment, his face contemplative. "Anyway, I asked because I was thinking about how it must suck sometimes to be the weaker sex." He looked at me. "I don't mean weaker like *that,* obviously. I just mean physically weaker. Smaller. To know that at least half the world out there is significantly bigger and stronger than you."

"I guess that might be a downside," I admitted. "But the upsides make up for it."

He nodded, looking at me. "Like what?"

"Being a mother," I said, promptly. "And I guess"—I thought for a minute—"being wanted in that way women are. Having the world lust after you. At least when you're young."

He laughed softly, and looked down. "Yeah."

My bosom swelled. Could he have thought I meant me? "And then, later," I continued quickly, "having someone devour you, the way your child does. It's actually a little terrible, but it's wonderful too. One of the highlights of life."

He nodded. "I can imagine," he said, as if he really could.

I sat back, curled my legs up under me on the chair. My shirt had fallen open again, but I didn't close it this time, and I knew my chest was flushed, my cheeks too. "Though I think as you age, power shifts," I said softly. "Women lose power, men gain."

"I don't know," he said. "I think women always have the power emotionally." His green eyes locked on to mine.

I swallowed. "Do you?"

He nodded. "They're more—they can express themselves better."

"More articulate."

"See?"

I laughed softly, aware of my body: warm, swollen, pulsing with temptation.

He was still looking at me, and now those two lovely pink stars appeared again under his eyes. "You're so nice," he said, and his hands reached for mine and held on, big and warm, and the warmth pushed through all of me.

I took a breath. "Well, so are you." I looked down then, suddenly shy.

He held my hands for a moment. And then I looked up, and he was still looking at me, his magnet eyes, and that was it, I couldn't get out. Our knees touched, and I melted, met him halfway as he leaned forward, and our lips brushed—lightly, sweetly—then parted again. My eyes closed.

I opened them. He was still looking at me.

*Oh god,* I thought, and I closed my eyes again, and this time, when our lips met, a current shot through me, so intense I gasped.

But he was waiting for me now, lovely rosy-white skin, sweet, opened lips. Once more, I leaned in, and this time his mouth was hot, hungry, barely restrained, and mine was too, and I opened it to him. And then panic. Panic. I pulled away, and somehow—somehow—I stood up, breathing hard. "I can't," I whispered.

He raised his eyebrows and blinked.

I pushed my hair back, shook my head. "You have to go," I said. "I'm sorry."

He turned to the side and winced, as if I'd physically slapped him, and let go of my hands, and when he looked at me again he looked sad and a little bit pissed off. "Is that how the magazines said to do it?"

"What?"

He shook his head. "Never mind. I'll go. If you want me to."

I almost laughed. "It's not that I—"

He stood up. "Forget it. I get it. You don't have to explain." He backed up from the table and began to walk toward the front door.

"Wait," I said, following him.

He kept walking.

"Wait!" I said again, and then I stopped in my tracks. The front door was opening, but Kevin wasn't there yet to be opening it.

Paul walked in, briefcase over one shoulder, suitcase in hand. He looked at Kevin, then at me, in my pajamas, then at Kevin again.

Kevin stopped in his tracks. "Hey," he said to Paul.

I was shaking. "Paul!" I said loudly. "Hi!" I went over and hugged him, too fast and too hard, a hug he only vaguely returned with his non-suitcase hand. "This is Kevin, our neighbor." I pulled away. "The one I told you about. Kevin, meet Paul."

"Nice to meet you, man," Kevin said. "Actually, I was just leaving. Take it easy." He walked out, closing the door behind him.

Paul watched him go. He turned and looked at me.

I smiled brightly, a regular Lucy Ricardo.

He frowned. "What was that all about?"

"What? Oh, Kevin? He brought over Hazel's little cup."

He put down his suitcase, then his briefcase. "What little cup?"

"She made a little pencil cup at his place, on his wheel. Remember? He's a potter. And he glazed it for her."

"Oh—that's *that* guy?" He looked around. "So—where is it?"

"What?"

"Hazel's pencil cup."

"Oh! Come on, I'll show you." I walked him back to the kitchen, pointed to the cup where I'd put it on the counter.

He went over and picked it up, turned it around in his hand. "Sweet," he said, smiling a little.

I exhaled. "How was your trip?"

He sighed, and I could tell he'd decided to give me the benefit of the doubt, at least for the moment. "Intense," he said. "Nonstop. But incredible. We have witness after witness who will testify about how great this guy is. His old landlord, his ex-wife . . . And black, white, male, female. His kid's former second-grade teacher."

"Wow."

"Yeah. So—that just adds to what we already have. The judge is giving us only two days for the hearing; he says he has a trial starting right after that. So we'll just have to run into the night those two days, if that's what it takes to get all our witnesses in. But we'll have a very strong case."

"That's amazing," I said, both meaning it and relieved to have successfully changed the topic. "You should feel fantastic."

"Well, I will when it's over."

"Did you have dinner?"

"I grabbed something at the airport."

"Want some ice cream?"

He considered a second. "Yeah, actually."

We went into the kitchen. Quickly, I swooped up the two tea mugs and dumped them in the sink, while Paul took off his jacket. He hung it on the back of the seat Kevin had sat in, then sat down in another chair—his usual one—and loosened his tie, a pretty blue and gold tie I'd given him a while ago. He was wearing a dark blue shirt, one I liked, one that looked especially good with the tie. I wondered if he'd thought of me when he packed it, when he put it on this morning. Probably not, I decided. "Oh," I said, as I scooped ice cream into a bowl, "I told Hazel you'd give her a thousand kisses good night. So you'd better eat fast and get started."

He smiled wearily, and I felt hideous, then, for deceiving him, for what I'd done here just minutes ago. "I missed her," he said.

I swallowed. "She missed you too."

"What did you guys do?"

"Me and Haze?" I scooped more ice cream into his bowl. "Celeste came over."

"You told me that last night."

"Oh. Right." The bowl was filled to the rim. I put it on the table in front of him. "And we, you know, went to the fireworks, and Hazel freaked out—did I tell you that?"

He shook his head no. "She did? What happened?" He looked at the bowl. "Yikes. Is that all for me?"

"She—" I suddenly felt too tired to tell him the story. "She didn't like the noise."

He went and got the spoon I'd forgotten to give him, sat down again. "And?"

I collapsed into the chair across from him, sat on my hands to keep them from shaking. "She ran away from our blanket." I shrugged. "And I had to follow her, through the crowd, in the dark, and then, you know, we had to come home."

He looked sad, and his sadness made me sad for her too. She could've used his sympathy yesterday. "Was she totally disappointed in herself?" he asked.

It was an interesting question, not the one I'd have thought to ask. "Yes, actually," I said. "I think she was."

"Poor thing. She must hate feeling so—terrified." He took a deep breath. "Maybe we should take her to see someone."

What he meant, of course, was, maybe *I* should take her to see someone. "Maybe," I said, halfheartedly. "If we really thought it would help."

"It couldn't hurt, could it?"

I shrugged. "I think it's biological. I think she has to outgrow it."

"Well, that doesn't mean she shouldn't have ways of coping with it now."

"I guess." I sighed. "I'll look into it."

"I will too. I'll ask around."

"Where, at work?" I couldn't keep the skepticism out of my voice. And I knew I was being unfair; after all, his salary supported my lifestyle, and he had to go to work to get the salary. But still. It's not as if I was telling him how to do *his* job.

He looked at me oddly. "Yeah," he said, finally, "or I could do some research . . . We could talk to Pansy too. She probably has some thoughts."

"I already know her thoughts. That I shouldn't have taken her to the fireworks anyway. She's too young, and they're dangerous, children shouldn't go until they're at least eight, blah blah blah."

He was still looking at me. "Maybe she has a point," he said.

"Maybe she does, but you know what, Paul? I don't particularly want to live that way. I'd rather expose her to things."

"Not if she's terrified, though, right? Why torture her?"

"Because, I think life should be lived!" I must have sounded slightly hysterical. "And I'm sorry, but I won't sit in my house for twenty years in a row because she might be afraid of something sometime. I'm not that self-sacrificing, and frankly, I don't think it would be doing her any big favors either, in the end."

He pushed his ice cream away, the bowl still half full. "I can see you're worked up about this, Elayna, so let's drop it for now."

"I'm *not* worked up!" I yelled.

He stood up. "Let's talk about it tomorrow. Okay?"

I tried to calm down. On top of everything else, I felt guilty, now, for putting Hazel through that last night. What a lousy mother I was.

Paul carried his bowl to the sink. "So where does that guy live?" He put his bowl in the sink, ice cream inside, and turned around.

"Kevin?" I stood up, reached around Paul for the sponge. "In the Tenement."

"Oh right, you told me that once. How come I never noticed him before?"

*Because you're never here,* I thought, but I said, "I hadn't either, till recently." I began to wipe the table, fast and hard.

"How did he get to know Hazel?" he asked—not quite casually, I thought.

I shrugged, wiping harder. "Just from seeing us around, I guess. He came over one time when we were out on the swing, and Hazel got all squealy over his dog. After that, he'd stop by with the dog—Sasha—to see her sometimes. And then he invited her up to make that pottery thing, so—" I shrugged again.

"But you went with her. Right?"

"Of course! *God,* Paul!" But I thought of yesterday, Celeste and me drunk, Hazel trotting off in her bathing suit with Kevin. I looked down and started scrubbing again.

"I'm sorry," he said, genuinely. "I'm sorry. Listen, I'm going up, okay? I'm wiped out." He paused. "You coming?"

"In a little bit. I'll just put this stuff in the dishwasher first."

He left the room, uncharacteristically leaving his jacket on the chair.

I went to the sink. I opened the dishwasher and began to load the dishes in, breathing fast. Shame was all around me, above and below, inside and out. What had my family done to deserve this? Nothing. Not one thing.

And then I thought of Kevin, leaning over the table, of the feel of his lips touching mine. I made for my chair and fell into it. Where exactly had he sat, and how, precisely, had he done it? I closed my eyes and reimagined it exactly as it had happened. His hands on mine, his face coming toward me, eyes bright and shining. His skin, his lips, coming toward mine. And in my mind—oh, in my mind!—I got to kiss him back, endlessly.

## Chapter Twenty-Two

For six days after that, I resisted. On the seventh day, I went to him. I couldn't take it anymore.

But let me backtrack.

Paul, of course, was working hard on the case. The hearing was scheduled for early September—just before Hazel went back to school—and we were supposed to go on our annual family vacation to Maine in early August. He would bring work along, naturally, but at least he was coming, and I knew by now to take what I could get. Our cabin was rented, the whale watch booked, the rocky beaches and cold ocean and penny-candy stores and lobster shacks and homemade berry pies awaiting.

Meanwhile, my father and Hazel were both pushing me to let her have a sleepover with him before we left. The next fashion show wasn't until after Labor Day, but he wanted her to experience true summer in New York, the die-hard days when most of his set went to East Hampton but he stayed and braved the stifling heat: the hot dogs and Italian ice vendors, the Lycra-clad Rollerbladers, the carousel and the Central Park Zoo. He wanted to take her on the Staten Island ferry, to see the Statue of Liberty and Belvedere Castle, to an outdoor puppet show in the park. He wanted to take her shopping, to let her experience the feeling of walking into an air-conditioned store full of crisp, vibrant clothes and have the sweat instantly disappear. In short, he wanted to do, with her, all the things he hadn't had time to do with me.

I said yes.

Pansy was canceled, Hazel's bag packed, the plans made. She would drive into the city with Paul in the morning; my father would pick her up at his office. The following evening he'd return her to Paul's office, and she'd come home with him. If he didn't think he'd get home before ten or eleven, I'd drive in and get her.

The day came. In pajama bottoms and a T-shirt, I walked Hazel out to Paul's car, kissed them good-bye, made her tell me my cell phone number yet again, just to make sure she knew it. Their car pulled away.

I went inside. It was funny, what came over me when Paul and Hazel left the house for a chunk of time and I was alone in it again. First—instinctively, not even consciously—I would take a deep breath, and I could feel it travel to all the parts of me that hadn't breathed since I'd last been alone: the parts I closed off, want to or not, when I was a mother and a wife, taking care of my family, constantly aware of other people's presence and needs. They were the same parts that allowed me, or caused me, to experience life fully and deeply, and as soon as they breathed again, the house felt different, smelled different, and I embodied it differently. *When I was a child, I thought, / Casually, that solitude / Never needed to be sought,* wrote the poet Philip Larkin. I moved through the silence and the dark, turning off radios and phones, and as I did, my mind opened up, and I began to think again, *really* think, not just go through the motions of life.

It was the same thought process, if not the same thoughts, that had, living alone in my twenties, threatened to overwhelm me; that had dragged me down and allowed me to get so far into myself that I could get stuck there and suffocate. But now, because they were short-lived and fleeting and reminded me of who I had been and still was—and, yes, because I had a family that loved me, because I was no longer alone *ultimately*—they were interesting and vital to me without being destructive. Ah yes, here I was again. And now I could feel my body—my tailbone, my inner ear, the space between my toes, the pores where my hair connected to my head. I could turn on music now, if I wanted, and actually listen to it, instead of hearing it as that much more background noise. I could hear my thoughts, for better and worse, and I could think about what I wanted, what *I* needed. *Me.* There was no one to judge me, no one for me to judge. My mind was utterly free. *Viciously, then, I lock my door*, Larkin penned. *And like a sea-anemone / Or simple snail, there cautiously / Unfolds, emerges, what I am.*

Of course, alas, I also had to do my work during most of my solitary time, which required a certain level of discipline that put a crimp in the freedom, though didn't obliterate it entirely. And anyway, work was its own relief and release. I fixed myself a peanut butter and banana sandwich on toast and sat down at the kitchen table to do it, falling asleep only once, briefly, my head lolling back on my chair, and getting up from my chair only once—okay, twice—once to use the bathroom, once to pour myself a bowl of dark chocolate chips, which I ate slowly, lovingly, one at a time, as I worked.

At two o'clock, I put down my pencil. I was spent, wired, bleary eyed, and restless, but I felt good; I'd gotten much of the job done, and I still had the rest of the week before it was due. I went to the computer and checked my email, ignoring all except one from Deborah, which I read and answered, and another from Celeste, which I read but didn't answer yet, saying Stephen had invited her to Paris for a few days, and what should she bring back for me? *So much for his wife and kids,* I couldn't help judging. I kept the email as new, then put on shorts and a T-shirt and headed outside, into the luscious heat, the engorged, bulging flowers, fat bumblebees dive-bombing, like tiny stunt pilots, through the balmy, almost turgid air. I jogged to and then through the town and beyond, until I got to the arty movie theater, the one for the yuppies like me. Two movies playing. After brief debate, I chose the French angst flick over the lesbian coming-of-age, and, with the $10 bill in my sock, bought a ticket for the five thirty show. I jogged back home, showered, ate leftover chicken, got dressed, then drove back to the theater and went in.

I was back home by eight. No one there. Cool, empty house. A message from Paul saying he'd be late, don't wait for him for dinner. Nothing from Hazel. I picked up the phone and called my father. "Devon Leopold," was his entire message, and then the beep. I left a long message for him and Hazel, spent a few minutes, but no longer, thinking about where they might be.

So now what? I went into the living room and sat down on the couch. Immediately, as it always did when I wasn't keeping it occupied with other things, my mind rolled on to Kevin, that passage in my brain now worn easy and comfortable, like a downhill slope, from extreme overuse. I thought, yet again, about that last night I'd seen him: first, of the kiss, that most glorious kiss, and then how I'd asked him to leave. Was he angry about that? He had seemed so, but I really didn't know.

I got up, went into the kitchen, poured myself some wine from the fridge. I took a few sips, topped it off, recorked the bottle. Then I walked to the front door and outside, back into the heat.

It was still light out; the sun was just starting to set, lazy violet and orange streaks faintly permeating the few silver clouds in the sky. I glanced up at his apartment. It was impossible to tell if he was home or not. I took another sip of wine and thought for a moment. Then I put the glass down on the front step—I'd be right back to drink it—and walked quickly toward his apartment. I would apologize. Nothing more, nothing less. I would say I was sorry things had ended so abruptly that night, I hadn't meant them to, I hoped he wasn't mad. And then I'd leave and come back home again.

I crossed the street, mounted his steps, knocked on his door. "Hang on," his voice called. My body went loose, and then mild panic kicked in. I turned to go—maybe I could get down the steps before he came, run back home and he'd never know it had been me. The door opened, and he stood there.

For starters, he wasn't wearing a shirt; for seconds, I knew, somehow, the instant I saw him, that only at the sound of the knock had he pulled on his pants. So: There he stands, hair, eyes, mouth, chest, belly button, bare feet, jeans. I tried not to look at his body—I hadn't seen it since that day I'd first met him—but really, how do you not? His nipples were small and tight despite the heat. His skin was milk white, Irish white, with the faintest light brown freckles, almost no body hair. He was thin in the flank, thinner than he looked in a T-shirt, so his ribs showed themselves, but his biceps were sweetly full, round and strong, like two ample oranges under his skin. Did the clay thing do that, or did he have barbells under his bed to keep them that way? His belly button: a perfect pink flap, like the clean inside of a knot on a balloon. He had a pale red birthmark on his left side, a few inches down from his underarm, about the size of a walnut, the shape of a koala bear. I took this all in with a glance, one I tried—unsuccessfully, I'm sure—to hide as I took it.

Could I smell him, or am I imagining this? He smelled like salty tomatoes on the deepest green vine, like wet, dark, cold clay. Like the cork of a bottle of red wine, like rising bread dough heavy with yeast. He smelled human and musky, not quite clean. Impossibly sexy. He smiled when he saw me. "Hey," he said, and he rubbed at the back of his neck.

"Hi," I said, and then, quickly, "I came to apologize."

"What for?" He blinked. "Here, do you want to come in?"

"No—that's okay." I thought of taking a step back from the door, but my body wouldn't do it. "I've gotta go back in a second."

"Oh." He looked into my eyes. "Well, I'm thinking, but I can't think of anything you did wrong," he said.

"Oh! Well, that's good." I laughed nervously. "It's just—that night, when—" I shifted on my feet, which, I realized now, were as bare as his. "Never mind," I said. "Forget it. As long as you're not mad."

He raised his eyebrows and smiled. "Nope."

"Oh—great!" I took a deep breath. "Well—okay. Bye." I turned to go.

"Wait," he said.

I turned back.

"That's all you came here to say?"

I nodded.

He laughed. "Okay." He put his right hand out toward me. "Friends," he said.

I should've nodded and left. "Friends," I should've said, and in fact I did say it, but then I did the other thing. I reached out my own hand, and I let it touch his.

He took it. Our fingers locked.

"Friends," he said again, much more softly.

And I couldn't let go. I couldn't let go of his hand, and I couldn't look at him. He brushed his thumb over the heart of my hand, fine sandpaper smoothing something away, and his fingers began to weave into mine, moving, moving, as if I were a piece of clay he was working. "You bite your nails," he said. "I noticed that the first time I met you."

I nodded, bit my lip to keep it from trembling, betraying me. Not that I had a prayer of succeeding. I was so utterly exposed, standing there. His hands pushed through mine, caressed, and the strokes woke my body. "I'm glad you came over," he said.

I didn't answer. I didn't trust myself to talk, to look up. But a question was forming in my brain, and before I could stop it, it had come out of my mouth. "Do you think," I said, and then I looked up, straight at him, "do you think kissing is adultery?"

He smiled. He raised one shoulder, let it drop again. "No," he said. "Not really."

For a second, I wondered if he even knew what the word meant. "Because that's—I mean, that's what I was trying to figure out that night you came over, whether or not it's—"

"It's not," he said, definitively. "I'm sure it's not."

I looked down.

"Come here," he said softly, and his words were a latch, releasing everything I was fighting to hold in. So I did it. I went to him, and I leaned in once more and touched my lips to his mouth, which was salty and soft and hard all at once, and suddenly he was over me and pushing against me, devouring my mouth with his. I could feel him shaking, and his excitement ignited me, sent a current of fire through my body. I moaned, and I felt myself falling, going down, but he caught me, held me, wrapped his arms all the way around my head and put his hands in my hair while we kissed, his mouth cold with beer and hard with youth and white teeth and I swear to god, I thought I would die. How many weeks of nights had I wondered if he felt the same thing, that same attraction I did? And now I knew, and I had him. He was mine.

He was kissing my ear, my temple, the pulse of my neck, the pulse of my throat, and everywhere he kissed, every time his lips touched my skin, sparks jumped through me. He pushed my face away and held it and looked at me, and then he kissed my mouth again and his tongue slipped over mine, his hands in my hair, on my back, on my face, and now it was as if I *had* died, died and gone to heaven—but no, something better. I was alive.

He broke away. "Come in," he mumbled into my ear, because, my god, we were still outside. And I felt his palms on the small of my back, pulling me.

I shook my head. I think I was crying by now. "I can't. I can't."

He kissed my wet eyelids, my swollen mouth. He was breathing hard. "Please?"

"Oh god, don't ask me that!" I pushed my face to his chest. Skin on his skin, his heart beating just underneath, arms around me. "Okay," he whispered. "I won't. I'm sorry."

We stood like that forever, forever and a day. Overhead: same old stars, same old moon, same old sky as always, a steady backdrop for humanity's fleeting pleasures, fleeting whims, for two humans below, clinging together, life's bliss, until I realized a car was on the way down our street, and I knew it was Paul's. "Oh, fuck," I said.

I pushed away from Kevin, unclasped from his embrace, and I turned and ran down the steps.

Paul's car was pulling into our driveway. I waited till it was all the way in, and then, knowing he'd take a moment to hear another line or two of whatever opera or jazz he had on, I shot across the street and in the front door of our house, up the stairs and then up another flight, to the third-floor bathroom, where I closed the door and turned on the bathwater hard. I tore off my clothes and got in.

It was freezing. Like a punch in the chest. I held my breath, adjusted the faucets quickly, waited for the hot to come through. Every part of me—face, heart, ankles, balls of my feet—was pounding. I adjusted it hotter, fumbled with the bottle of bubble bath and dumped in too much, lay back and tried desperately to stop crying.

Paul was in the house now. He would put down his keys and briefcase, take off his jacket, pick up the mail, then come looking. "Elayna?" he called, mounting the stairs.

I took a deep breath. "Up here."

The door opened, and in he came. "Hey," he said, smiling, and then, "My god, your eyes are bright red! I'm not kidding. Are you allergic to the soap, or something?"

I shook my head. "Just tired. I was reading all day, and then I saw a movie."

"Oh." He paused. "Which one? Was it good?"

"Um." I couldn't recall the name. Hadn't that been in a different life? "It was sad," I said, just to keep myself talking.

"It was? Huh. Who'd you go with?"

"No one. Myself."

He nodded. "Well, was it just a tearjerker, or worth seeing?"

"Um. Worth it."

"Good. Then maybe you'll go again with me."

"It was French," I said, quickly. "Subtitles. Angst. Women at the beach with good shoes and big stylish bags."

"Oh," he said. "Good, I can skip it. One less thing on the endless to-do list of life." But he smiled as he said it. He was in a good mood. I felt a pang of unbearable sadness. If he were miserable, it would somehow have been easier. He flipped through the bills, then looked back at me. "Anything good to eat?"

"You didn't eat at work?"

"We had a six thirty meeting that lasted hours. By then I just wanted to come home. Oh—it looks like I'll have to leave next Tuesday for Arkansas, not Wednesday or Thursday. That way, I'll have the extra few days if I need them, before we go to Maine."

My heart, that ruthless murderer, fluttered; an extra day with Kevin, perhaps.

"Too bad," I said, and then came the guilt, the shame, the water too hot, suddenly. "I could come down and make you some eggs, or something."

"Don't bother. Stay in the tub. I'll just grab some cereal."

"Are you sure?"

He nodded. "Oh. Your father says hello. It went fine this morning, with Hazel."

I couldn't believe I'd forgotten to ask. "So—" I swallowed. "She seemed happy to leave with him?"

"Thrilled."

"Well, great."

He was halfway out the door.

"I'll be down in a little bit," I said, as if sitting with him while he ate, as if scrambling him some eggs, would make up for sucking face with the boy next door.

"Don't worry," he said. "I'll be in bed by then." He went out, shutting the door behind him.

I slid down into the water. It was insane. I was so many people, so many different people, combined into one body—all of them crucial, vital, necessary. I was Hazel's mother. Paul's wife. I was alive and on fire for Kevin. *But clearly, I can never see him again.* I sat up straight, my shoulders and back suddenly out again into the cool air. *Never ever,* I thought—lest I be temped to do something that stupid, that utterly moronic, again. Because really, I was lucky. I'd stopped before things went too far, before any real damage was done . . . and now I would quit while I was still ahead.

I lay back again, submerged my shoulders once more in the heat. I thought of his mouth, of the taste of his tongue, the feel of the soft baby skin on the back of his neck. Of his hands on my neck. His mouth on my mouth, fingers tugging my hair, tongue in my mouth, filling it.

*Oh my god.* I went all the way under, made myself hold my breath, hold my breath, until I came up gasping for air.

# Chapter Twenty-Three

A week later, the doorbell rang.

Hazel and I had just come home from the pool, where we'd been all afternoon. She was still in her bathing suit. I wore a bikini top and sarong, an attempt at fighting the heat while also being young and hip, an attempt to show off my new body—I'd been running, running, every day in the sultry heat, or in the rain, water gloriously pelting my body—and not eating much, not on purpose, but I had no appetite, not depression this time, but the other thing, that chemical appetite suppressant, like no other . . . Anyway. The doorbell rang. And I knew it was him.

My brain registered first horror that he was here at my house again (what if Paul had been home?) and then absolute joy at seeing him, at the fact that he'd come. It had been his move, after all; I could not have gone to him again, or wouldn't have anyway. And of course, he could not come to me. But here he was.

Hazel ran to the door. "Kevin!" she screamed, opening it. "Hi! Want to watch *Mister Rogers* with me?"

"Heck yeah," he said. "Why do you think I came?" His eyes darted up to meet mine, avoiding my barely clad breasts. "Hi, Kevin," I said, casually, and I thought it must be a hundred degrees in here, and I wished I'd left on the air conditioner when we'd been out.

We went into the TV room. Hazel led him by the hand to the couch, sat him down bluntly, and climbed into his lap. I turned away. I couldn't watch. I couldn't watch on so many levels. Truth be told, I couldn't breathe. I went back to the kitchen, fell into a chair, fanned myself.

I could hear their voices. Her pointing out something on TV, him responding. Then: "I'll be right back. I have to tell your mom something."

No answer, which meant he'd picked a good time to leave, when she was glued to the show. I stood up. And there he was, in the kitchen. He opened his arms, and—*god help me*—I fell into them.

We kissed and we kissed. "I had to see you," he whispered. "I couldn't wait anymore."

"Shh," I said, because I wanted his mouth back, but I lived for his words. His waist brushed mine, new jeans, rough and dark. Then his hips. Something new, a step further than last time. My hips moved themselves out to meet his, and I felt him suck in his breath, and his hot hands squeezed the top of my arms, close to the shoulders, hard. And then his right hand came down, and his thumb brushed my right breast, and then my belly, the side of my hip, naked skin, above the sarong. I moaned.

"Mama!" Hazel yelled. "What are you doing in there?"

We jumped apart, as if we'd just touched a hot skillet. "What, honey?" I called, my heart jumping rope, doing peppers, fast fast fast.

"Could someone *please* come watch with me?"

"I'll go," Kevin said, like a parent whose daughter had called in the night.

"Me too," I said, like a guilty, adulterous mother.

We went. We sat down, on the couch, side by side but with a brick of space between us. Hazel—to my great relief—chose my lap to climb into this time. Our hands, mine and Kevin's, rested between us, inched closer, pinkies lightly touching, and I wondered if Hazel felt the heat inside me, pouring out through my skin, my pores, onto her own hot little body. How could she not?

After *Mister Rogers* we watched *Zoom.* A segment about a French girl, in Paris, who loved to dance. A segment about a blind boy and his Seeing Eye dog. A science experiment: putting oil and colored water in a jar, watching them separate and then swirling them together again, a tornado in a small, vivid universe. "I'm hungry," Hazel said, when the show ended. She turned to Kevin. "I'm having chicken nuggets. And buttered peas. Do you like chicken nuggets?"

"Chicken nuggets? Yup," he said.

"Want to eat over?" She jumped off the couch and grabbed his hands. "Can he, Mom? Please?"

I laughed nervously. "Hazel, I think he probably has better things to eat than chicken nuggets. And he probably doesn't eat dinner at six o'clock, like we do."

There was an awkward pause. The truth was, I needed him to leave. I was already worried that he'd been here this long. I was worried Hazel would see something in me and figure this out. I was worried she'd tell Paul he'd been here; well, of course she would, if he stayed for dinner, but if he left now, maybe there was hope. And—it was awkward, now. I was too turned on around him to be normal. I was flustered and bumbling, my emotions, my libido, displayed prominently.

Kevin searched me for an answer. He found it. "That's okay," he said, to Hazel. Did he sound disappointed? "I should go. Now that, you know, our shows are over."

Hazel frowned. "No!"

"Hazel," I warned.

She made a pouty face, but, lucky me, she backed down. "Well, can you come back tomorrow, then?"

He glanced at me. "Maybe," he said—hopefully, I thought.

"Good," she said. "Because the next day, we're going to Maine. So—I won't get to see you for a while."

He looked at me again, then back at her. "You're going to Maine?"

She nodded. "We go every summer. We stay at a lake, in a cabin. We can swim in there *or* in the ocean. The lake is better 'cause it's warmer and not nearly as wavy, and it doesn't sting your eyes, but I got a leech from it once. On my ankle. My dad had to pour salt on it to get it off me."

"Wow," he said, numbly—or was that wishful thinking on my part, that he was only half-listening, thinking about how he'd live without me? "That must have hurt."

"Nope. I mean, yeah, it probably hurt the leech. But it didn't hurt me." She laughed. She was still holding on to his hands.

"Well, that's good," he said.

"I know. We'll be back in nine days. Then a while after that my dad goes to Arkansas for his case, he's a lawyer, and he's trying to save a guy on death row, that's when they kill you because you killed someone else. And I have a fashion show in New York, with my grandpa. I'm wearing a miniskirt for one outfit, and high heels." She glanced at me. "Well, not *high* high. Medium. And then, the week after that, my school starts."

"Man," he said. "You have your schedule down pat, don't you." I wondered if he just wanted her to shut up.

"So come over tomorrow," she said. "And then not next week, but the—"

"Actually, I'll be away the week you get back," he said, cutting her off.

"You will?" I said. "Where are you going?"

"Well, first camping upstate with some friends, and then to my mom's." He addressed this to Hazel, as if she'd asked the question. "She lives in Atlanta, and she sent me a plane ticket to come visit her. Isn't that cool?"

"Where's Atlanta?" asked Hazel.

"It's in Georgia. Down south."

She frowned. "What are your friends' names?"

"My friends?"

"The ones you're going camping with."

*Go, Haze!* I thought.

"Well, there's Dave, and Ricky, and Reb—"

"Reb?" She laughed. "*Reb?* What kind of name is that for a boy?"

"Actually, it's not a boy. It's a girl. Rebecca."

My stomach clenched.

"You're going camping with a *girl*?" Hazel said.

"Two girls, actually." He smiled at her.

"Are they your—*girl* friends?" She put her hand to her mouth and giggled.

"No, they're not my *girl* friends," he said, amused, mimicking her. "They're girls, and they're my friends. But that's about it."

She nodded, satisfied, I suppose. "So that means I won't see you again until—" She paused, calculating. "The week after next?"

"Right," I said, and I wondered how I'd live without him. I wondered what he'd be doing camping, and what the girls looked like. Twenty-one, probably, stomachs twiggy and tight, skin rosy as cherries, gold hair glistening.

"But I'll see you tomorrow," Hazel said. "Right?" It was if she felt my urgency.

He looked at her. "Well, that's up to your mom," he said, his eyes on her. "I'm not sure if, you know, I'm invited."

"Of course you are," I said, and my blood flowed again, gushed.

He looked at me. "I'm supposed to work," he said. "But if I can get out of it, I'll be here."

Later, just before bed—we were reading *Ronia, the Robber's Daughter,* Astrid Lindgren's fiercely romantic coming-of-age masterpiece; Hazel and I were both riveted, captivated, mesmerized—my father called. He spoke to me for a moment—how are you, how's Paul, and so on—then asked to talk to Hazel, so I brought the phone to her room and handed it to her, in bed. She took it, pleased, and began to answer whatever questions he was asking. *Yes, no, yes.* She laughed, said something back. Yet another surprise: He was good with her on the phone, he knew how to engage. I went out of the room, brushed my teeth, came back. Hazel was chatting away. "We could do the one on the horse," she said. Pause. "Yeah. And the snow cone! A blue one, okay?"

"Does he have anything else to say to me?" I asked.

"Mom, shhh! I can't hear! What, Grandpa?" She paused, listening. "Okay. Wait—my mom wants to know if you have anything else to say to her." She listened, then turned to me. "No. Not unless you do."

"Oh. Um—I guess not. Tell him bye."

"She says bye," Hazel told him. "Yes. Okay. Bye from me too." She pressed the button to hang up.

I took the phone. She was smiling. "What did you talk about?" I asked, casually. "What were you saying about horses? You don't have to tell me if you don't want," I added, disingenuously.

"Oh. Um—he was asking me what photos I want to take next for my album." She looked at me. "We're making a photo album all of just me.

It's *so* cool. It's black velvet, I got to pick it out myself. We have *tons* of pictures already."

Did a red flag go up? I honestly don't remember. I climbed onto her bed and sat back against the wall, pulled my bare feet up and crossed them, Indian style, and said, "Really? What are they of?"

"They're of—I don't know! Everything! Blowing bubbles, eating candy, going to Serendipity. I'm the model, so—I get to say where we go, and I get to pose however I want. Or sometimes Grandpa just takes them, when I'm not really doing anything. Like, when I was ice-skating. Or one was at the museum, next to the Degas dancer."

"Huh. Are you allowed to take photos there?"

"I don't know, but Grandpa did." She laughed. "Oh, and one in my colored bubble bath, with a colored bubble beard. Grandpa has colored bubbles, they're *so* cool. They have like little rainbows on every single bubble."

"That sounds awesome." I shifted a little. "When did you take a bath at Grandpa's? In that bubble bath?"

"Last time! When I had my sleepover!"

"Oh. Right." We had talked surprisingly little about her two days with my father. She had told me what they'd done—carousel, zoo, "horsey-cart" ride—and that she'd had a good time. I hadn't pushed her for more information, content that they'd accomplished what they had, content to let details come out over time. And I hadn't spoken to my father, which I suppose wasn't odd; our contact had always been sporadic. Plus, I'd been preoccupied the past few weeks, my spare thoughts taken up with Kevin.

"Oh, and there's one of Godiva," she was saying. "He let me pick any candies I wanted, and then he took pictures of me eating them." She laughed. "They're funny. There's chocolate on my nose."

For some reason, that reassured me. I smiled. "He never told me about this album," I said. "Neither did you, actually. How come?"

"I don't know," she said, annoyed. She brightened. "Guess what? Grandpa's getting me a Polaroid camera for my birthday! He said I'll like to have the pictures come out instantly." She was sitting under my arm now, snuggling into me. I smelled her sweet hair, her soft skin. Her curls were getting thicker, longer. No more baby-fine hair. I ran my hands through it, softly, so I wouldn't pull the curls. "Tickle me," she said.

"Naah," I said. "You're much too old for that." I waited several seconds, for suspense, then jumped on her and tickled her frantically, listening to her beautiful, loud, racy laugh. When I stopped, we were both out of breath. "Haze," I said, keeping my voice as casual as I could.

She looked at me.

"Um—does Grandpa ever, like . . . does he ever do anything that feels, you know, embarrassing? That, you know, embarrasses you?"

"What do you mean?" She frowned.

"I mean, does he ever, like, ask you to do anything you don't want to do?"

"No!" she said. "Like what?"

I took a breath. "For example, when you're getting undressed," I said. "Does he give you privacy, or does he . . ." I stopped. "Never mind," I said. "Forget it."

"He gives me privacy, if I want it."

"Oh—*good*," I said, relieved. "And he doesn't ever, like, touch you, or—you know, in a way you don't want him to."

"Of course not! I mean, he *hugs* me, if that's what you mean."

"Well, that's good!" I said, too enthusiastically. "He *should* hug you!"

She glared at me. "Mama, Grandpa *loves* me!"

"I know, baby. I know he does, and that's great. He's an excellent grandfather to you. And you're lucky to have him. When I was your age . . . well, he wasn't the best father. I don't think he really even knew *how* to be a father back then. And now, in a way, I think he's making up for lost time, with you. And I'm so happy about that. I just—I want you to know that it's been a long time since he had a little girl, and now he's used to much older girls, the girls and women he photographs. The models. And sometimes little girls have different needs and, you know, limits, and he might not realize that. So if he ever does something you don't like or that doesn't feel right—you tell him you don't like it, and to stop. Okay? And then you tell me. Right away."

She looked troubled and maybe a little angry, and I didn't blame her. But there was more to say, and I felt like I had to say it, if only to get it out of my mind. "One time—" I hesitated, then dove in. "One time, when I was little, he took some photos of me that—well, that people thought were inappropriate."

"What's inappropriate?" She reached for Clod and hugged him to her face.

"Well, it just means that some people don't think it's right. Proper, or whatever. And when my father took the pictures, some people thought they weren't photos a father should be taking of a daughter."

"Why not?" She looked at me, wide eyed. "What was wrong with them?"

"Well, they were—I was wearing a nightgown—a grown-up nightgown, actually, more like a slip, it belonged to my mother—Grandma—and in some of the photos, some of my body was showing, and Grandma, in particular, was upset about it. *I* wasn't, really"—I took a breath and plowed on, absurdly—"but now, looking back, I do think maybe he shouldn't have taken them. Or at least, he should've asked my mother first."

"Why?" She stared at me.

"Well, because your private parts are *private.* So it should be up to a person herself, up to only you, if you want to expose them to a camera, but a child isn't old enough to make that decision for herself, so—"

"Then how would you ever have any naked pictures of kids?" Hazel interrupted.

"That's a really good point," I said. "I guess—it's not that it's wrong to have a naked picture of a child. It's the *way* it's shot. The photos of me seemed sexu—they seemed too grown up, to some people. To my mother. And that's why she felt they were wrong." I thought a minute. "Not that she said anything to *him* about it," I said, softly.

"Did *you* think they were wrong?" she asked.

"Yes," I said. "Or at least, I think so now. And it would bother me very much if he did that to you." I looked at her, hard. "Do you understand?"

She was frowning again.

I reached out to hug her, but she pushed me away. "You're talking too much!"

For a second I faltered. *How dare I, of all people, tell this child what's right and what's wrong?* "I know. I'm so sorry," I said. I took a breath. "Do you want me to read more?"

"No. I want to go to sleep."

I got down off her bed. I pulled her blankets up around her, tucked her in tight. Immediately, she kicked all of it back off except for the sheet.

"Listen," I said, tucking just the sheet around her now. "You don't have to worry about this. Your grandfather really, really loves you."

"I *know,* Mom! You *said* that!" She gave an exasperated sigh. "Can I just go to sleep now?"

"Yes." I bent down to kiss her. She turned her face away, so my lips grazed her ear. But as I rose, she reached up and grabbed my neck. "Good *night*!" she said urgently, and she smacked a kiss onto my cheek.

And still later, downstairs, in the dark, I put on an old mixed tape I'd had forever, something some boyfriend had once made for me: Bob Marley, Chris Smither, Bruce Springsteen, John Mellencamp, Vivaldi here and there. Slow, melancholy music, some of it romantic and yearning, some full of pain, bittersweet. I opened the windows and lowered the lights and moved around the room, slowly twirling. *Oh, the voices of passion.* This one was southern—twangy, male, hoarse—crooning on about love, how he's crazy in love, out of his head. His laugh caught in his throat, melted butterscotch, strong whiskey; windows down, hot wind blowing through your hair, eyes closed, saying, *yes, yes, yes,* because that's exactly what it is, he's got it just right, you'd follow this person to the end of the earth just to watch her—him—lie down and sleep.

My bare feet were cool on the floor. I thought about the first snow of the year, the pure silence of the flakes falling to the endless carpet of white. The cold air, the sweet, acrid smell of the flames from a fireplace rising into the night. Or the way it feels when you dive into a pool, split the still water and silently sink, down down down, into the loud, clear blue liquid mass, your arms pulling your body, sliding, gliding, smooth as a fish. Being alone somewhere that's usually full of people—a stadium, a school hallway—and feeling the space and quiet and solitude, the insignificance, and yet complete significance, of your minuscule self. Going back to a memory, a smell—calamine lotion, your grandmother's perfume—or a line of music, Led Zeppelin's "Stairway to Heaven," the first song you ever slow-danced to, in eighth grade, with some guy in a shirt that showed off his new muscles and Jovan musk splashed all over his neck; a guy you'd loved hopelessly, from afar, forever and ever, and then, my god, he asked you, *you,* to dance. Or biting into something rich when you're hungry: a ripe strawberry, sweet red juice filling your mouth; the first pull of a bottle of iced beer. Tasting cigarettes on someone's tongue in the cold, someone you crave, someone you can't live without.

I swooned in the dark. Tasted the pot from Kevin's mouth in my mind, and my body opened like a tulip in spring. The tape had ended; the room was silent and dark. I went to the window and looked out. His window was dark too. How odd, that he was so close by! Or maybe not. Maybe he wasn't there. Maybe he was out, off somewhere.

A car went by. Paul would be here soon. *Do something practical,* I thought. *Act your age.*

I went up to the attic and got down our two big suitcases. In my room, I took out my bathing suits: three old one-pieces and a new bikini I'd bought recently. I stripped off my clothes and pulled on the bikini. It was pale green, pretty, gently clinging. I looked in the mirror. *Is that me?* I pulled the tags off gently. Then I went into the closet and took out an old dress—brown, with tiny white flowers, hippie and romantic—that I'd worn the fall before Hazel was born, though back then I'd citified it over a tight black long-sleeved shirt and black leggings. Now, I dropped it on over just the bikini. It fell softly along my chest, rested at the top of my thighs, somewhere between too short and just right, depending on whether you were forty or thirty. And there I was, smack in between.

I shook out my hair. It was time to get it cut. *And who's gonna make me?* Paul's car pulled into the driveway. The engine shut off. And there it was: that mild wire of panic that buzzed through me every time he returned, as if I had just gotten caught red-handed doing something wrong. Quickly, I began to put things into the suitcase: dresses, shorts, T-shirts, running shoes. Downstairs, the door opened and shut. "Hello?" he called up, and I called back—hello, hello. It was 10:20. I kept packing. He came up, greeted me in person, went into the bathroom, came back. "Hey," he said, smiling.

"Hi." I smiled guiltily. "How are you?"

"Good," he said. "Really good. I'm starting to think I might actually get out of here on Friday with you and Hazel."

"Well, that's good," I said, and then, only half joking, "because I'm sure as hell not driving nine hours to Maine without you."

He shot me an amused look, then glanced at the open suitcase. "You started packing?"

I shrugged. "Thought I'd start early this year."

He began to unbutton his shirt, his white law-firm shirt: crisp, expensive, gold cuff links his grandfather had given him, an eccentric touch he employed now and then, which I'd always liked. "What's that dress?" he said, looking at me. He finished removing the shirt, tossed it in the hamper for me to take out and have cleaned.

I glanced down at myself. "Oh. It's old. Remember? I used to wear it to work, but with, like, work boots and leggings. Remember leggings?"

He laughed. "Oh yeah. God, 1992 at its worst. Or whatever year that was." He pulled off his pants, folded them neatly over the chair. He sat down on the bed in his boxer shorts. "It looks great on you," he said. His eyes scanned me, down, up again.

"Thanks." I smiled.

"What's under it? Do you wear it like that, or with something underneath?"

"I don't know," I admitted. "What do you think?"

"Like that."

I smiled again. "You think?"

"Definitely. What's underneath now?"

"Actually, a new bathing suit." I peeled off the dress to show him, sucking in my gut.

Paul nodded. "It looks great. Or, you look great *in* it, I should say. You really do. God, look at your body! You look better than when we first met."

I was eating it up—who wouldn't?—but then, in an instant, I realized the shift in his voice, and suddenly I wished I hadn't done that, let things heat up this way. "Thanks," I said quickly, and I reached for a big T-shirt, turned away from Paul and stripped off the bikini top and put the shirt on, fast. I pulled the bottoms off underneath it, yanked on white, cotton, not-very-sexy underwear. Paul climbed into bed, lay back on his pillow, hands under his head, watching me.

I went into the bathroom. I brushed, flossed, gargled with fluoride mouthwash. I rinsed my face, tweezed my eyebrows. My heart sagged. I put my hair in a ponytail. Wiped down the sink. *Okay,* I thought, and I went back to the room.

He was up. Up and waiting. "You know," he said, "we haven't made love in about a month. Maybe even more."

*Made love.* I hated that expression. What he meant was, we hadn't had sex. There was love, and there was sex. "Yes we have," I said automatically.

He shook his head. "I don't think so."

"Well, it's not like you've been lying around waiting for it."

His smile faded slightly. "I'm not *blaming* you, Elayna. I'm just stating a fact."

I didn't answer.

He watched me, waiting.

I turned out the light and climbed in, rolled onto my side, facing away from him.

He snuggled closer, threw his leg over my ass. I closed my eyes, wide awake. His hand began to caress the outside of my upper arm. Gentle caresses, back and forth. It felt like a bug, like a fly I wanted to brush away. I tried to endure it. Tried and tried, because I couldn't bear to be so mean. He kissed my shoulder lightly, and I knew what was next: His mouth would move down my body, maybe even get me off first—he'd always been generous about that—and then, just before he started *his* turn, he'd check in: *It's an okay time, right?* Meaning, not to get pregnant. And if it wasn't, he'd get up and find a condom and put it on carefully.

He kissed my shoulder again, a warm, gentle kiss.

"Stop it!" I yelled, yanking away.

"What? What's the matter?"

I had startled him, I knew. Guilt ripped through me.

"What was that about?" he said, finally. He sounded pissed off, and rightfully so.

I rolled over to face him, my own anger, rational or not, rising to meet his. "I just wanted you to stop touching me like that! I *hate* when you touch me like I'm some—some little *bird,* or something, some little creature you're petting. I *hate* that! It's so, so . . . *rote.* If you want to touch me, touch me *hard.* Like you mean it. Not just like—" Tears rose to my eyes. I brushed them off furiously.

He sat up. "Whoa," he said. He reached for his glasses and put them on in the dark. "Since when do you feel this way? Since when do you want to be—since when do you hate things to be loving?" He laughed a little, shaking his head, and I imagined his eyes rolling. *What the fuck do women want anymore, anyway?*

"I didn't say *loving,*" I said. "I said *gentle.*"

"Oh, what? So I'm supposed to slap you around? Gee, that sounds right up my alley." I didn't answer. He was breathing hard. "How long have you felt this way?" he said. "Because I've always been gentle, Elayna. Always. So what does this mean, that you, that you've had a problem with our sex life since we *met*? Because you know, I remember some good sex myself. Though maybe . . ." He laughed, a short, bitter laugh. "Maybe that was just me. Maybe I'm just one big fucking moron."

"No." I shook my head. "Not at all. Of course we've had good sex. Of course we have. We still do." It was true too. We did have good sex. Good *married* sex. When we had it.

Neither of us talked for a minute. I tried to formulate what I wanted to say, how to say it, but I didn't get very far. What should I tell him? And what was the truth? That I didn't love him anymore? But that wasn't true. I did love him. That I wanted a divorce? But I didn't, I didn't. I couldn't imagine life without him. That I didn't want to sleep with him because I wanted to fuck the boy next door, because this boy's skin made my skin come alive, alive in a way I thought I'd lost forever? *And oh, to be alive!* I thought of Celeste, wild and autonomous and alone.

"I'm tired," I said, a big, lame cop-out.

"You and me both," he said, copping out too.

"Let's just talk about it on vacation."

He was silent.

"Good night," I said, turning to him. His back was facing me now.

He didn't move, just mumbled something. Maybe good night. Maybe *Who are you, anyway? Because I don't even know you anymore.*

# Chapter Twenty-Four

But then, like all good married couples—at least, all those who can afford it—we went away. Kevin hadn't come back the day after we'd kissed in the kitchen, and by now, of course, that slight feeling of insult and disappointment and ambivalence mingled with enormous relief. Paul and I loaded our car and roof trunk with sheets and trash bags, hiking boots and sweatshirts, bathing suits and backgammon and chess sets and books, and, last but not least, our kid, and we drove up to Maine, where, in the driveway of the sap-smelling cabin nestled on Lake Ruckaho, pine needles under our feet, we unloaded it all and moved in. We had been coming here for years, and we knew well the antique stove and red-checkered curtains, the daddy longlegs that hunkered on the bathroom walls, the toads that congregated near the field of black-eyed Susans in back. The way you had to hold down the flusher, then let go, then press once more to get the toilet to fill up again.

In Maine, the three of us sat down to dinner in the cabin at night and had normal family conversations—or we went out to the Italian restaurant in town, where we ate spaghetti and watched the mail boat go by, the sky rides take off over the lake. This was Paul's time with Hazel, some of his only substantial time all year, and as always, as I observed them together—and as I had a chance to catch up with a relaxed Paul myself—I remembered exactly why I'd married him. He took her out on a whale watch while I went to a movie and had a long day alone in the town, and they came home red lipped and sand streaked, having seen "literally millions of whales." He took her fishing in the rickety old rowboat while I sat on the beach and tried not to fantasize about you-know-who. And after a few days, what desire I had left for him mostly washed away with the waves, replaced by love and gratitude for Paul.

So I sat on the beach and wrote bad poetry, about the water, the sky, the sea—natural things, *safe* things—all of it reminding me of why I hadn't become a poet: I couldn't get below the surface, couldn't succeed in describing something in a different or unusual way. I resorted, every time, to emotion and metaphor—not original, but obvious, trite. My love was not like a red red rose, but like a rose with thorns, dangerous, sharp . . . *Ouch.* I threw down my notebook and closed my eyes. Kevin was there in my lids. I forced them open again.

I got up from my beach chair. "Paul!" I yelled out to the dock, where he and Hazel were splayed flat, warming up in the sun. "I'll go get the lobsters, okay?" He waved back, a muted *Fine.* We were planning to boil them in the cabin that night—Paul's idea, something he'd always wanted to try. I was less than ecstatic about the prospect. I ate lobster, though only once or twice a year, but still, it was one thing to go to a restaurant and be served one on a plate—red, succulent, surrounded by lemon wedges and French fries—and another altogether to go pick one out of a pool and take it home to boil alive. But I was trying to be a Good Wife. *You should want your spouse's happiness more than you want your own,* I thought, remembering something a friend's rabbi had told her when she was preparing to marry. And off I went to comply.

At the Lobster Pound: tanks of lumbering purple crustaceans, thick rubber bands on their claws, piled on top of each other in abject misery. I tried not to look as the teenage boy, face sun-baked redder than a cooked lobster himself, reached into the tank to haul up my picks. "Any three," I said, turning away, and he did the honors, stuck them into white take-out boxes and handed the bagful to me. Outside, I put them in the backseat, then pulled away gingerly, twitching as though they'd already escaped and were crawling up the back of the seat. I felt worse with each mile, and by the time I got home, sympathetic claustrophobia was suffocating me.

In the end, of course, we couldn't do it. "You're gonna *kill* them?" Hazel yelled, when she realized. "In a pot of *hot water*? And *eat* them?" She burst into tears. I stayed silent but couldn't resist shooting Paul an "I told you so" look, and Paul—probably secretly relieved himself, in that "Be careful what you wish for or it might come true" way—rolled his eyes but stuffed the creatures back in their boxes and drove us all to the beach, where the three of us, checking that no one was watching, walked out on a pier and, after Paul clipped the bands on their claws (no easy task), poured them into the ocean, back to life. We stood there as they fell through the silvery froth and into the gently rocking black sea, moon beaming down from the black sky above, and I thought, *All the deep, dark, seemingly impenetrable things—sea, sky, moon, air—actually full of life and mystery once you get inside.* If *you get inside.* In the distance, points of color from the rides on a boardwalk somewhere, Ferris wheels, tilt-a-whirls, pirate ships. "Goodbye!" Hazel yelled to the lobsters, and we all said a prayer that they wouldn't get caught again, as they surely wouldn't end up with three suckers like us the next time.

I held Paul's hand on the way back to the car, feeling the sand give gently under my feet, the cold salt wind slap my hair against my face. Hazel was on his other side. "Thank you, Daddy," she said, from out of the blue, and he said, "For what?" and she said, "Saving the lobsters instead of eating them." Paul laughed. "Babe, I think you get the credit for that one; if it were up to me, right now I'd be wiping drawn butter off my chin." And we went to the diner and had grilled-cheese sandwiches instead, feeling virtuous and humane, and then we drove to the next town and took a risk on a local production of *Fiddler on the Roof,* and the man who played Tevye brought tears to my eyes when he sang, to his wife of decades, the mother of his daughters, and the woman to whom, way back when, his marriage had been arranged, "But do you love me?" And in the end, of course, she admits, "I suppose I do," and it's breathtaking.

We stopped for raspberry ice-cream cones on the way home, the three of us sharing a tiny round metal table in a big old wooden barn-turned-café, and when we got back to the cabin, we all declared it a perfect vacation day, a ten out of ten, before tucking Hazel tightly into bed.

"I wish I didn't have to sleep in here alone," she sighed, as I headed out of the room. I stopped and turned around. Uncharacteristically, I hadn't had to push thoughts of Oliver out of my mind all day, because I hadn't had them. "I wish you didn't too," I said, not sure if that was what she meant. She sighed, and seconds later, I heard her deep breaths of sleep, and I took my own deep breath and tiptoed away.

In bed that night—on our creaky, saggy, country bed—I snuggled up to Paul for the first time since our fight back at home. He stiffened for a minute, then relaxed and came right back, hardly (like most men, I imagined) one to hold the moral upper hand when it came to sex. One thing led to another, and I noticed he tried to be a little rougher than usual, my sweet, docile husband, and just the thought that he was trying, that he had made an effort about that, made me that much more determined to let this happen, this one small good thing. When he started to push into me, I felt him hesitate again—I knew he wanted to ask if the timing was okay—but to his great credit, he didn't, nor did he pull out at the end, as he'd done in the past when we didn't use anything. I suppose he'd decided to trust me, at any rate, not to do anything that might wreck the rest of the week.

The vacation was over before it ended; Paul's office called, and he stepped into the den to fire up his laptop, snapping at Hazel on the way for refusing to pick up her books from the floor. She deserved it, but still. And then the VCR broke, and then the rain came, three days in a row, until Hazel didn't want to do the library, the town, the grocery store anymore, and if I'd had to play Mancala or Clue or Guess Who? one more time, they'd have had to drag me away in a straitjacket. I stuffed all our dirty clothes—now damp as dishrags—into pillowcases, and Hazel and I drove to the Laundromat, stopping to buy ourselves cream-filled doughnuts, a coloring book, crayons. So she colored as the clothes whirled around and an old woman with a pot gut and tattoos on both biceps chain-smoked nearby, and I closed my eyes and there was Kevin, and this time, I let him stay, because he didn't have power over me anymore. It was over. I would tell him so as soon as we got home. And I thanked the powers that be that we'd all gone away when we had, that I'd had this chance to be gently slapped back into line with everyone's faculties still intact.

The machine when we arrived, eleven o'clock Saturday night: Celeste ("Bonjour! Back from gay Paris, call me!"), Pansy ("You didn't give me a written schedule before you left, Elayna, and I have no idea when Hazel's coming back. This is a professional day-care center, not a cage where you drop off your children any which time or day blab blab blab blab blab blab."), Clementine's mother, asking if we were going to the summer's-end sing-along at the school next week, which of course I'd forgotten about. A couple of hang-ups. That was that.

Paul was carrying Hazel past me, her head lolling over his shoulder, hair a squashed orange cloud. "I'll take her," I said, hanging up the phone. We did the transfer, him grateful, anxious to get the car unloaded so he could get back to work, me grateful for the sweet-smelling load in my arms, moist hands pressing my shoulders, bony knees stabbing my hips. Our house looked pretty but dirty, in that way you notice both the nice furniture in the living room and the dirt in the kitchen only when you've been gone. The fridge—modern, familiar, mine—was nonetheless desolate. Suitcases piled in the hallway, mail exploding out of the box. Ah, reentry.

I took the week slowly: returned the calls one at a time, did my work, did the laundry, restocked the fridge. I didn't call Celeste yet. Somehow, I couldn't face hearing about Paris, not that she was one to bore you with details of her trip, but I was trying to keep my mind out of the gutter, as it were, and refocused on the good, important things in my life—to make them be enough to sustain me. Paul was nonexistent, Kevin off on vacation, I supposed—at any rate, I didn't see him—Hazel back at Pansy's, glad to be there. In the afternoons, I picked her up and we went swimming at the pool, came home and made pasta and turkey dogs, watched our shows, read *Black Beauty*—crying when poor little Merrylegs died, rejoicing when Beauty found a kind home at the end—then took our cool shower and fell asleep together in her bed afterward. In the mornings, I awoke, well rested, at five and went out for a run while it was still cool and wet and steel blue, the flower beds islands of color in the dark, stretching and yearning toward the day. I came home drenched and invigorated before they woke up, and poured myself orange juice and escaped briefly into a book as the sun rose through the kitchen windows. It was the week before the final week of Hazel's summer break, the penultimate week, the proverbial calm before the onslaught: the sing-along and the fashion show and Paul's hearing and the rumblings of Hazel's school year, and all it would all bring with it.

Monday morning of week two—or the final week, depending on how you looked at it. It was Labor Day, but Paul had left for Arkansas and Hazel was at Clementine's and I was working. Or supposed to be. I sat at the table, unable to focus. We were doing an issue on the magical realists—Allende, Borges, García Márquez—who I must say didn't much interest me, and besides, since New York departed en masse at the end of August through Labor Day (all, it appeared, except the lawyers), anything I faxed or emailed to anyone today would sit idle anyway. The chocolate I had eaten was making me edgy instead of intense and passionate, as it usually did. I got up, stretched, and wandered to the front door and then out into the world, which was balmy, steamy, a steady shriek of crickets, the mature flowers almost fecal in their staggering smell, their desperation to display themselves before their buds wilted and fell away forever. I went down our walk and turned right. I'd cruise around the block, then try again.

I don't know what I was thinking, but it must have been good. I walked, head down, feet moving fast, brain so far off that I slammed into Kevin on the sidewalk. "Whoa," he said, reaching out to steady me. "Manic power walker. Watch out."

I looked up at him and gasped.

He laughed. "You okay?" Sasha wagged her tail at me.

I backed up. "Yes. God. Sorry." I reached up to my hair, down again.

"It's okay. Good thing it was me and not, like, some tree you slammed into." He smiled, then took a step back and gently assessed me. "Long time no see. Did you have a good trip?"

I took a deep breath, trying to slow my heart. He looked tan and handsome, yet oddly—thankfully—I didn't feel attracted to him. Immediately, I felt myself relax a notch. I bent to pet Sasha, giving my heart a little more time. He was a cute neighbor boy, nothing more. We were friends. No, not even friends, now. Friend*ly.* Yes, we'd toed the line, maybe even crossed it once or twice, but that was over, water under the bridge, and it wouldn't happen again. There was nothing to end, nothing to tell him.

I stood back up. "I did," I said. "How 'bout you?" And my voice was easy now, filled with relief.

"It was—it was good," he said. "Yeah. It was nice to get away." He bent to pat his dog. "I'm glad to be back, though. Sasha missed me. Didn't you, Sash." He put his hand on her nose, and she licked it. Was there something slightly different about him, slightly less confident? "And how's my friend Hazel?" he asked, and then he was the same as before, just exactly the same. I was the one who had changed.

"She's good." I took a step. "She had a great time in Maine." Another step, and he fell in beside me. We both walked a little. "We're glad to be back too, though," I added.

Could the talk have been smaller? *But this is right,* I told myself. *This is how one talks to one's neighbor and friend.* "She's all pumped up for the fashion show this Wednesday," I went on. "She's sleeping at my father's afterward, and then on Friday there's an end-of-summer sing-along at her school. She goes back next week, unbelievably."

We rounded the corner. I was boring him to tears, I was sure, the insufferable fool who actually answers, in detail, a question asked purely out of politeness.

"Man," he said. "I wish we'd had stuff like that when I was in school. I used to dread the first day. I'd have stomachaches for weeks beforehand."

"You did?" I slowed down a little and looked at him.

He shrugged. "I was nervous, I guess. I thought I'd get picked on." I must have smiled, because he said, "Like I told you, I wasn't exactly some Neanderthal. I was the kid who smoked weed in the janitor's closet, then snuck down to the art department to throw pots and flirt with the gay art teacher."

I raised my eyebrows. "But you're not—I mean—*were* you gay? Back then?"

He laughed. "God, no. I was granted that blessing. Otherwise, I'd be dead. My old man would've killed me." He shook his head again. "Nah, I just happened to like the guy. He was a decent dude. Unlike most of the teachers at that place."

So much for the small talk. We walked on for a while, silent. "Where are you going?" he asked.

"What? Oh. Actually, I was just walking around the block to try to jump-start myself. I'm supposed to be working."

"What are you working on?"

I shrugged. "Nothing too exciting. That's the problem. Magical realism, this issue. Not really my thing, especially in August."

"Oh, that's—what's his name. Gabriel García Márquez."

I looked at him. "You know him?"

"Love in the land of—"

"Cholera. Yeah. *Love in the* Time *of Cholera,* actually."

"Right. I liked that book."

"It's funny," I said, "I can't get into him. Maybe I'm too much of a pragmatist."

"I thought you were a romantic."

I blinked. "Did I say that?"

He nodded. "A while ago."

"Oh. Well, I guess I've changed." We both laughed, but the laughs were different: his amused, mine slightly nervous. *Had* I said that? To him? Christ.

Sasha lunged toward a squirrel, and after letting her go for a second, Kevin reeled her in again. "So, what will you do for two whole days without Hazel?" he asked.

"I don't know. Paul's gone too, actually. He has his big trial." I thought a second. "Maybe I'll just stay in New York, at Celeste's. Catch up on movies, or—"

"Wait." He looked at me. "You're going in this Wednesday?"

I nodded. The show was earlier this time—three o'clock instead of five thirty—so I'd need to have her there by one or two.

"I'll be there Wednesday too," Kevin said.

"You will?" It was casual, casual. Whatever I felt was buried deep inside me.

"I have to drop off some stuff for a client in the morning," he said. "And later, for dinner, I'm meeting a friend. In between, I've got hours to kill." He looked at me. "We should grab a beer or a coffee, or something."

I shifted on my feet. I thought, *What would be the harm?* I thought, *I don't need to see every single fashion show she's in.* I thought, *How long since I've lunched with a friend, a guy friend, in New York?* A black SUV blew past us and disappeared around the corner. I smelled gas, its fuel, and then its exhaust. "Okay," I said. "Where should we meet?"

He thought a minute. "There's a bar down on Thompson near Canal, a little hole in the wall called Billy's. We could meet there at, I don't know. Two? Three?"

"Three sounds good." I thought a second. "If you're not there by, say, three forty-five, I'll just assume you're not coming."

"Okay," he said. "I'm coming, though."

I let his remark slip right over my head, flutter away with the breeze. We were almost back home. "I'll leave you here," he said. "We've got a date with the park, Sash and I. See you Wednesday, if not before." Off they went.

I stood still for a moment. My brain felt slightly blurry, slightly buzzed. *The heat,* I told myself. *Summer in New Jersey.*

But Hazel would be home soon. I had work to do, work. I turned and headed back home, walking fast; eager, at last, to sit down and do it.

# Chapter Twenty-Five

Wednesday morning. I closed up shop, packed up Hazel for her overnight, drove us to New York, this time, and found a parking space on the Upper West Side. Then we took the subway down and met my father, who greeted Hazel with open arms, a Nikon-rimmed neck, and a red sun hat he'd bought for her. I left to meet Celeste for a quick lunch, the details of which I don't remember, except that she told me about Paris and more about Stephen and some about her new book, and I didn't tell her I was meeting Kevin afterward. At the time, I'm sure, I told myself it was purely because I knew she wouldn't believe me that it was innocent, that we were—really—just friends.

She invited me to stay that night at her place, and I told her I might, since my parking spot was good for two days. She gave me her spare key—"just in case I'm not home"—and we kissed and hugged and parted ways.

It wasn't raining when I started downtown, but the sky was white—not gray, not blue, but white, like cocaine—and as I walked, it morphed into a dark silver green, and, knowing it would pour, I swung into some little sports store and charged myself an overpriced waterproof hooded shell. The rain didn't actually start until I'd made it to a block from where Kevin had said we'd meet, and then the sky opened up and crashed down, and people around me and beyond, like startled roaches, scuttled for cover in all directions. I, in contrast, calmly put up my hood and stood at a corner waiting for the light, and a bike messenger, stopped with me, black bag over his shoulder, black skullcap glued on his head, said, "Now, there's a lady likes to get *wet.*" I smiled, the light turned green, he pedaled away, and I continued toward the bar, where, squinting into the mostly empty dark,

I spotted Kevin—in a booth, drinking a beer and reading the *Village Voice*—and I, squishing in my sneakers, legs soaked (I wore a just-above-the-knee skirt), pushing off my hood, headed over and slipped in across from him. "Hi," I said.

He looked up and smiled. "Hey. You're early."

"Am I? My watch broke. I've been early all day, for fear of being late."

He laughed. "Can I get you something?" he said, after a minute.

"Thanks—I'm okay. I just had lunch with Celeste."

"Yeah? How's Celeste?" He sipped his beer.

"She's good. She's all about her book, these days."

He nodded. He put down his beer and looked at me. "I wasn't sure you'd come."

I raised my eyebrows. "Why wouldn't I?"

"I don't know. I just wasn't sure you would."

"Well—here I am." I felt giddy. *The rain,* I told myself. *The water on my bare legs.*

He glanced at his paper. "I'm looking at movies. You saw *Dancer in the Dark* back when it came out, right?"

"No."

"You didn't? Wow. I thought I was the only one who missed that."

I shook my head. "I don't even know what it's about, to tell you the truth."

He smiled. "Me either. Just that it's supposed to be really good. Weird." He looked at the paper. "It's playing, for some reason—must be a revival. In—" He glanced at his watch. "Twenty minutes. You don't want to go, do you?"

"Sure." I stood up. "That sounds perfect. Can we make it?"

We ran, north and east, blocks and blocks, till we skidded into the mostly empty cinema, damp and panting. "Want popcorn?" he whispered, as the previews began, and I shook my head. We settled in to watch the movie, side by side but not touching, two friends out together, legal and aboveboard, no sweat.

Except, something happened. Partway through the movie, the story took a turn for the devastating, and shortly after that, a torrent was unleashed inside me. I sat there, a rag doll, face in my hands, tears streaming down my face. It was mortifying. I wanted to leave, but I knew if I did he would only follow me—and as bad as it was to be a mess in the dark next to him, it would've been worse standing out in the light. So I sat, and I sobbed, as I witnessed this sad boy with the slowly-going-blind mother who'd saved money from her factory job to buy him an operation without which he would suffer the same fate, and then, when someone stole her money and charged *her* with theft to cover it up, refused to lie about her innocence and was sentenced to death. A hideous hanging witnessed by her son. I sat, paralyzed except for my sobbing, staring at the screen in sheer misery.

Kevin handed me a napkin, which I used so completely that he handed me another one, who knew from where. He put his arm around me, a friendly, *hang-in-there* hug, and I turned away and huddled as far from him as I could, crying so hard I thought I might actually be sick, until the movie, the torture, finally ended. We sat as the few other people filed out around us, till it became obvious that we'd have to leave too. He had taken back his arm. I was holding my breath, imagining candy stores, yipping puppies . . . anything to move my mind to a more hopeful place. It was working, a little—but slowly. "Wow," he said softly, at one point, just to let me know that, if he wasn't exactly feeling my pain, at least he sympathized. He was as decent as he could have been. Finally, when the ushers began sweeping popcorn buckets from the aisles, he said, "Come on. I know somewhere we can go and just sit." He took my hand and pulled me out of there.

It was still raining, making the sky darker than the evening summer light would have had it, and I was thankful for the dark, for the rain, for the crowds of raincoat-clad people sandwiching us on sidewalks, engulfing us at corners. I left my hood off this time, letting the rain saturate me, wash the snot and salt from my face. Kevin still had my hand, and I clung to him as he led the way. He found the place quickly—small, dark, Irish, and crowded, this time, with almost-party-hour drinkers—and scored us a booth near the rear. "Be right back," he said, after depositing me in it. He made his escape, and I wondered if he'd ever come back, because I wouldn't have, if I were him.

I sat there. I knew I should do something to clean myself up, but I didn't have the energy to move. In the back of my mind—the *very* back, I know now—I wondered how Hazel had done in the show, whether she was at my father's by now or he'd taken her out for dinner. Kevin returned with two mugs of beer and a wooden bowl of shelled peanuts. "Bass ale," he said, sliding in. "If you don't like it, I'll drink them both and get you something else. I know the bartender."

I took a deep breath, tried to focus. "You do?"

"I used to hang here a lot, when my mom lived in town. We got friendly after a while." He smiled, almost sheepishly.

I sniffed. "Listen," I said, "I'm sorry for being such a jerk. I don't usually—I'm not in the habit of falling completely to pieces at a movie."

"Well, that movie was . . ." He shook his head. "I feel like a jerk for suggesting it."

"No! I wanted to see it too. I had no idea it would be—"

"What? The most mind-blowing, gut-wrenching flick you've seen since, like, *Platoon*? *Titanic*?" He pulled a small joint from somewhere, glanced around, then lit it and took a hit.

"Well—yeah, actually." I wondered how he knew *Platoon.* Had he even been born yet?

He offered the joint to me, but I declined; I had decided on vacation that, along with ending my relationship with him, I wouldn't smoke anymore. So instead, I inhaled his smoke. It helped. I ran my fingers through my damp hair, wiped my face on a napkin. "Let me pay you for the drink," I said, reaching for my purse.

He laughed. "You can get the next round. Which, like this one, will be free."

We sat for a while, watching boys shoot pool, surrounded by the white noise of the room, and eventually the place and the booze and his casual presence began turning my despair into a sort of cozy despondency, a buzzed half awareness that left me lulled and dreamy. I sipped my beer. Kevin gently stubbed out the joint, tiny now, and it sat in the ashtray, damaged but still with some life. I wanted to take it out and light it again. "Thanks," I said suddenly. "Thanks for being so nice to me."

"My pleasure," he said, after a second. He had an odd look on his face, one I couldn't quite read, and he continued to look at me until I had to look down. He got up again, this time for the bathroom, and suddenly I felt ridiculous. What was I doing here? Kevin reappeared and sauntered to the bar once again, leaned over, and said something to the bartender, a weathered-looking guy who laughed and slapped him lightly in the face. *When he returns,* I thought, *I will tell him I have to go, and then I will walk out of here.*

I took a final sip of beer and put down my glass. It was decided, then. Kevin was back. He slid in once more and looked at me, almost quizzically. "Feeling better?"

I nodded. "I am. Thank you. But listen—I should go."

I saw something flicker in his face, something subtle but absolutely there. "Oh—don't go," he said.

I blinked. Perhaps I said, *What?* Because he said it again: "Don't go. Please?"

Can I tell you what his words did? They shattered the wall of honor I'd been building for days, that I'd only just moments ago cemented. They shattered it into a pile of bricks, and then dust, and then they blew the dust away—*poof!*—just like that. "Don't go," he said, one more time, and I swooned in my chair. And my pilot flame ignited somewhere, blue and fiery.

I opened my mouth, but nothing came out. So I closed my eyes, and I mustered every ounce of resistance I had and created a mental blanket, which I dropped over that flame. Immediately, fire shot back through the blanket.

Kevin put his palms on the battered, clammy wooden table and leaned toward me. "I love being here with you, when you don't have to hide, you don't have to go anywhere. Is it okay to say that?" He frowned. "Well, fuck it. I said it anyway."

I could feel myself breathe.

"So now I might as well finish." He looked down at his hands, then at me again, his eyes hard and clear. "I just—I like you so much, Elayna. It's just how I feel. I felt it from that first day I saw you, and it hasn't really gone away. And I know, you know, that you're married, and nothing can ever really happen between us, but—I still feel what I feel." He looked at me, almost pleading. "When you were crying before, when you were all wet from the rain? I just—I feel like I want to *save* you, or something. Like you're this—this—whatever. You're the writer, you find the word." He took a deep breath. "So—now you can go, if you want, or tell me off, or whatever. I just wanted to say that first. It wasn't fair if I couldn't tell you. I'm sick of not being able to say it."

I sat there, not moving. He frowned for another few seconds, and then his face changed again, something gentler coming over it. "You know what I love about you?" he said. "This, right here." He moved his hand to the bone just below my shoulder, my collarbone or maybe clavicle, and pointed with two fingers, but he didn't touch me, just traced the bone slowly back and forth in the air, shoulder to neck and back again.

I breathed. I could feel his hands on my body even though he wasn't touching me, the way, when someone tickles the air near your skin, you feel the tickle and laugh. His not-quite-touch sent chills through me, raised goose bumps on my flesh. His fingers rose to my face, and now he did touch: with the tips of his fingers, he lightly traced the top of my left cheekbone from my nose to the side of my face, as if he were wiping away a tear or maybe just seeing what was inside of me.

That was it. Something opened deep in my heart or my gut, and everything that had been gathering, pent up, in there wound tightly, streamed out. My body moved itself forward, my arms reached out to him, my palms touched the sides of his face and pulled him toward me. He met me halfway, and then—who, I ask, had I been kidding?—we were kissing again.

And this time, there was nothing to stop us; no husband on his way, no neighbors, no daughter to protect . . . only a few happy barfolk, who, if they noticed at all, probably only cheered us on. My head was reeling, my mouth greedy as a baby bird's, my body pushing, yearning toward him, until the table, it seemed, was the only thing keeping us from merging into each other completely. We kissed and kissed. I drank him in, and I felt him do the same. And then he pulled away, his eyes locked on mine, and he slid out of his seat, and this time he came over and moved in next to me, and his arms came around me and I dissolved into him once more, and we kissed again, tasting and devouring each other, tearing ourselves apart so we could instantly come together again. "I want you," he whispered hotly into my ear. "I've waited so fucking long." His words, words uttered countless times in countless bars before, soothed and petrified and absolutely, completely lit me aflame. I moaned, and he kissed me harder, shaking fingers, warm palms. It was ecstasy.

Even now, I couldn't tell you which was more exciting: the exquisite, downright chemical deliciousness of him—his tongue, lips, earlobes, body, skin—or the utter thrill, the rapturous thrill, of him wanting me as much as I wanted him. I touched his cheekbones, his temples, his eyelids. I couldn't get enough. His hands moved to my breasts, both hands, together, and he touched me through my bra, through my shirt, and I moaned again, into his mouth. He made a noise, then took my hand and put it on his crotch, and I felt him, hard, through his jeans. Astonishingly, I felt myself salivate.

I pulled my hand off. "We can't," I stuttered. "Not here."

He moved away from me roughly. Immediately, I felt revealed and vulnerable, like a cut with the Band-Aid torn off—desperate to have him on me again. He slipped out of the booth one last time, grabbed my hand, and pulled me out after him. "Come on. We're getting out of here."

To this day, I don't know where he took me. Maybe the bartender's apartment, maybe some apartment-like hotel room. All I know: It was close by, it was dark, it was inside a small tenement building with a dirty entryway and a row of rusty metal mailboxes and a battered, slow, creaky old elevator you had to pull open and closed with a metal lever, by hand. He maneuvered me in, got us up, hauled me off at some floor. We kissed feverishly, our fast, deep breaths matching each other's, his hard, lean, thrummingly alive body moving to and with me. He produced a key from somewhere and put it into a lock and then we were inside a hot, dark room. I was rabid and dizzy, nipples tingling, breaths coming in bursts now, mixing with his.

Somehow in all this, I had the wherewithal—or, in retrospect, the lack thereof—to take off my wedding ring. I suppose, in my mind, or what was still functioning of it, I somehow believed that it wasn't as much of a betrayal to Paul if I didn't have on the ring; that, instead of cuckolding him and betraying our marriage, I could somehow be *un*married just for that night. At any rate, at some point between the street and that room, I took off the ring and slipped it into my purse. That must have been my last conscious thought. After that, my intellect pulled its own metal latch and slipped away to hibernate.

And then it was just me and my body, my libido and Kevin, and that room. Shades drawn, one small lamp providing light enough to make out a thick rug, a wooden desk, and a bed. Metal fan on, somewhere, pushing the hot air around. Kevin was pulling up my shirt, and I was clinging to his shoulders, trembling, fighting to keep myself vertical. My knees shook as his hands grazed my belly, my thighs—outside and in—and then my underpants, under my skirt. "Oh, please," I moaned, and he whispered, "What, baby? Tell me, tell me. I want to do everything to you."

My shirt was off; he pulled it over my head and dropped it to the floor. Then, his lips on my lips, tongue pulsing with mine, he pressed my nipples with his thumbs, through my thin cotton bra, then used the same thumbs to flick the cotton away, so my breasts tumbled out, into the hot room, into the palms of his hands. His mouth left mine and came down; he sucked one nipple, hard, and then the other, a jolt shooting through me each time, and then he slipped his hand up my skirt and touched me, with two straight fingers, through my soaked underwear. I came violently, buckling into him.

*Oh god.* I lay, still standing, on him and against him, all my muscles dissolved into sand, and he held me until I could breathe again, until I could stand on my own. And then I moved my mouth up, and my mouth found his mouth, and I tasted the smoky pink of his tongue, the sweet intensity and earnestness and pure loveliness of him. I started to tell him no one had ever made me do that before—not like that, anyway—but he shushed me and pulled off his shirt and now it was my turn to get to touch him. I lowered myself before him and tasted his skin: nipples, stomach, ribs. I flicked my tongue inside the rim of his underwear. He was breathing, heavy but quiet, eyes closed, concentrating; amazingly, I thought, he was standing stark still, trembling only slightly. I pushed his jeans down just a little, not unbuttoning them, so I could see his belly button, and then I pressed my tongue hard inside it. He moaned softly, a small, deep, "uh," and then he was quiet again, and his concentration, his focus and intention, reminded me of watching him work with clay. But now his hands were mine, curled into loose fists, resting at his sides, wrists facing me.

I unbuttoned his pants, and he opened his eyes and shoved the jeans down and stepped out, pants and underwear both, so his naked body faced me. I touched him, felt his velvety prick, the hardness of the flesh underneath, and then, at last, I took him into my mouth, tasting salt and bleach and gingery, naked male skin. His hands twitched and stilled; his head was back, his body erect, and the only sounds were his breath, long and hard and even, and the fan, whirring behind us somewhere. I held him inside me, moving just a little, letting him farther in, and in the dead quiet, I swear, I could taste his heartbeat, I could feel it and taste it inside him inside me.

For a long time, I just held him like that. Then, slowly, I began to move my mouth, gently at first, and then faster, more firmly.

He wrapped his hands in my hair, moving a little with me, and I tasted him in the back of my throat now, like citrus, the peel of a lemon, clean grapefruit skin. "Uh," he breathed, and he moved harder, faster, but then, suddenly, he stopped and pulled out. He took hold of himself and squeezed, closing his eyes for a moment. He opened them. "Wait," he said.

He disappeared and came back with a towel, which he spread on the rug. Then he pulled me to him and kissed me again, deeply, his body against mine as he slid off my skirt, unhooked my bra, got me out of my underpants. He pushed me gently onto my knees on the towel and joined me there, his breath hot in my mouth, in my ear. Then he turned me around, so my back was to him, and he held me like that, hands around my back and on my breasts, pushing his hips and his hard-on against my ass. "I love your body," he whispered. "You're a gorgeous woman. Perfect. Let me do something."

Gently, he pushed my shoulders and head to the floor, one palm supporting my stomach from underneath, so my back end stayed raised. He kissed my spine, my tailbone, goose bumps rising to meet his lips, and I hid my face in my arms, every part of me trembling. "I once made a sculpture like this," he said softly. "But you're so much more beautiful. Look at you. Look at this." He ran his palm over one side of my ass, down the back of my thigh, up between my legs. I shuddered, trying not to move, aware of my hard, heavy breath.

He kissed the base of my tailbone, and then lower, the edge of inside. I flinched. "Shhh," he said, but he moved his mouth down farther, reached my vagina, got his hands there from wherever they were and spread me apart and gently put his tongue in. I made a sound like a cry, and I felt myself falling, dissolving toward the ground, but he held me up with his hand as his mouth kept going. And suddenly I wanted him inside me, so badly I started to shake. I tried to sit up, but he held me, gentle but firm, and then I felt him there, a different presence now, and he pushed himself into me.

My body went limp, all muscles giving in as he thrust, hard, then harder. *Oh my god.* My insides opened up, letting him in, and I began to move with him. He reached around to the front of me and touched me again, and once more I came. And then he came, at last, again and again, exploding into me.

Afterward, we collapsed. I lay under him as our breath subsided, and I felt myself, in the dark, like a parachuter at dusk, slowly, slowly sinking. Down, down, through the crust of the earth, into the dark underground and beyond. I fell asleep. And I might have slept forever, spent and defiled, if the unthinkable hadn't happened.

My phone rang.

At first, I ignored it. He didn't move, and I didn't want to either. Couldn't, in fact. So though my body tensed, I kept my eyes closed and tried to block out the sound, or pretend it was part of a dream. It rang four times, and then stopped.

*Relief.* My body relaxed again, my mind still not quite there. Kevin lay on top of me, heavy, hot, unbudging.

My phone rang again, shattering the air. I jolted awake.

It rang again. I rolled out of his arms, pushing him off me. It rang a third time, from inside my purse, wherever the hell I had dropped it.

I stood up, dizzy, my heart beating furiously now as my eyes flitted around, trying to see. It rang once more, a hideous, horrible chime. My hands moved frantically, and then I found it, grasped it, pressed buttons, got it up to my ear. "Hello?" I panted.

"Momma?" Hazel said. "Mom! I want to come home!" She sounded close to tears.

"Hazel!" I pressed the phone to my ear. Kevin was awake now, sitting up, looking at me, blinking. I moved away from him and crouched naked near the floor, searching for something to sit on, to cover myself with. "Hazel, what's wrong? Where are you?"

"I'm at Grandpa's, but Mom, I don't want to sleep here anymore! Come get me!"

I closed my eyes, trying to think. "Did something happen?" I said, and my voice rose as my panic—her voice, my wet body, clothes strewn all over, *everything*—began to kick in.

She didn't answer.

"Hazel?" I said. "Hazel! Where's Grandpa?"

"He's in his room, watching a movie." She sniffed. "Where *are* you?"

"I'm—" I looked around. "I'm still here. In New York. But I'm downtown, so it's gonna take me a little while to get there. Okay? I'll get in a cab right now, though, and I'll be there soon. Okay?"

No answer.

"Okay?" I demanded, my panic growing. *Where the hell is my father?*

"Okay," she said, in the tiniest mouse voice.

I should have stopped then, I know, just gotten out of there and raced uptown. But I couldn't help it. "Hazel." I swallowed. "Did Grandpa do something to you?"

I don't even know what I was asking for, what I expected her to say, there in his house. Anyway, she didn't say anything.

"Okay," I said, giving up. "I'm coming. But listen to me. What's—what's Grandpa doing?"

"I told you! He's watching a movie. We were gonna watch it together. But I don't want to! I don't like it! And he called me a baby!" She sniffed. "I hate him. He's mean."

"Don't say that about your grandfather," I said, automatically. I swallowed. "What are you wearing?"

"Um—my new nightgown. It's pink flowers. Grandpa bought it for me before the video store."

"Well, get dressed. Put pants on, right now, and—"

"I don't have pants! I wore shorts here."

"Well, put them on, under your nightgown. Go in the bathroom to do it, if you want. Leave the nightgown on, though, don't take it off." I didn't really know what I was saying, but I needed to instruct something, and I liked the idea of her putting on more clothes, as opposed to taking any off. "And then," I said, "and then stay where you are now, and wait for me to come. Don't bother Grandpa. I'll be there as soon as I can."

"How long?"

"Ten minutes. No, probably fifteen. Or, or twenty. I have to get all the way uptown." I thought, with dread, of the traffic outside. "Maybe twenty-five," I said. "But I'll be there. I'm leaving now. Okay?"

She started to cry again, and I started crying too. "Listen," I said. "You don't have to hang up. But I have to put the phone in my purse, so I can go get a cab. I'll come back on the phone in a minute or two. Okay? Or you can press a button, and I'll hear the sound and come on as soon as I can. In a minute or two, I'll say hi to you again. Okay? And you say hi to me?"

No answer.

Kevin was standing up now, looking at me. He had pulled on his pants.

I found my purse, dumped in the still active phone, then put it down and began to find my clothes and get dressed. "I have to go," I mouthed, looking at him. I yanked up my skirt.

He nodded. "Is she okay?" he whispered. "Do you want me to come?"

I shook my head no to the second question; to the first, I thought, *Well, I'll find out, won't I.* And then I grabbed my purse, slid into my shoes, and ran.

# Chapter Twenty-Six

All God's wrath came down on me in the cab, which took fifty-five minutes to get me uptown. I'd chosen taxi over subway so I could keep in contact with Hazel by phone, but I paid the price in time and then she didn't respond to my voice anyway, as I'd told her to. "Hazel? Haze?" I kept saying into the phone, till the driver must have thought I was insane. I considered hanging up and calling back, but the line sounded live, and I didn't want to risk losing contact altogether, or getting the voice mail. Or my father.

So instead, in between calling out Hazel's name, I played every possible scenario in my head, each one worse than the next. He was taking off her nightgown. Fondling her flat little chest, and . . . I bit my lip till it bled. *Oliver is gone,* I pleaded to Whomever. *Please, please just let Hazel be okay.* I glanced out the window, willed the traffic lights to stay green until we could get even one block farther.

I made it at last, ran by the doorman with a quick little wave, and flew up the stairs when the elevator wasn't waiting there. At my father's door at last, I rang the bell. A lock clicked, and Hazel opened up. She stood there, staring at me.

I bent and hugged her, hard, closing my eyes. *Thank you thank you thank you.*

She shook me off. "That took you an *hour.*" She started to cry.

"The traffic was—Hazel, why didn't you stay on the phone, like I said?"

She glared at me through her tears. Then she turned and picked up her bag, which she'd packed up and left at the door. "Let's go," she said. She was holding Clod, and she'd put the shorts on under her nightgown, as I'd told her—I could see their lumpy outline—which made *me* want to cry, again.

"Where's Grandpa?" I said. I could hear the TV going, loudly, in his room.

She shrugged.

"Dad?" I called. No answer. "Stay out here," I told Hazel. "Sit on the couch. I'll be right back."

I walked down the hall toward his room. His door was halfway open. I knocked lightly. "Come in," he called, after a moment.

He was lying on his bed, wearing silver silk Calvin Klein pajamas; the bed—cherry wood, king size, dressed expensively in white—was made neatly, with large white pillows arranged on it. On his nightstand sat two bowls full of popcorn, and two drinks—one red juice, Hazel style, the other (lime wedge, a few melting ice cubes) a probable vodka and tonic—and I'm still astonished to recall that the sight of these props, his preparations for a party that wasn't going to happen, made me feel a stab of pity for him. I glanced at the screen he was watching. Little Brooke Shields, in a brothel. *Pretty Baby.*

My stomach rolled over. "Dad," I said slowly, "you didn't show her this movie."

"Not much of it, that's for sure." He didn't take his eyes from the screen. "She had little interest. I had thought we'd have a nice evening together, after an entire day of fashion show madness, but . . ."

Panic began to take over, panic laced with rage. "She's *six years old,* Dad! *Six!* This movie's completely inappropriate for her. It's about a *child prostitute*!"

He picked up the clicker and paused the movie, then turned to me patronizingly. "Elayna," he said. "This movie is about *life. Reality,* as opposed to some Disney fantasy. It's not gonna hurt her to watch it. It might even teach her a thing or two."

I stared at him in disbelief. "*What* would it teach her? What? How to, how to . . ."

He sighed, shaking his head as I sputtered. "Your generation is so hung up on 'appropriateness,'" he said. "You're so sheltered and self-righteous. Don't you see that it's a phase, a social trend? It's a marketing tool. And you know what? You're not doing a kid any favors to raise her like that, to keep her in the dark about everything from sexuality to the human body. Sex is beautiful. The human body is a beautiful thing. Why 'protect' her from that, as if it's some dirty secret? You might as well go back to the Victorian era." He looked at me, almost disgusted. "I didn't raise *you* that way."

For a second, I actually considered his words. *Was* my generation over-protective? *Were* we simply reverting to a time when beautiful things were considered shameful, when feeling what all humans naturally felt was something you had to do secretly, in shame? I glanced at the screen. There was Brooke, little Brooke, not much older than Hazel. And then I knew. There were lines, lines that shifted over the years, back and forth, closer and farther away. And you could toe them, step right up and put the point of your shoe right smack down . . . but you didn't go across. You tried to stop yourself. You *had* to stop yourself.

And I hadn't. I hadn't been able to.

My anger boiled. Anger at my father, for being obtuse and narcissistic. Anger at myself, for being downtown with Kevin doing what I did while my daughter was stranded up here. Anger at a world that would let me grow and birth a boy—a miraculous baby boy—and then take him away. *Oh, the heartbreak! The ruin!*

But when I spoke, my voice was firm. "You know," I said, "as far as I recall, you didn't raise me, period." My eyes shifted from the screen to him. His expression remained opaque. And that's when I noticed: Inside his silk pajamas, he had an erection, significant enough that I couldn't believe I hadn't seen it until now.

A wave of nausea broke over me, and the anger turned to rage. "You bastard!" I yelled. "You—you—how *dare* you? How *dare* you expose her to this? She's *six years old!* My god. And I trusted you!" I glared at him, eyes burning. "You should feel *sick*!"

I turned and ran for the bathroom, where I threw up into the toilet. I splashed my hands, wiped my face, and rushed toward the living room. But I stopped and went back to his room, one last time. His eyes were on the screen again. Who knew what he was thinking? "You," I said, pointing, but my voice was calmer now, "are a person who seriously needs help. And I hope you'll get it."

He wouldn't, I knew, any more than he'd admit he'd done anything wrong. He would never see it. Never. But he must know, I thought; on some level, conscious or not, he must understand. Sitting here alone, wifeless, loveless, glued to his movie, he must realize there was something amiss.

"Good-bye," I said, and my throat tightened once more, in spite of myself. I closed his door behind me. And I got my daughter and marched her out of there.

We took a cab to our car and got in. In the back, Hazel sat on her booster, thumb in her mouth, face buried in Clod. "Hazel," I said, "what happened at Grandpa's?"

No answer, thumb still in her mouth.

I turned back to her. "Was it the movie, or was it—was it something Grandpa said or, you know. Did."

No response.

"Haze? You have to tell me. I know you don't want to, but—"

"He didn't do anything." She turned to look out the window.

"Did he, um—did he touch you anywhere?" I pushed. "Or make you touch him?" I felt the nausea rising. Even saying it. "It's not your fault if he did, you just need to tell me."

She didn't answer.

"Hazel, please! I need to know this!"

She stared out the window despondently.

Hopelessness rose now to mingle with my anger, both quelling and exacerbating it. *Stop,* I thought. *This is the wrong approach. You don't know what you're doing.*

I would wait, then, to get her to someone who did. In the meantime, I needed to stay connected to her. "How was the fashion show?" I tried cheerfully, remembering only now that I hadn't yet asked.

No answer.

I turned again to the backseat. In the greenish light from the buildings, the cars, the traffic lights of the West Side Highway—lips open, eyes lightly closed, brow knit in thought—she was asleep.

Back in Jersey, I drove straight to the emergency room. Maybe that was extreme, but I had to do something, and I didn't know what else to do. The ER, of course, was its own kind of nightmare: Hazel was roused, questioned, examined, all so they could declare her physically fine. Relief more than surprise. My father wasn't a pedophile, despite his pedophilic urges, his narcissism and inappropriateness. But I also knew, and the ER resident confirmed this, that physical damage wasn't the only kind she might have. *Something* he had done—something more, I thought, than turning on a movie—had upset her enough to cry to come home when she'd begged to sleep at his place.

I would have to deal with that, somehow.

Home at last, I got her into bed, covered her with unneeded blankets and smoothed the hair off her face. I looked up, at her ceiling, at the invisible sky beyond, asking for something, *something*. Only safety, maybe. Then I staggered to my room, fell on my bed without brushing my teeth, without getting undressed or pulling down the covers or even getting a pillow to cushion my weary face. I didn't deserve one. Instead, I lay on my blankets, heart palpitating, letting the events of the day catch up with me, and the ecstasy of my afternoon canceled out the horror of my evening, or maybe the other way around, until my mind was numb and sleep reached down its soothing arms, dropped its soft, thick curtain on my mind, lifted me into its blank, empty bliss.

But in the morning—well. In the morning, after sleeping until she woke up naturally—only slightly later than her usual predawn hour—Hazel seemed fine. Tired, a little lethargic and hazy . . . but that made sense, given how late she'd been up last night. I observed her eat her Cheerios, chew and swallow her vitamin with a thoughtful little sigh. She was subdued, subdued . . . but that wasn't *completely* unnatural, and she didn't seem troubled otherwise. She poured more cereal, dumped her usual four spoonfuls of sugar on it. I didn't ask about yesterday and she didn't volunteer, and I decided to leave it alone, to proceed with our day—for right now, anyway. To wait and see if anything came out.

So I called Pansy to say we'd had a change of plans and would she by any chance have room for Hazel today, and she said yes; she never refused Hazel's presence, bless her heart, only complained when she didn't appear. And off she went, my sweet girl, with her bug spray and sunscreen, her sensible shoes and preservative-free, sweets-free lunch, to play dolls and house and wholesome games surrounded by childhood tunes from the 1950s. And I sat down and, as I'd always done for release and relief, I forced my mind onto my work, and anytime it tried to stray—anytime I was tempted to hit rewind and view yesterday—I shook my head and forced the thoughts away.

For several hours, I didn't leave my chair. Just as I was starting to resurface, Paul burst in.

He swooped into the kitchen and kissed me on the lips. He was holding a bottle of champagne, which he put down on the counter so he could pull me up with both hands and spin me around, hard and fast. "Stop!" I said. "I'm dizzy!" But I laughed.

He let go of me, grabbed the champagne again, and began to open it. "We were *flawless,*" he said. "We exceeded all expectations. The hearing went till nine o'clock both nights, but we got everything in. All our witnesses. They were—they were fantastic. God, I wish you'd been there to see it."

The few times we'd spoken on the phone since he'd left, he'd sounded restrained and tense, and he'd kept the conversation away from the hearing; I knew he preferred not talking about it while it was going on, that he'd rather talk at the end. Now he could let it out, and it was a relief for me as much, I'm sure, as for him. I couldn't remember the last time I'd seen him this happy. Maybe when Hazel was born. Certainly not since Oliver's death. I hopped up to the counter to sit until my head stopped spinning. "That's so exciting, Paul," I said, smiling. "Congratulations."

"Thanks. Oh, man. I'm so—" He shook his head. He was twisting the wire on the bottle. "I'm so pleased. The only way this could ever have gone better was if the judge overturned the verdict right there." He laughed.

I looked at him. "So—he didn't?"

He raised his eyebrows. "Um—no. He probably won't rule for another month or two, and then he'll do it in writing."

"Oh." I thought for a second. "And he'll overturn it then, though. That's what you're saying. Based on what you presented, and—"

He shook his head. "Actually, no. He won't overturn the murder conviction, even though it's obvious this guy didn't do it. These southern judges almost never do, and this one in particular. They have to get reelected, after all, and their constituents don't exactly like seeing murder convictions overturned. But we'll get a new resentencing trial. That won't happen for, oh, probably a few years, and meanwhile, our client's life is spared. And when it does happen, it'll be with a jury, not another judge. They'll be told our client was convicted of murder, and the question is whether or not to sentence him to death. Then the prosecution will present its case, and we'll present ours. And ours is excellent."

I was trying to grasp it. "So—say that goes well," I said. "Then what happens?"

He took out two champagne flutes from our wedding set, placed them on the counter, and resumed twisting the cork. "Well, if we succeed—which we have to—his term becomes life in prison." He gave the cork one final twist and out it popped, hitting the stove and rolling a little, resting on the counter. Champagne overflowed the neck of the bottle, covering his hands and dripping to the floor. He laughed a little, licking his fingers, then filled both glasses to the brim.

"So—then what?" I said.

"What do you mean?" He looked at me.

"I mean—then he's eligible for parole, or something. Or—whatever. Right?"

He made a doubtful face, then shook his head no. "He'd come up for parole a few years after that—he's already been in prison for seventeen years, remember—but that's pretty hard to get."

Something wasn't computing for me. "So you're saying—you're saying that even in the best-case scenario, this guy spends the rest of his life in jail?"

"Well—I don't like to think quite that far ahead. But yes, that's more or less how it'll probably go." He smiled, a little sadly, I thought. "I guess I thought you knew that."

"I probably did, at some point. We haven't really talked about your work in—well, years."

"No," he said, after a second. "I guess we haven't, really."

I was silent. I was thinking about the case. I knew I should shut up, but I couldn't help myself. "But—Paul," I said. "I mean, if he really spends the rest of his life in prison . . . what kind of a life is that?"

He looked at me. "It's a life," he said. "It's a life, not a death. *If* we can overturn it. But I don't have to worry about that right now." He handed me a glass. "Come on, celebrate with me."

I took the glass. I took a sip, then another. Then a third. "This is good," I said, trying to perk up for his sake.

"Yeah. It's on the firm. The cost of three sips of this swill could feed an entire third-world country, so—drink up."

I took another sip and put down my glass.

Paul finished his glass and poured himself another. "Where's Hazel?" he said.

"At Pansy's. She's there every day at this time."

"No, but—wasn't she supposed to be at your father's today?"

"What? Oh. Yeah, actually." My heart began to thump. It figured he'd remember. "She decided not to stay," I said, "so—I brought her home early. Last night."

"Oh." He took a sip of champagne. "So she went to Pansy's instead?"

"Yes," I said, relieved. "Pansy always has room, even though she always—"

"Let's go get her."

"What?"

"Let's get her! I miss her. I want to be with her. I have a day off; I want to spend it with my two girls."

I took a deep breath. "It's a little complicated. For one thing, Pansy'll freak if you pull her out."

He waved his hand. "Not a problem. I'll deal with her."

"Yeah, that's great. Then you go back to work and she takes it out on me."

He gave me a look. "Elayna," he said. "It's ludicrous that I can't take my daughter out of day care for one day to be with her parents because you're afraid of the day-care provider." He smiled. "Drink up, and then pack a bag with, let's see: bathing suits, towels, and lunch. In the meantime, I'll call Pansy, and then I'll get Hazel, and then I'll be back to pick you up. We're going somewhere fun. Where should we go? Oh—how about Six Flags? She'll like that, right?"

"Six Flags?" I laughed a little. "Paul, you have to be kidding."

"Not at all. That's exactly what I feel like. Something trashy and inane. It'll be like cutting school, only better, because I won't get in trouble for it. Well, except from the day-care provider." He looked at me. "Come on," he pleaded. "I'll take her on the rides and you can, I don't know, play games and win us stuffed animals. Or you can bring your book and read, if you want."

For a long moment, I didn't answer. I knew I should tell him about my father, tell him everything, just get it all over with—take his wrath and his help and his advice. "Paul," I said, but I stopped. *Not now.* How could I burst his bubble, ruin a chance for a fun, restorative day for the three of us? "Never mind," I said as he turned expectantly.

He smiled. "Okay. I'm calling Pansy now, then. Wish me luck." He picked up the phone and walked out of the room, champagne glass still in his hand.

I drank the rest of my own champagne. And once more, I turned off my mind as I went upstairs to pack.

So off we went, a day of rides and heat, of traffic and games and cheap stuffed animals and cheese steaks and fried mozzarella sticks dipped in chunky red sauce. It was nine thirty that night before we pulled back into our driveway, filthy, sticky, and spent, Hazel snoring in the back, her lips stained bright pink from her cherry snow cone, blue cotton candy speckling her hair. And as we did, I looked. I blinked and looked again. Kevin was sitting on our front steps.

The bottom of my stomach dropped out.

Through the window and the dark, I watched him watch us pull in. Paul, eyes bleary, driving toward the garage, didn't notice him.

We went in the back door. Paul carried Hazel. "Do you want to take her up?" I said, as he turned to transfer her to me as per our usual routine. I was trying to figure out how to do this, how to get out and talk to him without Paul noticing.

"Oh. Sure," he said. "If you want me to." He smiled at me, and then down at his girl. "Come on, sweetheart. Daddy gets to take you up tonight."

Her eyes sprang open. "I want Momma!"

"No, honey," I said, slightly desperately. "Daddy's gonna take you, tonight. He hasn't seen you, and he never gets to—"

"I want *you*!"

Paul looked at me. *What could I do?* If I took her up, I could have her in bed in two minutes and be back down to head off Kevin. If I tried to force her to go with Paul, it would be twenty minutes of her screaming bloody murder. "Come on, then," I said, taking her roughly. I started upstairs, sagging under her weight. The doorbell rang.

Paul looked at me quizzically.

I shrugged, then continued up the stairs, my heart thumping away. *Slow down,* I thought. *Do what you need to do.* I took off Hazel's pants and sat her, half asleep, on the toilet. "Pee," I ordered, turning on the sink to help her get the urge. I wet a washcloth. My hand shook. "Stop it!" she whined, as I tried to clean her mouth. She slapped at me, then wiped herself slowly, using about half the roll of toilet paper.

Voices downstairs: Kevin's and Paul's, talking. *Bang bang bang,* went my heart, but I forced my mind back to Hazel, now asleep on the bowl. I maneuvered her off, flushed, pulled up her underpants. In the bedroom, I ushered her into bed, pulled up her covers. "Where's Clod?" she screamed, suddenly awake.

*Clod. Clod.* I looked around desperately. "Here is he. Right here. Good." I handed her the donkey, then bent down to kiss her.

She smiled. "Good night," she mumbled, clinging to my neck. "Thank you for putting me to bed. I love you love you love—"

"Me too. Okay, Haze. Let go."

"Wait!" Again, wide awake. "I didn't kiss you on *both* cheeks!"

I bent again, and she planted one slow, long kiss on one cheek, and then on the other. "Okay?" I said, trying not to rush her. "I love you love you too. Good night."

"Who's at the door?" she said, her voice sleepy again.

"No one. I'll tell you tomorrow."

"Are you going out?"

"No! Of course not."

"Good." Her eyes closed. She flipped over, finally.

I turned from the bed. Paul stood in the doorway. I jumped, clutching my chest.

He was looking at me curiously once more. "That guy from across the street is here for you again," he said. "He's outside, on the steps. I tried to get him to come in, but he said he wanted to wait out there. He has his dog."

"Oh—Kevin?" I tried to sound casual. "Thanks. I'll go see what's up." I slipped by him, practically tiptoeing.

Outside, Kevin was pacing a little. Sasha sat, tense and erect, on our walkway, her leash slipped over the front rail. I stepped out and closed the door behind me. "What are you doing here?" I whispered, more harshly than I meant to.

He turned to look at me, the slight smile he'd produced when he saw me instantly fading. "I wanted to see you," he said.

I felt a pinprick of panic. "Listen," I whispered. "I—we can't really do this."

I saw his face melt; a scowl, like a boy's, crossed his eyes, his mouth. "Do what?"

The pinprick sharpened. "Anything," I said. "Any of it. What happened yesterday was—well, whatever it was, it can never, ever happen again. I'm really sorry, if you care. I should never have done that, to myself or to you."

"If I care? If I *care*?" His eyebrows knit, as if he were trying to contemplate what I was saying. "How could you think I don't care, Elayna? How, after everything that's happened, everything I said . . . how could you think something like that?"

"No—I don't think that! Shhh!" It was like dealing with Hazel, but exponentially worse. But this time it was all my fault, every bit. I grabbed the back of my hair and pulled, trying to think. "Listen," I said, finally. "I'll meet you tomorrow, and we can talk about all this. But I can't talk now, or here. I have to go back in."

He was frowning. "What time tomorrow? Where?"

"Um—" I tried to think. "I'll meet you in the park, after I give Hazel dinner. Six thirty. No, six forty-five. Near the pond. I'll, I'll get someone to watch Hazel. Mrs. Zuppo, or something."

He nodded once. Then he freed his dog and they slipped off into the night.

Above and around me, the heat was like a vice, crickets screaming. I opened the door and went back in.

Paul was taking a shower. I slipped out of my clothes, into a T-shirt and into bed. *What was that about?* I could hear him saying when he came in, and I could see his look, searching, casually interrogating me. I closed my eyes. I saw Kevin's frowning face, and then Paul, talking about the hearing. I saw my father, sitting on his bed in his pajamas, and Hazel, staring out the car window. I saw Oliver's little body, blue as a bruise. It was too much. Too much. The bathroom door opened. I closed my eyes and feigned sleep. And soon enough, a restless sleep came to me.

And then it was morning, another manic morning, all of us rushing in the usual ways. Paul left for work, and I got Hazel ready and off to Pansy's. Afterward, I drove straight downtown with my laptop. I didn't trust being home. *What if Kevin came back?* Fear played at my edges, and I kicked it away.

I picked up Hazel at two, and we went for ice cream, even though I couldn't eat, hadn't eaten all day. I was trying to observe her for signs of something, anything, amiss. We hadn't discussed my father again since Wednesday night, and I was loath to bring it up. And he hadn't called me, or her—not that I'd thought he would, and it was just as well that he hadn't, because I wasn't sure how I'd handle it if he did. "What did you do today at Pansy's?" I asked as she licked her cone and mine dripped down the base. It was raining outside too, a dreary drizzle that had come and gone all day.

She shrugged. "Nothing— Oh! We saw Clementine and her mom at the playground, and they asked if we're going to the sing-along tonight. We are, right?"

I slapped my cheek. "Shoot. I forgot. Um—yes. We can go."

"Good! Oh, and Mom! I need to get my school supplies! Clementine already got hers, at Rite Aid. She got, like, three notebooks, really cute ones with dolphins—well, one has dolphins, one has kittens, but I want sharks. Okay? And I need some pencils, and pens, and a glue stick and Sharpie markers—"

"Sharpies? What do you need Sharpies for in second grade—"

"Be*cause,* Mom! Like *everyone* has them!" She looked at me. "So *can* I?"

"I suppose so."

"Oh, thank you! You're soooo nice!" She dropped her cone on the table and ran over and hugged me, smearing chocolate ice cream from her cheek onto mine, and I thought, *Is this a child who's been through something horribly traumatic?* Maybe I *was* overreacting. Overprotective. Over-everything.

Three hours, thirty dollars' worth of school supplies, and a pair of new blue, Hazel-size sneakers later, we arrived home. Paul was there, sitting at the kitchen table reading the paper. "Well, look what the cat dragged in," he said, looking up.

I smiled, the familiar tug of guilt subduing me. "I should be saying that to you," I said. "What are you doing home at this time?"

"Hazel's sing-along is tonight, right?"

"Yes!" she screamed. "Are you coming, Daddy?"

"Of course," he said. "I wouldn't miss it."

"Yay!" she shrieked.

"Shh!" I said to her. "Go wash your hands." And, to Paul, "You remembered?"

He grinned and tapped on the side of his head. "They don't call me the Camera Kid for nothing."

I rolled my eyes and smiled in spite of myself. It was so nice to see him this happy. Guilt snaked through me, and then fear, the fear of discovery. So much I wasn't dealing with. "Oh shoot, this is supposed to be a potluck!" I said suddenly. "What the hell am I gonna make, in"—I glanced at my watch—"fifteen minutes?" I gave a sigh. "And I wanted to take a shower first, and shower Hazel, and—"

He stood up. "Go do it. I'll call for pizza, and we can pick it up on the way there."

I looked at him so gratefully; really, I wanted to cry. I rushed upstairs.

At seven fifteen, Paul called up, "Almost ready?"

I was dressed but shoeless; Hazel, wet hair still uncombed, was looking for the perfect footwear. "Uh—I have to find her shoes, and—"

"Why don't I go get the pizza," he said. "I'll pick you up on the way back."

"That would be amazing," I called.

I fought with her hair as she pawed through her closet, tossing things all over the room. "These!" she yelled finally, presenting a pair of mauve platform sandals, and then, "*Ow,* Mom. *Stop!* You're *killing* my head!"

I sighed, then dropped the comb on the rug. "That's it, then, that's the best I can do right now. We have to go."

The doorbell rang. "I'll get it!" Hazel yelled, tromping downstairs.

"It's just Daddy, picking us up," I said. "Grab your sweater and let's go."

I heard a car pull up in front. The horn beeped twice, a horn that sounded just like ours. I slipped into my shoes and went to Hazel's window to look.

It was our car, out there. I could just make out Paul at the wheel. So then who was at the door? "Hi, Kevin!" I heard Hazel yell, and then Kevin's voice, not happy. "Hi, Hazel. Is your mom here?"

For a moment, I was absolutely paralyzed. *Tick tick tick* went the clock, and my heart. And then I remembered. I had been supposed to meet him at the park. I grabbed my purse and flew downstairs.

He was standing in the foyer, frowning. "You weren't there," he said, the second he saw me.

"Where?" Hazel said. She looked at me. "Where weren't you, Mom?"

"You said six forty-five," Kevin said. "It's seven twenty. Were you coming? Or were you just gonna blow it off completely?"

And now I heard feet coming up the front steps. Paul appeared. He opened the door and looked at Kevin, then at Hazel, then at me. His look rested there.

"Listen," I said to Kevin, trying and failing to sound breezy, "we're actually on our way out right now. Hazel has a thing at her school, and we're running a little late."

Kevin folded his arms across his chest.

"Hazel," Paul said, "run outside to the swing. I'll be right out to give you a push."

"But, Daddy—"

"Do as I say," he ordered, and she rushed out, obeying him as she never did me.

Kevin looked down. Paul assessed him, and then me. "Is there a problem here?" he asked.

I shook my head. "No, no. It's fine."

Paul cleared his throat, and I could see him thinking, trying to decide what to do, maybe contemplating whether Kevin was a threat. And then he found his answer. "Tell you what," he said, and this was the lawyer talking now, all restraint and brains and strategy. "Why don't you two stay here and work out whatever you need to, and I'll take Hazel to the school. Elayna, you can meet us there as soon as you're done."

Neither of us answered.

Paul held my glance for a moment. Then he turned and walked outside. I saw him say something to Hazel, on the swing, and she hopped off and followed him to the car and got in. I watched their car pull away, and it was as if a piece of me went with it.

Slowly, I turned back to Kevin. On his face: some combination of anger, desperation, curiosity . . . and innocence. He was a child. A kid. *Oh my god,* I thought, and I took a step back from him. "Kevin." I swallowed. "Listen. You can't come here anymore. I, I'm married, and I have a family, and there's no way I can—"

"I can't believe," he interrupted, "that you would patronize me like this." He shook his head. "At least spare me that humiliation. Like I don't know you're married?" He looked at me hotly, his green eyes aflame. "Anyway, you didn't seem too married the other day." And then—astonishingly, to me, though I don't know why it should have been—he started to cry. "I don't understand women," he said. "I really don't. You pursue and pursue, you fall in love and make people love you back . . . and then, when you finally get the thing you want, you cut it off." He took a breath. "I mean, I know you have a family. I know that. But—" He looked at me again, his eyes glassy now. "I don't know how you can just let go of this."

I didn't answer. Of course he couldn't know. Of course he couldn't.

And I didn't know what to do. I felt horrible, hideous and disgraceful and, most of all, exhausted. "Listen," I said, looking down. "I messed up, Kevin—*I* messed up. Not you. I'm the one. I just never—I had no idea you—" I stopped. It all sounded absurd, hollow and clichéd.

I took a deep breath, trying desperately to form the mass of regret and sadness swirling in my brain into some sort of coherent thing to tell him. And at first, I couldn't do it. All those years of burying what I felt, of pushing everything, everything, deep into hiding. There were padlocks in there, rusty padlocks with long-lost keys. I searched every part of myself until I found them, and he waited while I turned the keys, one by one, till the locks popped loose and the doors they were holding creaked open, and suddenly I understood. I knew what it was, all of it. And I had to convey it to him.

"Listen," I said again, and this time I looked directly into his eyes. "You're—I've never met anyone like you. The combination of things, the charm and awareness and decency and *optimism* of you. And I lost myself in all that—or, rather, I *found* myself in it, because you made me feel things I hadn't felt in a long, long time. You helped me pull out of a dark place, a terrible, sad place. And I love you for that. I really do."

He'd been frowning, looking off to the side like a child getting yelled at, but something relaxed in him when I said that. I took another deep breath. "But—I have to put that part of me away, that part that loves you," I said. "I have to get rid of it, or find something else to do with it. Do you know? Because I have a love already, I had one before, and, and that's who I am now, I have a life full of people I love who are counting on me. And I've already hurt them so much with this, with this thing we've created, you and I. I've lied, I've . . ." I shook my head, blinking back tears. "And they can't be hurt any more. They've had enough pain already." I took a breath. "And now I've hurt you too. *God,* I've messed up. You have so much to give to someone, so much. But not to me. Because I can't give it back. And you need someone who can. You deserve it." I wanted to take his hand, but I couldn't, of course. I took a step toward him, closer but not too close. "I love, I've *loved* what we've had, it was . . ." I bit my lip, shook my head. "It was a miraculous thing for me, really. But it has to end now. And you have to help me end it. Because I don't think I can do it without you."

I stepped back. I had never been a poet. But it was something, at least.

He didn't respond.

I gave him another minute. And then I said, "I have to go. I'm due at Hazel's school. Forgive me." I pushed past him and out, leaving him there.

# Chapter Twenty-Seven

I must have made it to the school in record time. I found a parking spot—no easy feat—and ran in, past the walls of kids' watercolor paintings and sculptures of brains, past the brightly lit classrooms with their cheerful colored rugs and progressive, cutting-edge toys, many of which were only the old toys, our own childhood toys—wooden blocks and train tracks, glass marbles—come into favor again. I smelled chalk dust and sneakers, rubber cement and the lingering aroma of something baked, as the chorus of voices—men's, women's, and most notably children's—reached out to greet me. At the gym at last, I stopped just outside the doorway and glanced in, trying to catch my breath.

The place was packed, every spot on the floor taken by a parent, grandparent, or kid. The chorus leader, a zealously energetic former Broadway singer named Sky, was teaching the room a song, in Spanish, about the colors of the seasons, the colors of love. She had them singing in three-part harmony. I scanned the crowd until I spotted Hazel, sitting on Paul's lap on the floor. Clementine and Adele sat next to them, Adele holding a leash with Clementine's brother, Tommy, a toddler on chubby hands and knees, straining at the other end of it. I took a breath and was about to go join them when Paul glanced over and saw me. He motioned for me to stay put, then said something to Hazel, then to Adele. Then he got up and made his way through the crowd to get out to me.

I braced myself. He would ask about Kevin, of course. And I knew what I'd say. He was a friend, both mine and Hazel's, who had gotten a little familiar lately, stopping by unannounced. I had put an end to it tonight, and it wouldn't happen again.

The song was coming together, the voices in the room commingling, deep, middle range, high and sweet. *De colores son los pajarillos que vienen de afuera.* I saw Hazel and Clementine clasp arms. Clementine whispered something to Hazel, and they both giggled. Paul reached me, stepped out of the gym.

"Sorry," I began, before he had a chance to talk. "I was—it was—"

"Elayna," he cut in. "What the hell happened the other night?"

I blinked. "What night?"

"The night before I came home. Wednesday. Because Hazel told me—" He shook his head. "She told me something I know can't be true, because if it were, you'd have told me. She told me she went to the hospital." He looked at me. "What could she mean?"

The alarm inside me banged on, and this time, there were no keys to turn it off, to send me the words to try to make it right. "It's true," I said breathlessly. "We did go there. I took her, after my father's house. But everything was fine, it *is* fine. She's, she's totally healthy. And I was going to tell you—I mean, I *am* going to. I just haven't gotten around to it yet. I know that sounds crazy, but—"

He was staring at me. "What *for*?" he said. "Why did you take her there?"

"I just—I took her to get examined. I wanted to make sure she was perfectly safe. I mean, I knew she was, but—"

"Examined," he said, slowly. "Examined for *what,* exactly?"

I swallowed. "Let me just tell you the whole thing." I pointed to a bench farther down the hall, outside a classroom. "Come here, let's sit over here."

He didn't move. "Elayna," he said, with a calmness that scared me, "I want to know why my daughter went to the emergency room, and why I wasn't told about it."

I took a breath and jumped in. "She was supposed to sleep at my father's. You knew that, right? But around dinnertime—or a little later, around six thirty, I guess—she called me on my cell phone. She was upset, and she wanted me to come pick her up, right that minute. She didn't want to stay there anymore. And I thought that was weird, because she'd been begging for forever, to be allowed to sleep there." I paused, and now I heard the sounds of Hazel's favorite song, "Waltzing with Bears," starting up on Sky's accordion, and then the words of the first verse:

*Our Uncle Walter's not right in the head*
*He's been that way all his life, my mother said*

"Well, I told her I'd come right away," I continued to Paul, "because I didn't like the sound of her voice. I was still in the city, but it was rush hour, and I was downtown . . . anyway, it took me a while to get there."

*It's not that he's violent or falls down the stairs*
*It's just he goes waltzing, waltzing with bears.*

I reached out and pushed the heavy door closed behind him, muting the sounds. "And when I did," I continued, "I mean, when I got there, my father was in the bedroom watching a movie, and Hazel was—well, she answered the door right away, so she must have been sitting right there, waiting for me. She was mad I'd taken so long, and she seemed tired and sort of out of it—all of which seems natural now. She'd had a really long day." I looked at him for a nod, a show of agreement, but he was tight-lipped and blank. "But at the time," I said, "well, anyway, I went into the bedroom to tell my father we were leaving. And he was watching a movie, and it occurred to me that he'd probably tried to get her to watch it too, because there were two bowls of popcorn, and—"

He closed his eyes. "What movie?"

"*Pretty Baby.* You know, the one where her mother—"

His eyes shot open. "*Pretty Baby*? Are you fucking kidding?"

I swallowed. "It gets worse. He was in his pajamas. She was in hers too. A new pink nightgown he'd bought her." I was shaking all over now. Should I tell him about the erection? If I did, he'd hit the roof. But if I didn't, he'd never understand why I took her to the emergency room. I plunged in. "As I was leaving, I happened to glance at his—he had—ugh! I don't know how to say this!" I started to cry.

"He had what?" he whispered, and I could tell he almost couldn't bear to hear.

Beyond his shoulder, through the window in the door, I saw with near desperation that people had begun waltzing all over the place: teachers with teachers, parents with parents, parents with kids. I glimpsed Hazel with Clementine, twirling around. *Oh, to be in there with them!* "He had a hard-on," I blurted out, dragging my eyes back to Paul. "From the movie, I'm sure. That's all. And it's not like Hazel was in there. I don't think she watched any of it with him. I think she went out the second it got at all—I mean—because I'd told her before, I'd warned her that if my father ever did anything weird, that she should call me that second. And she did." I took a breath. "Anyway, I still freaked out a little. And then we left, and that was that, but, but on the way home I started convincing myself that, you know, maybe something—I don't know—that maybe he'd done something to her. I mean—I knew he hadn't, and he *didn't,* the doctors confirmed tha—"

"How can they possibly know?" he interrupted, quietly.

"Well, they can't know everything, obviously. But they examined her and found her in perfect health with no evidence of, you know. Anything. And they asked her some questions, and everything checked out fine. So—we went home and went to bed, and that was that. The next day—yesterday, that was—she seemed totally fine. I mean, you were with her all day too. Don't you think?"

He was looking at me intensely. "Let me ask you something," he said. "Did your father—did your father ever touch *you*? You know, *sexually*?"

"No! Never even close. Paul, do you think I'd let him be alone with Hazel if—"

"So then what *did* he do to you?"

"What?"

"What did he do, that he maybe shouldn't have? When you were a kid?"

"Well, nothing I haven't already told you. He took those pictures, me wearing my mother's nightgown. That's all."

He stared at me. "Do you know," he said finally, closing his eyes again, "what Hazel told me in the car on the way over here, about the other night?"

I shook my head, not trusting my voice.

"She told me she was 'modeling' for your father on the bed, doing model poses. In her nightgown. And then he asked her if she wanted to take off her nightgown, so he could shoot her in her underpants."

My blood went cold.

"And I guess she said no, or maybe something else, but I don't think she let him do it, though she wouldn't tell me that for sure. At least not in a way that convinced me."

For a second, I thought I might actually pass out. I thought of the photo album he was making of her, and, as in his apartment, nausea rose to my throat. How could I be so blind? I was sobbing. After a second—no, more like five or six seconds, maybe seven or eight—Paul reached out and put his hand stiffly on my shoulder. "You did the right thing to take her to the hospital," he allowed, quietly.

I sniffed hard. "Well, I don't know if I did. I just did what I—"

"I just wish you had told me all this," he said, a little louder. "I really—I still really can't believe you didn't."

"I was going to, Paul! It's not like there's been time. Yesterday you came in all happy, and then we ran off to Six Flags, and then today, you went to work early. I would have told you tomorrow, or even tonight. Much sooner if I'd thought anything whatsoever was wrong, but, but . . ."

My voice trailed off. He held me a second longer, then backed away. "We should go in," he said. "We can finish this later."

I wiped at my eyes, trying to pull myself together.

He was silent, watching me. A little too long. I looked up. He was staring at my hands. "Elayna," he said, "where's your ring?"

"What?"

"Where's your wedding ring?"

I glanced at my hand. Bright red flashed before my eyes.

The door opened, and Hazel burst out. "Come on!" she yelled. "Come in! The song is almost over!" She grabbed one of each of our hands and yanked us into the gym. "You guys dance!" she yelled. "I'm dancing with Clementine." She shoved us together.

The entire room—warm, festive, loud, packed with bodies—rang with the sounds of the song's final verse, as all those people—happy people, good people, earnest people, people who weren't letting their one remaining child pose for nude photographs and watch movies about child prostitutes, people who weren't having affairs on their husbands—as all these people, all these good people, danced around. Paul's hands stayed on me, but they were cold, cold as the dark, frigid night. We moved stiffly, like two frozen bodies. But I opened my mouth and forced myself to join in the song:

*Well we begged and we pleaded, "Oh please won't you stay?"*
*Managed to keep him at home for a day*
*But the bears all barged in and they took him away*
*Now he's dancing with pandas,*
*And he can't understand us*
*And the bears all demand at least one waltz a day.*

Paul let go of me abruptly; my hands fell to my sides. But there was one last verse of the chorus, and he saw that now; he'd let go too soon. He stood for a second, floundering. And then, as if recovering in a trial, he stood up straighter, and he walked calmly over to Hazel and Clementine. He bent down and said something, and they smiled and opened their arms. Carefully, Paul picked them both up at once. And while I stood there and watched, he twirled those two little girls, heads thrown back, mouths open in laughter, and the room around me danced with him and the girls to the words:

*He goes wa wa wa waltzing, waltzing with bears*
*Raggy bears, shaggy bears, baggy bears too*
*There's nothing on earth Uncle Walter won't do*
*So he can go waltzing, wa wa wa waltzing*
*He can go waltzing, waltzing with bears.*

# Part Three

# Chapter Twenty-Eight

It's the oldest story in the book, of course; I'm not here to rewrite history or humanity, only to give you my little version of it. It was me versus my daughter, me versus my marriage. I chose me. But of course, my daughter and my marriage were also part of who I was.

But that's not it, really. Maybe it's more that I chose one part of me over another, and both were precious. My eyes over my ears, a hand over a foot. Heart over brain, libido over heart. Passion over security.

But—that's not it either. Because I *didn't* trade in the security, I didn't sacrifice my family life—at least not willingly. I was no Celeste, foregoing financial stability, steady love, and the glory of children for the right to give in to every passion and whim. It's more like this: From the vast array spread before me, the sparkling smorgasbord brimming with the most tempting and delectable trifles of life . . . from those, I'd had to choose, and I hadn't. I hadn't chosen. I'd taken everything, and now I would suffer the consequences.

Saturday morning, the day after the sing-along. Needless to say, I had not found my ring, and—along with desperately trying to figure out what to do about that—I was trying to keep Paul from getting wind of that fact. So I avoided him altogether, slipping downstairs early, waiting for Hazel to awaken so I could observe her for unusual behavior once again, and then, when she did make her appearance, hauling her off to the grocery store, library, pizza place. By the time we came home, Paul was out for a run; by the time *he* came home and slipped upstairs for a shower, Hazel and I had gone on a bike ride. We came home to find Cindi and Zach, who'd stopped over. Which brought us to late afternoon.

It was one of those early September days that feels more like October: a chill in the air, a splash of yellow leaves on the trees, sprung from nowhere. Cindi and I proceeded to the front steps, where we sat while Hazel and Zach swung in arcs on the swing, Hazel's long and graceful, Zach's more wobbly. I was vaguely despondent, and not a little anxious—still, I think, trying to formulate an emotion that would be appropriate at the culmination of the events of the past few unbelievable days—while Cindi, chewing gum, flipping her hair this way and that as if a bee were trapped in it and she wanted him out, described her apparent breakup with Joey, which had happened last night.

"It was *horrible,*" she said, pronouncing it so the first syllable rhymed with "far." "I feel *so* bad, because he's still the sweetest guy." She sighed and looked up. "I told him, I'm like, 'Joseph, you've gotta understand. I love you as a friend, you're my total soul mate. I'm just not attracted to you anymore as a *boy*friend.'" She took an enormous black scrunchy out of her purse, then flipped her hair forward and inserted the accessory to form a ponytail on top of her head that cascaded like a waterfall down both sides of her now deeply tanned face. Watching her, it occurred to me that the sun was the one thing she wasn't anorexic about; she soaked it up like a plant, letting it, yes, fry her outside, but also no doubt nourish all the cold, starving parts inside too. "I'm like, 'Maybe down the road we can go out a little, or whatever,' " she said, picking at the hair at the base of the ponytail now, loosening it if only to have the chance to redo the whole process shortly, "but—I don't know, Elayna. We're just incompatible. I mean, all the guy wanted to do was have sex! And after a while, I was just, like, get *off* me! I couldn't stand it. I mean, it's not *him,* don't get me wrong, I *love* his body, he's totally ripped. But I'm sorry, I just can't have sex two, three times a weekend. It's *repulsive,* after a while. Don't you think?"

"Mm," I said, absentmindedly. I replayed the events of the night with Kevin, not the sex, but the parts that pertained to my wedding ring. It could have fallen out in the elevator, I supposed—with all the jostling that had been going on—though more likely in that apartment. When I dove for the ringing cell phone, before I heard Hazel's voice calling for me.

"I mean, don't you think?" She was looking at me.

"Sorry, what? I didn't—"

"I was just saying, don't you think two or three times a weekend is a lot? I mean, isn't that a tiny bit, like, *compulsive*? My shrink thinks it's downright psychotic. Dysfunctional, at the very least. She thinks he probably had attachment issues as a—"

"I don't know," I interrupted. "That doesn't sound like so much, two or three times a weekend. I mean—not at the beginning, anyway."

"Well, but this *wasn't* the beginning! We've been together, like, a *month* now!"

If it had fallen out in that apartment, maybe it was still there: in a corner somewhere, or peeking out, like a Wonka golden ticket, from the edge of the rug. Or the person—whoever's apartment it was—had found it. He or she probably still had it. "Huh," I said, trying to sympathize, realizing Cindi was waiting for an answer, and then I couldn't resist adding, "Well, Cin, you never much liked sex at all, did you? I mean, regardless of how long y—"

"It's not that I don't *like* it," she snapped. "I like it as much as the next person. It's just, you know. There's more to life than one's physical pleasure. Don't you think?" She turned to face me. "Take you and Paul, for example. You have to admit, sex isn't exactly a priority. Is it? I mean, where is it on your"—she put her hands up and formed quote marks—"Big List? Like, tenth? Fifteenth?"

"It depends on the month," I said, honestly. "But, Cin, that's a little different. Paul and I have been together seven—no. Almost eight years." Our anniversary was coming up, I realized. September 19.

"Well, but at the beginning," Cindi practically pleaded. "Not the *beginning* beginning, I mean, but—you know. After a few months."

"To tell you the truth," I said, "at the beginning, we did it all the time. We couldn't wait to get our hands on each other." I would have to ask Kevin if he could ask the person. Not something I looked forward to.

Cindi shrugged, annoyed. "Oh, whatever. You were always way more into sex than I was. Remember what a slut you were as a kid?"

"I wasn't a *slut*," I said, half laughing, but I stopped. *Had* I been?

"Anyway," she said. "My shrink will say I did the right thing. I know she will. I mean, why stay with someone you're not attracted to. Right?"

"Right," I said.

"So, if you know any other great guys . . ."

I looked at her. "Well, don't you think the same thing would happen again? I mean, if the problem is that you—"

She sprang up. "Zachariah," she bellowed, "get away from that street! This is not like our block! Cars come fast around here!" She watched him a second, then sat back down and turned to me. "Not if I fell in love," she said, defensively. "Not if it was real love, if it—"

"Well, it was real love with Peter, wasn't it? I mean, you did marry the guy and have his kid."

She frowned. "I married him because he was a father figure to me, the father I'd never had in Daddy. And of course, that's exactly what undid us, according to my shrink. His fathering me. I got tired of being patronized." With one huge, hyper motion, she yanked out her ponytail and redid it exactly as it had been. "Anyway, that was a mistake, that whole marriage. We were totally wrong for each other. He never understood me. He never quite *got* the things I value, the things that make me click."

"Like what?" I said, genuinely curious.

"Well, like—like *beauty,* for example. The value of the beauty industry, and how it can take a girl with really, really low self-esteem and make her feel good about herself. That's a good thing, Elayna! Did you know that in war-ravaged countries, one of the first things women ask for, after they recover physically, is hair products and makeup?"

"Hair products?" I looked at her skeptically.

"Well, not *products,* so much—I mean, I'm not talking about, like, *styling gel.* But a *brush.* A brush, a tube of blush . . . something to fix themselves up with. And once they do, they're on the road to recovery, psychologically as well as physically." She smiled a little. "That's one thing Joey did get. The value of looking good when it comes to trying to *feel* good. He understood that body-mind connection." She shook her head, looking sad. "If only I could've stayed attracted to him. He was such a—goomba," she said, using a word her oldest friend, Angela, had used constantly throughout our entire childhood.

I stood, if only to make her shut up. "Haze and Zachy," I called, "want some macaroni and cheese?"

"Yeah!" they both screamed from the swing.

I turned to Cindi. "I'll go put on water."

She stood too. "Let's all go in. I could pick at something myself. Do you have bagels? Oh my god, I'm *so* craving a spelt bagel with nonfat cream cheese right now."

We gathered the kids and herded them inside. It was close to six thirty. "I wonder where Paul is," I said, suddenly.

"Oh—he went to the movies," Cindi said.

I looked at her. "He did?"

"He told me to tell you. Sorry, I forgot. Some documentary about the Civil War, or something. He said he'd be back around seven thirty."

"Where was I when he said that?"

"Up in the bathroom, I think. He was heading out. He just asked me to tell you."

I felt a stab.

"Listen, do you mind if I call my girlfriend Chrissie? I think we might go out tonight, if I can find a sitter. Her cousin Leo is in town, and she thinks he and I might, you know, have some stuff in common." She smiled.

I rolled my eyes. "You don't need a sitter, Cindi. Zach can stay here."

"Really? Are you *sure*?"

"Of course. I'm home anyway." I was in no mood to plead and beg.

"Oh my god, Elayna. You're awesome. I brought his overnight bag, just in case."

She ran out for the bag, came back, and made a loud call on her cell phone while I fed the kids. Then she said good-bye and left as I herded them upstairs. "We're getting in our PJs early tonight," I told them, pulling off their clothes. "You can go out and play for five more minutes, in your PJs, for a special treat. Then one story and straight to bed."

"Mom, *why*?" Hazel yelled. "It's, like, *four o'clock*!"

"It's past seven, Hazel, and you were up late last night. I want you both absolutely snoring by eight, because Monday's a *school day*! Your first day of second grade! Remember the poem? 'In winter I get up at night / and dress by yellow candlelight . . . ' "

" 'In summer, quite the other way,' " she screamed, " 'I have to go to bed by day'!"

"Right. No more talking." I felt exhausted, suddenly, almost unable to go on.

They brushed their teeth—or rather, I brushed their teeth, after somehow getting back to my feet. Then we all went outside for the day's finale, the gloaming—streaks of deep pink and rusty magenta, yellow and ocean blue sky—which I couldn't bear for them not to see. Zach ran back to the swing, Hazel following. She helped him climb on, then began to push him.

I sat down. They never got tired of this. Not when they were together. *Two kids are so much less lonely than one.* I thought of Paul, out at the movies alone, and again, that stab of fear. What was I going to do about the ring? I thought of Kevin, and sadness tingled through me. I let it sit for a moment before shaking it away. I had told him the truth. I had done the best I could. Hadn't I? Now, I had to think about the ring.

A car turned onto our street. I watched to see if it was Paul's, but it passed. A moment later, though, his car did appear. I waved as he pulled into the driveway, but he didn't wave back. He parked in the garage and went in the back door. Sitting on my hand so he wouldn't see my lack of a ring, I waited for him to come out front to say hi, to tell me about the movie. With every minute he didn't come, my heart grew a little heavier. We hadn't said a word to each other all day. And last night, after the singalong, he had gone straight to bed. He hadn't said anything about Kevin, and I wasn't sure whether to be relieved about that or terrified.

"Come on, babies—bedtime!" I called, standing up.

"Noo!" they yelled in unison, and then they both broke into giggles.

"Right now," I said. "I'm counting to ten. One, two . . ."

They both squealed and ran past me and into the house.

I got them settled together in Hazel's bed, a chair next to it this time, so Zachy wouldn't fall out. "I want Daddy!" Hazel said as I kissed them good night. "I want *him* to read me my story. *Daddy!*" she screamed.

"Yes?" he called from the bedroom; obviously, he'd been listening for his cue.

"Would you read our story?"

"Sure," he called. I stood up, and he appeared. I smiled at him, but he passed without looking at me. "How about *Are You My Mother?*" he said to the kids.

"Yeah!" they both screamed.

My heart sagged.

I went downstairs. I stood, alone in the hall, and thought for a second. Paul would be occupied with reading for at least a few minutes. It was now or—who knew when?

It was a stupid thought, I know. Okay, idiotic. *Really, what was I thinking?* Only this: I had to get that ring back. If I did—*if I do,* I thought, and don't ask me why—*maybe it will save my marriage.* And for one moment—just one—it occurred to me that maybe Kevin had it. That maybe all I had to do was ask.

So I went. I walked outside, across the street, and up to his apartment, where I knocked on the door, three times, fast.

Sasha appeared, wagging her tail, and then Kevin. He looked at me, and I could tell he tried not to register anything. He opened the door and stood there, in the doorway.

My heart reached the ground and set up shop there. "Hi," I said, swallowing. "Listen, I'm so sorry to bother you—"

He looked terrible. Pasty skin, dark circles under his eyes. In them too. His eyes themselves, those beautiful green eyes, were dark and angry, gray as a storm. I almost couldn't bear to look.

"Listen," I said again. "I'm—I'm sort of in trouble because I lost my wedding ring the other night, in New York. And I'm pretty sure it was in that apartment, the one we went up to, because, because I took it off on the—" I blushed. I looked down, trying to collect myself. "Anyway, I need to get it back, as soon as possible." I looked at him again. "Do you think you could call whoever's apartment that was and ask if they—or I mean, I could call, I could do that myself, if you could get me the number."

He watched me, not moving. Behind him, I saw Sasha walk away, lie down in her spot. "I don't have the number," he said.

I stood still. We both did, for another moment, a year.

"Okay," I said finally, and I turned to go.

"I'll see what I can do," he said.

I turned back with a rush of relief. "Thank you," I said. "Thank you so much."

He nodded once. And then he closed the door in my face.

# Chapter Twenty-Nine

At home, Paul was downstairs, sitting at the kitchen table. "Oh!" I said, rushing in. "They're asleep already? Should I kiss them good night? Because I thought they'd still be—"

"I have two questions," he said.

I froze.

"What's going on between you and that guy?"

I cleared my throat. "Nothing," I said, and I meant it.

He continued to stare at me, his expression unchanged.

I shifted on my feet. "So—what's the other one?" I said. "You said you had t—"

"Where the fuck is your wedding ring?"

My mouth opened, then closed.

"That's what I thought," he said.

He got up and moved past me, out of the room.

He didn't say a word to me all the next day. He kept himself busy, watched the news during dinner, went to bed while I cleaned up—unheard of. I didn't know what to do, so I wrung my hands and did nothing.

Monday morning, Hazel was up by six, preparing for her first day of second grade—or rather, her first half day, since her school believed in starting with two twelve o'clock days. By six fifteen, she'd picked out an outfit and put it on; then, amazingly, she let me brush her hair. "I want braids," she said, and I silently followed her command. At the end, she was a carrot-topped, green-legged Dorothy, complete with red sparkle shoes I'd gotten at Payless for $6.99. "Go show Daddy," I said, unable to contain or hog my bittersweet pleasure at the emergence of this grown-up schoolgirl from my ratty-haired baby princess.

She rushed into our bedroom. I hovered outside, hoping desperately that Paul and I could at least have a moment of bonding over this.

I heard him say something, and her laugh. I walked in. "Doesn't she look awesome?" I said.

"For sure," he said, in his "I'm talking to Hazel, not you" voice. He slipped by me, out and into the bathroom.

I drove her to school. I stayed for an hour, helping her set up her cubby and box of spare clothes, then glitter glue an artful name tag. When I left, I went to a coffee shop and buried myself in my work. By the time I left at 11:55, I was awash in magical realism—that leap from the real to the extraordinary, that crazy jumbling of time . . . both things I could've used right then in my nonmagic real world.

I got to the school at 12:02. Close enough. The classroom was packed—parents, students, tensely smiling administrators, infants ogling from mommy slings—and the place was buzzing with first-day-of-school excitement, everyone wanting a piece. I wormed my way through the halls, greeting parents I knew. In Hazel's new classroom, I glanced around. "Where's Hazel?" I asked the teacher, finally.

"Oh—hey, Elayna. Her dad picked her up a little while ago. A few minutes early, actually. He said they had plans today."

My breath stopped.

"Hey, stranger!" Adele, Clementine's mother, moved in, and the busy teacher slipped away, onto the next needy parent. "I hardly got to see you the other night!" Adele said. "I was fixin' to be able to catch up with you a little, but—"

"Oh—I know," I said, fighting for composure. "Paul was mostly with her that night. I had something I needed to deal with."

"Oh, Paul. What a sweetheart. Clementine just loves him."

I tried to smile. "Thanks. Anyway, we'll have to have coffee, or something." I was dying to get out of there now.

"Definitely. Hey—speaking of the devil, where *is* little Haze?"

"Paul got her," I said quickly. "I forgot they had plans today. I'm sure he told me, but . . ." I smiled weakly. "The early Alzheimer's again."

"Tell me about it. I can't even remember my own birthday. Which is probably not a bad thing, come to think of it." She cackled.

Clementine ran up then, and I took the opportunity to bolt. "See you," I called.

I drove home fast. In the car, in the driveway, I turned the motor off and sat. *Think,* I told myself. *Where would he have taken her?*

I turned on the car again and backed out of the driveway.

I went to all the kid-friendly spots in town: toy store, coffee shop with the hot chocolate she liked, ice-cream place. I drove by the park, went into the library and even the kids' indoor gym. (Paul had once deemed it "a giant petri dish.") No dice. Back home, I called his office, just in case they'd gone there. Naturally, Marisol answered.

"Hey, Marisol, it's Elayna. Is he there, by any chance?"

"No—he took the day off." She sounded surprised. "He didn't tell you?"

"Oh—I'm sure he did. I probably just forgot. He picked Hazel up from school, so he's obviously around. I'm just trying to figure out where they went."

"Well, if I hear from him, I'll have him call you."

"Thanks. I'm sure they'll be here shortly." I hung up.

I paced the house. *Don't panic,* I told myself. *He's punishing you. But wherever they are, they'll be back by tonight. He knows she has school tomorrow.*

I found my sneakers, put them on, and barreled outside, walking fast.

I headed down the block. It was cool and breezy out again, today mostly overcast. I passed the Zuppos' house, the wilted remains of the faded lily garden, and moved on. Above me, clouds seemed to gather in an angry mass, and I felt that the heavens, all the heavens and all of humanity, were enraged with me. I stood for another moment. Frustration gripped me, and I wanted to scream. I turned and began to run down the street, and then around the corner, running and running, block after block.

Back home, heading in, I noticed the mail, overflowing out of the box. I took it in to dump on the table and ignore, but something caught my eye and I pulled out a white envelope, my name stenciled perfectly on the front in my father's immaculate black print. My hand shook as I held it, my anger rising. With everything else that had happened, I'd thought very little about the things he'd done that night, but now it all came back to me—the movie, his erection, and *had he really asked Hazel to pose in her underwear*? *My god.* I ripped open the envelope. A photo dropped out, landing facedown on the floor. On the back, again in his writing: *"Hazel and Elayna, New York."* I picked it up and turned it over.

It was the shot he'd taken the day of the first fashion show, when I'd kissed her good-bye. It was a gorgeous photo, intimate and lovely. I looked at it for a long time. It was his way of apologizing to me, I knew, the closest he'd ever come.

I put the photo on the table, and, still looking at it, picked up the phone. My hand shook as I pushed in his number.

I didn't expect him to answer, and either way, I didn't know what I'd say. But he did pick up, and when I heard his voice, my own found its way. "Dad," I said.

"Oh hello, Elayna."

He said it as if nothing had ever been wrong. I shook my head. "I don't—I don't know how you can say that like that," I said, my voice climbing a scale with each word.

He sighed. "Elayna. You're still upset, I presume."

"I'm *still* upset? *Still*?!" I gripped the phone. "Oh, what, you thought I'd just, what, *forget* about it all after a day or two? Forget the fact that you begged me to let you spend time with my daughter, and then you, you violated her, not to mention my trust, and then—*then*"—I almost laughed, it was so unthinkable—"you came this close to making the same mistake that you did with *me* twenty-eight years ago, the mistake that—"

"Elayna," he said calmly. "I really don't know what you're talking about."

I rolled my eyes, furious. "Those pictures you took of me as a kid, wearing Mom's red slip."

"Oh, yes. The ones that so enraged your mother. Your mother, egged on as always by your silly sister and her—"

"Don't try to blame it on Cindi!" I yelled. "Or on Mom! Those pictures were completely inappropriate, they were—"

"*Inappropriate?*" He sighed. "That's in the eye of the beholder, Elayna. Perhaps for your mother they were, though I suspect she might not have thought twice about them if your sister hadn't started the witch hunt. As for me, they were no more 'inappropriate,' to use your generation's favorite word, than capturing a child in all her beauty and naiveté, her childlike innocence. That's really all that was for me, Elayna. I was frankly somewhat stunned when you girls all reacted as if I'd led some pornographic—"

"Well, what about Hazel?" I'd stood up and was pacing around the kitchen now. "Did you or did you not ask her if you could shoot her in"—I stopped, stood still—"in her underpants."

"Did I—oh. That." He laughed a little.

"How *dare* you laugh?" I sputtered, and I wanted to hurl the phone to the floor.

"Elayna, that's really not quite how it happened. My god, if I didn't know better, I'd think you were accusing me of pedophilia."

"*Am* I?" I said evenly.

"I certainly hope not."

"Well, then what the f—what the hell do *you* call it? You rent a highly sexual movie and try to show it to a child—"

"You're right," he conceded. "It wasn't the best movie for her. As I recall, she wouldn't even watch it. Said it was 'boring.' "

"Thankfully! And she wouldn't take off her pajamas for you, either, would she."

"No. She had little interest in either. In fact, she had little interest in any of the movies I'd rented. I offered her another when she didn't like that one, but she—"

"You did?"

"Of course. I'd rented three or four, not sure what she'd like. I started with the most sophisticated, which I guess is where I went wrong, but I was happy enough to work my way down. But by then she seemed only to want you. So I let her go out and call you, and I watched the movie myself and stayed out of her way."

I paused for a moment. I didn't disbelieve him. And if he was telling the truth, idiotic though he'd been, it was at least less offensive than before. "Okay," I said. "So what about the underwear?" My voice shook.

He sighed once more. "She was leaping all over, jumping on the bed, then complaining she was hot. 'Sweating,' I believe is what she said. So I asked her if she wanted to take off her pajamas. I admit, the idea of shooting her in her little panda panties didn't displease me, but neither did shooting her in the twenty million other poses I shot her in. She's a ravishing child, but again, the beauty of shooting a child half clothed, or nude, for that matter, is that every viewer will see something different, depending on what he or she brings to it. If it titillates you to look at a child in her underwear, well, fine. But don't assume—or not assume—it titillates the photographer as well. Because all I'm doing is capturing on film what's already out there."

I shook my head. Oh, he was exasperating! But I confess, his words mildly reassured me about what had gone on that night.

I had made my way into the living room, and now I sank into a chair. The fault was mine; I knew it now, clearer than ever. Because I had known all along exactly what my father was—really, he hadn't done anything more or less than he'd ever done before—and I'd left Hazel with him anyway. I had failed to heed the warnings of my conscience, of Cindi, even of Celeste, instead risking Hazel's safety for my own desires. I had failed to protect my own daughter. It was the worst sin any mother could make, a crime for which there was no forgiveness. And how was that any less terrible than anything he did?

I took a breath. "I have to go now, Dad," I said. "I'm gonna hang up." And I did, though I knew then, unlike at the beginning of the call, that we would go on, he and I. Because that's what we did. He was my father, my family. Hazel's grandfather. But I knew this too: As long as I was alive, he would never be alone with her again.

Tuesday morning, just after sunrise. I woke up in that same chair, body stiff, running shoes still on, and for a second I felt the relative bliss of disorientation. And then I remembered. *Hazel is gone.* I got up. Washed my face, changed my shirt, and headed over to the school.

I parked in the back of the parking lot and watched the cars come in, one after another. Not Paul's. At eight thirty, the late bell rang. *Maybe you just missed them,* I thought, trying to stay calm. I got out of the car, went in a side entrance, sneaked down to her classroom. The kids were sitting in a circle; her teacher was demonstrating how to crochet. I scanned the circle. Clementine, Destiny, Sage, Aidan, Jenny, Willow. No Hazel. Not anywhere.

Back in the car, I sat shivering with fear. Was this a missing-child situation? *But she's with Paul,* I told myself. It didn't reassure me. I thought about going to the police, but I couldn't imagine. I got out of the car, paced around it, got back in, and closed the door. "FUCK!" I screamed suddenly, smacking the steering wheel. I beat it and beat it, until my hand was bruised and red, soon to be black and blue.

I sat for hours. I couldn't quite believe he wouldn't bring her at all, so I sat there until I had proof. At noon, the children streamed out. I waited until every last child who'd come out had gone home. No Hazel.

I thought for a second. And then I did something I still can't quite believe: I went to Pansy. Not Cindi, not Adele, not even Celeste. Pansy Dougherty, domestic educational facilitator. I thought then it was maybe because she was the closest, both proximity-wise and to Hazel. But I realize now it's because I knew that, like a mother, she'd do what I needed her to. First, tell me I was awful—dole out the punishment. Then, help me fix it.

As it happened, she did neither. My eyes were red and swollen when I knocked on her door; my hair, my body, my dirty, wrinkled clothes, still unwashed from my run yesterday. When she saw me—through the window, of course—she frowned, then opened the door. "I thought Hazel was tomorrow!" she said. "She's welcome to come today, but I don't have her down, just so you know. Are you sick? You look like you're coming down with something."

I shook my head. "She's not coming today. She's not with me. I just—I thought maybe I could talk to you."

She looked at me for a second. "Well, come on," she said finally, ushering me in. "The boys just went down for their afternoon naps, thank god. A little early today, because they were all exhausted. They stay up until all hours of the night with their parents, and then who pays the price? Me, when they're fit to be tied the next day." She closed the door and bolted it. I glanced into the darkened den, saw three lumps on the floor under blankets. "I miss my big girls," she was mumbling, "because Hazel and Cherry are my helpers, for sure, though I don't mind saying, it's not so bad having just the three boys. I can put out the trains and everyone's happy, none of this, 'We want the *dolls,* Pansy, *pleeeeeze?* And the *dress up*!'" She laughed suddenly.

Inside, it smelled like beef cooked with some sort of grain: meat loaf, maybe. "Sit down," she said, motioning to the chair. "Want some juice?"

I looked at her gratefully. "Thanks. If it's not too much work."

"Please. One more thing's not gonna kill me." She went into the kitchen, returned with two plastic cups and handed me one. "I don't mind taking a load off myself," she said, sinking into the other chair. "I've been on my feet since seven AM. Let me tell you, chasing three three-year-old boys around is no piece of cake. Giving them breakfast, cleaning them up, making sure they all make their poops." She stuck her nose up proudly.

"I know," I said. "I don't know how you do it."

"Well. You do what you have to, in this life. And there's no glory in being a martyr about it either, believe me. You don't see me complaining, do you?"

Obediently, I shook my head no.

"I'm not saying I'm some sort of a saint," she acquiesced. "Everyone has to vent now and then, don't get me wrong. I'm just saying. I work hard, and I reap the rewards. I've been a domestic educational facilitator now for—"

"Twenty-two years," I interjected.

She laughed. "Where's Hazel?" she said suddenly. "Didn't she have a half day yesterday and today?"

I nodded. "Paul went and picked her up yesterday, though he didn't bother to tell me. And then, today—" I stopped.

"What?" She looked at me.

I shook my head. I began to cry, silently.

Something changed on her face, but she spoke with calm authority. "What happened?"

"I'm sorry," I choked out, but she shook her head. "Now now," she said, after a second, and she reached out and patted my arm. "It can't be that bad. Come on, drink your juice. Come on. You'll wake up the boys."

I took a sip from my cup. Grape juice, the kind I'd had as a child: dark, sweet, and rich. I sipped again.

She nodded. "Good. Now tell me. What happened?"

I told her everything then—or almost everything, anyway. I told her about Kevin, my father, the fashion shows, Hazel's phone call to me. I left out the actual sex with Kevin, and my father's erection. But I told her I'd met Kevin in the city, and that Hazel had been with my father, who'd been inappropriate—just as, yes, she'd predicted—and I should have known he might be, and I'd forged ahead anyway. I told her about the movie he'd tried to watch with her (though I stressed that she'd been smart enough to leave the room and call me), about him wanting to photograph her on the bed, that I'd found out because Hazel told Paul, who told me. "Nothing terrible actually happened," I said, as much to myself as to her. "But it *could* have."

She nodded again, oddly silent for a change.

"And Paul knows all this," I said. "Not everything, but—enough. And he's so mad at me."

"Phew," she said softly.

I nodded. It was an enormous relief to have told her. "And I know—I know I deserve whatever happens," I said. "But I'm so worried, Pansy. What if they don't come back? And where are they? It's so unlike him not to take her to school!"

She sat up straight. "He didn't take her at all? Did he call her in sick?"

"I don't know."

"Well, let's call the school and find out." She got up, went into the kitchen, worked the phone until she'd talked to someone. "He did call," she said, reemerging. "That's a good sign. At least he's rational." She looked at me. "You're lucky. He cares about Hazel. And let me tell you, that's not something you want to mess around with."

"You're about the billionth person to tell me that lately." We sat quietly for a moment then, her thinking, me staring miserably at the rug.

"Listen," she said, finally. "They'll be back."

I almost sobbed with relief. "How do you know?"

"Because. He's not the first guy on earth to blow his top, believe me. I bet he brings her back tonight." She gave a firm nod. "I'm ninety-nine percent positive."

"Oh god! Do you think?" Immediately, I started to cry again. I buried my head in my hands.

"Shh," she said. "Come on. Don't get your cage all rattled about it again. That's not helping anyone here."

Once more, I tried to pull myself together; it seemed as if this was all I'd been doing for weeks. From the other room, one of the boys cried out. Instinctively, I started to rise, but Pansy reached her hand out to stop me. "He'll go back," she whispered, and she was right; in a second he was quiet again. We sat for another moment. I looked up at Pansy, sitting back in her chair, legs calmly crossed, holding her cup of grape juice. "Tell me the truth," I said softly. "Do you think I'm horrible?"

She gave me a look. "Don't be overdramatic. You're no more horrible than anyone else. We're all human, after all." She leaned back a little. "You made a mistake. A bad one, but—it could've been worse. And you know what, Elayna? Everyone makes mistakes. I tell the kids that all the time. How else can you learn? And most of us make at least one that does some big mondo damage in our life."

"Well, *you* didn't."

She cackled. Immediately she covered her mouth to squelch it. "Don't even get me started," she mumbled, and she got a dreamy look, no doubt happily reliving whatever terrible thing or things she'd done. "What's important, though," she said, suddenly, "is not to let it happen again. Let your mistake teach you. Every cloud has a silver lining, you know."

"Right," I said, and then, "But how can I? I wasn't looking for it. I wasn't looking to have an—an af—not that I did," I added quickly. "But being with this guy made me feel so—so—" I took a breath. "I didn't really think I'd ever be able to feel that way again, after Oliver. Do you know?"

She nodded, smiling a little.

"How could I resist that?"

"Well, maybe you *couldn't,* that time. But you can next time. And you will." She looked at me. "How?" she continued, like a teacher leading a class. "You fight it! You fight it with all your might. You fight it because you *want* to. Because what you have isn't worth losing. And if you want to fight it, you'll be able to. If you don't?" She shrugged, like, *Your loss, fool.* "The good thing," she said, "is that time helps you fight it. At some point, you wake up and smell the coffee. You tell yourself, 'Okay, I'm older, I've had my fun. Time to grow up, already. Time to stop being such a narciss—nar—' "

"Narcissist."

She sniffed. "And after that, you look at your husband in a new light—maybe just because he's stuck with you all these years." She laughed loudly again, this time forgetting, in the passion of her lecture, to muzzle herself. "For me, it happened around fifty," she said. "Just a few years ago. I learned to—"

Another noise from the sleep room, but this time, Pansy got up promptly. "Nap time's over for Hector. He won't go back this time around, he's put in his forty-five." And sure enough, he whined a little more as she entered the room, stepped around the other two sleeping bodies, and picked the boy up. She came out with him wrapped sausage style in a blanket, sat down and held him, swollen lipped and dazed, on her lap.

I stood up. "I should let you get back to your kids."

She nodded, and her face was all sternness again. "I'll see Hazel tomorrow, then, like always," she said. "Right after you get her from S-C-H-O-O-L."

I nodded gratefully. "Yes," I said. "See you then."

I went home again, back to my empty house. I thought I should eat—I couldn't remember the last time I had—so I stuck some bread in the toaster, then promptly forgot about it as I wandered around, restless and distraught, looking futilely for my family. I sat down in the living room chair and fell asleep again, but startled awake seconds later, it seemed, to the sound of screeching brakes. I rushed to the window, but there was nothing out there.

In the end, I went out again. I walked for two hours, in the sun and the haze. Back home, I took the toast that had popped up hours ago, spread peanut butter on it, took a dry bite. I turned on the kettle, chewed and swallowed, put the toast down on a plate. The water boiled, and I poured myself a mug of tea. Leaving the toast behind, I took the tea out to the living room, the mug shaking as I carried it.

I went to the window and looked out. The air was motionless; the swing hung empty and still. Like a scene from Joyce's *The Dead.* Beyond—well, who cared what was beyond? I turned back into the room, flicked on the TV, flicked it off again.

I went upstairs, then into Hazel's room. I looked around. Bed unmade, drawers open, a pair of pants—inside out with underwear still inside them—on the floor, along with strewn Mr. Potato Head parts, stuffed animals. I picked up the pants, separated the underwear out, and threw them both in the hamper. I got some water and watered her little spider plant. I started to pick up Mr. Potato Head, then changed my mind and left it there, just as she had.

I went to her bed and sniffed her pillow. Her sweet, musty scent filled my head, and I sniffed again, longingly. Something fell to the floor. I reached down and gasped. *Clod!* I picked him up and hugged him, burying my nose in his fur. For the first time, I felt a twinge of real anger at Paul. Nothing I'd done justified taking her away without her Clod. He was making *her* pay for *my* mistakes.

I pulled back her covers and got into her bed, curling up so I fit. Then I stuck Clod under my face, leaned into his clammy softness, and fell into blank, heavy sleep.

# Chapter Thirty

When I awoke—in the morning, sun streaming through the window—Hazel was staring into my face. "Mommy!" she screamed. "Momma! Momma! And *Clod,* oh, Cloddy!" She grabbed the donkey, then jumped on me, kissing me and pulling my hair. I reached out and held on to her with all my might.

"Momma!" she yelled breathlessly. "Me and Daddy went to a *hotel*! It had a real live pool, and then another little burning-hot pool that was really wavy and bubbly! And it had all these little bottles of stuff in the bathroom, and my own shower cap! Daddy said I could *keep* it!" She looked at me. "Can I?"

"If Daddy said so, yes," I croaked. I kissed her eyelid.

She pulled away. "Yay! But, Momma, I missed you *so much!* I was crying and crying last night! Daddy had to take me out for ice cream to cheer me up, and then he let me watch TV, like, *all night,* because I was all wired up from the chocolate, he said."

I grabbed her face and kissed her hard on the cheek.

"Ow!" she shrieked, but she was smiling. And then, "Why are you in my bed?"

Before I could answer, Paul appeared in the doorway; I felt his presence before I saw him. I sat up and looked at him, rubbing my eyes. "She wanted you," he said, bluntly. He turned and walked away.

I jumped out of bed. "Look, I'm still dressed from yesterday!" I said to Hazel. "How convenient. All I need is shoes and a hairbrush and I'm good to go."

She giggled.

"Come on," I said. "Let's go downstairs and have waffles. I'm starved. And then we should get you ready for school, shouldn't we. You missed yesterday!"

"I know. Daddy said it was okay, just that once. But I want to go today! I want to see my friends! I haven't seen them, like, *all summer*!" She sniffed dramatically.

"I know, baby," I said. "We'll get you there."

Downstairs, I toasted her two waffles, drenched them in syrup, and sat watching her eat, savoring the sight of her sticky-lipped, filthy little face. When she was too full to eat more, I wolfed down the rest. Then we both brushed our teeth.

I got her to school right on time. "Hey, Hazel," her teacher said, smiling. "Are you feeling better?"

"Yes thank you," she said, shocking me.

By the time I got back home, Paul was gone. I picked up the phone and called Pansy. "You were right!" I said, when she answered. "Hazel's back! But—"

"Oh, hello, Elayna," she said, in her domestic educational facilitator voice. "Exactly. So I'll see her at twelve ten, then, today being Wednesday half-day."

"Yes. Right. But, Pansy? Paul's gone now! He brought Hazel back home, but then he left again."

"Right," she said, professionally. "Exactly. He'll be back."

A glimmer of hope. "Do you think?"

"Believe me," she said, a hint of familiarity sneaking into her voice, "they don't stay away long. Well—unless they meet another W-O-M-A-N, particularly a much younger one. But that's a whole 'nother thing. *That's* when you have to worry. Otherwise, he'll be back. Because you-know-whats can't stand being alone. They need a warm B-O-D-Y in the bed with 'em at night. Trust me on that."

I stood there for a moment, considering her words. I thought of Marisol, but I quickly dismissed that. A flirtation was one thing, but Paul was too original to leave his wife and take up with his secretary. "Well, then," I said, finally, "when do you think he'll—"

"I'm sorry, Elayna, but I can't talk right now. I have three three-year-olds waiting for their cheese sticks."

"Oh—right," I said. "Okay. See you later, then, I guess."

"Don't forget sunscreen. We may have outside play today, if the weather holds."

I thought about saying Hazel wasn't coming today; how could I let her go when I hadn't seen her for so long? But then I decided it was probably better for everyone if I stuck to the routine. "Okay," I started to say, but I stopped. The thing was, I really did want to spend even a little time with Hazel after school, if only to catch up with her.

I decided to compromise. "Though actually," I said, trying to sound firm, "Hazel and I have a lunch date today. I can bring her over afterward—around two-ish—or we can skip today, it's up to you. I'll pay you either way, of course, and I'd understand whichever you choose, but—"

"That's fine," she said. "Two is fine. See you then." She clicked off.

*He'll be back.* I played her words in my head through the morning, the afternoon, the evening. Evening morphed into night, and then into another morning. "Where's Daddy?" Hazel said, munching her cereal.

"At work," I said promptly. "I guess he had to leave early today."

She nodded and took another spoonful.

Morning, on into afternoon. I wanted to call his office, but I didn't dare. If he wasn't there, Marisol would know he wasn't home. And if he was, she'd put me through to him, and what would I say? Whatever it was, I had to say it in person. And he had to come to me to hear it, he had to be ready. I would just have to wait.

Still, I couldn't bear not knowing if he was at work or not. For a second, I actually considered going into the city and sneaking up to his office to see for myself. And then something came to me, someone who could help me. I racked my brain for his name . . . and there it was, filed right between Hazel's allergy prescription and Hazel's shoe size. Graham Jackson, the Brit, of the lopsided, close-set blue eyes. I grabbed the phone and called the law firm, asked for his extension. His secretary picked up. "Can I speak to him?" I asked. "It's Elayna Leop—Elayna Slade. Paul Slade's wife."

"Hold on, let me see if he's here," she said, as if there was any chance he wasn't. I drummed my fingers on the table. A second later, he clicked on.

"Hey-lo, Elayna," he said. "Long time no speak. Are your eyes still as deep and mysterious as the Adriatic Sea?"

I smiled a little. "Deep as ever. Listen, Graham? I have a favor to ask."

"Ask away."

"Well, Paul and I—I need—" I stopped. This was harder than I'd anticipated. "I just need someone to go look and see if Paul's there," I said, spilling it out. "That's all. Just if he's in today. But I don't want him to know I asked."

"Let me guess," he said. "Marital spat and you can't call and ask his secretary, lest she find out he wasn't home this AM, like the good hubby he supposedly is."

I blinked. "Exactly, actually."

"Say no more. No, say one more thing. Your phone number. I'll do some research and call you right back."

I gave him my number and hung up. Minutes later, the phone rang. "He's present," he said. "Clothed in a dark suit, red tie, well-pressed white shirt. Appears in good health, if a tiny bit piqued. At time of observation, he was engaged in reading the sports section of *The New York Times.*"

I let out my breath. "Thank you."

"Anytime, love. If I can be of further service, don't hesitate."

"And what do I owe you for this stunning feat?" I said, trying to keep up the banter for one more line.

"The pleasure of several moments of your lustrous conversation at the next company shindig."

I smiled. "The pleasure will be mine."

That night, at six sharp, Paul called to talk to Hazel. I saw his office name on the caller ID, and I knew he wanted either both of us or just her, so I let her pick it up—he'd ask for me afterward, if he wanted to. Then I walked around the house straightening things—books, CDs—while they talked. I don't know what he told her about why he hadn't been home, but whatever it was, it did the trick. At the end, I heard her say, "Want to talk to Mom?" Pause. "Okay, I'll tell her," she said, and then, "Bye! I love you."

I wandered into the kitchen. "He said he'll call you later," she said, reaching to hang up the phone.

"Thanks," I said, casually.

He didn't call later. But the next night, again at six, there he was on the caller ID. He and Hazel had their conversation, then hung up once more.

Saturday morning. Hazel didn't ask where he was, and I didn't bring it up. Instead, over coffee, I told her that we were going to cook a nice dinner tonight. If Daddy got home to eat it with us, great; if not, we'd save some for him.

And we did. We went to the grocery store, came home, and made baked chicken legs with butter and salt, a side salad, and plain pasta. At six o'clock, we sat down and ate it. "I guess Daddy will have his later," Hazel said, chewing.

I swallowed. "I guess," I said.

Sunday morning. No Paul. Hazel and I took a long bike ride. After a while, we stopped to get egg-salad sandwiches, which we ate at the park, lying on the grass near the shimmering duck pond, ducks pirouetting crisply around it, perhaps knowing their days were numbered here before flying wherever it was that ducks fly when the cold descends. It was a gorgeous fall day; a few leaves drifted through the air and settled somewhere, the leaders of their soon-to-be handsomely, artfully, maybe a bit sadly falling autumn pack, forming piles of burning red, orange, yellow on the curbs for the children to crunch around in as the sky grew bluer and the weather colder, as people began to hole up inside with their families. *And what's yours*? I asked myself, and I answered, *Two girls left, two boys gone.* I stopped eating abruptly, my stomach suddenly a knot. "Can I give the rest to the ducks?" Hazel asked, pointing to my discarded half sandwich. I nodded and watched her take it and run for the pond.

She came back with chattery stories about the ducks. Finally, she was quiet. I lay back, letting the sun warm my face, and she lay back next to me. "Mom?" she said.

"Hmm?"

"How come Kevin and Sasha never come see us anymore?"

I sat up. "What?" I said, stalling for time.

She repeated the question.

"I think Kevin's been working a lot lately," I said. It was lame, but what could I do? I had to tell her something.

"Like Daddy?" she said.

I smiled a little. "Yes. Maybe."

"Everyone's gone," she said, after a moment. "There's hardly anyone left. Daddy, Kevin, Sasha, Oliver . . ."

My throat tightened. "I guess that's true. But some of them will be back."

She nodded, but doubtfully. "When will Daddy?"

"I hope soon. But either way, I know he'll keep calling you."

She frowned. "I want to visit him!"

"Daddy? Well, the thing is, I don't—"

"Not Daddy! *Kevin!* And Sasha!"

"Oh. No," I said quickly. "We can't."

"Why not? Maybe he's back from work now."

I sighed. "It's hard to explain, Haze. Sometimes you just have to give someone space." I thought a second. "But we could write him a note, if you want."

"Okay," she said.

I breathed a sigh of relief.

We biked home and put our bikes away, then got out paper and markers. Then, while she made a card with a silver dog on it, I wrote Kevin my own note.

*Dear Kevin,*

*Hazel wanted to write you, which gave me an excuse. I hope this note finds you well.*

*I also hope you can believe that I never meant to hurt you. Though, why would you, really? After all, I didn't believe you were planning to pick up the dog poop way back when. I do now, though. Is it too late to say that?*

*I reread this Blake poem the other night and it made me think of you:*

*He who binds himself to a joy*
*Does the wingèd life destroy;*

*But he who kisses the joy as it flies*
*Lives in eternity's sunrise.*

*Do you like it? Not too snooty, right?*
*I wish you so much luck and happiness.*
*Love,*
*Elayna*

Hazel had finished her own note. *Dear Kevin,* it said. *I mis you. How is yor dog? I hop you dont have to much work. I love you. Love, Hazel Leopold Slade.*

We took our notes and put them in an envelope. We sealed it and wrote "Kevin" on the front. Then we walked it across the street to his house. "Shh," I said, as we tiptoed up the steps. "I don't want to bother him."

"Because he needs some space," she whispered back. "Right?"

I nodded. We dropped the envelope in his mailbox and went back home.

Late that night, when I went to lock up the house, to look one last time down the street for Paul, I noticed something white sticking out of the screen door. I opened the door to get it. It was the same envelope we'd put our cards in, but "Kevin" was crossed out and "Elayna" written on it.

It was sealed. I tore it open.

Inside was my wedding ring.

# Chapter Thirty-One

Monday morning. No Paul. I consoled myself. He had called Hazel every night. He was working. He was okay, and she was okay. And right now, that's all that counted.

As for me, I would wait. He would come back when he was ready. Or he wouldn't. And if he didn't—but I couldn't let myself go there. Not yet.

So I waited. Tuesday morning. I dropped Hazel at school, drove back home. I took a shower, first hot, and then, when that made me oddly dizzy, cold enough so I shivered. It woke me up, at least. In the mirror, I stared at my body. Legs sticklike and goosefleshed, stomach puffy. I hadn't exercised, hadn't eaten . . . I was a mess. My breasts ached; my arms felt simultaneously heavy and frail.

I went downstairs, made a cup of tea, and sat there, not sipping it. I had no work to do, which always set me at odds. I glanced at the paper; with Paul gone, I was more up on the news than I'd been since before Hazel's birth—perhaps because, not having him to clue me in on the world, I felt obliged to clue in myself. But today, it couldn't hold my interest. I got up, went out to the back porch, stared out into the distance. *So this is it, then,* I thought, without wanting to. *The culmination of eight years of marriage.*

I thought of calling Cindi or Celeste, but I couldn't bear the thought of Cindi's smugness ("All men are dogs. You're better off without one."), and I didn't want pity or consoling from Celeste. I didn't deserve it. I wandered back inside, then through the house and out the front door this time. Mrs. Zuppo walked by—pacing spritely, I might add, raising alternate fists and strolling at a clip.

"Hi, Mrs. Zuppo," I called, suddenly anxious to engage.

She turned and grinned. "Elayna! How you doing?"

"Okay. You?"

"Eh. Can't complain."

"That's good. You look great, by the way." I was being friendly, but as I said it, I realized it was true.

She shrugged and waved her hand. "Thanks, hon. I did actually lose some weight, finally. Twenty pounds, give or take."

"Twenty pounds! Good for you!"

"Yeah, well. That damn doctor wouldn't get off my back, so." She laughed. "I went on Weight Watchers, finally. It's not so bad, once you get used to it. It's the walking I hate, but—" She shrugged. "I'm getting used to it."

I felt suddenly, surprisingly happy. "Well—I don't want to keep you," I said. "But that really is great news."

She nodded. "Thanks. Give my love to the baby, okay? Tell her to come see me. I have the pizzelles she likes."

"I will." I waved, and off she trotted. But I felt a wave of nausea then—hungry, no doubt—and I went back into the living room to sit until it passed. *Twenty pounds,* I thought. *Good for her.*

Hours later—Hazel had just gone to bed—I was back in the exact same spot. I should have been exhausted—I had been all day—but, like last night, I wasn't tired now . . . or maybe *too* tired, or too anxious, to sleep. I stared out the window. Swing trembling, black sky. No one coming. No husband, no father. No Paul.

Wednesday morning. I got Hazel up, mechanically dressed her, packed her a lunch. Then I sat down to eat breakfast with her, or to watch her eat, at least. Suddenly, I felt I could barely keep my head up. "Eat up, baby," I said, envying her youth, her obliviousness, until she said, "How come Daddy didn't call me last night?"

I sat up straighter. "I don't know," I admitted. "But I bet he'll call you tonight."

"Are you *sure*?"

"No." We were quiet a moment. "But I'm *confident.*"

"What's confident?" she asked.

"Well, it's—"

I heard a sound down the hall. We both turned around.

Paul walked into the house. He turned and closed the door behind him.

"Daddy!" Hazel shrieked. "Daddy!" She leaped from her seat and ran to him.

I stood up, stunned. However much I'd always believed he'd come home—*How could he not?* I'd asked myself, over and over—now that he was standing here, I couldn't quite believe he had. He looked like crap, I have to say. As bad as I felt: strung out and worn weary and altogether pathetic. No matter. I'd never seen a prettier sight.

Hazel flew into his arms. He embraced her, and they stayed like that for a long time, neither one making a sound. I stood nearby, waiting, drinking in the sight—the fantastic sight—of his strong fingers on her wild, curly hair. *Thank you,* I said to whoever had done this. *Thank you thank you thank you.*

He looked at me then. I met his gaze. His eyes searched my face, and then down my body and quickly back up. And I saw what he'd noticed, and I saw it register in his eyes. My wedding ring. On my finger, where, save for one brief time, it always had been.

I moved to hug him. I couldn't help it. I reached around him and Hazel and held on to them tight, even if they didn't hug me back.

We had it out that night, of course. He was taking a shower, and I knocked and went in. "Hi," I said, sitting down on Hazel's step stool.

He was washing his hair, and he didn't stop, or answer me. Through the glass shower door, I watched his hands work. The soap ran down his shoulders, his chest, through his dark torso hair. His body was so familiar: the gentle slope of his stomach, his muscular thighs. His strong back, his deep olive skin. I had missed him so much. For a second, I thought about stripping and hopping in with him. But I didn't have the nerve, so I sat there watching.

He finished rinsing and turned off the shower. I reached for his towel and held it toward him, and he took it and stepped out. I watched as he dried himself off. "A little privacy would be nice," he said, and I wasn't sure if he was kidding. Anyway, I didn't leave. My stomach felt tight—a tightness, all through my abdomen. It would be there until he forgave me, I knew. *If* he did. "You missed a spot," I said, as he dried his back, and I stood up to help him, but he moved away. "That's okay," he said. He walked out.

I followed him into the bedroom. He dropped his towel, pulled on a pair of boxers (*Since when?* I thought; he had always slept naked), hung his towel on the hook in his closet, and slipped into bed. His hair was dark, curly, damp. He lay down, then sat up again. "Shit," he said. "I didn't brush my teeth."

He got up and went back into the bathroom. I followed him again, this time standing in the bathroom doorway.

He brushed and brushed. I swear, he brushed more in one night than I did in my whole life combined. "Listen," I said finally, because I couldn't wait anymore. "I just want to say this. I'm so, so sorry for—for everything that's happened. And I know you're mad at me, and I totally understand that, but maybe we could just—"

"*What?*" He said it loudly, toothpaste still in his mouth. "You *what*?" He turned to me and laughed once, bitterly, mouth white with froth. Then he turned back and spit into the sink. He rinsed with Hazel's pink cup, then blew back past me, into the bedroom.

I followed. "I understand," I tried again, "that you're mad. And I want to apologize."

He shook his head, laughing silently this time, and his anger and hatred went through me like a chill. "You know what, Elayna?" he said. "Save your breath." He slipped into bed. "Because nothing you say will make me forgive you. Nothing. Ever."

He might as well have hauled back and punched me. I started to cry.

He shook his head again. "I don't—I don't even know what to say to you. You betrayed me and you humiliated me. I don't know what happened between you and that guy, but whatever it is, it's, it's—" He shook his head. "I feel like a fucking idiot. An idiot." He looked at me, his eyes burning with hatred. "Why?" he said, finally. "That's what I don't get. Why would you? I've been so loyal, so fucking—"

"Because I needed something." The words weren't planned, and frankly, I wasn't sure where they were coming from, but there they were. "Maybe because of Oliver," I said. "Or maybe not. But I needed something, Paul, and you couldn't give it to me. Or wouldn't. I'm not blaming you, and I'm not saying that's an excuse. But I think—I think—I do think I did try to ask. Because after, after Oliver died . . ."

He was watching me, at least. Listening, maybe. I felt an inkling of hope.

" . . . I needed to *talk* about it with you," I finished. "We needed to talk, or to grieve together . . . to do *something*. You know? And then we needed to start over, somehow. Start a new baby, maybe, or—or not. I don't know. But you wouldn't do it! You wouldn't connect, and I couldn't either, I guess. But at least I wanted to *try*. I know that. And I think I *did* try. But you, you were never here, and even when you were, you—"

He turned away, and I felt my hope fade again. I thought, *This is the wrong approach if you want to make up*. Though I'm still not sorry I said it.

Anyway, I tried again. "Paul, I didn't love him," I said. "And I don't love him now. I only ever loved you." It wasn't completely true. I *had* loved Kevin, in a way; I didn't think I'd lied to him that night. But it wasn't the way I loved Paul. Paul was my love, the father of my baby. Babies. Paul was the one.

He looked at me, a little clipper flat on its side, wind knocked out of its sails. "I'm working every waking hour to save a man's life," he said, "yet my own life feels dead. Just—dead. You killed it." He was crying now too. I looked at him, imploring, but he shot me a look of pure bitterness. "I wasn't gonna come back, you know."

I nodded, tasting my tears.

"I did it for Hazel," he said. "That's the only reason. And I'm not staying."

I nodded, swallowed. "I hope you do, though."

I thought I saw a glimmer of something then in his eyes, the tiniest crack in the ice. He lay down and turned away from me, slid as far as he could to the other edge of the bed. But I clung to it, that glimmer. It was all I had. Hazel, and that.

That was six months ago. It's March now, but outside is still gray and white; no sign yet of spring. The weather outside matches the mood in our house. Paul is often angry, except around Hazel. But he's still here. Some days, I'm optimistic. Some days, I sense spring. Other days, it's miles to go. Miles or years or decades.

But I stand up straight, whenever I can. Paul is my love, my love, the love of my life, and I like to think that no matter what happened, I'm still his. And marriage—the real kind, the kind Celeste can't imagine—*our* marriage . . . well, I like to think it will survive this. Because despite what I destroyed, despite what I wrecked, so much remains. And this, it seems to me, is what the commitment is for. I needed to find that wedding ring for myself as much as for Paul.

Four days after he returned—on the day of our eighth anniversary—Haze and I made him a cake, and I gave him a card with a picture of a smiling baby glued inside it. "I love you," I wrote at the top of the page. "Me too," I had Hazel print below that. And then, in tiny type, in a bubble coming from the baby's mouth, I printed, "Me three!" If I'd known then what I know now, I'd have made that baby's bow pink. As it was, I made it a neutral, lively grass green.

Reading that card, Paul's eyes grew wide; for the first time since he'd returned, he looked at me with curiosity more than bitterness. "It is true?" he asked. "Are you—"

I nodded, smiling weakly. The abdominal tightness hadn't been stress after all. The aching body, puffy stomach, sore breasts . . . it all made sense now. The dizziness, the exhaustion. I was on the verge of puking every minute, night and day. "About six weeks," I said.

I could feel him calculating back—right back to Maine, on that saggy old bed. Believe me, I'd already done the math, over and over again.

Still: "Is it mine?" he said, and again, that flash of hatred.

I flinched only inside. "Of course," I said, evenly. "How could you even ask?"

I knew how. But I thought that was the best answer to give, and as soon as I gave it, I saw I'd been right. He stood up a little straighter then.

It's March outside, as I said. And I'm glad. I'm not ready to give birth, to leave the nest of our house, the log fires Paul's started to make night after night—when he's home, yes; but I don't think I'm deceiving myself in saying he's home more often now. Not always, but often. He's trying. We all are.

By late spring, the baby will come, and that'll be a whole other thing. I'm nervous, of course. But I try not to think about what could go wrong, and I never, ever talk about it. The Queen of Denial, Cindi would say, but there's a fine line between denial and staying optimistic, and I'm willing to toe that line. I know what could happen, because it did. But that doesn't mean I have to think about it. At least not more than once.

At the moment, that's not hard; there's too much to think about that's gone right. A new baby, dive-bombing inside me. A healthy seven-year-old, growing taller and more aware by the day. A husband who's still here. *Time does not bring relief,* wrote Edna St. Vincent Millay, but she was wrong in this case—though the relief is incremental, a snail slowly crawling, and sometimes it's one step forward, three steps back. Like I said, there's a part of Paul that will never fully trust me again—and that's a terrible thing for a husband to have to wield, and a hideous scar to have in a marriage. But we move ahead anyway, damaged, maimed, growing older but wiser too, we hope, every day. The scars are part and parcel—so why wish them away? A shiny coin never used, a package left perfectly wrapped . . . you never get to see what's inside, never find out what that money can buy. That's what I tell myself, anyway. And it helps. The important thing is to get up and move again. To keep going, let time proffer its salve.

In the end, I think that marriage, like life, is amorphous and nebulous: something that changes and changes and then changes again. And the changing . . . well, that's part of what keeps it alive. Mine still is, my marriage, and to me, it's because it has heart—that one thing poor Oliver lacked. I made two of the biggest mistakes you can make, and we're still together. *That's* what overwhelms me. *That's* what's romantic. It was loyalty over fidelity. I fell, and Paul picked me up, even though he's the one I crushed when I did. What more can someone ask? *My love, my love.* And I won't fall again. I'm no Devon Leopold, even if I am his daughter.

So—we take things day by day. That's the plan, anyway.

The funny thing is, I think it's Celeste's plan too, more or less. "How's *le* baby?" she asked, when she called me last week.

"Fat," I said. "Hyperactive. Robbing my body of nutrients, energy, and vitality. Getting on my nerves, literally and figuratively."

"That's what I love," she said. "A mommy who tells it like it is, for a change."

"Yeah, well." I sniffed. Month seven of a stuffed-up nose. "How's *le* lover?"

"Home with *le* wife." She sighed. "Woe is I."

I laughed. But then I had to ask, just one more time. "Celeste, doesn't that make you a little . . . sad?"

"Of course," she said. "But I *like* to feel sad."

I tried to relate. And I could, a little.

"Anyway, it goes with the turf," she said.

I didn't answer. I was feeling sad for her.

"Don't pity me, Elayna," she said, reading my thoughts. "It's why I write. It's *how* I write. And I need to write—"

"Ow!" I said.

"Oh come on. I'm not *that* pathetic."

"No—it's not that. The baby just kicked."

"Oh." She paused. "No offense, Elayna, and you know I love Hazel to death, but—something human growing inside you, kicking your kidneys, your spleen? That's way creepier than what I'm doing, if you ask me."

I just smiled. Sometimes, you keep your mouth shut.

As the months proceed, as the goldengrove unleaves, as my belly grows rounder, here's another thing I've learned: There are many ways to find passion, to be transported. It doesn't have to disappear as you age, settle down—and in fact, maybe the older and more settled you get, the more places you learn to find it. And you learn which ones you can go to, and which ones you can't. I'm still learning, every day. The smell of a lily, the crack of a bat against a ball, the sound of a lone, muted trumpet in the night . . . those are all yes. In a pull of cold water, in watching a young couple kiss. All the things I already had. They were always right there. But at first I wasn't able to see them—grief clouded my eyes—and then, when I did, they weren't enough, or maybe it was too late by then.

One more thing I've learned: Life doesn't have to be an opera, constantly dripping with high drama. There's enough tragedy without trying, thanks—so may as well leave the opera to the stage, and youth to the young. *Be regular and ordinary in your life so you can be violent and original in your work.* That's a quote I displayed back in loftier, more ambitious days. And now? This is enough. My husband, my babies, poetry.

Speaking of babies: I've seen Kevin lately walking with a girl—petite, eyes like upside-down half-moons, short cranberry (yes, *cranberry*) hair. Last week, outside, I saw them, walking with Sasha, and I waved. It was the first time Kevin had seen me in months, and I thought I saw his eyes widen as he took in the human basketball under my shirt. I was too far away to see if he smiled, so I simply told myself he did. Did he wonder if it was his? I'll probably never know. But I have a feeling he knew the truth. Yes. Surely he did. Otherwise, he wouldn't have stopped coming around.

Anyway, that day, next to his pretty little girlfriend, he waved back.

And that was enough. Really, that was perfect.

# Acknowledgments

My deepest gratitude to the following for their generous and thoughtful help with this book: David Herrington, Bill Newman, Dan Zulawski, Susan Squire, Joan Berzoff, Deb Addis, Marjorie Braman, Vera Jones, Robbie Myers, Reneé Wetstein, Mary-Claire Phillips . . . there are others, and you know who you are. I do too.

Additionally, and perhaps especially, heartfelt thanks to the astonishing poet Tony Hoagland, who let me borrow his beautiful title so I didn't have to steal it.

And to Elizabeth Kaplan: smart, savvy, loyal agent.

And to my editor, the charming, witty, wise, and thoroughly wonderful Brenda Copeland, and to the lovely Amy Tannenbaum. And to Sarah Branham, Emily Bestler, Jodi Lipper, and Judith Curr, for coming through so perfectly at the end.

And to my mother and sisters, Bette, Judy, and Amy, who read parts and drafts of this book again and again and offered support, editing, and advice. And my father, LBH, for his enthusiasm and steady supply of ibuprofen and Voltaren pens.

And to Kate Christensen, who makes the writing life ever less solitary and more fulfilling by being available day and night with effusive encouragement, brilliant thoughts, and passionate and invaluable friendship.

And finally, to Dan Jones. For all of the above and everything else.